Redemption

RICHARD BURKE

ORION

Copyright © Richard Burke 2006

The right of Richard Burke to be identified as the
author of this work has been asserted by him in accordance
with the Copyright, Designs and Patents Act, 1988.

First published in Great Britain in 2006 by
Orion Books, an imprint of The Orion Publishing Group
Orion House, 5 Upper St Martin's Lane,
London WC2H 9EA

1 3 5 7 9 10 8 6 4 2

All characters in this publication are fictitious and any resemblance
to real persons, living or dead, is purely coincidental.

A CIP catalogue record for this book is
available from the British Library

ISBN (hardback) 0 75285 769 X
ISBN (trade paperback) 0 75286 824 1

Typeset at The Spartan Press Ltd,
Lymington, Hants

Printed and bound in Great Britain by
Clays Ltd, St Ives plc

www.orionbooks.co.uk

Always first, my love and thanks to Valerie and Daniel. Living with a writer is far from easy. My thanks also: to Will Aslett, Paul Campbell and Cindy Hanegraaf for their comments on early drafts; to Kate Mills for her insight, support and endless patience; to Euan Thorneycroft for excellent advice, generally given over an excellent lunch; to my *sifu*, Master Lam Kam Chuen for the art of *tai chi*; to the staff of Pentonville Prison for ideas and advice; to Peter Richardson for advice on the banking system; and to Larry and Tia for lending me their names, but not their characters, for charity.

This book is for Daniel, who was once called Eyelash.

Before

One

You watch. You plan.

You are not accustomed to this, and so you are careful, cautious. This must be perfect. It can only happen once, and there are . . . requirements.

There are patterns to learn. He gets up at six thirty, she at seven fifteen, then the girl as late as she can. Bed is ten thirty for all of them, but the girl switches her light on again sometime before eleven, and stays awake secretly until the small hours. You know these habits, because you have hidden outside their house, you have timed the switchings on and off of lights, charted the shadows moving from room to room.

You watch their days, too. He leaves for work, then the girl for school, then the woman, headed for whichever office she is working in this week. He walks to work, but frequently gets a taxi home. She takes the Tube. The girl walks.

He always takes the same route. He grabs a doughnut from the café across from the prison before he goes in. You know the interior, you can imagine him moving through it: he strides through the clamour and shuffle of the wings, marches the corridors, stops to pass the time with officers, puts a hand on an arm here, offers a joke there, or a reassurance. You have watched him do it. He has passed you on the wings, a man from a different world, full of himself, full of certainty.

She is different. Once a week, she travels by tube to St Mary's Hospital. You have waited with her in the corridors, watching her nervously twist a lock of hair around a finger – twist, tug, twist, tug, chewing it in the corner of her mouth, pretending to read the same page of a magazine for an hour or more. You have been outside, waiting for her, as she emerges, nervous and uncertain, sweat misting her upper lip even on the coldest days. (This makes you smile. She is scared. Good.) Sometimes he comes with her, and you cannot go so close. But still you watch. Private money is paying for those sessions. You find that interesting.

And then she goes to work. She is a temp: she works in different places from time to time, and that makes things harder. But that is why you have prepared. Because there can be no error. There is a balance to be gauged – eye for eye, life for life, dream for broken dream; the implacable algebra of revenge.

You watch from the doorways of vacant houses. You are a passer-by, coat collar casually turned up. You watch. You wait. And you prepare.

Monday

Two

The dream woke him because he had nowhere else left to go. He had done something, saved someone, but the men who came did not believe him. He had seen it in their eyes. And now they had come for him, and—

Matthew Daniels dragged his eyes open.

In the half-light, shadows drifted on the ceiling. The curtains lifted and sank on a slight breeze. Where they parted, he could see the trees outside, nodding. Cars whispered past. A distant alarm sounded and then stopped.

Someone calling in his dream. Someone accusing him.

Charlotte's back was pressed against his side. It was hot, tacky with sweat. The sensation was still strange to him, even after more than a year. Asleep, Charlotte was a furnace. Awake, she fizzed with relentless, irritable energy. Sometimes it tired him. Sometimes, he just wanted a little peace.

Second love. The shadows on the ceiling nodded wisely at him, as if they knew exactly how he felt. He wished they would tell him – because sometimes he had no idea.

Careful not to wake Charlotte, he eased himself out of bed and slipped behind the curtain to avoid spilling light into the room. Charlotte stirred briefly, then silence returned. The street was flat and grey in the morning light. A woman emerged from the gate of a house a little further down the street, hauling on a tubby labrador. She was bundled in layers of tweed and wool, and had a scarf wrapped tightly about her head. The dog was grey around the muzzle, and barrel-shaped; it hurried after her on stiff fat legs. He could hear its claws ticking on the pavement. Beads of rain sparkled dully on the rows of parked cars. A little way down the road on the far side, a car with silvered windows gleamed a little brighter than the rest.

Somewhere near by, next door perhaps, a mobile phone rang and was not answered.

He fought his way back through the curtains into the room. Luminous digits on his bedside table told him it was twenty past six. There was no point in going back to sleep. As he took his dressing gown down from the hook behind the door, Charlotte's came off too and flopped loudly to the carpet. She didn't stir.

Her face was crumpled against the pillow, angled back, so that she was facing him perfectly. The one eye he could see was firmly shut; the other was obscured by a scrunched-up cheek. Her mouth was open, and strands from her bob of dark hair hung across her teeth. A high brow curved seamlessly to the tip of a small, elegant nose. Her hair swept down around her cheeks to meet the soft line of her jaw. She wasn't angular in any dimension. She was rounded everywhere.

To Matthew, she was beautiful. She preferred to call herself fat. That always made him laugh, because if you looked at it the wrong way, it was sort of true. He didn't look at it the wrong way; but for her, of course, that wasn't the point.

He loved watching her sleep. When she woke, that rumpled face would come alive with laughter, and her clamped-shut brown eyes with sparkle with mischief. And her smell – a heat that rose from her that would be almost a taste – apples, yeast, vanilla. And her voice, a high-pitched bell.

Yes, definitely love. It felt all the more precious for having won it twice.

Downstairs, he sat in the kitchen, listening to the morning's news on the radio, cradling a cup of tea, soothed by a dawn chorus of pigeons, traffic and aeroplanes. There was something special about this hour, about the near-peace of London's restless streets, with Charlotte and Em safely asleep upstairs. He found it reassuring. The world waking around them today was the same world as yesterday; it would be the same again tomorrow. Even the ceaseless drone of the news on the radio reinforced the illusion: the more sensational the story, the more familiar it seemed. The world was a big, dangerous and miserable place – but not this corner of it. Here, he could shut it all out. There was peace, of a sort – and he vowed, as he did every morning, that nothing bad would ever happen to either of them, come what may. He would not allow it. Not again.

At ten past seven, he took her a cup of herbal tea. Em's alarm was ringing. As he passed, there was a grunt from behind her closed door, and a thump. The ringing stopped. In the main bedroom he set down the tea, switched off their own alarm before it could ring, and kissed the top of his wife's head. It was now the only part of her poking up above the covers.

'Morning, darling. Ten past.' A sleepy groan answered him. He chuckled into her hair. 'Mmm. I know the feeling. Tea's on the table.'

'Oh, *yum*,' she muttered. 'Tea.' She rolled away from him and wrapped the covers tighter. 'Go away.'

He bounced onto the bed beside her. 'What, *really*?'

'Matthew, I'm asleep. Go away.'

He slid a hand under the covers and ran it down her back. 'Ve can do zis ze easy vay, or ze hard vay.'

She arched away from him. 'Matthew! That's cold! You – you—' She ran out of words. A few seconds later, she peeped out fuzzily at him. 'I could go off you, you know.'

He kissed her on the forehead. 'See you downstairs.'

On his way down, he rapped on Em's door. 'It's quarter past.' There was no reply. There rarely was. 'Em?'

Muffled by the door, he heard her shout, 'All *right*!'

He shook his head. Teenagers: they were either asleep or in a foul mood, you could take your pick. She was awake now, which meant she was in a grump.

'Downstairs by half past, please.' He hurried on to avoid the inevitable response. Her ranting pursued him down the stairs – which was good, because it meant that she was alert. There was a chance she'd get out of the house on time today.

Charlotte was first down. She pecked him absently on the cheek, and sat nursing her tea, clearly still half-asleep. Matthew made himself busy with the toaster.

He called over his shoulder, 'Sleep well?'

She groaned. 'Still sleeping. Why am I so tired?'

'That's easy. Too much sex.'

She sniggered, reluctantly. 'Once was all it took.'

There was an envelope on the counter by the toaster. He tossed it onto the table. 'Here. You must have missed it on Saturday.' That wasn't true. He'd found it half-hidden behind a pile of recipe books. It hadn't got there by accident.

She eyed the envelope, scowling, then slid her finger under the flap and ripped it open. She stared at it for a long time before pulling out the letter. She glanced at the header hastily, then slid it back.

He brandished the butter knife at it. 'From . . . ?'

She scowled. 'None of your business. A bill. My mobile or something.'

He smiled at her sadly. He had seen the hospital's red logo. She avoided his eyes for a beat, then muttered, 'Oh, all *right*.'

She made a show of pulling the letter out again and scanning it. 'Yeah,' she said. 'Bill.'

They both contemplated the lie for a while without talking.

The toast popped up. Matthew buttered it, then looked hopefully in a cupboard full of mugs. 'Where's the Marmite?' Ever since Charlotte had moved in and started rearranging the cupboards, he had been unable to find things. Truth be told, he hadn't been much good at finding things before, either; but now, everything seemed to move on a daily basis.

She didn't answer him. When he turned to look at her, she was studying the envelope, and softly biting her lip. Matthew felt a pang, partly of sympathy and partly of something sharper: whatever Charlotte was feeling, all too often she forgot that he might be feeling it, too.

'Charlotte?' She looked up at him, unease scored into the lines of her face. 'The Marmite?'

She smiled weakly and pretended to throw the envelope at him. 'Morning.'

Em appeared in the doorway wearing green pyjamas and a bleary frown. She assessed the scene, then stomped over to Matthew. She eyed the buttered toast, then yanked open the cupboard next to the one he had been looking in and plonked the Marmite on the counter in front of him.

'*Feuhl*,' she muttered, in a passable imitation of Inspector Clouseau in *The Pink Panther*. She poured herself a bowl of cereal.

'I know a *feuhl* when I see one, Kato,' he shot back, narrowing his eyes to cunning slits and then crossing them, 'and I am looking at one right now.'

She chuckled, and slumped at the table with her cereal, blowing Charlotte a kiss that was carefully designed to seem insincere. Sprawled over the bowl, her mouth full of cereal she mumbled, 'So you'll pick me up at one, yeah?'

It wasn't clear who she was speaking to, but Charlotte bridled instantly.

'*What?*'

'One's early. Doesn't finish till five.'

Charlotte blinked heavily, controlling her obvious irritation. 'First, Em – pick you up from *what*? And second – one o'clock? On a Monday? Absolutely not.'

'That's *so* not fair!'

Matthew's job in these – frequent – situations was to forestall the argument. 'Em, what are we actually talking about here?'

She rolled her eyes at him. 'Hello? Just, like, the disco I told you about?'

Why did Em's generation, like, make every statement sound like a question? This was not the moment to ask.

Belatedly, he remembered a discussion a week ago:

– *Dad, can I go to this club on Friday next week?*
– *Depends which club.*
– *It's open night. Patch is going.*
– *Which club, Em?*
– *It's an open night. Patch's sister's boyfriend's trying out as MC.*
– *What's an MC?*
– *Dexter. He's wicked.*

There had been more to the conversation, but it conveyed no information helpful to anyone over the age of fourteen. What it had boiled down to was that Em wanted to go to a disco – on a Friday, she had said – and she had agreed to give fuller details later, either to Charlotte or to him. Clearly, she hadn't.

'Is this that thing you were telling me about?'

'Yeah. At the Palace. Dexter's MC.'

'Dexter?' Matthew raised an enquiring eyebrow.

Em sneered contemptuously. 'Dexter? Like, Patch's sister's boyfriend? *Der!* '

Em fancied Dexter. Dexter was buff, apparently. And fit.

'You said that was on Friday,' he pointed out.

'Yeah. Like, they're *really* going to let *Dexter* do a *Friday*?'

'And I didn't say you could go. You were going to tell me more about it first, or Charlotte.'

That was enough for Em. 'That's *typical!*' she howled. 'So, like, there's no point even going now, is there?'

'No one's said you *can* go yet,' Charlotte reminded her.

'I didn't ask *you*.'

Charlotte's face flushed. 'Now, you listen, young lady—'

'Right, that's it,' Matthew said sharply. 'Em, you do *not* speak to Charlotte like that. The answer's no.'

Em threw her spoon into her bowl and pouted at the tablecloth. 'Why are you *doing* this to me?'

'One more word from you and you'll be grounded for the week.'

'I *hate* you!'

He held up a finger. 'One more word.'

Em glowered at the table. Charlotte stood, wordlessly, and stalked out of the room. Matthew sighed. Why did it always come down to a choice between them? Couldn't they see how ridiculous—

He heard Charlotte's keys jingle and the front door opening. Shit.

Hastily, he muttered, 'Finish your cereal, Em.'

He caught the front door just before it closed. 'Charlotte?'

She stopped on the short path to the street, her back to him.

'Are you OK?'

She didn't move.

'Charlotte?'

She turned. 'What do *you* think?' she hissed. Her face was mottled with anger, and there were tears in her eyes.

Matthew looked momentarily confused. 'But—'

'Oh, *spare* me.' She turned away from him again and opened the gate. He hurried after her and caught her arm.

'Darling, listen—'

She twisted her arm away from him. 'A little support would have been nice. But you have to just pile in there and take control, don't you?'

'What, you mean with Em? But I—'

'I'm not some little *kid*, Matthew. I can fight my own battles, thank you.'

'Charlotte, that's unfair. I was just—'

'Oh, *is* it? Well, I'm so sorry, Mr High-and-bloody-mighty. No one told me you were the only person round here who was allowed to decide things.'

'Come on, darling, be reasonable.'

For a moment, she looked like she was going to explode. Then, suddenly, she was dangerously calm. Coldly, she said, 'Goodbye, Matthew,' and walked away from him.

He called after her, 'Darling? Where are you—'

'Oh, for – I'm going to *work*!' she yelled, without looking back. She upped her pace, and, within a minute, she was gone.

Matthew rubbed his forehead wearily, and headed back indoors. Arguments were not his favourite way to start the day, particularly when he had no idea what they were about. He closed the front door thoughtfully. One way or another, things had been tense for more than a year now. And even if it was understandable – sometimes – it was wearing. It had been a while since she had stormed out, though: she knew he found it difficult.

He trudged back into the kitchen. Em was eating his and Charlotte's toast.

'Sorry,' she muttered.

He shrugged. 'Me too.' He waved a hand vaguely after Charlotte. 'She's . . .'

Em rolled her eyes at him and tossed Charlotte's letter over the table towards him.

From the hospital. Her appointment for the scan.

'Dad, you are a *feuhl*,' Em said gently.

Three

Charlotte sat in a tube train on her way to work and let guilt and nausea wash over her. Her anger had not lasted long. She knew that Matthew was right, she had been unfair. But the fact that he was right was part of the problem. Why did he have to be so *reasonable* all the time, so considerate – no, worse, so patronising? His concern for her left her with no space of her own, and no way out except to force him away.

Worse still was what lay behind it. He thought she couldn't see it, perhaps he couldn't even see it himself; but it was there. She could see in his eyes that he was still uncertain. He had changed himself, to make her happy. And now he was no longer sure who he was supposed to be. He was scared.

So, unfortunately, was she.

Dear Ms Daniels, the letter had read. Stupid bureaucrats. She was *Mrs* Daniels. She had once been Ms Logan. She had changed, too.

An ultrasound scan has been arranged for you at St Mary's Hospital at 9.15 a.m. on Friday 23 May. Following the scan, we may have to admit you for surgery. Please bring an overnight bag with you in case surgery is required. Please do not eat or drink for 12 hours before your scan . . .

Friday. Five days from now. Four, really.

The letter went on: it told her where she should report to, what documents she should bring, that it might be necessary to take blood samples. If surgery was necessary, she should arrange for someone to collect her the next day. The letter didn't bother to point out that, if things went badly, she should also arrange for someone to be there to pick up the pieces.

The Tube was saturated with the stench of people. She kept her eyes closed, and breathed through her mouth, as lightly as possible. It didn't help much. A woman five seats along from her had doused herself in Opium perfume. Oily fumes coated the back of Charlotte's throat. There was sweat, aftershave, the thick dark grease that had soaked into the seats over decades, the scent of newsprint rising like acid from the cheap paper.

She sank into herself. And remembered the day, more than a year ago, when everything changed.

She has been rushed from the GP's surgery to the local hospital in a taxi. They have taken blood, and scanned her uterus and ovaries with compassionate efficiency. And still, she has no idea what is going on. Now, she waits on a long line of chairs in a corridor, for someone to tell her what is happening to her that has made her period go on and on, and made the cramps so bad that occasionally she moans aloud.

Matthew has forced her to go to the doctor. There, she has waited an hour for a gap in his appointments. He has pricked her thumb and dipped a stick into the drop of blood, frowned, and then rung reception to ask for a taxi to take her to hospital. He has told her nothing. Now, here at the hospital, the nurses and doctors have told her nothing either. She has asked – and they have told her that she is here so they can find out what the problem is, and that when they know they will tell her. Now she waits, uncertain and afraid.

The corridor is silent. There are flurries of activity: small flocks of doctors suddenly sweep into view, white coat-tails flapping, heels squeaking on the rubber floor, and vanish through doors with scratched metal kick-plates. Through other doors, she catches glimpses of machinery, strange white shapes in the centre of empty spaces.

She waits. And she is afraid.

A heavy period shouldn't mean you have to go to hospital. You don't need a scan for it. There must be some problem with the coil that she and Matthew use for protection. She hates the coil, the idea of a metal spike inside her – but she hates the Pill more, and they have long since given up on condoms and caps. The last thing they want is a baby. Charlotte is thirty-seven. Her biological clock stopped ringing long ago. She is used to a life free of attachments and consequences. It has been a hard decision to agree to live with Matthew – and she still finds it hard every day – but at least it's just the two of them, and the almost-adult Emily, whom Charlotte adores, who is so sweet to her, and who loves her father so much more than he can see. And he doesn't want a child either, or to marry. They are both independent souls. They control their own lives. It suits them both to be the way they are – attached but independent, unmarried but together, there for each other, but without demands or expectations. And besides, Matthew has Em – sort of.

But now the coil has gone wrong, hasn't it? It has gone adrift and pierced something. It has got infected and her womb is failing to cleanse itself. Or something. She must wait to find out, in this corridor, alone.

She wishes she could ring Matthew and tell him what is happening – which is nothing – but there are signs everywhere demanding that she turn her mobile off, and she doesn't know where the pay-phone is, and she doesn't dare leave, in case they come for her while she is gone.

She waits, and wonders if they have forgotten that she is there. Perhaps the scan results have gone adrift, and are floating free through the hospital, transferred from one orange cardboard file to another, with no one knowing why, or who, or what, or anything.

'Ms Logan?'

A dumpy woman with curly hair and thick-rimmed glasses is peering hopefully down the corridor, as though it is full of potential Charlotte Logans, rather than entirely empty except for her. She stands, and the woman smiles tightly and darts off towards a blank door, glancing expectantly over her shoulder to make sure she is following. She opens the door and motions Charlotte inside.

It is a small room, with just enough space for a desk and a couple of chairs. Charlotte sits. The woman follows her in, sits in the other chair, smiles distractedly, and then bends over her notes. Then she sets them down and turns to face Charlotte. There are bags under the woman's eyes. She looks exhausted. She can't be more than twenty-five. Charlotte wonders how she finds the time or energy to look after herself. When does she do her washing, her shopping? The woman smiles again, this time more sincerely, and Charlotte detects something uncertain in her eyes – and the thin pulse of fear and anticipation that has been throbbing inside her for the last hour becomes a sudden rush.

Whatever this is, it's bad.

The doctor opens her mouth, then pauses for thought. Then, in an abrupt, clipped voice, she says, 'Ms Logan, I'm afraid you have lost your baby.'

Charlotte opens her mouth to speak. What baby? she wants to ask. And what do you mean, *lost*? But she cannot find words, and a strange panic swells inside her.

It is only later, coming back from the hospital on the bus, nursing a secret in her belly, and another in her heart – feeling as though she might break at any moment, and wondering why the preoccupied faces of the men and women crammed around show no trace of care or sympathy – it is only then that she comes slowly to realise that the child she has just lost is a child she has always, desperately, wanted. That the doctor has taken away a hope she never knew she had within her.

The Tube stopped, and she half-woke, scanning instinctively for signs to tell her which station it was. There were two stops to go. Fine. The train set off again.

A foot from her nose, a wall of overcoats swayed with every jolt of the train, wafting air towards her. They obscured the adverts mounted above the seats opposite, which might have helped kill at least a few minutes. She closed her eyes again, fighting rising nausea. Why did businessmen wear overcoats in May anyway?

But it wasn't just morning sickness and the constant fatigue. What really ate at her was fear. What would happen this time? She would lose this baby too, wouldn't she? Or the doctors would decide she needed the operation – and then that would go wrong. Or Matthew would change his mind: heaven knew, he'd been reluctant enough to try in the first place.

And what would she become afterwards? When Matthew had left, taking Em with him; when these few nauseating weeks of pregnancy had been reduced to a fond, sad memory? She would be Charlotte Logan again. On her own. Fiercely independent, and utterly lost. Pregnancy, it seemed, did not agree with her; and she was a moody cow anyway, even at the best of times.

It wasn't Matthew's fault. He was only trying to tell her that he cared. She would ring him and apologise. Later, though: give him time to realise what he had done wrong. No one flourished by being smothered.

She would ring him after lunch. Let him worry for the morning. Let him learn. It was obvious to her – and, she suspected, even to Em: Matthew needed to learn how to live dangerously again. Not that any of that really mattered. Because, she reflected, the truth was that she loved him. Why else would she be carrying – for now, at least – his child?

The train slowed towards her stop. She stood by the doors, and watched the tunnel walls flicker by.

Since leaving the Ville, Charlotte had worked as a temp, unwilling to put in the hours of travelling that would have been involved if she had accepted a transfer, and not at all sure what other choices were open to her. But having a tedious job with no future was the least of it. So much had changed. Everything, really.

Work, for the last two weeks, had been at a legal firm specialising in messy divorces. She was typist and receptionist to an obnoxious man called Thomas Chandler. After less than a day there, typing out endless letters of litigation, she'd had her fill of accusations and marital posturing. The clients the firm dealt with seemed to her to have had little enough wealth in the first place: by the time it had been divided, and the lion's share taken by Chandler, there was often nothing left for the separating couples except the bitter satisfaction that their once-beloved was as badly off as they were. Couldn't they see what love *was*? Because it certainly wasn't to be found through lawyers whose only interest was in conflict. She didn't want to type letters on their behalves, she wanted to march into their houses and shake them until they understood what they were doing; that their tireless desire to destroy could only, in the end, hurt themselves.

She knew this in the only way you could ever really know anything: she had been there. When she thought about what she had done a year ago, when Matthew had first proposed, she shuddered. The only reason they were still together was that he didn't know. But it was only a matter of time – and what then?

One moment's madness – walking out, furious, unsure what she really wanted – a moment she regretted deeply; and it still threatened to change everything in her life. It always would. Charlotte Daniels lived every day waiting for the axe to fall.

After her first week at Thomas Chandler and Associates (although there were no associates that she could see), she had told the temp agency that she'd had enough, and they had promised to find her something new. By the end of this week, with luck, she would be moving on.

And, with luck, she would still be pregnant. And still with Matthew.

She pulled her mobile out of her handbag, and flicked through the contacts list. Once, the number had been labelled *Matthew D.* Now it was labelled *Home*. She studied the number – *her* number – then she snapped the phone shut again. Later. After lunch. For now, let him stew. She might not be perfect – but neither was he. He wasn't at home anyway, he was at work, and he'd have checked in his mobile at reception.

Nevertheless, he was a good man – in many ways a brave man, for taking on someone as screwed-up as she obviously was. And she loved him, and she knew that he loved her, and he had found falling in love every bit as hard as she had. She had always been conscious of the ghost of Rachel, his first wife, hovering somewhere in the dark corners of their growing relationship.

She placed her phone back in her handbag, among the detritus of her life: lipstick, tampons (so pointless just now, but carried out of habit), eyeliner, purse, a keyring with a light on it, a pen and a pad of paper . . . And buried near the bottom, the bottle of aspirin and the pen-injector for her heparin: blood-thinners, prescribed by the miscarriage clinic, who had told her that there was no guarantee that the drugs would help her, none at all. Wait for the scan, they said. The scan's the thing. If it's positive, then probably the drugs will see you through. If it's negative, we operate. And the operation may work, or it may not. She didn't want to think about it.

It was lunchtime. Better to think about food – if she could keep it down. She ignored the lights flashing on the switchboard, closed her handbag, and headed out to buy a sandwich.

The traffic fumes were a welcome change from the stench of industrial carpets. She turned onto a small road that cut behind the block where the office was, heading for a sandwich shop she had discovered towards the end of her first week there. Halfway along it, there was a shut-down pub with boards on the windows; at the far end, there was a tiny corner shop, with rows of mouldy-looking vegetables on a rack outside. The rest of the street was houses, all of them blank, half of them cracked and in disrepair, a few of them boarded over. There was no one on the street, except for a man a little way behind her. He was hunched in an overcoat despite the warmth of the day. She didn't pay much attention to him. She was adrift in her own thoughts.

Had she looked, she might have seen his face; but it would have told her nothing. He was just a man, trudging the same street, perhaps walking slightly faster than her. He would catch up with her soon. Had she been paying attention, she might have noticed that he would reach her at about the point where a white van with blacked-out windows had pulled up at the kerb in a gap between the ranks of parked cars. As she approached, a man hopped out and slid back a side-door. He buried his head inside the van, and stayed there. Had she been paying attention, she might have thought that he was waiting for something.

She noticed nothing. She didn't notice that the road was empty, apart from the man behind her – he was close now – or that the man in front, leaning half-inside the van, was doing nothing. This was just one of the countless lulls in the busy life of any London street. She wasn't surprised when the man walking behind her finally closed the gap, just as she drew level with the van.

The man who had been leaning into the van's interior straightened, and stared at her. He took a step closer to her.

Then the man behind her tapped her on the shoulder.

She was so far away, adrift in her thoughts, that she jumped when he touched her. Then she remembered where she was. This was Notting Hill. This was just a man. He was lost, or she'd dropped her purse. Or something.

She turned to face him, not noticing the other man, now behind her, closing in. The man she was facing showed her a row of gapped and yellowing teeth.

Instinctively, she smiled.

Four

He strode hard, walking off his anger. The spat with Charlotte had been ridiculous. So, she was worried about the scan: well, so was he, but he didn't use it as an excuse to scream and shout at her. Couldn't she *see* that she was being selfish? Things had been rough for the last year and a half, for both of them; but snapping at him was hardly going to improve things, was it? Why should *he* be the one to make all the effort?

He knew the answer to that. It was because he was the one who most wanted to make everything right. Somehow, after the miscarriage, that had become the deal: supporting her had turned into a full-time job – not because she necessarily needed it, but because he needed to be sure of her. But over the last year, he had come to realise that the best thing to do if she was in a mood was just to let her get on with it.

His anger at her behaviour might just as easily be directed at himself. He was too bloody sensitive. Charlotte accused him of taking himself too seriously, and she was right. Charlotte was not Rachel – a truth he knew full well, but all too often ignored.

But it was so unjust. Whenever Charlotte and Em argued, they demanded that he take sides – and what could he do? He had nearly lost Em after Rachel had died. He had nearly lost Charlotte after the miscarriage. Even the slightest threat that he might drive one of them further away from him was unbearable. To be fair, the choice was not really his to make. Charlotte was stubborn enough when she was upset to deliberately do things that she actively didn't want to do – if she knew it would hurt. On at least one occasion, she—

Well. He had told himself he would never go there. What would be the point? What was done was done, and dwelling on it helped no one. He was sure she regretted it, and, really, he didn't want to know. Really. It was best for such things to fade and be forgotten. In any case, it was too late to raise it now. It was already history. It would fade. One day.

But when they had pointless rows, like this morning, it was hard to believe that she had truly changed. She had behaved unreasonably, and he had been suckered into playing his old habitual part. So, they were both different kinds of fool. Whoever said love was easy?

It didn't matter. Later they would laugh about it.

It was a bright morning full of grey people shuffling resentfully to work along gritty streets. Only he seemed aware that the sun was shining. Pigeons peered down from the outcrops of the buildings. A female on the pavement pecked at invisible specks of food, ignoring a male who strutted round her in a club-footed dance. The air was sharp with fumes. The busy clatter of the streets was a pleasure to him. London had so much energy, was so crammed with life. Matthew breathed deep and relished it.

He glanced at his watch. She would have calmed down by now. She would probably call later this morning, embarrassed and apologetic. Then he would bring flowers home, for both of them.

He stopped at his usual café a block away from work, and bought a doughnut and a cup of black coffee. It was always revolting, but marginally *less* revolting than the powder-fine instant he would have found in the staff kitchen. He shoved all thought of Charlotte aside and strode briskly on. There was work to be done.

The Ville's entrance loomed above him, a once-cream arch, now greying. It was strangely out of keeping with the building hiding behind it: it made the place look more like a town hall than a prison. Glimpses of razor wire high on the parapets gave that illusion the lie. A tattered plant sprouted from a crack some thirty feet above him, and a single butterfly danced fitfully around it.

In the reception area, the officer manning the gate looked up from behind a glass screen.

'Morning, Guv.'

Matthew smiled cheerfully at him. 'Morning, Bernard. Short straw again?'

Bernard Jenkins' laugh had a sarcastic edge. He wasn't much amused. Not many officers enjoyed working the front desk: visitors to the prison were often less controllable than the inmates. Jenkins was a short, tough cockney with skin the colour of stained wood. He

22

had been overlooked for promotion countless times because, despite his apparent popularity with other officers, he showed no flair for the job. Matthew felt like a hypocrite passing the time of day with him, knowing that he had passed judgement on the man's career behind his back – but that went with the territory, and, in any case, Jenkins did not seem to bear a grudge. He just plodded on, treating all and sundry with the same incomprehensible mixture of good cheer and studied ill-grace. He seemed pleased whenever he was noticed, though – and so Matthew always made the effort.

'Are your daughter's results in?' he asked. She had some rare blood disease. There had been talk of tests.

Jenkins beamed back at him. 'Doctor says she can go back to school whenever she's ready.'

'The all-clear, then?'

He nodded eagerly, his eyes misting slightly.

'Bernard, that's great news. You must be—'

'Not half.' He smiled. 'You all right, then, Guv?'

'Hmmm?'

'Only you look a little . . . You know.'

Irritated that his preoccupation was showing, Matthew forced a smile. 'Oh. Still half-asleep. Need this coffee.' He held up the polystyrene cup. Jenkins gazed at him, his eyes completely blank – waiting for something more, perhaps.

Uncomfortable, Matthew muttered, 'Best get on,' and waved his ID fob. Jenkins released the gate lock. Once through the double-gate system, Matthew stopped at another grille and exchanged the fob for his key-set.

He also handed in his mobile phone. No one was allowed phones inside the prison: the inmates got everywhere – on cleaning duty or catering, in transit from one wing to another – and a mobile phone left lying around was an irresistible prize.

As he left the reception area, Matthew heard Jenkins mutter something, amplified but indistinct. It didn't sound complimentary. The officer Jenkins was working with laughed coarsely. Perhaps the morning's row was more obvious on his face than he had thought. Everyone knew Charlotte, of course. They had met here, and worked together until she finally decided she couldn't handle her double life. Pentonville prison was a small, often incestuous world.

He headed across the small courtyard that separated the entrance area from the admin corridor. As he entered this, the sounds of the wings beyond folded over him: the clatter of gates opening and closing every few seconds; the echoing shuffle of thousands of shoes, moving, always moving; the endless, chaotic human traffic of the Ville. The prison's huge hollow spaces were filled with voices, prisoners calling between the landings, squabbling over the pool table at Association, yelling from the distant reaches of the building's vast spaces. It was chaos, controlled: the apparent mayhem of a machine too complex for easy comprehension, but functioning perfectly.

Her Majesty's Prison, Pentonville: the Ville, to all who knew and loved her – which, by and large, meant the staff, because the inmates would rather have been anywhere else than here.

But to Matthew it wasn't just a prison, it was a job. He was one of twenty or so governors, all answering direct to *the* Governor, Mark Thornton. He had his very own shabby office, with too few shelves and a flickering strip-light which he had been trying to get fixed for over a year. He had reports to file, staff to reward and reprimand, policy documents to draw up and review. And meetings, endless meetings . . . His job was to keep his part of the machine working smoothly. Some of the individuals he was responsible for were extremely unpleasant – not all of them prisoners. But that was his job, both a challenge and an irritation.

It was a strange job, in its way. The pleasure was all in the professionalism, and in friendships with colleagues, not in what you actually did, which was to regulate the lives of convicted criminals. There were no triumphs in prison, no miracle cures, no intense one-on-one relationships that could transform a man from criminal to upright citizen. Most of the inmates had been inside more than once; most of those that hadn't would be.

There were exceptions. Sometimes, rarely, you encountered inmates who were genuinely different. Not the misguided souls who never should have been there, the men with one too many traffic convictions, as keen to please as a puppy, and as confused. Not them, they were sad, but not interesting. But occasionally you ran across someone who stood apart. Who was self-possessed. Thinking. Aware. And, if you were extraordinarily lucky, they were *good*.

Matthew had met one once. He had trusted him, believed in him, even. He had recruited the man to help with a minor drugs problem on his wing that had threatened to get out of hand. The men responsible were caught, but Matthew had seen the project as a failure. Because, by then, he had seen the *man* as his project, not the drugs. A strange and charismatic man, who had shafted Matthew comprehensively – but, perhaps, fairly . . .

Sometimes Matthew wondered where he was. More often, he reminded himself that, in the end, the best course was not to get involved.

Charlotte had loved working at the Ville – in part, he suspected, because she had never taken it as seriously as him. She had been a rank or two below him, mostly because she was five years younger than him rather than through want of talent. When they had met, he was nudging the top of the Officer grade. She was utterly professional, but never took herself seriously. She was so unlike Rachel. She was dangerous, and funny. She had spoken to parts of him that he thought had died years before. She made him laugh.

The day's first task had a name. He was Larry Tysome, and he sat glaring at Matthew as though he belonged under a stone in a swamp.

'Larry, I do understand that it's been hard for you . . .'

Tysome snorted. 'Oh, *hard?*'

'. . . but it's been – how long?'

'Sixth of December, she died.'

'The sixth of December *a year and a half ago*, Larry.'

The man's eyes swam redly. His grief was still sharp after eighteen months or more. Matthew understood that all too well. Rachel still haunted him after eight years. Tysome's grief would never completely vanish – but he was out of time. He had obligations. His work had been unacceptable for far too long.

Matthew flicked the document he held. It was a formal list of Tysome's misdemeanours and shortcomings: promises made at his last appraisal and not delivered on, minor but regular breaches of conduct, consistently turning up late – as he had yet again this morning. He had kept Matthew waiting for twenty minutes.

'Larry, you're just not pulling your weight, I'm sorry. You're still having trouble relating to your colleagues. You've been rude and, frankly, aggressive to several of them. And I have to tell you, Larry, that your attitude to the inmates leaves a lot to be desired. You don't seem to have got anything from the retraining course we sent you on – and, um, that other course . . . Dee?'

He looked over at Dee Somers. She was Tysome's personnel officer, here to see fair play because this was a formal disciplinary meeting. She was whippet-thin and eagle-nosed, and she looked at the file in front of her over red-rimmed glasses on a string.

'Personal Bereavement in the Context of the Workplace,' she said. She looked up brightly. 'Three half-days.'

Matthew nodded encouragingly at Tysome. He chose not to look encouraged. Matthew sighed inwardly. Why was it that five per cent of his staff took up eighty per cent of his time? Most people were competent and just got on with the job, but there was always a Tysome or two in the mix. And, however much Matthew would have loved just to sack him, he couldn't.

'We *care*, Larry. We want to help. That's the point. But you have to do your bit, too. And we've been here before, haven't we? Too many times.'

Tysome gave little away, other than a narrowing of his tiny eyes. His face was long and slightly chubby. A weak chin faded into a fat neck. Wispy brown hair receded over a shiny forehead. The face was lifeless, the mouth slack, the brow unmoving and uncreased. His skin was grey and damp. His wet blue eyes were set piggily above the bulging flesh of his cheeks; they peered out at Matthew shrewdly. He could almost see the calculation in the man.

'Larry, we need to sort this out. We can't go on having these chats with you for ever. This has to be the last time.'

He slid an envelope across the table towards him. Tysome stared at it, but did not touch.

'It's a formal warning,' Matthew said.

He hated this. The man might be irritating and, increasingly, a liability – but throwing the book at someone was always unpleasant. He detested causing misery, even to an insubordinate curmudgeon like Larry Tysome. At the same time, it was a relief that there were rules and structures; it meant that this was in no way personal. To confront this man's inadequacies and confusions without the comfort of a formal role would have been unbearable.

'I'm sorry,' he said gently – and managed to sound as though he meant it.

Tysome's podgy face stayed slack, but his eyes narrowed again, and watered a little. His clasped hands slithered over each other as though he were holding a bar of soap. He licked his lips. He frowned. He said nothing.

There was a tap on the door. Mark Thornton poked his head into the room, took in the scene, and muttered an apology.

'Just a quickie, Matthew. About the walkthrough tomorrow. Nip in when you're done?'

The walkthrough was a dress rehearsal of an upcoming visit by a minor member of the royal family. Hordes of equerries and other royal hangers-on would be going over the Duke's route, the plans for meals, security arrangements, availability of specially cordoned-off toilet facilities, and anything else they could think of. The prisoners would have to be locked up for the duration of the site survey, which was bound to cause ructions. Nevertheless, the visit was an honour, and the preparations were a welcome break from routine.

Matthew gave his boss a tight nod. 'Five minutes, OK?'

Thornton's teeth flashed as he smiled, and dimples appeared, set deep against the hard line of his jaw. Without the grey at his temples, he would have passed for thirty. 'See you shortly.' He nodded at Dee, who blushed. He cocked his head at Tysome, winked unconvincingly at Matthew, and left.

Dee rolled her eyes at Matthew, pretending she found his charm a little too much. When Matthew grinned at her, she concentrated on the pad on her knee, her face still a little flushed. Reluctantly, Matthew took the point. Thornton flirted shamelessly with women. When Charlotte had worked here, she had been no exception. She had lapped up the attention, and lavished it back. Truth be told, he had been relieved when she decided to leave. Then there was the miscarriage, and everything had changed.

Well. He would bring her cornflowers. She loved those.

'Matthew?' Dee smiled at him, and his attention snapped back to the room.

Had Tysome said something at last? Possibly. He was looking at him blankly, waiting. The envelope containing the formal reprimand was untouched on the desk in front of him.

Matthew bit back his irritation. Stare how he might, Tysome surely recognised that this procedure had one inevitable conclusion. The system could no longer tolerate his shortcomings. He had been warned. Attempts had been made to reintegrate him. Now, slowly, with great caution and propriety, the system was pushing him from the nest. It had to happen. He was failing to do his job properly. The life of the prison came before the needs of any individual member of staff.

'I think we're done, don't you, Dee?'

She nodded. He turned back to Tysome, who was still staring at him.

'Larry, I'm sorry things have gone this way. Let's try to sort it out, yes?'

Tysome gazed at Matthew and at nothing, as though he just happened to be in his line of sight.

'Larry?'

The man shook himself awake, and seemed to shrivel slightly. His shoulders drooped.

'Larry, read the letter. When you've read it, if you want to discuss anything, or if you feel you need arbitration, then either Dee or I will do whatever we can to help. OK?'

Another impassive look: intensely annoying – and a little unnerving. How could anyone care so little for their work?

Matthew stood, picked up the envelope and firmly handed it to him. 'Any time, OK, Larry? Let's get this sorted.'

Tysome dragged himself to his feet. He was at least four inches taller than Matthew, and considerably wider, but his frame had no stature to it; he was a small man, despite his size. His lips quivered a little. Then he took the envelope and left. Matthew thanked Dee, chatted with her for a minute or two, and saw her off.

Once he was alone, he rang Charlotte's mobile. There was no reply. Ridiculous, really. It was still down to her to make the first move. He didn't leave a message. It was a moment of weakness even to have rung.

Still, he wished she had answered. It would have been good to hear her voice.

Five

S he woke slowly, dreaming the room before she was fully aware
of it: strange, echoing, grey. Concrete, perhaps. A spiky mattress, smelling of damp and spores and something altogether
less pleasant. Then there was a violent roar – some monster enraged
in these strange caves, or perhaps an explosion, or an avalanche, or –

A plane.

Then another. This time, a shadow flickered across the room as it
passed overhead. There were panels of grimy glass let into the roof.

Her head hurt. She felt sick. She forced her eyes open and pushed
herself upright on the bed. The effort made her dizzy, and she leaned
back against the wall behind her, with her eyes closed again, until the
feeling passed. The wall felt cold, and sharp edges of peeling paint
dug at her scalp.

Too real. Not a dream, then.

She opened her eyes again. The room was bare and large, and the
walls had once been white. The enamel was yellowing, and falling
away in thick, hard scabs. The ceiling was high – twenty feet at least
– and its many ridges were supported by a lattice of metal struts.
There were strip-windows in the roof, but they were tiny, and so
caked with moss and filth and bird droppings that she couldn't see
the sky through them: they provided a muddy glow.

She closed her eyes again, and took a moment to digest her situation. Real. Not a dream. Which meant her memories were real, too.

*He pushes her into the van. He hits her hard on the cheek. When she
comes to, the van is racing at terrifying speed, jolting and battering her.
She lurches towards the door, but it is locked. She screams at the driver to
stop. He ignores her. The man who hit her is next to her. She attacks
him. She flails at his face and arms, while the van rocks them both with
every turn. He scowls at her, unruffled by her blows.*

Then he hits her again. She is dazed, and he wrestles her down flat onto the floor. He lies on top of her. She struggles – until he snarls, 'You want more?' The driver watches the action in his mirror.

The man on top of her bares his stained teeth. His breath is stale, heavy with cigarettes. He reaches over her head to the ledge behind the seat and gropes for something – a plastic bag with a zip-seal. It holds what looks like soggy cotton wool. He takes a deep breath before he opens it. Then he whips out the pad and holds it over her nose. She smells it the moment it comes out of the bag: pungent fumes, penetrating, a thick, stringent, chemical smell. She tries to hold her breath, but her lungs are empty to start with.

They want to kill me. I'm about to die.

She tries to buck him off her. Fails.

'You done there, man? That stuff stink, y'nah?' The driver spits into the footwell, and opens the window.

The man on top of her doesn't reply. His grin grows rigid. His eyes bulge. He bears down harder on her, rams an elbow into her solar plexus. Her chest begins to heave and spasm. She fights not to gasp – then shudders and draws a breath. It is thick, and sharp and heavy and—

The room. Concrete. Cold. Planes overhead.

She forced herself to stand. Her shoes crunched on the gritty concrete floor. She eyed a chemical toilet in the corner. Bad news: it meant whoever those men were, they intended her to be here for a while.

There was a door, a metal one, white-painted and peeling. It had a window made of safety glass, cross-hatched with wire. Thick strips of metal had been welded across it on the outside, about five inches apart. The door gave onto a corridor. Mounted just outside was what looked like a tripod. Bizarre, but undeniably there. There was a door opposite hers, this one solid, with no window. A metal plate marked it as room 143. If she pressed herself against the glass and squinted sideways, in one direction she could see a stretch of the corridor – more doors, blank and numbered – and in the other direction the corridor's end. An old grey filing cabinet filled the end wall, battered and leaning to the side, with one drawer hanging open and the mangled remains of a metal venetian blind draped over it.

The door, of course, was locked. She slapped on it, and called out.

'Hello?' Maybe someone was waiting outside the door.

She was answered by the roar of another plane.

'Hello? *Hello?*'

She bashed harder at the door. The sound boomed around the room, but the glass did not give.

'Let me out! Hello? Someone, let me *out!*'

No one came. Who was she shouting at? Given how she got here, did she really expect them just to shuffle up sheepishly and release her? Ridiculous. She was here, and she was alone.

There was the bed she had woken on, a wooden divan with the drawers removed. The material covering the frame was ripped and mouldering. The mattress smelled of ammonia and stale urine. There was a pillow – brand new, overstuffed, and without a pillow-case. There was a duvet, also new, and also coverless.

She stood in the middle of her prison, and yelled at the top of her voice, 'Bastards! You *bastards!*' Her voice bounced from the walls, and the silence afterwards was more oppressive than before.

Her watch told her it was past four o'clock. She had been unconscious for more than three hours. No wonder her head was pounding.

She threw herself at the door again, battering at it with her palms until they stung. Every ninety seconds her yells were drowned by another plane.

'You stupid, stupid bastards! Let me *out!* Can you hear me? *Out!*'

Nothing happened at all.

The bed stank of urine. The unused toilet stank of plastic. The room smelled of damp, although the concrete floor was dry and skimmed with dust.

Inside her, she could feel the uncertain presence of her baby – Eyelash, she called it, because that was how big it had been at their last scan two weeks before. If things went well on Friday she would start calling it Blackberry. It was their little joke, hers and Matthew's. It was their way of keeping the worry under control. Eyelash made her stomach lurch, not because she moved – it was a she, she was sure of that – but because of the unfamiliar processes going on down there. She could *feel* her. Every moment of that was precious.

She breathed as slowly as she could, searching for calm. They would release her before the morning. And by Friday, this would all be a memory, a bad dream. She would go to the scan. They would operate if they needed to. Everything would be fine.

Five o'clock came. Then six. The minutes were marked by the screams of planes.

At six fifteen, a man appeared. He was wearing a balaclava that covered everything but his brown eyes, and the dark skin around them. He wore jeans, stained shoes with high, rounded toe-caps, and a shabby black T-shirt. Tendons rolled over each other beneath the brown velvet skin of his forearms, and he walked with the wide gait of a man looking for trouble. Worse, he was not one of the two men who had snatched her. And then there were three . . .

He carried something metal on his shoulder. For a moment she thought it was a gun. But guns don't have lenses and a brushed-chrome finish.

The man holding it didn't look at her, only at the camera's screen. His gaze flicked up towards her briefly – casual, disinterested. Then he looked back down to the camera, gauging his shot.

'Please . . .' she said.

He didn't reply. He concentrated on the camera.

'Who are you? Let me go. Please. Don't – you won't . . .'

When at last he spoke, his voice was rough and strangely high. He pushed the video camera closer to her face, and said, 'Aren't you going to smile, then?'

Six

'*I do* hope she's OK.'

It was the fifth time Amanda Thornton had said this in the last fifteen minutes. She wrung her slender hands and perched even closer to the edge of her armchair, sitting unnaturally upright, with her knees tucked to the side. She was, Matthew thought, an entirely artificial woman. Her cheekbones were so high and stuffed that the skin was as shiny as plastic. Her hair was the perfect honey blonde that you can only buy, not be born with. It had been crafted into a fly-away bob that made her look as though she possessed her very own portable wind machine. A fluffy angora top completely failed to keep most of her belly hidden. She could get away with it – just. Impressive for someone in her forties. On another woman, it might even have been sexy; to Matthew, the overwhelming sense that her look had been designed was completely off-putting.

'You don't think anything *awful* has happened to her, do you?' she twittered. Her eyes were as bright and nervous as a bird's – and as empty. The concern on her face was, Matthew suspected, probably more for the fate of the beef Wellington than for the whereabouts of his wife.

He mumbled something about how he was sure that Charlotte was fine, and she'd probably just got stuck on the Tube – just as he had on the previous four occasions.

Amanda Thornton nodded jerkily, and clasped her hands tighter on her lap. 'Mark will be back soon,' she chirped.

Oh good, he thought. *There's something to look forward to.*

Matthew had been looking forward to spending the evening with Charlotte: comedy on the telly, a bowl of pasta and a glass or two or wine; apologies mumbled and accepted; sitting together on the sofa, half-embraced. After the fracas over breakfast, that was the plan.

He had completely forgotten Thornton's invitation until he received an email halfway through the afternoon: *7.30 all right?*, and Thornton's address. Only then had it come back to him. Two weeks ago, a brush in the corridor, a brisk, friendly greeting:

    – Oh, and Matthew. How do you fancy bringing that gorgeous wife of yours over for a spot of supper? Mrs T's dying to meet you both.

    There is little Matthew can say. The idea fills him with horror – but Thornton is the boss. This is politics, not pleasure.

    – That'd be great, Mark. We'd love to. Thanks.

    – How are you fixed for Monday week?

    – Er . . .

    But he knows there is never anything booked on a Monday. And even if they don't do it then, they will have to do it soon.

    – Sounds great. Thanks, Mark. I'll check with Charlotte, but I'm sure it's fine.

    But he doesn't want to check with Charlotte. He knows what she will say. Since the miscarriage – no, since he proposed to her – she has changed. These days she sees him as shallow and dangerous. Where he has always found the man uncomfortable, Charlotte, who used to love to flirt with him, now finds him repellent. He does not ask her why. He does his best not even to ask himself.

    So, he nods at Thornton and smiles – and wonders how he can tell his wife that they must spend an evening with his boss. Back in his office, he rings her, but there is no reply. He doesn't want to break the news in a message, so he tries a few more times, without success. Then, when he gets home, he finds Em and Charlotte at each other's throats – and by the time he has made peace between them, and then told himself that he will say something tomorrow morning, because now is not the time, and then rushed through another argumentative breakfast . . . it has slipped his mind.

    Understandable, perhaps. He had hoped since the moment he heard that the invitation would go away. Understandable, yes – but forgivable?

'I do hope she's all right,' Amanda Thornton said again.

    It was already eight fifteen. *He* hoped she was all right, too.

    He smiled shortly at her, and sipped from the small tumbler of beer she had served him. The glass was only half full. He would probably have been given more liquid if he had asked for a whisky.

'Mark had some things to deal with at work,' she went on. 'He rang. You know how it is.' She had told him this before, too. Twice. Light conversation wasn't her strong point.

'Of course,' he agreed. He pretended to sip his beer, unsure what else to say.

Thornton had left the office at least an hour before he had – though he probably had no idea that Matthew knew that. There had been a sudden half-important crisis on D Wing, little more than a disagreement between two inmates: on his way back to his own office, Matthew had poked his head round Thornton's door to let him know that a formal report would have to be submitted. Thornton's secretary, Anne, had told him that the boss had left early.

Amanda Thornton nodded eagerly, and smoothed her already-smooth skirt.

'I . . . I'd better . . . You know . . .' She pointed in the direction of the kitchen and mimed something vaguely culinary. 'Yes . . .' she muttered. 'I'll just . . .' She stood uncertainly, opened her mouth, closed it again, and scurried away.

He cradled his glass and surveyed the mock-classical decor. Squares had been painted in gold on the cream walls to suggest panelling. Old prints of hunting scenes and hansom cabs hung everywhere – except where there were gilt mirrors or over-large flower arrangements. He perched on the edge of his chair – if he had sat back in it, it would have swallowed him – and contemplated his boss's taste, such as it was. Charlotte was going to hate it.

If she ever got there.

He had arrived home early, bearing a bunch of cornflowers, knowing that Charlotte would have been home for an hour or more. Most likely, she would be upstairs in the bedroom having a rest, or perhaps a bath. She tired easily these days. With luck, she would have got the message he had left on her phone, and would already know about the Thorntons; and if he was *really* lucky, she wouldn't even be angry about it.

Music, if you could call it that, thumped through the house. It was angry, miserable and uncompromising – a fair match, in fact, for the girl who was playing it. He called upstairs, 'Em, quieter please!' It had no effect. Probably she couldn't even hear him. He'd have to go up in a minute.

'Charlotte?'

Again, there was no reply. She probably couldn't hear him either.

He put the cornflowers in a vase in the kitchen. The stems gave off a bitter-dry scent until the water swallowed it. They looked wonderful: intense, chalky and fragile. They dominated the room, and filled it with pale blue light. Even with Em's music scraping at his senses, the room felt tranquil. He sat for a few minutes, taking pleasure in the simple fact of being home, and of knowing that the two most important people in his life were here too – beyond his sight, upstairs, but close. He pulled a single flower from the vase, and padded upstairs.

He knocked on Em's door as he passed. 'Volume.'

He heard a muffled, 'Sorry,' and the sound faded fractionally. 'More.'

He heard her feet thump crossly across her room. The sound reduced to something that was merely loud.

He clamped the cornflower between his teeth, knocked and opened the bathroom door, and made a grand show of swooning romantically against the wall opposite the bath.

She wasn't there. Nor was she in the bedroom.

He went into what had until recently been the box-room: Em had scrawled *Eyelash's Room* on a piece of paper, decorated it with ink-drawn flowers and a one-toothed baby, and stuck it to the door. The walls were a patchwork of colour samples – baby pink, baby yellow, baby blue. Piles of baby clothes, still wrapped and in their shopping bags, lined the edges of the room. Clothes bought by Charlotte, colour schemes pondered by her, as though buying baby outfits and painting walls might somehow prevent another miscarriage.

Poor Charlotte. The last year had been rough.

She was not there.

That left the garden – although it was a cool grey evening, and he could think of no earthly reason for her to be out there. He peered out of Eyelash's window. Opened it. Leaned out to check that she wasn't directly below. There was no one in the garden.

He rapped on Em's door, noticing as he did so that the music had got louder again.

'*OK*, Dad!' He heard her clump across the room again, and then the music stopped entirely. More clumping, and the door jerked open. 'Satisfied?' she snapped.

He gazed back at her mildly, not rising to the bait. She lowered her eyes.

'Sorry.'

It made him want to laugh. There was something so appealing in her sudden meekness. It was a reminder that his little girl was still in there somewhere. Not that he saw much of it these days.

'Have you seen Charlotte, poppet?'

She shrugged, unhelpfully.

'Well, has she called?'

Eyes still down, Em muttered, 'How should *I* know?'

He glanced past her into the room. On her dressing table sat a rough ceramic bowl in brilliant blue, inset with glittering stones. It held a candle. A thin line of greasy smoke rose from it. The flame guttered for a moment in a breeze too slight to notice, then steadied.

He felt a small, bitter lurch. The bowl was the last thing Rachel had ever given her. Em had seen it in a shop, and loved it. Rachel had gone back the next day and bought it for her.

In his more introspective moments, he wondered if the distance between them had less to do with puberty than with this bowl – or with Rachel, and Charlotte. But he could hardly freeze his own life for her sake, could he? On her bad days, she seemed to expect him still to be grieving. Well, he *was*, and he always would. But to expect it to dominate his life? That was just . . .

Childish.

Therefore, also forgivable. She was still young. At her age, every wound was fresh. But he wished sometimes that she would put that bowl away in a drawer, stop lighting the candles – and get a life.

Em shifted her weight uneasily and studied the floor.

'Are you sure she hasn't rung?'

Em glanced uncomfortably at the candle behind her, and then nodded.

He persisted. 'You've no idea where she is?'

She shook her head and bit her lip. The message was clear: no, she knew nothing about where Charlotte was, and she would very much like it if he could leave her in peace. He did.

He sat on the edge of the bed and rang Charlotte's mobile. He got the answering service. Her tone was bright, the words familiar. 'Hi. Charlotte here. Do leave a message and I'll call you back. Bye.' She always said 'Bye' in a sing-song. It made him smile.

He waited for the beep. 'Hi, darling, it's me. It's five past seven. I'll have to leave at quarter past to get to the Thorntons'. You did get the message I left, didn't you? We're there for dinner. So I suppose I'll see you there.' He gave her the address, then went on. 'Darling, are you OK? I'm sorry about the thing this morning – you know, with the scan. Just . . . Yeah. Call.'

There was probably a hold-up on the Tube. She was stuck in a tunnel somewhere, with the driver mumbling incomprehensible updates through the tannoy.

It had been nearly eight by the time he arrived at Mark Thornton's house in Islington. He sat outside in the car and called her again on his mobile. No reply. He left another message. He rang the London Underground information desk. There were no problems reported on the Tube. Perhaps she was working late. He found her current office number on a scrap of paper in his wallet. Naturally enough, no one was there.

The house was huge – impossibly so, for a prison governor's salary. Matthew had heard rumours that Thornton's wife was wealthy, but had thought nothing much of it until now. Climbing the stone steps towards the immense front door, though, he found himself wondering what else he had heard about Thornton might be true: that he did more than just flirt with other women; that his wife had found out about his affairs, and had . . . Well, what *would* you do? There were as many answers to that one as there were gossip-mongers at the Ville. Besides, this was all information that Matthew had no desire to know.

Reluctantly, he rang the bell, thinking about accidents. Maybe Charlotte had been clipped by a bus, or pushed onto the rails at a tube station. She had been mugged. He dismissed each idea. She was late, that was all. There could be any number of reasons. He could hardly start ringing round hospitals and police stations just because her phone was switched off and she was a little late for dinner.

Amanda Thornton answered the door.

'Oh! You must be Matthew. How – how lovely . . . Mark's not back yet. Something at the office. He'll be here soon, I'm sure. Where's your wife – Charlotte, isn't it? I thought she . . . But, look at me, with you on the doorstep. Please. Come in . . .'

They waited together for nearly half an hour, he cradling a glass of beer he could have finished in a gulp, and she fussing, flitting back and forth to the kitchen, and smiling at him as though he might be tempted to bite her.

At twenty past eight, a key rattled in the front door, and then it slammed closed. Mark Thornton called out a cheery hello. His wife bustled out of the kitchen, twittering questions and information at him in equal quantities – what had kept him so long, he'd kept their guests waiting, well, just one guest because Charlotte wasn't here yet, and she did hope nothing bad had happened to her, and did Mark think she should serve the crème brûlée in individual ramekins, only she was worried because it hadn't set quite as much as it said in the book, and—

Matthew tuned them out. *Where was Charlotte?*

Dinner, predictably, was an uncomfortable affair. Thornton was in a foul mood. He snapped at Amanda over the size of Matthew's drink, then busied himself in the kitchen, managing to give the impression that the time his wife had spent there had been entirely wasted. At one stage he called along the corridor, 'Sorry, Matthew. Be with you in a minute. Nightmare day.'

Five minutes later, he abandoned Amanda in the kitchen and came through, bearing two large glasses of beer and a sympathetic grin. After ten minutes of uncomfortable small talk, she called them through to eat.

'Oh, I do hope she's all right,' she said nervously. Again. She set a hot plate in front of him. 'I've left hers in the oven. Do you think it'll get too dry?'

Matthew had no idea, and opened his mouth to say so. Thornton laughed.

'Really, Amanda. *You're* the cook, not him!' She pouted at him, and he mock-groaned. 'Darling, it'll be *fine*. Anyway, if it's dry, then it's dry.' She nodded uncertainly and headed back towards the kitchen. Thornton eyed Matthew. 'No idea at all what she's up to?'

'None.'

'She's not gone off me, then? Not hiding at home, refusing to come out and play?'

Matthew smiled, weakly. Thornton's words were often hurtful – but only just, and always open to a more innocent interpretation. Still, if something hurt, it hurt, regardless of the speaker's intentions. 'No, no,' he said. 'Of course not. She's just . . .' He shrugged.

Thornton's eyes creased. 'Always a worry, eh?'

Matthew bit back a savage response. Why should *Thornton* think of Rachel? It was just his own anxiety. This was just some blokish, misplaced joke about women.

It's called charm, Matthew. You might want to try it sometime.

One of Charlotte's unkinder cuts.

Thornton frowned, concerned. 'Listen, if you're worried, want to give her a quick buzz before we tuck in?'

Gratefully, Matthew slipped into the hall, and tried Charlotte's mobile again. He left a message – not the one he would have liked to have left – *get me out of here* – but a brief expression of concern. With the Thorntons listening, what else could he say?

When he returned to the table it was to an uncomfortable silence, as though they had been whispering behind his back.

He spread his arms. 'No reply. I'm so sorry.'

Thornton grinned. 'Nonsense. She'll be stuck on a bus or something. Happens to us all – eh, Mands?'

Amanda sat with her eyes cast down, her food untouched, saying nothing. She nodded meekly – and then silence returned.

There were sporadic attempts at conversation. Thornton wanted to know if Matthew had watched the game on Saturday; Matthew had no idea which sport he was talking about, let alone which match. So he asked Amanda about her work. She told him that she didn't work, and it was amazing how busy life was anyway, she didn't have *time* to work. The conversation died again. Amanda's turn. She wanted to know more about Charlotte, she'd heard so much about her. Thornton laughed loudly, as though this was the funniest question he had ever heard, and then answered on Matthew's behalf.

'Office romance, they were, these two. Lost me a bloody good officer, Matthew did. Sexy too.' He twinkled at Matthew, who did his best to respond in kind. 'Seriously, though,' Thornton continued, 'you did well there.'

'It must have been my turn to get lucky,' he answered – and immediately worried that it had sounded sharper than he had intended. His hosts showed no sign of taking it the wrong way, though. He concentrated on staying quiet, and worked his way through a soft and flavourless lump of crème brûlée.

After half a cup of coffee, he made his excuses and left.

He called Charlotte's mobile again the moment he was in the car. Voicemail again.

There was a reason, of course, whatever it was. She had arrived home too late to get back out to the Thorntons', perhaps. Perhaps she just hadn't been able to face it. Either way, now, she was sitting at home in the kitchen waiting for him. She hadn't answered or returned his calls because the Thorntons might overhear.

He rang home. Em answered, with music in the background.

'Yeah?'

'Em, it's me. Has Charlotte—'

'Get *off*, Dad! Patch is going to play Dexter's gig down to me.'

Matthew was confused. 'Play what?'

'*Da-ad!* Dexter? The gig? The one you said I couldn't go to? Get *off*!'

'Em, if Charlotte's there I really need to—'

'She's with you. Like, you were going out with her? Remember? Now, *please*! I really really *really* need—'

'She hasn't come in and gone back out? Rung? Nothing?'

'She's not *here*, Dad! *Pleeeease*!'

'Tell her to call me when she gets in.'

Reluctantly, he rang off, and began the drive home.

Perhaps it was the baby. She had lost the baby. She had miscarried again. She was huddled in a corner somewhere, hugging herself, sobbing, unable to ring him, unable to bear even the thought of him. No more playing at mummies and daddies. A return to silences and arguments fought for no reason, and her attacking him not because he had done anything wrong, but simply because she hurt. A return to Charlotte disappearing into the night, reappearing in the morning, weeping and apologetic and offering no explanation at all.

The only light in the house was in Em's room. Their phone was cordless: she would have taken it into her room with her. Obviously, she had not had any reason to come back out. When he went inside, he was surprised not to be assaulted by her music. Perhaps she was on the phone, listening to Dexter's 'performance'.

He went round the ground floor, drawing curtains and switching on lights. In the kitchen, he poured himself a beer. He picked up the downstairs phone, and briefly activated it, listening to see if Em was using it. She wasn't. He hung up, without dialling Charlotte's number. Ten minutes later he gave up, and rang her again. After three rings, it kicked over to her answer machine. He had left too many messages already. He texted her:

Where are you? Getting worried. Love you

Then he waited.

She wouldn't leave him, would she? Frictions over the breakfast table were hardly cause for a divorce, however unhappy she was underneath it all. He buried the memory of her last walk-out. A night away, no explanation . . .

No, it was the baby. She couldn't face telling him. She had fallen over and something had jabbed her in the belly and –

Or she was in some kind of trouble. She was lying bleeding somewhere. She was already under the surgeon's knife, an emergency operation to save her life. She'd been raped, arrested, mugged . . .

He did his best to ignore his fears, and did not altogether succeed.

It was Rachel, all over again. She hadn't come back. She had just walked away one day, leaving a six year old alone in her room. He had piled Em into the car. They had searched and searched. And in the late twilight of a summer day, they had found her. He had waded out into the lake, and . . .

And he had lost her. He had nearly lost Em, too. The grief, the fear – and then the slow, deliberate grinding-down of all he still held precious. The police. The social workers. Em designated as being *at risk*. The disciplinary hearings at work.

But that was the past. This was different. It had to be.

He texted Charlotte again.

Missing you. Where are you?

He sat, waiting. The house was brightly lit, and silent. The clock jolted round, minute by minute – and uncertainty gave way slowly to a rising tide of anxiety.

He thought of the police: *Are you sure you had no idea, sir? You'd been arguing hadn't you, sir? Are you sure it didn't just get out of hand, sir? Are you happy to repeat that in court, sir?*

Bastards, the lot of them. Their precious procedures mattered more to them than the human beings they dealt with every day.

Of course, he was very aware of the question this raised. What made his own job any different from theirs? After all, he too was obliged to follow rules and protocols rather than intuition. On one occasion, he hadn't. He had chosen to trust someone, to take the . . . informal route. The result had been ruinous – not for him, fortunately, but for the victim of his trust. A principled, brilliant and dangerous man. A name he wished he could forget.

But there *were* differences between what he did and the police. The men Matthew looked after in the Ville had already been found guilty by judge and jury. All that remained was to carry out the terms of their sentence. The police, on the other hand – and he had no doubt that they would deny it – acted as though *they* were the judges. When they claimed that they were just doing their job, the truth was that they could target whoever they chose – and from that moment on, that person's innocence or guilt was irrelevant, because their sentence had already begun. They were in the system, and the system would slowly and impartially process them – so many hours in a holding cell for questioning, Social Services called because there was a child involved, suspension from work, damage to your reputation . . . All without trial, just part of the process.

Just doing our job, sir.

At least Matthew worked with people who'd had their day in court. Barring the – very, very occasional – miscarriage of justice, he dealt with people whose guilt was not in question. The police, though, worked with *suspects*. And the taint of their suspicion was enough to threaten what little you had left – your daughter, your job . . .

The difference, simply put, was that the police were bastards. The lot of them.

It was nearly midnight, then, with no word from Charlotte, before Matthew finally decided that, bastards or not – who else could he call?

Tuesday

Seven

It is eight years ago. Matthew is troubled. Emmie is nearly six – and, since her birth, Rachel has never quite been the same. He remembers their elation immediately after Emmie was born. He remembers the daze after that, a time when it felt as though they would never sleep again; Emmie howling, howling, and the slow grind as you are worn down to a nub, the functional, barely conscious remnants of what you were.

Change nappies. Feed her. Hold her while she screams at three in the morning, in whatever room is furthest away from your other half, because they need to sleep, and next time it will be their turn. Change more nappies. Feed her.

And Rachel: drowsy-happy at first; then bleak and exhausted, just as he was. Then . . . something worse. Rachel in a place she could not find a way back from. A place where no light shone at all, where you did what you did because it was in front of you and it was your job. No joy. No laughter.

When Emmie first smiled – when Matthew jiggled her excitedly, and she smiled again, a grin that crookedly cracked her face – Rachel's lips had tightened slightly. Yes, she said. She's smiling. Then she got up from the bed and took her from him. She needs changing, she said. And she took her into the next room.

He talked to his friends. They laughed sympathetically. Post-natal depression, they said, and they dandled the fourth or fifth of their huge brood on their knees. Just takes time. It'll be fine. And their urchins gazed at him, with chocolate smeared round their mouths.

At home, Rachel changed nappies. She fed Emmie. She sat and flicked ceaselessly through television channels.

Emmie was two when they finally saw a doctor. After that, there were pills for Rachel, then counselling, then psychotherapy. And at home, she fed her daughter, kissed her husband dutifully when he came home from work, and sat, waiting for something that never came.

And now Emmie is six. When Matthew demands it – when he needs it enough – Rachel smiles, or makes love, or walks with him and discusses changes to the house, or the troubles of his career. When Emmie comes home with star stickers for her school work, she kneels next to her daughter and talks about it earnestly. They paint together, go to the zoo.

And when she is alone, when she has fed them both, and Matthew is deep in paperwork in the study, and Emmie is in bed, she sits and she stares. She scans through the television channels.

Flick. Flick.

One night, when he knows that she is awake, staring at the ceiling, and she thinks he is asleep, he whispers to her. 'I love you,' he says softly. He can feel her awake next to him, and he says, 'I love you.'

She does not reply.

She takes the pills. She sees the psychotherapist once a week. But in the years since Emmie first came into their lives, Matthew has slowly come to understand that Rachel, the woman he loves, is afraid of the dark in a way he will never truly understand.

Emmie rips open the thin translucent paper and pulls out the bowl inside. It is blue, and stones are set into it. They sparkle in the evening light.

'A present,' Rachel says – and Emmie squeals and hugs her. Rachel presses her face into Emmie's hair and breathes deeply. 'Love you,' she whispers.

Across the top of their daughter's head, as she babbles excitedly and turns the bowl over, and traces the sharp stones with her fingers, Rachel catches Matthew's eyes. She sees the pain there, and she turns away.

He searches for her.

It is twilight, late. It is the middle of summer, and the hazy glow of London in the evening hangs over the common.

He calls for her, holding Emmie's hand too tightly. She struggles to keep up as he marches through the thick grass. 'Rachel? Rachel!'

There are birds, still singing although it is nearly ten – and Rachel

48

has been gone since six at least, because that is when he came home from work and found Emmie crying in her room, with a puddle of wee on the carpet, because Mummy had told her she must not come out, not for anything. Emmie, howling.

He has fed her. Cleaned up the mess in her room. Told her everything is fine, and let's find Mummy, shall we?

Rachel does not have many friends. He rings them. They haven't seen her. He dumps Emmie in her car-seat and drives to the common.

Last night, he had argued with her – or tried to: she pulled away. Switched on the television.

Flick.

Now, he strides the common, calling. There are places where they always walk together, places she loves.

'Rachel? Rachel!'

It is late. Everyone has gone: even the walkers, exercising a dog, smoking a cigarette, escaping for a moment from the life they are about to return to. There are tussocks of grass, grey rushes, clumps of trees. The paths are gravel and mud. He rushes along them, worried now, tugging Emmie along behind.

There is a red shape, a dress, and dark hair spreading. Two leather heels break the surface. He leaves Emmie on the shore and wades into the lake alone. The water is chest-deep by the time he reaches her, and warm and streaked with slime; and he struggles to lift her, to turn her pale face to the surface. Water slides from her mouth, her nose. He babbles at her. Emmie screams at him.

She is white, so pale.

He drags her towards the shore.

Later, much later, when he has run, with Rachel limp across his arms and Emmie dragging behind, howling – when he has called an ambulance and the police from his brand-new mobile, and has staggered towards the nearest road – later, as they wait, he looks at his daughter, and he sees in her reproachful face the one truth he is more afraid of than any other. She blames him. He did this to her.

Later still, with Emmie upstairs asleep, he sits, and he switches on the television: anything to take away the silence. He scans through the channels, searching for anything that will lift the gloom, or perhaps deepen it.

49

Flick.

Flick.

In the morning, the police will come, and ask their endless questions – and, even then, with Rachel not twelve hours dead, he will see suspicion in their eyes. They will question how she died. They will question whether Em, his daughter, the one treasure he has left in the world, is safe in his care.

And he will discover a new fear inside himself. Overpowering. Crippling. The failure to save. The fear that he has made himself alone.

Eight

Eight years ago – and still the memory of Rachel's death crept over him whenever he was stressed and alone. As a result, the twenty minutes between calling the police to report Charlotte missing and the police actually arriving were . . . disturbing.

By then he knew that something was badly wrong. The desk sergeant had explained the procedure. The first step was to check if any reports had come in about her: she might be in hospital, or a police holding cell somewhere. She wasn't. That ruled out muggings and accidents.

On the phone, the desk sergeant had politely said, 'Not wanting to pry, sir, but have you and Mrs Daniels fallen out or anything?'

Matthew blinked. 'I beg your pardon?'

'Only, you'd be surprised how many missing persons turn out to be – well, taking a breather, let's say. Could be an argument. Maybe they're just a bit depressed. Not being rude, sir, but can you think of any reason why—'

He didn't mean to lose his temper, but the man's comments were uncomfortably close to the bone – and, at the same time, utterly wrong.

'Would I *really* be talking to you if I thought that was the explanation? Are you suggesting I can't tell the difference between an argument and a potential emergency? I'm a prison governor, for goodness sake!'

The sergeant didn't bother to reply.

'Sorry,' Matthew muttered. 'But – no, there's no reason why she'd be gone.'

The sergeant continued, undeflected, his tone exactly as if Matthew had never spoken. 'All the same, sir . . .'

'Look, Officer, I understand what you're getting at, but the answer is, no. There's a bit of friction in any relationship – but there are no serious problems, OK?'

At the other end of the line, he heard the officer suck breath. 'I see . . .' There was a series of sharp clicks – a pencil tapping on a desk, perhaps. 'Well, then. You're a prison governor, you said?'

'Yes.'

'*O* . . .' tap, tap '*Kay* . . .' Then, brightly, he said, 'Well, I think we'd better send someone round, sir, don't you?'

Matthew hung up, and waited, in the uneasy company of his own imagination. At least this time, they couldn't threaten to take Em away from him.

The police sat in his kitchen, their caps set on the table in front of them, each cupping a mug of tea that they never drank.

'Do you have a photograph, sir?'

He was startled, even though the question was an obvious one. He glanced around the room nervously.

'Somewhere, yes. I must have.'

Charlotte dealt with the photos – because, she said, he never got round to putting them in albums. Well, neither did she: they were all crammed in a drawer somewhere, still in their packets. He could visualise the drawer, but he couldn't remember where it was.

As he rummaged through the kitchen units he talked, to fill the silence. 'I'm sure you're right. She'll be back any moment . . .' He wasn't sure of that at all.

'Of course, sir. Still, it's best to be safe, isn't it?'

It was hardly reassuring that the first thing the police had told him was that they had to consider the possibility of kidnap. They asked if he had received any threats or demands. He hadn't. Had he heard from anyone about her? No. Was he sure? Yes. No girlfriends, old boyfriends? *No.*

And there's no one from the prison who'd got it in for you, sir? An ex-con with a grudge, that kind of thing? That one gave him pause. *I know where you live, Guv; I'll be seeing you.* But threats were just the normal background noise of prison life, they were part of the job. He had a good relationship with most of the inmates, and a reputation for fairness. There were always a few troublemakers – but that was hardly surprising, and nothing new. Occasionally he did run into ex-inmates in pubs or shops – because the Ville sat in the middle of its own catchment area, and the majority of the inmates lived within a few miles of the prison – but there was never any trouble. Invariably, ex-cons were not foolish enough to risk another stretch inside.

So. No threat from the prison that he could think of. In fact, there was no reason for Charlotte to be gone at all. She just was.

The police insisted on speaking to Em. She was still awake, despite the hour, reading, with headphones on, and a fresh candle trailing smoke from her blue bowl. She attempted to challenge him – until she saw the look on his face. Ungraciously, she tore off her headphones and followed him downstairs. Once there, she protested, in her bolshiest tone, that she knew nothing, that it wasn't her fault, and that she wasn't Charlotte's keeper. She also asserted that Charlotte had a fearsome temper, and who knew what she was capable of? The junior officer solemnly noted this down. Restraining an impulse to slap Em hard, Matthew ground out something like, 'I think that's a bit extreme, Em, don't you?' Em rolled her eyes at him, and chewed gum. When she was quite sure that she had made her point, she flounced out, swaying her hips a little for the younger policeman, who concentrated earnestly on his notebook while his ears went pink.

The older policeman smiled knowingly. 'It does get better, sir. Generally when they're about thirty.'

Matthew smiled tightly back.

They assured him that they took all missing persons cases very seriously, especially those involving At Risk Groups – that meant him, apparently – but there wasn't much they could do until they were completely sure that Charlotte was in fact missing. And that, they told him, could take a day or more. In the morning they would track down her boss and find out if he could shed any light. But really, sir, they said, there was not much they could do. You'd be surprised how many so-called missing persons just turn up the next day, sir, they said.

That was when they asked for the photo. After some rummaging, he found one of the two of them, smiling, on a recent walk in Epping Forest. He was a head taller than Charlotte, and his cheek pressed against her hair. She leaned against him, laughing – because he had pinched her bottom just as their friend pressed the shutter. Her eyes sparkled with mischief, and her cheeks were bunched high.

'Thank you, sir. Excellent.' The older police officer made a show of studying it. He glanced at his watch. 'As you said, though, sir, I'm sure we won't be needing it. Most likely she'll turn up before morning. We'll drop in again tomorrow morning around nine, see how things stand.'

They left, having accomplished precisely nothing. Despite their original talk of kidnappings and At Risk Groups, their visit had clearly been a cosmetic exercise. He might have expected as much, after what had happened with Rachel.

It was almost one o'clock. He tried Charlotte's mobile. There was no reply.

He cracked another bottle of beer, and waited. The bottle sat untouched on the kitchen table, fizzing quietly in the silent house.

When the phone rang, he jumped so violently that his arm nearly knocked over the bottle.

'Charlotte? Hello?'

The line hissed and popped. Perhaps she was drunk and she had dropped the phone. Maybe it had switched itself on in her pocket. She'd talk in a second.

'Charlotte?'

His own voice echoed back at him emptily. He stared about the room, confused. The clock's second hand ticked on one more notch. An amplified scraping sound caught him by surprise – as though something was rubbing against the microphone at the other end, or someone had breathed on it too heavily.

Then there was a voice. A man's voice. It was harsh and guttural, and it spoke in an amplified whisper.

It said, 'Calling the police was a big mistake. Anyone would think you didn't want to see her again.' Then, before he could frame a response, the voice continued, 'You *do* want to see her again, don't you, Matthew?'

It took him several seconds to digest what was happening. Some-one . . . *had* her. As much for time as anything else, he hissed, 'Who the hell—'

'Hardly going to tell you, now, am I?'

'You bastard, what have you—'

'Temper, Matthew.'

'What do you want? Where is—'

There was a sound at the door: the flap of the letterbox.

The voice said, 'You should be receiving a package any minute now. Watch the video.'

He rang off.

Confused, and badly rattled, Matthew dialled 1471 as he made his way to the front door. An automated message told him that the call had come from Charlotte's mobile.

On the doormat, there was a tape.

Nine

'*P*lease . . .'
    She is confused. Scared.
    '*What . . . ?*' *she whispers.* '*What . . . ?*' *She falters. Her eyes flick around the room.* '*Why are . . . ? Who are you? Please. What do you want?*'
    She is fully clothed, sitting coiled on a shabby bed in a concrete room – but she seems naked. Her voice echoes off the walls. There is fear in her unsteady gaze.
    '*Who are you?*' *she asks again. She is trying to sound brave, but her voice is uncertain.* '*Why . . . ? What . . . ? What do you . . . ? Why are you doing this?*'
    The camera's view widens. Whoever is holding it is backing towards the door. Charlotte is small and uncertain, perched on a bed in a concrete room.
    '*Wait!*' *she yelps.* '*Please! What do you want? I – no! Wait!*'
    A door closes between her and the camera. It has a glass panel. She is standing now, and terrified. As the door snicks closed, she comes closer. She is still calling to the man, but it is barely audible now.
    '*No! Wait! Please!*'
    The camera wobbles as the man sets it on its tripod, just outside the door, pressed close to the glass. His shoulder obscures the picture for a moment, and the automatic focus makes the image swim. Then he is gone, and the picture sharpens again, and his receding footsteps crunch crisply on the grit of a concrete floor.
    She is at the glass now, pressed against it.
    '*Wait! Come back! Please! No – I – I—*'
    She squints sideways, trying to see where her captor has gone.
    '*Please, no! Let me out!*'
    She batters the glass. The sound is thin and distant. Her palms are

pressed against it. They show brilliant white. For a moment, the camera struggles to adjust.

'What do you want?' she yells. But there is no reply.

Her eyes flicker across the camera and then, uneasily, around the room. She steps back, bites her fist. Whispers something to herself. She is completely unaware that her other hand has strayed to her belly and is rubbing it gently. Her eyes are wide. She is confused. Hesitantly, she backs away from the door and the camera, and searches for a corner where she cannot be seen.

She disappears from view.

The sound from inside the room is faint and scratchy. Every minute or so, for some reason, there is a deafening roar that blankets out whatever sound might be on the tape.

Then, after a time, Matthew hears the distant, unmistakable sound of a woman crying.

How dare he, whoever he was? What was he hoping to accomplish? What kind of sick maniac would make Charlotte suffer like that – and then send him a tape of it?

The answer to that was obvious: someone from the Ville.

I know where you live, Guv. I know where your wife is right now. Might just pay you a visit when I'm out, Guv.

Thousands of prisoners: eight hundred or more at any one time, a hundred coming or going every day. It could be any one of them. But why?

He rewound the tape and played it again.

'Who are you?' Charlotte said to him. 'Why . . . ? What . . . ? What do you . . . ?'

Someone she didn't know, then, despite her own years at the Ville. Or someone in a mask.

'Who are you?' she whispered, terrified. A strange roar drowned out all other sound for a few seconds. Her lips mutely said, 'Please . . .' The roar faded.

He was desperate to reach out to her, hold her. She needed his reassurance, his strength. She was afraid.

The phone rang. He paused the tape before he snatched it up.

'Want to know what happens in the next instalment?' the voice asked.

'Let her go.' Matthew's teeth were clenched. He could feel his pulse beating in his head.

'You'll like it,' the man said. 'There's more . . . action.'

'You sick bastard, don't you realise—'

'Unless you get the police out of it.'

'What do you—'

'No police, *Matthew*. All right?'

He paused, groping for some element of this insane situation that he could control. His initial rage was restrained now: now, he was thinking. Who was this man? How could he reach him? What could he do to change this?

At last, he said, 'What do I have to do?'

'No one must know. Not your girl, not the police. No one. That's the deal.'

He couldn't help himself. It was tantamount to encouraging the man, but he had to know. He said, 'Or?'

There was a pause before the man answered. 'You know the answer to that, don't you?'

'Listen, she's *pregnant*! If you think—'

'Put off the pigs, or you lose your wife – again.'

The phone went dead.

Desperately, he dialled Charlotte's number. It kicked through to voicemail. He rang off, dialled again: same result.

Again. Again.

He thought, furiously. There had to be a solution. Somewhere, there was an answer. He had been on courses about hostage situations. There were procedures, proven approaches: be calm, speak normally – sympathetically, even. Extract what information you can, but never take action yourself. Keep the hostage-taker talking until the professionals arrive.

The police would believe him now, of course. He had the video. They would leap into action.

Just like last time.

How big did you say the life insurance payout was, sir?

The fools had trodden over his grief – and Em's – in size-twelve boots and had only let go, grudgingly, when they were forced by an expensive lawyer to accept that they had no evidence at all. His return to work had been unpleasant: the staff greeted him with caution, the inmates with delight.

He didn't *want* the police involved – but, given the situation, what was the alternative? They were coming back tomorrow morning at nine whether he told them about the tape or not. And whatever his opinion of their methods, at least they would know what to do . . . Eventually . . . Once the proper forms had been completed . . . Once they had harassed him and Em to within an inch of their lives, on no better grounds than that they were associated with the problem . . . After all that, they *might* just drag themselves into motion, and try to do some good.

By then, they would be searching for a corpse.

He needed time. If he could resolve this himself, there would be no need for the police. If this could be dealt with quickly, then his chances were better alone.

What to do in a hostage crisis: do *not* panic. Do *not* give in. Establish a line of communication. Keep the man talking. The hostage-taker is afraid. He wants it to end. He wants a way out: help him find it safely.

He remembered the woman who had run the hostage course. He could still hear her strident voice. He could see her pacing, see her flip-chart full of selected highlights. Some ideas were underlined, others scribbled out in red. *Get their confidence – good. Ask what they want – not good – remember, you're in charge, make them want to work with you.* He remembered her final tap of the pen on the chart-paper, marking an end to all constructive ideas from her audience. Teacher knows best. But then, Teacher's beloved wasn't in the hands of an unknown maniac. This wasn't work. This was personal.

Shocked by his own uncertainty, Matthew reached again for the phone. When Charlotte's answering message had played, he spoke. 'If you want to keep the police out of this, you'll have to help me. As things stand, the police are coming back tomorrow morning at nine. I'm prepared to put them off if you tell me what you want. If it's at all possible, I'll get it for you. But keep her safe, you hear. She's pregnant. The baby's at risk. There are drugs she has to take. If she's harmed, or the baby, all deals are off.' He checked the kitchen clock. It was almost four in the morning. 'We've got less than five hours to sort this out. Call me.'

He sat in the kitchen, under the harsh ceiling light, staring at a now-flat bottle of beer, and a vase full of cornflowers. Waiting.

At quarter past, he rang again. It rang out, never even switching to voicemail. Angrily, he rang again. There was no reply. And again. How could the man be so *stupid*?

It became a routine. He waited five minutes, then rang. Another five minutes. Another call. He couldn't even pretend that he was grinding down her captor with the torture of a ringing phone – because for all he knew, it wasn't even ringing. But if the phone was off, when he switched it back on, Matthew wanted his to be the first voice the man heard. Whatever he wanted, Matthew would need time to sort it out – or, if it was something unacceptable, time to work out what to do next.

At five, her mobile responded, and he heard her voice: 'Hi, this is Charlotte . . .' When it was done, he said, 'There's four hours now. Whatever you want, I swear I'll try to sort it out. But you need to talk to me *now*. There's not much time. Ring me. I'm waiting.'

Five minutes later, he rang again. The call switched through to her answering service. After another five minutes, it did the same.

Then his own mobile beeped, signalling a text message. It was from Charlotte's mobile. It read:

You want her to stay pregnant – you stop ringing

Matthew almost threw his phone at the wall in frustration. The man was mad, brutal, incoherent, incapable of thought. Why wouldn't he just *talk*? He must want this to be over. They both did. Didn't he understand that he was destroying his own chances of success?

Not to mention the life of Matthew's unborn child.

He gathered his thoughts and texted back.

Police come at nine. What do you want me to do? I can pay if it's money

Three minutes later the phone rang – and a now-familiar voice whispered, 'I thought you'd never ask.'

Ten

S he sat on the bed and waited. Planes came over every ninety seconds, low and oppressively loud. Each time, the roar filled the room. Sometimes their shadows fell across the windows in the roof, and for an instant the yellow glow that seeped through the filth would flicker to darkness – so fast that every time it shocked her, and left her panicked, reeling with an intense awareness that she was alone. Captive, and utterly alone.

She was normally home by half past five. That was when someone would have first missed her – Em, back from school, usually in a strop about something or other, and demanding to be fed. Would Em raise the alarm? More likely she'd grouch off to her room thinking all the adults in the world had it in for her, and that Charlotte's absence was a deliberate personal slight. If Em was anything to go by, it seemed that teenagers had a limitless capacity for blaming others for their every woe. Not Em, then: Matthew.

If he was on a normal shift, and assuming (optimistically) that there wasn't some crisis, he got home at about six thirty. He would have rung her. Absent-mindedly, she groped for her bag, and found nothing but the nylon-covered pillow. She stood and scanned the room again. No bag. No phone. No call from Matthew.

Cautiously, she skirted round the thought that, also, she no longer had her drugs. It was only just past midnight. She wouldn't need them until the morning – and the possibility that she might be forced to spend the rest of the night here was . . . unthinkable.

No. Matthew would have missed her, and when she didn't answer her phone, he would have raised the alarm. He was always fussing over her, worrying if she so much as twisted her ankle. Half the police in the country would be looking for her by now. Another unwelcome thought made an appearance: Yes, they'll be *looking* for you. But when will they *find* you?

Another doubt, less worthy, crept into her thoughts, too: what if he didn't call the police? He had only ever mentioned them with contempt – and after what they had put him through, she could hardly blame him. Still, this was different. He would have called them, wouldn't he?

She picked up the pillow and squeezed it experimentally. It was so densely stuffed that her hands bounced. Still, the duvet looked all right. She wrinkled her nose. Shame about the bed. She would have to sleep on the floor.

Except it wouldn't come to that, would it? Because the bastards who had snatched her must have a plan. They had probably already made their demands. Matthew would have checked with her office and discovered she hadn't come back from lunch. And the moment he realised that it was not some bizarre hoax, he would have called the police. So, by now the alarm had already been raised. They were already negotiating. And whatever it took – money, a siege, whatever – it would surely be over before morning.

Yeah, Charlotte. Right.

So, who were they? What did they want? She hadn't really noticed the men until it was too late. They had just been people on the street – one black, one white, she thought, but she was not even sure of that. They were just faces, just people. Except that they had taken her prisoner, and there had to be a reason.

There was one obvious reason. Matthew. What else could it be? He had done something – or had the power to do something. If you rose high enough through the ranks, you made enemies. It had been bad enough at her level. There were threats – but you rapidly learned that threats were just the posturing of powerless men, struggling to find ways to assert themselves in an environment where their every move was rigidly controlled. The first time, it scared you; the second time, you wondered about it a little; the third time, you laughed.

But Matthew was a governor now, albeit a junior one, and that made a difference. Now, he was making the rules. He controlled access to parole. He could strip inmates of their privileges if they misbehaved. He had power. Charlotte knew that, at work, Matthew was fair-minded to the point of obsession. Mostly, he was well liked, by prisoners and staff alike. But it only took one . . . Or, in this case, three. And these goons had worked out that the best way to get to him was through her.

She shivered. Thank heavens they hadn't gone for Em.

What did they want? A prisoner released? A fat cheque? If it was money, he would find it. If it was to do with the prison, they might discover that his hands were more tightly tied than they thought. And that would mean a siege, and drawn-out negotiations through a megaphone . . .

If, that was, they could work out where she was being held.

All she had were questions – and, at the end of every line of thought, the nagging fear that this could go very badly indeed.

She shouted. Nobody came.

She shouted again.

Time passed. Endless time, marked by the relentless drift of the hands of her watch. There was a naked bulb hanging on a long flex from the high ceiling. She couldn't reach it, not even nearly. The light was bright and flat, and it filled the room. There was no switch for it that she could find. Just beyond the glass in the door, the video camera watched her, unblinking. A tiny red light shone just above the lens.

She banged on the glass. Shouted for help.

She jammed her fingernails in all around the door, probing, dragging, tearing until her nail-roots bled.

Time passed, and the camera watched. The light hung steady in the airless room. The glass refused to shatter, the door would not give.

She was hungry. She hadn't eaten since lunchtime. She yelled at the camera. 'When are you going to feed me? I need *food*, you bastards!' The camera watched impassively. She turned away. Prowled the room, caged.

Walls. The door. The bed, which stank. The chemical toilet. Walls. The door.

She banged the glass. Shouted for help. Waited. Looked again at the camera.

'I'm *hungry*! Do you *want* me to starve?'

The camera recorded it all. Sheepishly, she realised that no one would watch it until later – or, perhaps, at all. Although the red light was on, she hadn't seen anyone change the tapes in all the hours she had been here. Perhaps they had done it while she was hiding in the corner; but she had prowled around the room frequently, so surely she would have heard, or caught them at it? She thought about that, and decided that it might be best to assume her captors *could* somehow change the tapes without her noticing. Because the alternative was that the red light on the camera was a lie – and there was no-one watching her at all. She banged the glass one last time, more in disgust than in hope, and yet again sought out the one corner of the room where the camera couldn't follow her. Then she waited. Because what else could she do?

What would Matthew do? What *was* he doing? How long ago had he decided she was missing – properly missing, not just storming about somewhere? He was always so careful to give her as much space as she wanted. It infuriated her: that cautious, methodical voice he put on, the patronising tone that he thought signalled respect. Small wonder that she'd lost it with him a few times and slammed out of the house. But now . . . How much 'space' would he give her before he began to worry? How much more before he actually *did* anything? At work, Matthew was a man of action; at home, he was . . . well, still at work. But what passed for managerial incisiveness at work could sometimes be oppressive at home. It wasn't always – far from it – she would never have fallen for him otherwise – but it was *there*. He was playful, inspirational, sensitive, thoughtful – and then, suddenly, this detachment would come over him. He would become intense, unsure, methodical, vulnerable.

He was too wise to explain to her that it was to do with Rachel – but she knew. Em had it too. That same hunted look. As though they were the victims, not her.

How long would Matthew play the victim before he realised that his new wife, mother of his child-to-be, was in trouble?

It was a shock when she realised that she was creating a scene – and he wasn't even here. If she had been at home, perhaps she would have been storming out about now – and they say it takes two to make an argument . . .

Matthew was strong. He was clever, incisive, mature. He would be doing . . . something . . .

She only had to wait.

She was woken from an uneasy doze by the scream of a plane. A howling, ear-bursting, grating scream – then a hollow, fading roar. She stared blearily at her watch. It was four thirty. The small patch of sky she could see through the high windows had begun to turn grey. Another plane came. A brutal scream, the roof shaking, the dangling light strangely unmoved. The roar vanishing to silence. Then another. Another. Another. Every ninety seconds, an endless, repetitive, agonised scream.

She huddled under the duvet in the room's one unobserved corner, unable to crouch, unable to hunch herself up too far – because of the baby, because of that awful imagined feeling of pressure against her belly. So she huddled, crumpled sideways, her knees bent tight, and tried, desperately, to wrap herself away from the terrible noise that hammered through her every minute and a half. The floor was hard, gritty and cold. Shards of peeling, hardened paint scraped at her back.

Briefly, she sobbed.

Later, after she had stopped, when the terror had become familiar, she began to get angry. Or, at least, she tried to. Who was this man? What gave him the right to . . . to . . . ?

And another lurch of fear would take her, or another plane would shatter her attempt at concentration.

She battered at the door. Shouted. Nobody came. She moved to a different corner. The camera watched her. She kicked angrily at the bed. She regretted it immediately. Fumes of ammonia curled up the back of her throat. She made a dash for the toilet.

It was an empty plastic tank with a flimsy lid. There were none of the usual treatment chemicals in it. In between spasms, she decided that this was to prevent her harming herself by drinking the stuff. Still, for now it was one less stench to contend with.

But then, unless they fed her, there wasn't going to be much more real sickness, was there? Just nausea and fear.

He came for her again at half past six in the morning. She saw his shadow at the door, and stood hurriedly. He peered in through the bars, his face reduced by the balaclava to darkness and the whites around his eyes.

'Get away from the door,' he yelled. His voice was over-loud, despite being muffled by his woollen mask.

She stared at the man, and didn't move. She was nowhere near the door.

'You listening?' he bellowed. 'Stay where you are.'

She nodded, and spread her hands to indicate she was going

nowhere. He eyed her for a long second, then bent to unlock the door.

This time he left the camera outside. He slipped in as quickly as he could, locked the door behind him and put the key into the back pocket of his jeans. He dumped a plastic bag on the floor at his feet. Then he stood and stared at her.

He was slim and quite short. Wiry muscle braided his bare fore-arms, writhing beneath a dense carpet of tattoos, blue against the dark brown skin. He stood bow-legged and bow-armed, like a cowboy on the draw. His stance was wide, his eyes narrow, his breath heavy.

Charlotte had no idea whether she was more terrified or annoyed. She stared at him, uncertain what her gaze betrayed. His eyes slid away from hers. If she hadn't been so tired, perhaps she would have laughed. It was almost as if he felt guilty about something.

'What you looking at?' he growled.

'Sorry.' She looked away. There was no point antagonising him.

'You all right?'

Charlotte nodded meekly. Then, suddenly more angry than afraid, she glared at him. 'No I'm bloody not. Would you be?'

Muscles twitched in his arms like tightened ropes. The balaclava was too small for him: it covered his whole face except for the eyes, but it was stretched painfully tight. It didn't cover his neck at all. Tendons jerked on both sides of his adam's apple. A few wisps of curled black hair escaped from the neckline of his shirt.

'I can't help that.' The man strode over to stand in front of her. Still distracted, Charlotte wondered about his eyes. It was strange, how little they gave away. They darted around, sometimes, or narrowed slightly; but was he agitated, or was he just avoiding looking at her? She couldn't tell without seeing the set of his mouth, the crease of his eyebrows, the way he held his jaw.

He leaned towards her and said confidentially, 'I might have to hurt you soon.'

He winked. Her mouth flapped while her thoughts tried to catch up with what he had just said.

'I . . . you . . .'

'Might have to hit you,' he explained. 'In the belly.' His voice was completely neutral, as though this were a conversation about going to the bank in his lunchbreak. 'Or do it another way,' he added. 'Depends.'

She wished she could speak. She wanted to speak. She wanted to scream at him. Nothing would come out of her mouth. She wrapped her arms around her stomach protectively, and he nodded, as though he had expected her to. He stood, tense and confident, and stared at her legs.

'My baby . . .' she whispered.

He sniffed, and scratched savagely at a point just below his left shoulder. 'Yeah. Well, that's the point, innit?'

'But—'

'Stop whining!' he snarled, vicious suddenly. 'Stupid cow.'

He stalked away from her and wandered round the room. He leaned towards the toilet to inspect it from a distance, tapped the bed-frame speculatively with the toe of his boot. He sniffed again, philosophically, and leaned against the wall near the door. She watched him, mesmerised.

'What, are you thick or something?' he growled. 'I said *depends*, didn't I? Said I *might* hurt you. Depends.'

Charlotte was struggling to make sense of his words. It wasn't that she didn't understand them – their meaning was horribly clear – but it was still incomprehensible to her. It was unreal. She was supposed to be at home, waking up, rolling over to find Matthew already risen but the bed still warm, fighting the day's first waves of nausea, lying in bed with one hand resting on her warm belly, feeling for the small life inside. She should be bickering with Em, or trying to hold down some breakfast.

The shriek of another plane clawed at her ears: this one lower than most, the sound more agonised. The man scuffed idly at the floor, traced a lazy arc with his toe cap. It sounded like sandpaper being ripped.

With a cold lurch, she realised that he didn't care at all. It didn't matter to him that she was pregnant, because to him she was just an object. He was talking to her, yes – but only because it entertained him to see her confusion.

'Depends, see,' he said again. His eyes were locked on hers now.

'What depends?' she asked feebly. Then, only slightly more defiantly, 'Who the hell are you?'

Her question was swallowed by the roar of another plane, but he seemed to understand. He pushed himself up from the wall and stood over her again. She smelled stale sweat and hot skin. A tiny muscle ticked for a moment in the outside corner of his eye. He held himself utterly still.

'What depends,' he said softly, 'is whether I hit you.' Again, the eyes narrowed in amusement. 'Wanna know what it depends on, do you?'

He was studying her. Self-consciously, she tugged her skirt down over her knees. His eyes flicked down, then drifted back up to her face. There was something intent in his gaze, something hungry; and she knew that what he wanted from her was fear. He wanted to hear her beg. And, very nearly, she did. Her terror was real enough, but, even fogged by fear, she was aware that he would not stop just because she begged him. If she gratified him, he would just want more. She had to show him that he couldn't reach her, that, whatever he did to her, *she* would remain untouched.

'Fuck off,' she said weakly – and began to sob. How could she pretend she wasn't scared? And her baby – her precious little girl, or boy maybe, a small red-faced bundle in soft white clothes, and the rich smell of its skin, the smell of her own baby; and the grunts as she fed her, and the love rushing out of her and into her baby daughter, and –

And he was going to rip all this away from her, for a moment's amusement.

'Just . . . just fuck off . . .'

He bent down towards her, and his breath smelled of cigarettes, even through his balaclava.

Suddenly, she was screaming. 'Get *away* from me! Get away!' She struggled to her feet, and shrank away from him along the wall. 'Just . . . just . . .'

He straightened and watched. She reached the corner of the room and huddled there, transfixed.

He pulled something out of his pocket and rattled it to get her attention. 'Or I could just keep these.'

She squinted at his upheld hand. He was holding a bottle of pills and a pen-injector. Her drugs.

'No . . .' she moaned. 'No, I need them. They're for . . . Please. My baby needs them.'

He stayed completely still, examining her.

'My baby,' she whispered. Her hand drifted over her belly, feeling for the bump that wasn't yet there.

His dark eyes sparkled. 'Depends.'

'But – but – you just said—'

'What it depends on,' he said savagely, 'is whether I get a call.' His gaze raked her. 'I'm on a payroll. It's down to the boss, not me.' She heard him laugh, soft and low. 'What *I* want . . . That's different.'

Those eyes. Smoky black. Glistening. Something in them, something . . . He drifted closer, and she yelped. He stopped.

'Maybe later,' he said in a whisper. As though there was something intimate between them, something he didn't want the camera's microphone to detect – if it was even on.

He was only a few feet from her. He scanned her from toe to head, slowly, scratching his shoulder. As his hand dropped back to his side, he let it slide over the muscles of his chest, sculpted by the tight material of his T-shirt. He leaned towards her, as though he was about to confide in her. When she moaned again, his eyes creased.

'You're sexy when you're scared,' he said. 'I like that.' Then he turned sharply away and headed for the door. He picked up the bag he had left there and, without taking his eyes off her, emptied it onto the bed. Then he unlocked the door, and surveyed her one more time before leaving. Above them, a plane howled, and its shadow flicked briefly across the room. Into the silence it left behind, he said, 'See you, Charlotte. See you soon.' His voice was soft and reflective. Then he tossed the aspirin and heparin towards the bed. 'For now.' And he left, locking the door behind him. The medicines bounced when they hit the mattress. The aspirin bottle stayed there, the injector spilled onto the floor, clattering. She stared at it, horrified, wondering how fragile the mechanism was. Perhaps that tiny crash had been the vial breaking.

She stayed in her corner for what seemed like hours. In reality, it must have been ten minutes or so, because seven planes came over. Then, still only half-convinced that he had gone, she edged across the room into the camera's dispassionate gaze.

She retrieved the bottle and the injector, and took half an aspirin, trying to take comfort from the bitter fizz on her tongue before she swallowed – and failing. She held the injector as though it was a knife. What if it *was* broken? How long could Eyelash survive without? There was no way to know. The doctors hadn't even been sure the drug would make the difference in the first place. It was just a precaution until Friday's scan. She pressed the injector into a fold of skin on her stomach. She couldn't feel whether the needle delivered a dose or not.

The bag had held a large bottle of water and a few pieces of pre-sliced bread, which were now lying loose on the revolting mattress. She sipped at the water, and tossed the bread as far away from her as she could. Then, clutching the medicines to her as though they were the most precious things in her world, she sank slowly to the floor, her back against the mouldering bed, and let the camera watch her as she wept.

Eleven

Five hundred thousand pounds. An impossible amount. Not that the man cared about that.

'Not my problem, is it?'

'But I *can't*,' Matthew had pleaded. 'I just don't have it. I'm a prison officer, not a movie star.'

'Governor. Prison governor.'

'A governor, not *the* Governor. I earn less than thirty thousand a year.'

'Better start saving, then, hadn't you?'

'Look, I just can't find that amount of money. I can't.'

There was a pause. Then the man said, 'How much you got then?'

Matthew's thoughts raced. There was his joint account with Charlotte – a couple of thousand there; his own savings account – maybe ten if he was lucky; the building society account he kept untouched for a rainy day – that had twenty in it, from the death of an aunt a couple of years ago. Thirty thousand, then, to be safe.

'Twenty-five,' he said. 'That's all I've got. Take it all. Just—'

The line went dead.

Furiously, he dialled Charlotte's number. It switched straight through to voicemail. Listening to her voice, waiting, when he needed the man to talk to him was almost unbearable.

After the tone, he hissed, 'You have to understand. I can't. Find. Any more. That's *it*. If I could, I would. Where am I supposed to get half a million? This is madness.' Well, yes, it almost certainly was. But shouting at a madman would get him nowhere. He had to keep him talking. 'Look, I am not rich. Sorry, but that's just the truth of it. I might be able to get thirty, thirty-five maybe. *Maybe*. But that's it, that's all I can do.' He checked his watch. 'The police are here again at nine. Neither of us wants them involved. We've got until then to sort this. Thirty-five. It's all I can get.' Uncertain, he rang off, and waited.

The return call was immediate and short. The man snapped, 'First wife leave you nothing, then, did she? Your house worth nothing, is it? Tough.' He had rung off before Matthew could reply.

Instinctively, Matthew hit the redial button – and then hung up. He needed to think about this. The truth was, he could hardly claim that the house was valueless – or that Rachel had left him destitute. The man had obviously done his homework. At a guess, the house was worth around four hundred thousand, and he owned it outright, because the endowment policy had paid off the mortgage when Rachel died. And after a battle in the coroner's court, when the verdict of death by misadventure was returned, another life insurance policy had paid out eighty thousand. And she had left him more than a hundred thousand in cash – savings he had never known she had, an inheritance from her parents, who had both died before he'd even met her. All that money was set aside for Em's schooling, all of it held in a trust. In principle, if he liquidated everything he possibly could – and if he could find some way to pull the money from the trust – he was worth over six hundred thousand pounds.

In reality, he was only worth the thirty-five he had already offered. How could he sell the house in time? Even raising a new mortgage on it would take weeks – and the loan would be calculated on his income, not on the house's value: it would be nowhere near enough. Say they offered him a mortgage of three times his income, that would give him eighty-five thousand, give or take – and the money would arrive a few weeks from now . . . and then there was the trust money. There were other trustees, co-signatories: how could he persuade them to sign the money away? And even if he could, selling the investments and converting the cheque to cash would take weeks.

The truth was, he could raise at least a substantial part of the money the man wanted – but he couldn't do it *now*. There wasn't time, not for any of them. Even if the man said he was prepared to wait – and how unlikely was that? – his nerve would break. Chances were, he would kill Charlotte rather than risk holding her so long. He *might* just give up and release her – but that was a gamble. It was common knowledge – he must have heard it on countless news stories: if you don't find them within the first two days, the chances are that you won't find them alive. Besides, there was something in the man's voice. He didn't seem hurried or stressed. He seemed, if anything, *satisfied*, as though he was actually enjoying this.

And perhaps that was the one ray of hope. Because if some sick part of the man *was* enjoying it, then – just perhaps – Matthew could buy some time.

He dialled again, and after Charlotte's message, he spoke. 'You're right. I hadn't thought of the house and things. Some of the money is out of reach – it's in a trust, not legally mine any more – but there's the house, and my savings . . . But it's going to take weeks to turn it into cash. We can't wait that long, can we?'

We. Textbook stuff. *Take the initiative*, the teacher had said. *Show them that you're on their side, that you're helping them find a way out. That's how you turn them. They want all the help they can get.*

'I can try,' Matthew said at last. 'In the morning. I can try for an emergency loan against the house. Cash in my insurance policies, get what I can out of that trust. Plus there's the thirty-five I told you about. If it all works, I might be able to raise a hundred, hundred and fifty. That's all I can do. *Maybe.* But turning that into cash . . .' He stopped, thinking hard. It really *was* all he could do – but was it enough, and what happened if it wasn't?

There was a beep as the voicemail kicked out of record. He rang again. There was one more thing. 'The police,' he said into the silence. 'How do I put them off?'

Then he sat and waited, trying to think through how he could make this work, and realising that there was very little hope at all.

After half an hour, a text came through:

Hundred and fifty cash by six in evening

It should have been a kind of relief. It wasn't. It was a set of impossible tasks. He texted back:

Police?

The reply was terse:

Wait

73

Out of options, Matthew sat in the kitchen's harsh light, paralysed, wondering what he could possibly do. He spent almost an hour staring at nothing at all before he realised that he would have to have a detailed plan. There would be no time for mistakes. He must prepare secondary plans for every possible contingency: what if the bank couldn't find the deeds to the house, or insisted on a cooling-off period before they would issue a loan? There were a hundred pitfalls – and sitting contemplating them like a rabbit in a car headlight would save no one. He must plan around them all.

He switched on the computer in the study, thanking providence that he had recently agreed to Em's incessant demands for a broadband connection. The old dial-up connection would have blocked all incoming calls, and he couldn't have risked closing any potential line of communication to the kidnapper. Now, he could search the net for information about banking procedures without that risk.

Time passed at the internet's irrational pace. Tracking down the information behind each link was an agonisingly slow process that usually ended in failure. And yet, for all his impatience, the hours blurred by. By the time the sky outside the study window had begun to lighten, revealing grey smears of cloud against a pale haze, he had learned almost nothing. There had been a few nuggets about same-day money transfers buried deep in the pages offered by some regulatory body or other; the standard three-day clearing system could be circumvented, apparently, by using a system called CHAPS. But the rest of the information he gleaned had been less reassuring. Banks generally limited the amount of cash they would issue to a customer to a few thousand unless they had been given several days' notice. Cashing in a life insurance policy could take anything up to two weeks. And even with the deeds to a house already in their possession, most banks insisted on a land search to confirm ownership before they would lend money secured on it. This wasn't legally necessary but, as one website had put it, it was 'reasonable business practice'. In short, despite his frantic calculations earlier, almost none of his potential wealth was actually available to him.

There were only two ways forward. He would have to hope that the bank manager was prepared to set aside 'reasonable business practice' and simply trust him. Or else he would have to persuade the kidnapper to change his mind.

Who was this man? There were clues. It seemed he was less concerned now about the police. Matthew's stomach turned when he saw the clock in the corner of the computer screen: it was six fifty-four already, they would be here in two hours. Who could be that unafraid of the Law? Either someone who knew how to control the situation or a fool. Matthew spent every day in the company of criminals. He knew from direct experience that there were very few masterminds amongst them. Most of them were in prison because they had done something stupid, acting first and thinking later. They were driven by their emotions, or by an upbringing that they simply didn't have the ability to rise above. So, which type was he dealing with – a genius who knew how to manipulate the police or a madman? He hoped the man was a genius. Because if he wasn't, anything could happen.

More clues: the voice. The man spoke in grunts and whispers, which meant he did not want to be recognised. He had a cockney accent, so he was a Londoner. He knew about Matthew's past, and that Rachel had died. A lot of people knew that – but not everyone.

It was someone from the Ville.

That pretty much ruled out the possibility of a criminal master-mind. Instead, it was a fool who had learned about Rachel's death while he was inside and thought he'd found a way to take the money she'd left. So, he was looking for an ex-con from the Ville who was dangerous, vindictive – and stupid. Well, that narrowed it down, didn't it?

Know where you live, Guv. He must have heard that once a week since he joined the service.

He shut down the machine and returned to the kitchen, throwing away the untouched beer and making himself a strong cup of black coffee. Without any expectation of success, he tried Charlotte's mobile, twice. It kicked through to the answering service. Ten minutes later, there was a text.

Told you to wait

He wrestled with his memory. Who, out of all those people, could have done this? There were names – some of them violent madmen, a few more considered, methodical, and perhaps therefore more dangerous. Nine or ten names, perhaps, from eight years.

What he needed was an informer, someone to be his eyes and ears, someone who could look at the list with him and tell him which names were Yes and which No. Most, if not all, would inevitably be Maybe. But the point was that his imaginary spy would know what rumours had flown. Perhaps one of them had bragged about his plans before he was released, or had shown a particular interest in the gossip that had swirled about Matthew after the police had finally lifted their suspicion and his precautionary suspension had been rescinded. He didn't need a generalised suspicion of these few potential kidnappers, he needed detail. But he knew from costly experience that even the most apparently moral and earnest convict was a dangerous liability. At bottom, he had finally accepted, men who committed crimes were unpredictable, unreliable and a hazard to everyone's health. It was a lesson he had learned from a man he had trusted, but only for a while. So, he was stuck. Even if he had been able to find someone who could tell him more about the men on his list, he knew that whatever the man told him would be part lie, part wish-fulfilment, and wholly self-serving. What it would almost certainly not be was the truth. To a convict – any convict – the truth was plastic and slippery. It could be moulded or, just as likely, you could discover that you were no longer in possession of it at all.

Besides, how was he going to find someone to fill the role? He had only ever seen the potential for an honest, constructive working relationship with one convict in all his years in the Prison Service – and his relationship with David Gordon had lasted months, at best . . .

He shook away an image, or tried to: a man writhing on the floor in the wash-room, howling; another man lunging, snarling; an officer sent crashing into a wall by a casual flick—

Well. He couldn't find David Gordon now even if he tried. Just as well. Because he was almost desperate enough to ask for his help.

He wrote some names down, then crossed a few off. Seven men, all of them brutal, unthinking and greedy, and most of them raving maniacs. One of them was threatening to kill his wife and his unborn child. And, it seemed, one of them would be watching when the police came, not much more than two hours from now.

There was no time. There was nothing he could do. For the first time since he had dragged his first wife from the water so many years ago, Matthew Daniels understood what it was to be the victim of a situation that was entirely beyond his control.

It was only when he heard footsteps on the stairs that he jerked up his head and realised that over an hour had passed. It was ten to eight, and he still had no idea what to do. And, within the minute, his daughter would be demanding to know where her stepmother was.

'She rang last night. Well, more like four in the morning. Her friend, um . . . Deborah. I don't know if you ever met Debbie . . . Anyway, she rang Charlotte last night, apparently. She's been taken in to hospital. Some kind of cancer. Anyway, it's bad. Days to live. Terrible. And Debbie needed a hand to hold.' He puffed out heavily. 'Who wouldn't? So, Charlotte's been in hospital most of the night, in Oxford. Couldn't use her mobile, of course. There are signs everywhere, you have to keep it switched off.'

It sounded lame even as he was telling her. Em watched him, ignoring the bowl of cereal in front of her.

'Anyway,' he added, after a pause, 'panic over. Well, for us anyway . . .'

He found it hard to meet her eyes.

'Yeah,' Em said. 'Whatever.' She cast her eyes down, and toyed with her food.

'She sent her love,' he said desperately. Despite her belligerent behaviour, he knew that Em was very attached to Charlotte. She had spent years with no adult female company until Charlotte had arrived in their lives. He had always felt guilty about that.

'Yeah, right,' Em replied. 'Great.' Her tone belied her answer.

She shoved in a mouthful of cereal, and ignored the crumbs that fell onto the table. Matthew had wiped them up before she swallowed.

'She did,' he said. 'Sent love.'

'Oh, leave it *out*, Dad. I'm not a bloody *kid*!' Em pushed away the half-finished bowl and scraped back her chair.

He was unsure whether she was talking about the cereal or his lie. While he worked on a reply, she muttered, 'Fine, see you this evening,' and stalked out of the room.

When the front door thumped shut behind her at eight twenty, it was a relief.

*

The doorbell rang less than three minutes after Em had left the house. Typical of the police to turn up early when they weren't wanted. What the hell was he supposed to do now? Matthew trudged towards the front door.

A woman squeezed past him with a bag of groceries, pecking him on the cheek as she passed.

'Sorry, darling, forgot the keys.'

She glanced around her, frowning, then headed down the hallway towards the back of the house.

'Has anyone rung?' she called over her shoulder.

Her voice was airy and high-pitched, with no particular accent. She was short, about Charlotte's height, well-built but not fat, she had shoulder-length black hair, and he had never seen her before in his life. The worst of it was, somehow he wasn't at all surprised.

He followed her down the hall. 'Who are you? Where is she?'

In the kitchen, the woman dumped the shopping bag on the worktop and reached for the kettle. She smiled brightly at him.

'Police not come yet, then?' He shook his head. She narrowed her eyes, then nodded and filled the kettle. 'And there's no one else here? The girl's gone?'

He spread his arms to show her the empty room. She stood in his kitchen, with his kettle in her hand, and her eyes laughed at him. She put the kettle on.

'Who the hell are you?' Matthew asked. He was weary. This was too much.

'I'm the girl who's here to get you out of the hole you got yourself into, darling. All right? I'm Charlotte – aren't I? Leastways, that's what you're going to tell the fuzz when they get here.'

'The hell I will,' he snapped. 'You're going to tell me where she is, and who the bastard is who's got her and then—'

'Oh.' She held up a manicured finger. 'Nearly forgot. Got a little present for you.' She fished a slip of paper out of her bag, and slid it across the table towards him. 'Compliments of the missis.'

It was a print-out of their latest scan, the one where the nurse had told them the foetus was the same size as an eyelash. They had heard its heart, a high-pitched, slippery pulse; and they had squinted at a field of grainy black and white blobs, trying to discern the tiny creature that loomed so large in their imagination. Charlotte had carried the print-out in her bag ever since. Looking at it now, he still couldn't see where Eyelash was – but he knew what the picture meant. It was a threat.

'Please,' he said, his voice catching. 'Where is she? Is she all right?'

'She will be if you're a good boy. Otherwise . . .' She shrugged, disinterested. The kettle boiled. She picked it up and turned to him. 'So. What's it to be?'

What choice did he have? With the baby, there was no halfway house. There was no room for bluffs or a waiting game. None at all. Either Charlotte kept it or it was gone. Helplessly, he nodded. She giggled lightly, came over and gave him another kiss, on the lips this time. Then she waved the kettle at him.

'No, darling, not that. I meant tea or coffee?'

They waited. She sat, he stood, opening and closing his fists uselessly. He could feel the heavy beat of the blood in his ears, and a draining heat behind his eyes. Idly, she traced the wood grain in the kitchen table.

She glanced up at him. 'Nine o'clock, they're coming, yeah?' She checked her watch, wrinkled her nose, then concentrated on the table again.

He wanted to roar at her. Instead, what emerged was a hoarse whine. 'Where is she? Please. Is she safe?'

She slapped the table, hard enough to cut him off.

'Leave it – *darling* – all right?'

She lifted her eyes and fixed him with a glare that was suddenly cold and full of menace. After a beat, she flashed him a dimpled smile, then her face slumped back into neutrality.

'*Work* with me, darling,' she said. She sounded like a drama teacher.

When the police came, she held him back and went to answer the door herself. He followed a few paces behind. She opened the door and was instantly all smiles and bustle, convincingly nervous and distracted. She never quite met the officers' eyes, but she kept patting her hair and glancing sideways at them. She had their full attention.

They stood uneasily in the hall.

'I'm *so* sorry for the trouble,' she burbled. 'Really, I feel such a *fool*. It just never occurred to me that Matthew would call the police.

I mean it was just a little tiff, that's all.' She laughed skittishly, and peered at them from behind her hair. 'You must think I'm an absolute monster.'

'Just glad there's not a problem, miss,' said the man.

The woman officer, his senior, sighed. '*Mrs* Daniels,' she said pointedly, glaring at her associate, 'you do understand that we took Mr Daniels' report very seriously.'

'Oh, absolutely,' the woman gushed. 'I'm *so* embarrassed. I was just a little miffed. That's all it was. I mean, who even *cares* about—' she glanced coyly at him and giggled '—do you know, darling, I can't even remember what the argument was about? The washing up? The ironing?' She shrugged, then leaned closer to the police-woman. 'I overreacted. One of those times, I'm afraid.'

Matthew snarled inwardly, whilst smiling at the police officers. She couldn't have been much less subtle if she'd proclaimed out loud that it was her time of the month. Then, suddenly and over-whelmingly, the miserable irony of the excuse the woman had chosen smashed home and left him reeling. No 'time of the month' for Charlotte. Not now.

Since this woman's arrival, he had been numb – functional, but not truly aware. Now, he felt real fear rising inside him, and struggled to control it, in case the officers detected that there was something wrong.

The policewoman, to her credit and his horror, showed no sympathy for the impostor's story.

'Mrs Daniels, you are aware that your husband gave us a photo of you to help us look for you?'

The fake Charlotte frowned. 'Well, no, but . . . Well, he would, I suppose.'

The policewoman nodded and continued. 'I have to tell you, Mrs Daniels, that meeting you face to face is rather a surprise.'

She handed the woman an A4 sheet, a crude colour copy of the photograph he had given the police the night before, blown up to show only her face. Her hair – *Charlotte's* hair – was dark. Her bones were heavy, her eyes blue. The face's overall shape was broadly oval. There, the similarities ended.

The stranger took the photo and studied it. Then she turned to him, giggling.

'Is this the one you took in Norfolk last summer?'

No. It wasn't. It had been taken by an old friend of Charlotte's, Giles, just a few weeks ago in Epping Forest.

He muttered uneasily, 'It was the only one I could find.'

The woman slapped the photo onto his chest, so that he had to grab it, and laughed merrily. Conspiratorially, to the policewoman, she said, 'You lose ten pounds, grow your fringe out, buy a whole new wardrobe – they don't even notice!' She slipped an arm round his waist and hugged herself close to him. 'You silly old chump.' She nestled her head under his arm.

'Norfolk?' The policewoman smiled at her.

The stranger squeezed him harder. Painfully hard. Her nails dug into his side. 'Last summer,' she said. 'I was an eighteen then. Can you believe it? I'm aiming to be a fourteen for the summer.'

Very deliberately, she swayed him backwards and forwards, peering out at the police officers from under his wing. He did his best to grin oafishly. That, at least, wasn't difficult. Everything else was agony.

As though on impulse, 'Charlotte' grabbed the photo from the policewoman, and held it next to her own face, pointing back and forth between the two.

'Eight months,' she said proudly. 'Nine pounds.'

The policewoman studied the photo and the real face.

'Congratulations,' she said eventually.

'Well, it's not really enough,' bubbled the stranger, still holding him tightly. 'And, frankly, a little *encouragement* wouldn't go amiss . . .' She rolled her eyes towards him – and she, and both the police officers, laughed.

'Charlotte' pounced. She slapped her forehead.

'Oh, where are my manners? I haven't even offered you a cup of tea.'

She looked from one to the other, as though she wanted them to stay more than anything in the world.

'Thank you, Mrs Daniels, but we'd best get going.'

The policewoman – and it was only now that he suddenly realised that he had made no effort to register her name – folded her notebook and the pair took their leave.

The moment the door had closed, the woman winked merrily at him. 'Got a message for you, darling,' she said softly, 'from the boss.' She leaned a little closer to him, and whispered, 'No more fuck-ups. Got that?'

Matthew nodded mutely. He had never felt so powerless in his life. She nodded back, her face uncomfortably close. 'Because if you talk to anyone – *anyone*, yeah – then, trust me, the boss will know. And you know what happens then, don't you?'

She waited until she was sure he had got the point. Then she yelled, loudly and angrily, for the benefit of their departing guests, '*Norfolk?* Matthew, that is the worst photo of me we've *got*! I am *so* not impressed!'

She held up a finger and tiptoed into the front room. He follow-ed. Through the net curtain, he saw the police officers laughing to each other as they climbed into their car and drove away.

He was still watching them when he heard the front door click. She was almost at the gate by the time he had registered what was happening. He dashed out onto the street.

'Wait!'

She didn't look back. She glanced casually along the road before crossing it at an angle.

'Where *is* she?' He was yelling, on the street. He didn't care. 'I need to talk to her! What do you want?'

She pulled a mobile from her handbag, held it to her ear, and trotted briskly away on high heels.

'She's *pregnant*!' he screamed after her. '*Please!*'

She turned the corner at the road's end without looking back, and was gone.

Twelve

e sent a text message:

Police gone. Trying to get money. Use mobile number not home

Then he went to the nearest branch of his bank and asked to see the manager. It took several arguments and an agonising three-quarters of an hour's wait but eventually the Great Man agreed to see him.

He was not a day over thirty, and his office was hardly more impressive than Matthew's own. They sat on poorly stuffed chairs made of brown tufted nylon, uncomfortably close to each other, and waited through an uneasy silence while Matthew tried to work out what best to say.

'Mr Daniels,' the man said at last. 'I'm afraid I really don't have much time . . .'

'I've been with you for twenty-five years,' Matthew said abruptly.

The man frowned, and Matthew suddenly realised that he didn't even know his name. There had been a brief introduction, but he hadn't been paying attention because he had been too focused on what he needed to achieve.

'Well, yes,' the manager said, still frowning, 'and customer loyalty's important to us. That's why—'

Matthew had spotted the name on a plaque on the desk. 'Mr Jarvis, I desperately need some cash. Today.'

Mr S. F. Jarvis, MBBA, whatever that meant, Stoke Newington Branch, creased his brow again. 'Well, the cash points can dispense up to—'

'A *lot* of cash.'

Jarvis made a show of biting back his irritation. 'Well, the cash points will dispense five hundred pounds. If it's more than that, then you have to—'

'I need a hundred and fifty thousand. Today.'

For a beat, Jarvis just stared at him. Then he laughed, the patronising chuckle of a man who desperately wanted to say, 'Really, my dear Mr Daniels . . .' but who didn't dare because he was talking to a man at least ten years his senior. The boy still had spots, for heaven's sake. He'd barely left home.

Matthew glared at him, and said softly, 'No joke, Mr Jarvis. This is serious and urgent.'

The furtive look of a told-off schoolboy crossed the man's face briefly, and then was gone. In its place was the hard, businesslike exterior of an Important Man. 'May I ask what this money is for?'

'No.' Matthew immediately regretted having snapped.

Jarvis's eyes narrowed. 'Because I can think of very few legitimate reasons for needing that kind of amount in cash.' He glanced down at a thumbnail, and began to pick round the edges of it fitfully, avoiding Matthew's eyes. 'We don't issue large amounts of cash at short notice, I'm afraid, Mr Daniels.' He looked up again, his fingers still intertwined and picking. 'And by "large", I mean anything over five thousand pounds. There are good reasons for the restrictions.' He counted them on his fingers. Matthew saw a bead of blood swelling on the side of his thumb. 'Fraud,' Jarvis snapped. 'False accounting. Money laundering. Large withdrawals are usually to do with one or other of them.' He stared coldly at Matthew, who looked puzzled. Impatiently, he added, 'Create an account, withdraw the money as cash, use it to open another account elsewhere . . .' After a moment his eyes flicked uneasily downwards, and he hid his bleeding thumb inside a fist. Then his gaze returned to his client, his lips thin and his skin mottled with anger.

This was going badly. Jarvis was a little man with too much power – and if he suspected that was Matthew's opinion, even for a second, then it was all over.

'I . . .' Matthew offered, wondering what he was going to say next. What would Jarvis accept? 'Look, I'm sorry. I'm just excited. It's . . . an investment opportunity. A once-in-a-lifetime thing, really. But the man wants cash today, or he's got another buyer.'

Back in control, Jarvis raised a superior eyebrow. 'Shares? Bonds? I'm sorry, but it sounds to me like you're being taken for a ride, Mr

Daniels. You should only buy these things through a well-established source. We can offer—'

'It's a painting.' Immediately, he wondered if it might have been wiser to claim it was a car. Too late. Besides, he knew absolutely nothing about expensive cars – and the still-spotty man in front of him might turn out to be a boy racer at heart. Trouble was, Matthew didn't know much more about fine art than he did about cars. And, unlikely as it appeared, there was always the chance that Jarvis was a connoisseur. He decided that the only safe course was to choose a name that Jarvis could never have heard of. 'It's a . . . Thornton,' he explained. 'You know, the abstract expressionist. Post-war. I mean, he's second-tier, obviously, but who can afford a Pollock these days?' He tossed the comment away, smiling as though the joke was shared.

Jarvis's expression remained unchanged. 'Are you an expert, then? A collector?'

Matthew managed to keep his smile in place. 'Well, one tries, you know . . . Expert? No. More of a keen amateur. But a Thornton—'

'Because I have to tell you, Mr Daniels, that this all sounds highly unlikely. Insisting on a same-day cash sale—'

Matthew butted in hastily, groping for another made-up name. 'It's a well-known dealer. It's . . . Logans in Bond Street. Do you know them? Very well respected. A friend of mine works there. They've been doing this house clearance. Apparently the executors are keen to liquidate the estate as quickly as possible. Cash today better than a good price tomorrow, you know, that sort of thing. And—'

'*Cash*, Mr Daniels? Not a bank draft? Not a CHAPS transfer?'

Matthew shrugged. 'Cash.'

Jarvis clasped his hands and stroked his lips with the knuckles of his thumbs. There were scars and scabs on a few of the other fingers now displayed. 'I find it very hard to believe that this is above board.' Briefly, he sucked at the blood seeping from his nail, his eyes never leaving Matthew's, as though he was doing nothing out of the ordinary at all. His cheeks flushed slightly.

Matthew scented failure. He could hardly put pressure on the man for a nervous habit: it wasn't the sort of weakness that would change a bank manager's mind over a cash dispensation of a hundred and fifty thousand, it was just . . . unpleasant. He hid his desperation as best he could, and shrugged again. 'Well, to be blunt, Mr

Jarvis, isn't that my call? If I get ripped off, then I get ripped off. It's my money.'

Jarvis scowled. 'I thought we were discussing a loan, Mr Daniels. That would make it *our* money. The bank's.'

Shit.

'Oh, absolutely,' Matthew blustered. 'But if it was secured against the house, say? I mean, I know you'd never take the *painting* as a guarantee.'

Jarvis's hands were buried in his lap again. He raised an eyebrow. 'A mortgage? Well, there are a few checks to run before—'

'You already hold the deeds. And there's no mortgage at the moment. So . . .'

Jarvis shook his head, slowly, as if it was heavier than it was. His lips were a tight line. 'Proof of income,' he said. 'Confirmation from the Land Registry. I'm sorry, Mr Daniels, but we insist on these things for good reason.'

If he thought it might have made a difference, Matthew would happily have threatened to strangle him. He'd have held a sharpened paperknife against that man's neck, and demanded that all the cashiers empty their tills. Instead, flatly, he said, 'Then it comes down to trust.'

As he had known it would.

Jarvis nodded, and Matthew detected something like sympathy in his expression. 'Banks are not very good at that, I'm afraid. There are guidelines. They're very clear.'

Matthew tried to look relaxed, and failed. 'No exceptions? With the house as security, you've got zero risk. And the whole point is, this is cheap. I could sell the thing tomorrow for nearly double.'

Jarvis shook his head and stood, holding out a hand that had only recently had the congealed blood sucked off it. Matthew took it. His desperation hid his disgust.

'Give me a couple of hours to consider it, Mr Daniels. We'd be delighted to help, if we can. But please, don't get your hopes up too high. Even if we agree to help you, I doubt very much we can release that much cash on such short notice. It would leave us with no float at all. So unless we can order it in . . .' He pursed his lips, thinking. Then he shook his head. 'Slim chance, if I'm honest. And that's *if* we agree to help.'

Matthew thanked him, trying for a balance between humility and businesslike confidence, gave him his mobile number, and walked back out onto the busy, sunless street, wondering who he could possibly turn to if Mr S. F. Jarvis, MBBA, withdrew his only, fragile hope.

What worried him was that he already knew the answer – and it meant he was about to embark on a very dangerous path indeed.

Thirteen

Monk was not his real name – but David Beresford Gordon was long-since dead, whatever those in authority chose to believe. In the early years, while he was still running, he'd had several names, but he had been Monk now for twenty years or more. And what did a name matter? Names were ephemeral. They were an illusion. They suggested that it was possible to know someone – and it was not.

Monk moved with the air, he moved with the light, and he did not move at all. Even as he stepped – forwards, a sweep to the side, forwards again, back – his feet were as rooted in the ground as a tree's. His fingers fluttered like leaves in a drifting breeze. His knees and body swayed. His head and arms were weightless scraps in the currents of the air. He moved and was still, and the two were the same. Monk danced the strange, slow forms of *Tai Chi*. His skin shone blue-black in the warm afternoon light.

His thoughts moved, too: the drift and flow of memory:
– *she said, love – David, she said, I love –*
– *a knife in sunlight, the man's face staring, wise and dangerous –*
Fragments. Ancient things.

His memories were riverweed, caressed by the water, always rippling, flowing . . . And one day the riverweed would be gone – one day, even the current would be gone – but, always, the channel would remain. The moments of Monk's life flowed through him and past him, events long gone, events yet to be. He grew in time. And the channel that guided his life, the flow of who he was, the weed, the river, the tree, the leaves and earth, the root – all merged into a single Thing: *Tai Chi*.

Stillness in movement, movement in stillness. A meditation and a martial art. The name of China's most famous symbol, the *yin* within the *yang*, the whole that encompasses all things. Monk moved, transformed, at the still point of the restless world. For this moment, for as long as his *Tai Chi* continued, he was free.

A braided blue thread circled one wrist. A small shell dangled from it, swaying with his broad, subtle movements. A cowrie shell: its texture and colour long since leached away by the slow wash of time. A gift.

– *it will keep you safe, David* –

– *I love you, David* –

– *David, I* –

And she had told him the truth. It had kept him safe. But not her.

The cowrie caught the light as he whirled, with infinite slowness, from one posture to the next: a dull gleam, for a pain that was as sharp as ever. It was part of the lesson of *Tai Chi*: the past is always with you – and so is the future. A life is a single thing. It is whole and complete. Within each life there is a perfect balance, whether you are aware of it or not.

In Monk's life, there had been betrayal. There had been violence, death and grief. These things were within him and part of him. It was time for the pendulum to swing. There must be yin to balance the yang of the memories that burned him still. There were wrongs to be made right.

And it would come – because the future and the past were one and the same: they were part of one great circle that all souls completed with their body's death. It was only our limited senses that told us different.

The process of redemption had already begun. All he had to do was wait.

Fourteen

He walked home, desperate for his phone to ring and dreading the prospect. The kidnapper would want news of the ransom. Or it would be the bank manager, refusing the loan. When at last it rang, it was neither of them.

'Yes? Hello? Is she OK? The woman came. I—'

'Oh, you're there then.'

It took him a moment to recognise the voice.

'Oh. Tia . . .'

'Yes. Your assistant. From the office. You remember what an office is, don't you, Matthew? It's where you're supposed to work.'

Tia Hannaford was effectively his secretary, although her title these days was Administrative Assistant. She was a prematurely middle-aged woman with a spinster's taste in cardigans and an acid tongue. She liked to think that she mothered everyone in the office, but it was the kind of parenting that most of them were glad to avoid when they could.

'Matthew? Matthew!'

He had forgotten about work completely. On a normal day-shift, he was generally in by eight thirty.

He groaned, 'Oh . . .'

'Exactly,' Tia said tartly. 'Sleeping off a hangover after supper with Mark, are we? He's been here since eight.'

He sighed, to buy himself an extra second to think of something to say. Tia wasn't playing.

'For goodness sake, Matthew! Mark's climbing the walls!'

Matthew bit back his words. Now was not the time to express his opinion of Mark Thornton.

He decided that the same story would do for work and for Em. 'Look, I can't make it in just now, Tia. Charlotte's got this problem—'

'Oh, Matthew – it's not the baby, is it?'

'Gosh, no,' he said, instinctively – and then regretted it: the baby would have given him the perfect reason to be taking time off. In a way, it was even true.

'Is she OK?' Tia asked.

Wincing at the horrible falseness of his own words, he mumbled, 'Yes. She's fine. Only, she got called away. A friend of hers . . . It's . . . a cancer thing.'

'So, that's why she didn't go to dinner last night?'

'How do you—'

'Mark told me. He popped in to ask where you were this morning. Twice. I'm sorry to hear Charlotte's friend's got cancer, Matthew. But that keeps you at home *why*, exactly?'

He felt a sudden urge to tell her. She would be shocked and supportive. She would take the initiative. She would tell Thornton and the other senior staff. They would know exactly what to do. They would call the police . . . And that was the one option he could not afford to consider. Even if the police were the best people to help him – and what he had seen on the last two encounters gave him no faith in them at all – the chances were they would not believe him now. They were convinced they had seen Charlotte, just hours ago. By the time he had explained the situation, played the video to them, begged them to review her mobile phone records, jumped through the endless hoops they would want before they were satisfied that this wasn't some prank, or a sinister plot of his own – how many days would have passed? What would have happened – to Eyelash, to Charlotte? Even contemplating such possibilities horrified him.

He realised now, far too late, that, when he had complied with the woman that morning, he had burned his bridges. Now, he must do this alone.

'I'm going to work from home today, Tia.' He spoke in a rush, improvising. 'I spent a lot of time talking with Charlotte on the phone this morning. And I'll have to be back early for Em, of course.'

'Matthew I really think—'

'Tia, really, it's pointless me coming in. There just isn't time. I'll work here.'

'So, I'll just cancel the Duke's walkthrough, then, shall I? Ring and tell the equerries who are coming in that the planning meeting's off?'

He had forgotten about that. The practice walkthrough for the Duke's visit was scheduled for twelve, with sandwiches and a post-mortem at one thirty, and more inspection time afterwards if it was needed.

Sandwiches . . . When was the last time he had eaten? Last night with the Thorntons, he realised; but he'd hardly touched his food, and since then, he had been awake all night. A few polite nibbles at a leathery piece of beef and half a ramekin of crème brûlée were hardly sustaining. But how could he devote time to making sandwiches when his wife was held hostage by a maniac who would hardly even talk to him?

Tia waited him out. What had she been talking about? Yes, the precious royal walkthrough. He stared at the living-room walls, groping for inspiration. They had been vibrantly painted by Charlotte. Her absence bled them of all colour. They were daubed, not decorated.

'What the hell's got into you, Matthew?' Tia said at last.

She was furious. He could hear the future in her voice: if he stayed at home, she would make a point of ringing every quarter of an hour with some trivial query or another. He would leap at the phone with every ring, thinking it was *him* . . .

He didn't have the energy to fight the massed might of the Ville's bureaucrats as well as the bastard who was holding Charlotte . . . let alone Mr S. F. Jarvis from the bank. Besides, what was he going to do at home all day? He would wait, and hope, because he had already done all that he could, and every moment of silence would add to his fears. Looked at from that perspective, work would be a welcome distraction.

'Oh, to hell with it, Tia,' he muttered. 'You win.'

'Well, you'd better be quick,' she snapped back.

He hammered up stairs and changed for work. There was no time for a bath. The finely scented equerries of the royal party would just have to live with the smell. He swept up his briefcase and his mobile phone. Back in the living room, he jabbed the record button on the answering machine, and spoke, nervously and fast.

'This is Matthew Daniels. Look, I had to go in to work. No choice. You can reach me on my mobile.'

Then he called the bank and asked to speak to Jarvis. He was in a meeting, the receptionist told him, and offered to take a message. Reluctantly, Matthew left his name and repeated his mobile number. 'I was just wondering if he was any closer to a decision. It's . . . urgent.' He was miserably aware that the woman probably dealt with hundreds of people saying the same thing to her every week.

'I'll tell him you rang,' she chirped.

He didn't really believe her.

He drove to the Ville. The day was bright, now, the air sharper. The hard faces of the buildings he passed gave the light a brutal intensity. The street's many facets blurred to a single grey glare. What went on behind these façades? All those lives: how many lived daily with fear, and could say nothing? His own face was just one of thousands, each with a story, and each isolated from the rest. He was drowned in the traffic's harsh roar.

He parked, and headed towards the Ville's main entrance. With the gates hanging above him, he paused, suddenly uncertain. He was going to have to break one of the prison's most rigid rules, because there was no way on earth that he was prepared to be parted from his mobile. He tugged at his jacket, hoping to disguise the imperceptible bulge where his phone hid in his pocket. It was only a small thing; the presence of a mobile in a governor's pocket for a few hours would hardly bring the Ville to its knees. But in the Prison Service, security was everything – and that depended absolutely on the rigid discipline and integrity of its staff. Only complete consistency allowed them to maintain order amongst eight hundred potentially unruly inmates. Taking his mobile inside went against years of ingrained habit. He could *feel* how wrong it was.

Still, he was going to do it – wasn't he?

'Morning, Boss.' Bernard Jenkins was manning the doors again. Matthew muttered something at him distractedly, and fumbled for his pass and key fob. Jenkins waved him on, smiling. He thanked him, and put his fob in the exchange tray, and waited for Jenkins to fetch his key set. Once it dropped through, he grabbed the keys and turned to go.

'Sir?'

Matthew turned to look at him, pretending puzzlement, with his heart thudding.

'Phone, sir?'

'Oh . . . Yes. Thank you. Half-asleep.'

Jenkins gestured at a neat stack of checked-in mobiles on his side of the glass. He returned to the counter and made a show of fishing in his pockets.

'No, I . . . Nope. Must have left it at home.' He shrugged absently.

Jenkins frowned at him, then nodded. He headed for the door. 'Sally's back at school,' he called. Matthew turned and cocked a head at the man, confused. What was he talking about? 'My daughter,' Jenkins said. 'Sally. She's back at school.'

'Oh . . . Yes, great.'

Jenkins looked confused. His cheery smile faded. Matthew walked to his office as fast as he dared.

Tia Hannaford was in the office, but it was otherwise empty. The other five members of his unit, the officers, must be out on the wings. It was a relief.

'How lovely of you to drop in.' Tia eyed him sourly, then returned her attention to the screen in front of her. 'Mark's furious,' she said, without looking up. 'Raving about how it was Charlotte last night and you this morning.' She glanced up at him briefly, then turned her attention back to the screen. 'Is this friend of hers OK?'

'No, Tia. She isn't,' Matthew said coldly.

Tia shrugged indifferently. 'Still, you weren't going to help her by moping around at home, were you?'

He eyed her angrily. She arched her eyebrows, and mouthed 'Mark!' at him irritably. He held up his hands in defeat.

'OK, OK, I'm going.'

Wearily, he stood. The appearance of the strange woman this morning seemed days ago. The prospect of actually having to work now, carrying out normal everyday duties as though nothing at all was wrong was . . . was . . . He couldn't make it make sense. It was ridiculous. It filled him with helpless anger.

By the time he reached Mark Thornton's office, he had his frustration almost under control. He knocked.

'Come.'

He went in, reluctantly. Thornton looked up at him from the documents on his desk, and studied him intensely.

'Matthew, you look like shit,' he said bluntly. 'You didn't drink *that* much last night, surely?'

'Sorry, Mark. Just tired, that's all.'

For a moment, as he had with Tia on the phone, Matthew found himself hoping that Thornton would see through his words and force the truth out of him. Then it wouldn't be his responsibility any longer. It was being responsible that was intolerable – and being alone: no one to share the burden, to offer ideas, no one to tell him that what he was doing was *right*. He shrugged the feeling off angrily. Self-pity was no help at all.

Thornton stared at him for a beat, then said gruffly, 'We'll discuss that later. The Duke's mob get here at twelve. Are you set?'

Surprisingly, he was. Under other circumstances he would have spent the morning touring round to make doubly sure, but the preparations for this preliminary visit had been weeks in the making. Assuming everyone was where they should be, it would be fine.

'Set,' he replied. And then he drifted. There was something dream-like about being here, about doing these insanely irrelevant things . . .

Thornton peered at him suspiciously, 'Are you sure you're all right, Matthew?'

He attempted a smile. 'Fine: And thanks for last night, by the way. Charlotte sends apologies . . .' He faded again. Shrugged.

Something danced in Thornton's eyes – amusement, perhaps. 'Tia says Charlotte's been called away. Good news, eh? I was beginning to think you two'd had a domestic.'

Matthew did his best not to glare. This was hardly the time for games – not that Thornton could possibly know.

'No,' he said miserably. 'Just, this friend's got cancer . . . She was stuck in the hospital. Couldn't ring.'

Thornton wrinkled his nose at him. 'Well, you take good care of her, Matthew. There's others who'll have her if you don't.'

'Well then,' Matthew answered more sharply than he meant to, 'if they're coming at twelve, I'd better get ready, hadn't I?'

Thornton grinned at him. Perhaps, if he had been a different kind of man, Matthew might have felt able to confide in him. As it was, he left the office with the heavy awareness that he had just closed another door.

Fifteen

Every minute spent showing the Duke's equerries and body-guards around the prison was unbearable. He explained, introduced, ushered – while inside, he fought endless tides of questions, waves of paralysing uncertainty. And one question in particular: did he dare to do the one thing that remained open to him? How desperate would he have to be before he could talk to a man like David Gordon? The idea was not just ridiculous, it was actually intolerable. And yet . . .

Gordon had served his time. In the eyes of society, he was a free man, equal to any other – so why was he not in Matthew's eyes? The answer was that Matthew knew the man and society did not. A snatch of memory played through his mind: David Gordon, seen through the jumpy, grainy frames of a CCTV camera, smashing a palm into one man's chest so hard that he flew – literally flew – into a wall; whirling, an elbow cracking across another man's cheek, the arm folding fluidly around his neck . . . Three men, hospitalised in less than twenty seconds. This was not a man you would ever consider worthy of trust – although, before, Matthew had. And in a way, he had been right: Gordon had certainly solved the problem. The cost had been too high, though. He was unpredictable, uncontrollable and capable of quite extraordinary violence. And, however society now chose to describe him, the man was a criminal, and always would be. He had committed murder. It was not a fact that could be rubbed away by twelve years in prison: the murdered man would remain dead, however much time Gordon had served.

How much 'collateral damage' – as Gordon would doubtless think of it – was acceptable, if the result was Charlotte's return? There were principles at stake – and that was agonising, because principles were an irrelevance, compared to recovering Charlotte unharmed. This wasn't *about* principle; it was personal. The trouble was, principles were there for a reason. Ignoring them led to ruin. If Matthew turned to David Gordon, he would be in his debt, whatever the outcome. That was absolutely unacceptable for a prison officer – let alone a governor: the officer could be coerced into doing things that were not just improper, but were, quite probably, downright dangerous: drugs for inmates, or special favours, even a good word to the parole board. It could not be allowed to happen. Of course, from time to time, it did – and the consequences were always bad.

Besides, what guarantee did he have that Gordon could help him? He only had the man's word – and that, he knew, was worth nothing.

'The proper way is not always the right way,' Gordon had told him once. He had been standing in that odd pose he so often took up when he was in interview, his knees bent, his hands waving about somewhere in front of his face. *Chi Kung*, he'd called it. Matthew called it irritating. 'One day you will understand this,' Gordon continued. 'You will realise that, whatever you think, it is what you *do* that expresses your Self. You can only do what you do. Your limitations teach you to be free.'

Matthew had been reprimanding him for putting three men in hospital at the time; he hadn't paid much attention to the man's mystical ramblings. Instead, he had snapped at him, reduced him to Basic Compact, and extended his time on the Isolation Wing. David Gordon, the man who insisted on calling himself Monk, had thanked him courteously, turned his eyes inwards, and settled deeper into his disturbing bent-kneed pose.

It was a year or more later, when Gordon was being transferred to a lower category prison, that he had murmured to Matthew, 'You live in a prison of your own, Matthew. What will you do if, one day, you find you need my help?' He had stood in his cell, absolutely calm, watching Matthew with unwavering eyes. Then he had gathered his small armful of possessions and as he passed Matthew, he had paused and gazed up at him. He said, 'I live in a different world from you, Matthew. I will come.'

The wing officers had escorted him away.

Matthew had always lived an entirely un-mystical life. He had been glad to forget the man – or try to. David Gordon was trouble, although, Matthew was reluctant to admit, he had rather liked him. He clearly had principles, even if they were strangely expressed and dangerously open to violence. And Matthew had sensed that Gordon was troubled by something that he couldn't confront. Something had driven this man into his strange, dangerous and lonely life. He couldn't help thinking that, if his own life had taken another path, their roles might somehow have been reversed.

As he showed the visitors round the prison, they bombarded him with questions that any of his officers could have answered, and that only a child – or perhaps a Duke – would be interested in. How many prison officers will be manning the second floor on C Wing? There was an easy answer to that: who cared? His Highness the Duke is keen to meet some inmates, but he wants to be sure it isn't a type who might tarnish his reputation. Well, whatever. The Duke wants to meet a selection of staff after the tour, but he will require a ten-minute refreshment break beforehand. Fine. We'll get a bucket, just like the inmates have. Not.

As he was ushering the party out of A Wing and towards the catering block, his phone vibrated in his pocket. He grabbed it so fast that it was in his hand before it began to ring. He hit the receive button before its first chirrup was done. The equerries and guards looked irritated: they had all been asked to check in their phones when they came in. The two officers accompanying the group stared at him, horrified.

'Don't ask,' he muttered at them. He checked the screen. When one of the officers opened her mouth to challenge him, he snapped, 'I said, *don't*!'

The call was from Charlotte's mobile. He mumbled 'Wait' into the receiver and headed for the nearest private room. There was only one private room on each floor of the wing: the Principal Officer's work station. The PO today was Oliver Walsh – a solid, unimaginative type. Matthew kicked him out of the room and then shut the door.

'I'm here,' he said. 'Is she all right? Listen, what do we need to—'

There was no reply, just a deafening roaring sound.

'Hello?'

The roar began to fade.

'Hello? Hello? Is she all ri—'

A now-familiar voice interrupted him.

'Having fun, then?'

He was confused. 'Fun? What are you . . . ? No. Listen—'

'Poncing around at work, while she sweats it out all on her lonesome?' The man paused. 'I could be doing anything to her, couldn't I?' He chuckled.

Fury reared up in him. 'Listen, you bastard, if you touch a single—'

'You want to watch that temper of yours, Matthew. I told you before. It could get you into trouble. Or her.'

Before he could answer, the roar started again. He had to shout to be heard.

'Listen, she's *pregnant*, you bastard. You *know* she's pregnant.'

The man said nothing. Then, with the roar still building, there was suddenly silence.

Matthew stared hectically about the room, searching for something to latch onto, anything that made sense. There was a desk with a newspaper, a plastic chair. There was a print on the wall of a castle, nestled amongst posters outlining procedures and protocols: In Case Of Fire, In Case Of Breakout, In Case Of Violent Incidents . . .

Nothing that told him what to do In Case Of Your Wife Being Kidnapped By A Madman With No Desire To Talk.

His phone beeped again – this time the signal for a picture message. The picture loaded painfully slowly.

It was a picture of Charlotte's face. Her expression was bleak and completely neutral. Her eyes were puffed with lack of sleep. She looked . . . resigned. It was an expression he had only ever seen before on news broadcasts: it was the face of victims, hostages, the disappeared, the lost.

There was text to accompany the picture. It read:

Have taken away drugs. Next I hurt her

Matthew kicked savagely at the door. He had never felt so frustrated in his life, or so desperate. Immediately, the door opened, and Oliver Walsh peered in.

'You all right in there, Guv?'

'Never bloody better. Piss off.'

'Sir, with respect, you should check that phone in immediately.'

Matthew stared at Walsh long enough to make a point, then swept past him and out. What madness had possessed him to be here in the first place? As he approached the group he had been showing round, an equerry – Major General Someone-Or-Other – barked, 'Daniels, *really*, this is unacceptable. Please show at least a *little* respect for—'

He left the royal entourage bleating in his wake and headed straight for the exit, waiting distractedly while Larry 'Helpful' Tysome, relished the time it took to unlock the gate. Eventually, he stood aside – slowly – to let Matthew pass. His eyes were lifeless, and his face was as slack and sullen as a schoolchild's. That was fine. It was all irrelevant.

As he left reception, Bernard Jenkins sang out, 'Bye, Boss. Mind how you go.' The man's laughter followed him out of the building.

He rang the bank the moment he reached his car. When he finally fought his way past Jarvis's assistant and reached the man himself, he was far from happy to be disturbed.

'Mr Daniels, I said I'd ring you when I'd made a decision. I'm in a meeting at the moment.'

'Look, I just need to know. Can you tell me how long until—'

'Mr Daniels, when we decide, *I will ring you.*

'I'm just worried about the time. It's getting late.'

'I'm aware of that. Now, please—'

'OK. OK. Sorry. I'll . . . just wait.'

Jarvis rang off without replying. Helpless to do anything else, Matthew put the car in gear. *Wait*, said the kidnapper; *wait*, said the bank. And meanwhile, Charlotte's drugs had been taken from her – and soon he would 'hurt' her, he said, whatever that meant.

And what if he *didn't* wait, the kidnapper? What if, while Matthew scrabbled together whatever money he could, the man had already dumped her somewhere, or left her locked in that room without food or water, or taken her to the river, tied chains round her ankles . . . ?

He had no way to know, and no way to control it. His future was in the hands of a bank manager and a man who was, he suspected, entirely prepared for murder. Already, he could feel Charlotte drifting away from him, their tiny unborn child slipping into the dark.

It took him an agonising half-hour to negotiate the traffic – longer than if he had walked. The car slid slowly along bright, busy streets towards an empty house.

There was a pile of post on the doormat. He picked it up and scanned through it. There was one letter for him – a financial report from a small investment – and the rest were for Charlotte. Grimly, he put it on the stairs, on top of yesterday's pile. It was where they always left the post for each other; normally, it only accumulated into a pile if one of them was away. Charlotte already had ten or more items waiting for her, most of them mail-order catalogues: she loved to window-shop from home. He did his best to ignore the pile. She would be here to deal with it, just as soon as he had the money together – if he ever did. The kidnapper would buy the deal. It would be fine.

In the living room, there was a message on the answering machine. He hit the button.

'Mr Daniels? Stephen Jarvis here. Just to let you know our decision regarding your request. I'm afraid it's a No. It runs completely counter to several sections of the banking code – and given that the loan would be, effectively, unsecured, I'm afraid we all felt—'

Matthew had already fumbled for his mobile, and was frantically jabbing numbers. In the background, Jarvis was still droning on about how he remained a valued customer: angrily, he yanked the power cord out of the wall. The stupid, moronic, imbecilic *fool*. He *knew* how important the money was, he *knew* to call on the mobile. And the stupid twit had—

'HSBC, how can I help you?'

He asked for Jarvis and breathed deeply while he was on hold. Shouting would get him nowhere. At least they had agreed to put him through.

'Mr Daniels?'

'Mr Jarvis, listen. I need to talk to you about—'

'Mr Daniels, I'm afraid our decision is final. I'm sorry to disappoint you.'

'But, what if I—'

'*Final*, Mr Daniels. We simply cannot agree to lend you money on the terms we discussed. Perhaps if you could call in again sometime, we could discuss arranging a facility for future opportunities—'

Matthew rode over him. 'So, how much can I have now, right now?'

'I'm sorry? Oh . . . Well, as I just said—'

'No, I mean, how much of my *own* money can I withdraw? Immediately. Today.'

Jarvis drew in a long breath. 'You do realise that I shall have to report this, don't you, Mr Daniels? In all honesty, this does look highly suspicious. I have no choice but—'

'Fine. Report it,' Matthew snapped. 'Now how much of my money are you holding? I want it all in cash, today.'

He heard keys being tapped. Over the noise, Jarvis said, 'Well, we only have a limited cash reserve—'

'Then get more. How much? Today?' There was a pointed silence, except for more tapping. Matthew tried for a more conciliatory tone. 'It's a deposit for the painting. With luck, if I can put a fair whack down, he'll hold it for me.'

Tap, tap. Pause. Tap.

At last, Jarvis said, 'There's one account here with you as signatory called the Emily Daniels Trust. *Is* that a trust fund, Mr Daniels?' When Matthew agreed that it was, he went on, 'Well, you can't touch that, then, obviously. Let's see, the other accounts—'

Matthew jumped in, hoping he didn't sound too desperate. 'The trust's taking a part share. An investment. I've cleared it with the other trustees.'

There was a significant pause before Jarvis responded. 'Well, since you're the signatory, I suppose . . .' Tap. 'Mr Daniels, I have to say, I am not at all happy about this.'

When had he learned to sound so old? Matthew wondered. Perhaps there was a school for bank managers somewhere that drilled it into them.

'I understand,' he said briskly. 'You're not happy. But the trust wants to invest in art, OK? It's an opportunity. I explained.'

There was a sneer in Jarvis's voice when he answered. 'Well, let's just hope that this painting's all it's cracked up to be.'

There was more tapping. Matthew held his breath. At last, Jarvis announced, 'Twenty-eight thousand three hundred and twenty pounds. I've left a few pounds and pence in the account, just to keep it active.'

A lot of money – but not a hundred and fifty thousand. Would the man accept it? He'd have to, for now, and Matthew would try to find the rest tomorrow. He thanked Jarvis profusely, who told him tartly that the bank would have the cash ready for him in half an hour provided Matthew produced acceptable ID, and that he would be reporting to the police within the hour.

As soon as they had rung off, Matthew called the man, ignoring Charlotte's voice on the message, and explained the situation as calmly as he could. He needed to know where to leave the money he'd been able to raise so far – and he needed to persuade the man not to give up on him. 'It's all I can do. There isn't any more, I swear. Getting more would take weeks. But we'll work something out. Just don't . . .' He didn't want to even mention the alternatives. He began to prepare.

How do you carry twenty-eight thousand pounds in cash? What would it weigh, how bulky would it be? The films he had watched over the years were no guide: a million could fit in a briefcase, or a few hundred thousand could require several sacks. In the end, he settled for a large overnight case, with his briefcase and several plastic bags inside it.

It took him more than ten minutes to find his passport.

As he was preparing to leave the house, a text appeared on his phone:

28 buys you till tomorrow. Interest only. 150 still to pay

He sighed out a breath he hadn't realised he was holding. A day's grace. It was only deferring the nightmare – and in many ways making it worse – but a day was a day. Something could change. He could find the money – somehow. But if the banks wouldn't lend it to him, then how? And if he couldn't find the money, then who should he turn to?

A memory crept into his thoughts, unwanted, of a man standing perfectly still, his eyes distant and at peace. *I live in a different world from you, Matthew. I will come.* No. He would have to be utterly desperate to turn to him. While there were any other options at all, he wouldn't go there. But he *was* desperate, wasn't he? The voice nagged at him. You know you need information. Well, where else are you going to get it? It's either that or find the money, isn't it?

Angrily, he pushed the thoughts away and turned back into the house. There was one more thing he could try. In the living room, he pulled Yellow Pages down and hunted for loan companies. He'd seen the adverts on television often enough – up to thirty thousand pounds, no questions asked; need cash now? For up to twenty thousand, just call . . . He found them listed as Credit Agencies, page after page of garish ads, photos of men and women smiling in front of new conservatories, or in hospital beds. None of them offered enough to get him out of trouble – but if he rang several in quick enough succession, perhaps he could get money from each of them before his credit listing was changed. And then, maybe, if he also pulled as much cash as he could from his credit card, maybe . . . Faced with the ads, and the smiling faces, his brief burst of optimism faded.

. . . and maybe not.

There wasn't time to make a list, so he tore the pages out of the book. He would work through them on the way to the bank.

Before he reached the front door, the phone rang. It was the house line, not his mobile, and he hurried back to answer it. If the man wouldn't accept the money, then—

'What the hell are you playing at, Matthew?'

Not the man. It took him a moment to register that it was Mark Thornton.

'*Matthew?*' He was clearly furious. 'I asked you—'

'Yes. I heard you, Mark.'

'*And?*'

'And I'm not *playing* at anything, Mark.'

He didn't have time for this. He knew he needed to keep up appearances, but, really, what did any of this *matter*? It was just Thornton posturing, throwing his weight around so that he could feel important. To hell with him. He had to get to the bank. He had to call everyone on the pages he held, quickfire, bang bang bang. He had to work out what the hell he would do if this failed.

'Matthew, you just walked out on the Duke's entourage – without a word of explanation or apology, I might add. What the hell's got into you?'

The kidnapper could be ringing him now, unable to get through. If the line was engaged, maybe he wouldn't bother trying again.

'I have to go, Mark. I'll explain later.'

'Matthew? *Matthew!* If you—'

He interrupted. 'Look, it's *personal*, Mark. And I have to go. Now.'

Thornton shifted his tone. 'Well, if it's personal, Matthew, that's fine. I understand. But still, you shouldn't—'

'I'll call you later.'

'Look, if you need—'

Matthew hung up the phone, and headed for the bank.

Sixteen

As he walked, he worked through the list of loan companies. The first, predictably named A-Loan, respectfully declined to help. 'Yes, sir, it does say *No Questions Asked* in the advert – but that only applies when verifiable security is being offered against the loan – say if you were buying a car, and you offered the car as security. May I ask what you need the money for, sir?' He wasn't going to try the art trick again – they'd want some form of proof that the painting existed. He told the man that it was for private reasons. 'Well, in those cases we do require proof of income, sir. If you can get a statement from your employer – hard copy only, we don't accept email or faxes – then we should be able to approve the loan tomorrow and have the money for you by the end of the week . . . Well, the amount depends on your income and your credit risk . . . On that basis, sir, we'd be looking at – I'm talking hypothetically here, sir, subject to confirmation . . .' he sucked his teeth. '. . . fifteen? Maybe twenty. Cleared into your account Friday. No? OK, sir. Thanks for calling A-Loan.'

The next company, AlphaDebt, told a similar story. And the next. He reverted to the art story. The fourth company said they would accept part-share of a painting as security, but only after an independent valuation. He dropped the art idea again.

By the time he had reached the end of the list, he had persuaded just three companies – provisionally – to make money available to him the next day on the strength of a fax from his personnel officer at work confirming his income. All three required forms filled in and signatures appended; either he could visit their offices during working hours or they could put the forms in the post. It was nearly four o'clock already, and the nearest of the firms was on the other side of London. Worse, between the three of them, they had only agreed to lend him twenty-five thousand. There seemed little point. He had thanked the sales people, and told them, Perhaps tomorrow.

He signed for the money in a little room, under Jarvis's hostile gaze – and when it came, the pile was tiny. In fifty-pound notes, twenty-eight thousand pounds didn't take up much more space than a couple of thick paperbacks.

'They are marked notes, Mr Daniels,' Jarvis said crisply. 'And we've kept a register of the serial numbers. The police will be able to track them through the system.'

'That's fine,' Matthew answered, thinking, let them. Perhaps, when this was over and it was safe to tell them what had happened, they would be able to track down the bastard who had taken her. Apparently, the police had decided not to pursue the case. 'A watching brief,' Jarvis had muttered, before busying himself with the paperwork, his not-quite-acne glowing bright against his collar.

Matthew left as quickly as he could, with the money in a bag in the briefcase, and the briefcase still inside the overnight case. Outside the bank, he rang and left a message for the kidnapper – and received a text back:

Will collect from coffee shop round your corner. Half five

Matthew knew the place. He and Charlotte sometimes went there on Saturday mornings. He had half an hour to get there.

It felt much heavier carrying the case homewards, as though a few hundred sheets of paper made all the difference. And, in a way, they did.

The coffee bar was a couple of streets from the house. He sat at a table outside, sipping at a double espresso, with an impossibly large amount of money in a case at his feet. When his cup was empty, he began to feel exposed. Everyone was surely sneaking glances at him, wondering what he was doing there with no coffee and a large case. He dragged the case inside with him when he went to buy another cup. Luckily, no one took his table while he was in the queue. He sat again, in the company of his own scattered thoughts.

How was Charlotte coping? Did she talk to this man, or did he leave her alone? How much did she know about the ransom demand? She would be thinking the same thoughts as him, tracing the same paths to getting the money. Perhaps by now he would have told her about her temporary stay of execution – or perhaps she just sat and waited, as helpless as he was. She was strong, that much was undeniable. But it had always been a brittle strength, and the miscarriage had broken it. Since then, in place of her inner reserves, she seemed to Matthew to have coped with the world by using anger. When she was fragile or challenged or unsure, her response was rage. He smiled to himself sadly. Generally, the rage was directed at him. In the last year or so, since her last major outburst, it had become a game, of sorts: she did her best to keep it in check, and he did his best not to be hurt by it. Because they had something that was far stronger. Love. The dogged will to be happy together.

In her room, wherever it was, whether the man was there or had left her alone, she would be fighting uncertainty, in the knowledge that she was loved. It was the only comfort he could think of – for him as much as for her – and it was nowhere near enough.

'Darling, sorry.' The woman had pecked him on both cheeks before he was fully aware that she was there. He was enveloped in half-familiar perfume, and the woman sat down opposite him heavily, smiling the same false smile she had used so well that morning. 'I can't *believe* I left it at your place!' she gushed, fanning herself as though it was hot. A cool breeze swept away the cloud of perfume, and briefly lifted her bobbed hair. 'You did bring it, didn't you, doll?' She looked at him, eyebrows arched. Unhappily, he nodded at the case beneath. She clapped her hands against her cheeks. 'Oh, thank *goodness*. This evening's going to be enough of a nightmare anyway, even *with* the frock.'

She dragged the case towards her, swung it round, and extended the pulling-handle. 'Darling, you're a lifesaver.' She pressed a splayed palm towards him, every inch the dizzy socialite. 'Don't get up, will you? Stay and enjoy your coffee.' She air-kissed him from several feet away. 'Must – *mwah* – dash, darling – *mwah*. Soon, yes? See you!' She winked at him, turned and trotted away, with twenty-eight thousand pounds in tow.

Matthew sat rooted to his seat. A slow fury gathered inside him. How could a woman care so little? And if she didn't care – then what was going through the kidnapper's mind? He was calculating, deliberate – and mad and evil. He couldn't buy him off – that much was now obvious – but how could he hope to fight him?

The answer stared at him out of his own memory, with soulful blue-black eyes, and his body held unnaturally still. As all the money he could possibly raise in time disappeared round the street corner, he finally gave up the struggle. With profound reluctance, he reached for his phone.

Seventeen

She knew nothing. What was happening? Well, she would find out in due course, she would just have to wait. The question that vexed her most, and kept her mind usefully occupied, was: who was he?

He was almost familiar to her. She was sure she didn't actually know him; it was more as though she had half-noticed him somewhere from time to time, or she had heard his voice before. She couldn't be sure even of that, though; perhaps she was imagining it. She had only heard a few barked instructions from him, and only seen his deep black eyes, and his skin almost as dark, and his wiry frame – and she had dwelled on those things, because what else was there to do? Most likely, she had seen him at the Ville. He was one of the thousands of inmates, the carefully blank faces that had formed a constant backdrop to her work there.

This whole thing was about Matthew. One of those faces had it in for him, or they reckoned he could change something they wanted changed – and their best route to him was through her.

Or else, it wasn't about him at all. Maybe, somehow, it was about her . . . How could she know? The room offered no clue. Even the planes were silent on the subject. There was just a face she half-recognised, or imagined that she recognised.

At least he had let her have the drugs. There was hope in that. For the moment at least, he wanted her and Eyelash alive and healthy. It was something to cling to.

She found ways to mark the time, to give some kind of structure to an existence that had already become at once dreary and terrifying. It was four thirty in the afternoon, a little more than a day since she had woken here. Twenty-four hours.

There were other landmarks, too. Her scan: she had to be at the hospital this coming Friday at nine in the morning. So, as long as she could get out of here within the next – concentration was hard with the planes howling over; it took a while to work it out – sixty-four hours and thirty minutes, then her baby would be in safe hands. If she could keep her alive that long. Or him.

She held her belly and crooned, 'Hold on, sweetheart. I'm here. It's OK. Nothing to be scared of. He's just a silly man, that's all.' She tried to keep her tone bright. 'He'll let us go soon, you'll see.'

She wished she could cry, but she was beyond that now. Nothing that she felt, nothing that she thought, could make the slightest difference. This morning, she had tried singing. She had marched around the room, ignoring the camera – and had realised how little of any one song she really knew. She would start a verse, then falter after a few lines, mumble something vaguely tuneful until she reached the chorus – and then be stumped. It made her feel foolish, and that made it impossible to become absorbed by what she was doing. And then, every ninety seconds, the impersonal scream of another plane swallowed the sound, and left a hollow space in its wake, an inescapable reminder of her situation. She couldn't forget, not even for two minutes. There was nothing to do, and nowhere to explore except the inside of her own frayed mind.

She sank into herself. The cycle of thought became shorter and shorter, a blur of anticipation, uncertainty, fear and expectation . . . And then even that vanished, leaving her devoid of real awareness, consumed by a dull churn of abstract emotion. Each hour was a dry, empty horror. It dragged past like footsteps shuffling across the gritty floor of her prison.

She knew the walls now. She knew their peeling yellow enamel, their film of grimy condensation. She knew the roof, its window panes mired in pigeon shit and moss. There was a kind of safety in limbo. This was her fortress.

Time, broken into the ninety-second beats of passing planes.

Twenty-four hours.

Already, the toilet stank. It hunched in the far corner of the room, biding its time. Every time she thought of it, bitter threads of bile rose in her throat. It was almost reassuring: it meant that, for now at least, she was still pregnant. Sometime soon, balaclava-face was going to have to empty the thing.

It was raining. Drops ticked against the metal sheeting of the roof.

The air, when she could bear to take a breath, was heavy and hot, unrelieved by the drizzle.

There was a pattern, of sorts: the man had come the night before, he had come again in the morning: he would come again this evening. What was left of this morning's food lay on the floor in a corner: a paper plate with half a crispbread on it, some Marmite in a plastic tub that had once held coleslaw, a plastic knife, a bottle of mineral water. She had forced herself to eat, for Eyelash's sake.

There was nothing now, not even fear any more, not really. There was just horror, and the absence of hope. Was it just a day since she had so confidently thought that rescue was hours away?

Matthew wasn't coming. He would have found her by now. The man was keeping her because he still had a use for her – but whatever his purpose, it was clear now that it would take time to achieve. And if he didn't succeed?

It was this that paralysed her. His eyes were wide and dark, and full of . . . not anger exactly. Pleasure and fear. He was unstable. He might do anything.

She would never be a mother. The eyelash-sized person inside her would never grow to see the love in her mummy's eyes.

Perhaps Matthew hadn't come because he didn't want to. He had always tried to hide it, but she had seen the look in his eyes when they talked about Eyelash, when they made plans. The baby was for her, not for him. And, when he had asked her to marry him – the day she had stormed out – that was because she knew the proposal was made out of charity, not love. She was a burden to him, a problem in his life requiring constant careful manipulation to be solved. He touched her uncertainly, as though she were a bomb that might go off at any second. And he was right, she was; his attentiveness drove her to explosive fury.

And when he had asked her, when he had so carefully and methodically implied that something as stupid as a ring on her finger might take away all the misery of losing her baby – she had . . .

She had made one single, terrible mistake.

She had never told him, but she had seen his face when she walked back in the next morning. No wonder he hated her – even if he didn't know, not for sure. No wonder he wasn't coming. He would be happier without her. She would die here, and never be able to tell him that she was sorry.

But she was torturing herself, and she knew it. It was just her own regrets. He loved her – too much, perhaps, too overwhelmingly; but he loved her. He would be frantic. He was negotiating with her captor. When the man came again, it would be to release her. Or maybe Matthew himself would unlock the door.

Or maybe another night would close in while the planes yammered above her, and morning would come, another day, then the afternoon – and then she would have spent forty-eight hours here, and there would be just forty left before the scan.

She sat on the cold gritty floor, devoid of plans, wavering between hope, horror and emptiness.

The man came at six. Hot black eyes stared at her through the glass. She faced him defiantly. Satisfied with what he saw, he turned away and began dismantling the video apparatus. 'Boss says he don't need it no more,' the man said gruffly through the glass. 'Waste of bloody time in the first place, if you ask me.' Charlotte watched uneasily. So. Something had changed. She searched for something to say, and found nothing. He was playing games with her; why else make a show of discussing her own predicament with her? She refused to be his accomplice. *He* was abusing *her*. Finished, the man eyed her suspiciously before unlocking the door and standing in front of her, staring.

'Toilet needs emptying,' she said at last.

He laughed. 'Your fault for using it.'

'You *animal*,' she hissed.

His eyes scowled at her from behind the balaclava. Brow furrowed, he reached an arm around himself and scratched savagely at a point below his left shoulder. It was a gesture that reminded her of someone – no one important, just . . .

'Yeah. An animal,' he said. He sniffed loudly. 'So?' His eyes raked her. When she folded her arms self-consciously, he chuckled.

'Brought food,' he said after a while. He made no move to offer her the plastic bag he was carrying; she made no move to take it. 'What's the matter? Not hungry?' His eyes probed her. He sniffed again. 'You will be. Soon enough, you'll be begging me for it.'

She wished that she had the courage to spit at him – but how could she? She needed him. He controlled her world. How long would she last if he took away her food, her water? How long would Eyelash last?

'Thank you,' she said meekly. She kept her eyes down. Today, he was wearing shabby trainers below frayed black jeans. The trainers were white, and spattered with pale mud.

'That's better,' he growled. He moved closer and held out the bag. Then, when she reached for it, he pulled it away again. 'Ah-ah-ah. I want a *proper* thank-you.'

She dropped her hand to her side, studied the floor. She bit her lip. She wanted desperately to back away from him to find a corner – but there was already hunger in his voice, and she knew the man well enough by now to know that he fed on her fear.

He dumped the food bag on the floor and came closer – too close. His chest almost touched her breasts. She could feel his heat on her skin, smell the tobacco on his breath, the sharp odour of sweat on his face, the blunter scent of builder's dust in his clothes.

'I'll let you into a little secret,' he said. His voice was thick and coarse. 'You're lucky. See, the boss doesn't want you hurt. Wants the money first, don't he?'

The boss? He'd said that before. It hardly mattered now, though. For now, she was safe. They were just waiting for money, and then . . .

The man pressed his face closer. 'Here's another little secret,' he said. 'Don't matter what the boss wants, does it? Cos he ain't here.'

She recoiled. She could sense his satisfaction when his words had the effect he wanted. Small, inarticulate noises escaped from her. 'You – he—'

'See, the way I look at it,' he went on, almost under his breath, 'the boss isn't gonna want to keep you for ever. So I got to get my fun in while I can.'

When he touched her, she yelped – and his eyes hardened. He traced her collarbone with his fingertips, then let his hand slide slowly down towards her breasts. He squeezed one of them, hard. She whimpered and tried to pull away. As she jerked backwards, his hand closed on her blouse and yanked her towards him. He snarled at her, and grabbed her throat, forced her head up until she was staring into his masked face. His eyes were wide and intent on her. The force of his grip jammed her mouth painfully shut.

From between clenched teeth, she hissed, 'Fuck – off – you – disgusting—'

He clamped a hand over her mouth. 'Temper, temper.' His voice was an ugly caress. With his other hand, he let go of her throat. His fingers trailed downwards, over her neck, her chest, her belly. They scrabbled at the waistband of her skirt. He grunted as he worked, the sound muted by the balaclava.

'Do you know how long I've wanted to do this to you? Do you? That smug look you always had on your face. I just wanted to slap that smile off you, rip off that uniform, see what you look like. I'm gonna fuck you till you scream.'

She couldn't speak: the hand was still over her mouth. *Uniform?* Then he *was* from the Ville, no question now. If she could just talk to him, maybe she could—

His fingers slid inside the waistband of her skirt. Stroked downwards over bare skin. 'This job's a fucking gift.' He sighed as he reached her knickers.

She bit his hand as hard as she could, and flailed at his face. He howled and jerked his arm away. '*Ow! Bitch.*'

She dodged past him and ran to the locked door, battering her hands against it as loudly as she could, screaming incoherently for someone, anyone, to come.

He dragged her back into the room by her hair, drew her upright by it, and plunged his fist into her solar plexus. She gaped at him for a breathless instant, her eyes bulging, then she crumpled, her chest spasming, and curled at his feet. He crouched comfortably beside her.

'That wasn't smart, sweetheart. Next time you make me hit you, I'll do it lower.' He waved his fingers in front of her face, and said in a sing-song tone, 'Bye bye, baby . . .' He leaned closer – and between her pain and fear, she found a moment to be grateful that she couldn't breathe, because at least she was spared the smell. She might even have laughed at that – if her lungs had been working. Instead, she could feel herself fading. 'No food for you, doll,' he murmured. As though it was an intimacy. As though he was making love. 'Not until you learn how to be nice to me. So you'd better have a think about what you're going to do for me tomorrow, hadn't you?'

She drew in her first gasping breath, then convulsed as her lungs closed down again.

He laughed. 'Here,' he said. 'Something to get you thinking.'

With every sign of pleasure, he licked a finger. Then he slid it deep into her mouth.

Over the sound of her own retching, she heard his laughter, the sound of his keys in the lock, the crisp, bright footsteps in the corridor as he left.

She knew that there were things she needed to concentrate on, things she had to understand and react to, things he'd said. Don't need the camera any more; I've wanted to do this for ages; you in your uniform; boss says, the boss says, the boss, the boss . . . But concentration was impossible. Her chest heaved for air, her stomach clenched and unclenched, her throat was on fire.

She watched herself from a vantage point somewhere near the ceiling, a small lost figure, paralysed by her own weakness. And she knew, distantly, that if they were going to survive this, Eyelash and her, then she could no longer afford to wait. No one was going to rescue her, not in time. She would have to save herself.

Eighteen

Monk had never bothered learning to drive. He didn't see the point. The events of his life moved at a speed of his choosing. He slid through London towards Matthew Daniels in a taxi, towards a location he had chosen partly because it was secure, but mostly because of what it meant.

As he travelled, time unravelled in his thoughts. For Monk – and for anyone, although most people never realised it – past, present and future were only different patterns within one cloth. What changed as you sensed time passing was merely the part of the pattern you chose to gaze at. One of Monk's many patterns concerned Matthew Daniels. Threads of this pattern extended outwards through time. The patterns were discernible in their first meeting. Other threads of it stretched far into the future. He had known, the very first time they met, that he and Matthew Daniels were linked.

He closed his eyes and allowed recollection to take him.

It is five years ago, and Monk has just arrived at Pentonville, transferred from Whitemoor, the category-A prison that has been his home since he was sentenced for murder seven years ago. It does not matter to Monk where he is: there is no one who might visit him, no one who cares how to find him; there hasn't been since he was fourteen. In the thirty-four years since, he has been almost entirely alone – and he has learned that it does not matter where you are. It does not even matter who you are. Identity, purpose, circumstance: such things are without importance. There is only the yin and the yang, the shade and the light; what matters is how you move between them.

This is what he knows. This is what he believes. And one day, perhaps, it will also be what he feels.

– David, I –

– help me, David, oh David –

He sits in an interview room in Pentonville prison, in a chair in the middle of an empty space. He is flanked by two prison officers. Facing him from behind a metal-legged table is the officer in charge of the wing he will be staying on. His name is Matthew Daniels, and he gazes at Monk with brisk compassion. There is a file on the table in front of him, which he does not refer to once.

'Fifteen for murder,' Prison Officer Daniels says matter-of-factly, 'with seven served.'

Monk does not reply: he has not been asked a question.

And what is there to be gained by telling this man that he is innocent? That he was trying to save the man they claimed he killed? The police had never believed it, nor had the judges at his hearing or at appeal. And Monk has his own reasons for accepting punishment. He was innocent – this time; but he is a murderer nonetheless. Besides, there is a man that he swore long ago to protect.

'The Ville's a little more comfortable than Whitemoor, David,' Matthew Daniels continues. 'I'm sure you'll be fine here.'

'Monk,' says Monk. David is no longer his name. David Beresford Gordon died a long time ago – or should have.

– the sunlight through the window –

– and, David, she said, David, I –

David Gordon died when he was fourteen. Monk is forty-eight.

'I prefer David,' Matthew Daniels said bluntly. 'It's your name.'

Monk does not reply. David is *a* name. It means nothing. It is the name of a boy who should have died. And whatever name they call him, a Monk is what he has become. He owns nothing, lives nowhere. He lives within himself, and contemplates the innocence he lost so very long ago. It is only fitting that he should live in a cell and do penance. He has chosen this path – or it has chosen him. Let Prison Officer Daniels call him what he will.

He surveys Monk, his lips pursed. He leans forward and flicks the file in front of him. 'Excellent record,' he says. 'Cooperative. Signs of remorse . . .' He frowns. 'But you refuse to retrain for release. Why?'

'Because what I need, I have,' Monk replies. 'I will never kill again.'

It is true – although Matthew Daniels understands the words differently from their true meaning.

He laughs. 'I should bloody well hope not!' He looks at Monk with amusement in his eyes. Monk does not respond. The sparkle fades – and at that, Monk smiles a little, inside.

Everyone at the Ville knows Matthew Daniels' story. His wife died. Killed herself. The police thought he had killed her, because of a massive insurance payout. He was suspended while he was under investigation. Then it turned out that he was innocent. The man who returned to work was haggard, and barely able to cope. He had become kind, to the point of weakness – but inside, there was a core of steel that had never been there before. He was a dangerous man: talked like a pussy cat, bit like a tiger. A man to respect and to fear.

And, since his new cellmate told him this story, last night, just after he had arrived on the wing, Monk has known that this is a man he can understand. He has never met him, and already he knows Matthew Daniels to the core. Because he too is a man made dangerous by grief – and by the terrible, paralysing knowledge that, despite your innocence, it is you who are to blame.

Now, Monk sits motionless in the interview room, and lets his body's senses ripple outwards towards the man in front of him. He feels the taut shifting of the officers on either side of him, a hot tingle against his skin. He reaches further, with senses for which there are no words – and he can feel the softness beneath Matthew Daniels' steel. There is a stillness there, the stillness of a man who knows that moving will not ease the pain. The pain is something in his bones. It is a friend. There is weariness there, too, a slow ember within him. Monk looks with his eyes, too, and sees in the hollows of the man's face an echo of what he has already sensed inside him: set against the exhaustion, there is a rigid will. Matthew Daniels lives with uncertainty, grief and despair. He fights it every day – and, mostly, he wins.

But perhaps, Monk reflects, he can sense these things in Prison Officer Daniels because he knows them already. These troubles are his own companions too. For all their manifest differences, he and this man walk the same path.

With a frustrated sigh, Matthew Daniels gives up staring at Monk and looks instead at the file in front of him, still closed. He clucks his tongue as he thinks. Then, suddenly, he leans forward.

'David,' he says, 'I think I need your help.'

Later – months later – Monk is in Segregation. He has a narrow cell that is all his own. He is here because he is dangerous. He has put two inmates and one prison officer in hospital – because he did as Matthew Daniels asked. There was a drugs problem on his wing: he needed an informer, a man who could help him pinpoint the people responsible: suppliers, dealers. Matthew Daniels needed to know the whole chain before he could take action. Monk found this out for him.

What he found is that one inmate, Louis French, was given the drugs by his girlfriend during visits. One particular officer, Officer Holt, who was occasionally in charge of supervising visits, enjoyed blowjobs from her, in exchange for turning a blind eye. Recently, though, Holt has become the mule. French's friends in the outside world have been piling on the pressure – because he wouldn't want anyone telling his missis or the Governor, would he? Holt now carries in the drugs, and he is terrified.

Monk had done the legwork. He has played the troubled addict, used his senses and his wits – and he has relayed everything he has discovered to Matthew. (He thinks of him as Matthew these days; he knows there is a connection between them and that one day its meaning will become clear.) He has no regrets about informing, because it is the right thing to do. Because the drugs that French peddles are brutal destroyers of lives – and because Monk wants a future, one that lifts him from the mire of grief and crime that has been his world.

Matthew is grateful. He collaborates with the police on a sting. Angus Holt is apprehended along with one of the men who supply him. French is charged and segregated.

Then, two days later, two men attack Monk in the wash-room. One of them has a knife. The two men are now in hospital, along with the officer who tried to pin Monk down, not realising that unless Monk remained free for a few more seconds, his throat would be cut.

Now Matthew, newly promoted to Junior Governor, stands in Monk's single cell, shaking his head in frustration. Monk is unperturbed. He stands in *wu chi* – a static posture that gathers energy to him, connects him to the roaring power of the void – and contemplates the man in front of him. It is clear that he is wrestling with anger. Such emotions are the privilege of power.

'I am grateful,' Monk says to him mildly. He cannot think of him as Governor, or Mr Daniels. Already he knows him too well for that. He nods at his narrow cell.

Matthew frowns. Monk is teasing him, he thinks. 'It's for your own safety,' he says.

Monk laughs inside. His lips hardly move as he murmurs, 'I could be bounded in a nutshell and count myself a king of infinite space.'

Matthew snaps. 'Spare me the Shakespeare, David. I know you're a clever bastard. That, heaven help me, is why I chose you in the first place.' There is fury on his face, and horror. 'That, and the fact that I believed you when you said you wanted a second chance.'

Monk does not reply. What is there to say?

'You put three people in hospital, David!'

Still, Monk says nothing. Because what Matthew has said is a statement of fact. He senses Matthew's energy, strangely cool and watery, rippling and crackling, cold sparks over his skin.

Monk could kill him with a single swift blow, not that he would ever choose to: Matthew seems unaware of both the risk, and of his own safety. He is too angry.

'You let me down, David,' he says wearily. 'You said you wanted to change.'

'You said you would protect me,' Monk returns.

'You attacked one of my officers, David! You could have killed him.' But Matthew is defensive now.

'He tried to restrain me,' Monk says simply. 'I did what I had to. There was no lasting damage.'

Matthew will never understand the full meaning of this: that Monk is absolutely in control of himself. If he intends to kill, he kills. If he intends to injure, he injures. If he wishes to jolt someone just enough that they leap backwards because of the pain, then that is exactly what happens. If he had wanted to hurt the prison officer more seriously, he would have.

'I did no damage,' Monk repeats. What he means is, Trust me.

But Matthew cannot trust him, not now. Instead, he stares at him, full of horror and full of fear. He cares too much, wants every outcome to be happy for everyone. It is a feeling that Monk understands. He understands it because he too has suffered that same torture, he too has howled in outrage at the night. Monk knows what it is to want to make everything right once more. Matthew wants to control the world, and Monk wants to withdraw from it; but their reasons are the same. There are ghosts to lay to rest.

He remembers a sunlit day long ago. A day when a girl told him she loved him, and when he loved her. Then the men came, and she screamed, and he did nothing because he couldn't, and she died.

Riverweed.

Matthew is angry at what he believes is Monk's indifference. 'For goodness sake, David! At least look at me! Give me one good reason why I shouldn't ship you back to Whitemoor.'

There is nothing Monk can say that can prevent Matthew doing this, except to show remorse. Remorse is an emotion that Monk finds hard to understand, because every action he takes is simply an expression of his nature: he cannot be anything other than himself. He fought because he had no choice. Perhaps another man would have acted differently – but then it would be another man, not Monk. Monk is true to himself. There are no regrets.

That, at least, is the theory.

'I didn't mean to,' he says. He lets humility creep into his voice. 'They attacked. I defended myself. I've been a martial artist since I was twelve. I just . . . reacted.'

'Bullshit, David!'

The irony is that he is telling the truth. But in Matthew Daniels' eyes, he senses anger at a world that can never be set right.

And Monk knows at that moment that the two of them have a future. It is through Matthew that Monk will find a way forward. And it is through Monk that Matthew will begin to learn, and at last grow away from his pain.

It is some years later. Monk stands in an abandoned space of weeds and concrete and broken glass. His posture is *wu chi*, drawing the energy of the world into himself, merging with it, becoming one. He feels the currents of the air, and the subtler currents of his own awareness. He is a trout, motionless in a stream. He is the gull, soaring above the cliff top on unmoving wings . . .

His mobile rings.

He had forgotten to switch it off; but there are no accidents in Monk's life, no coincidences. If he has left his mobile on, it is for a reason. He will discover that reason when the time is right. Perhaps he will discover it now.

He presses the energy he has gathered down into his belly, then he walks to the half-demolished wall where he has left his jacket. He takes the phone from a pocket, holds it to his ear, and waits.

There is a voice at the other end. 'David? Hello, David?'

Monk does not reply. He knows this voice. It belongs to a man who, until recently, was his jailer.

'David? It's Matthew Daniels. From the Ville. I don't know if you can hear me, but if you're there, I . . . Well. I got your number through the parole listings. Not that they know I'm ringing you . . .'

Interesting. He waits.

'David? Listen, I need your help. Badly. David?'

Monk smiles to himself. Most definitely interesting. And, of course, there is no decision to make at all.

'Speak,' he says softly.

There are no accidents in Monk's life, no coincidences. There is only Destiny.

Nineteen

Rachel Miriam Daniels. Beloved wife of Matthew, mother of Emily. Her dates, chiselled into the dark slate: she had been thirty-four when she died.

Her grave was better tended than most of them but still it suffered from neglect. He had stopped laying flowers years ago, and had planted bulbs and roses. The plants had never really thrived. He used to visit once a week, on Friday, on his way to or from work, but it had been harder since he had been with Charlotte: it was a slight to her, to concentrate too hard on Rachel. Besides, he had found that he didn't *need* Rachel's memory as much, now that he had a future again. He had come to accept long ago that Rachel's ghost would always haunt him; he felt that she would have rather approved of Charlotte. But still, most Fridays there was a moment as he hurried past the graveyard when he remembered, and when he left her grave behind, it felt like a tiny act of betrayal. Sometimes, he simply didn't remember – and that was even worse.

Grass had grown up thickly around her stone since he had last been here. For the most part, he managed to keep it clear of the weeds that threatened to encroach from neighbouring plots – nettles, brambles. Eighteen months ago, someone had sprayed their initials over the stone. He had scrubbed at it for hours, with every chemical he could find. Faint white and yellow smears still looped across its face.

Why had David Gordon insisted on meeting here, of all places? It was proof – as if proof were needed – that his misgivings had been accurate.

He had explained to Gordon on the phone – no, he was going to have to call him Monk now, wasn't he? – that Charlotte was missing, and that he wanted Monk's help with some information. He hadn't mentioned that she'd been kidnapped. He had asked if they could meet. Gordon – *Monk* – had offered to come to the house. Matthew had hurriedly explained that this was a bad idea. It was obvious that he was going to have to tell Monk more than he wanted to.

'Someone's watching me,' he confessed miserably. 'They mustn't know I'm meeting you. It'll have to be somewhere else.'

There had been a long silence while Monk digested this. Then he had asked, 'Where is your wife buried? Your first wife.'

It was a deliberately cruel act. Matthew was in no position to argue with it.

'Drive,' Monk had said. 'Park a few streets away, then walk. If they follow you, you'll know.' *They?* A disturbing thought. 'Unless they want you to see them, they'll have to wait outside,' Monk went on. 'Too visible if they come in.'

He couldn't fault the logic – but there were countless other places Monk could have chosen.

Hastily, he scribbled a note:

Em – Had to pop out, sorry. I'll prob be back late. Grab some food. Love you always. Dad x

He stared at the words until they blurred.

There was a guilty relief in knowing he would not have to confront her when she got back from school. The more she saw of him, the more she would realise he was lying to her about Charlotte's whereabouts. Sooner or later, she would have to know the truth; but she was too young for this. How could she understand that this was directed not at her but at him? That he was protecting her? How could she believe that when he lied to her, avoided her, deliberately drove her away? Just to keep her safe and happy. Just for love.

When this was over, he would explain, and apologise. It would have to be enough. For now, though, he had a meeting to go to.

There was an elaborate tomb near the cemetery's far end: a Gothic extravagance, now crumbled and boarded over, daubed with initials, in huge sweeps of black and green. Monk was waiting for him on its far side, hidden from the road.

'Did anyone follow you?'

Matthew shook his head. Monk gazed at him, unblinking.

He was surprisingly short – no more than five feet seven – and slim, but he stood with a looseness that somehow made him seem larger. His shoulders were utterly relaxed, his arms hung limp, his knees were unlocked. There was no effort to puff himself up. He looked as if he would sway in the slightest wind. But he had presence. He commanded the eye.

A deep scar ran the length of his face. It notched one eyebrow, then traced a jagged line down his cheek, and left a deep cleft on his jawline near his chin. The skin around it was plump and puckered.

But it was the eyes. There was such calm in them, such certainty, that somehow even his disfigured face seemed entirely natural. They were mild brown against his intensely black skin. His gaze was soft and unwavering.

'Some might say that you hung me out to dry,' he said finally.

Matthew shifted uneasily. 'You broke the rules, David.'

'Monk.'

'Monk. Whatever. Look, you helped nail the drugs thing, and I was grateful. But that didn't mean you suddenly had the right to go around assaulting my staff.'

'He put me in danger.'

'I don't *care*, David! What you did was wrong. You got punished for it, exactly the same as anyone else.'

The man stared mildly at him. 'Monk,' he repeated.

Matthew bit back an angry response: the man had a talent for being almost immediately irritating. But he needed him.

'Look, prison is tough, Monk,' he said bluntly. 'It's supposed to be. But we treated you fairly. You knew the rules. I'm sorry if you had a rough time, but you're the one who put yourself in exile.'

Suddenly, Monk was right in front of him, facing him from less than two feet away. An eyeblink before, he had been ten feet away. As Matthew's awareness caught up with his presence, he had a belated impression – more a memory – of a whirling form, a blur of fluid movement; but he was already here. He was perfectly still, absolutely relaxed. The fear that now rushed over Matthew arrived far too late to help. Monk stared up at him, his scarred face utterly impassive.

Softly, he said, 'That is true.' He drifted away again, scanning the wasteland of graves. There was something bleak in his stare, an emptiness that Matthew found disturbing. When he spoke again, his tone was harsher. 'Someone has taken your wife. You don't know who, and you cannot go to the police.'

'How did you know—'

'Because you told me she is missing and that you were being watched.' He faced Matthew, and his lips twitched: perhaps in amusement, perhaps anger. 'And now you need my help.'

Warily, Matthew said, 'I just need information. Nothing else. Someone with contacts.'

'What makes you think I can help you?'

Matthew's frustration boiled over. 'Look, you're all I could think of, OK? Trust me, I'm no happier about it than you are.'

Monk pursed his lips thoughtfully, and Matthew waited for him. Scraps of paper and plastic lifted in the breeze, then settled. Monk ran a finger over the stone beside him, tracing the barely visible lines of an inscription. Lichen flaked away under his fingers.

Matthew sighed. 'I'm . . . sorry. I didn't mean that quite how it . . . Look, the truth is, I'm desperate.'

'You must be.'

He ignored the jibe. 'I need to know who's doing this. He won't talk to me. He just . . .' He held up his hands, as though he could somehow grasp the word with them. 'Well, he wants more than I can possibly raise.' Monk raised an eyebrow. 'It doesn't matter how much, David! Monk. Sorry.' Monk's fingertips rasped over the lichen-crusted stone. 'Look, it's a hundred and fifty thousand, OK? Cash. If I had a couple of weeks maybe I could raise it – maybe – but that bastard wants it tomorrow. It's already cost me thirty grand just to keep her alive until then. I can't reason with him, he . . .' Frustration got the better of him, and he tailed off. He held up his hands again, helpless. 'I need information, Monk. That's all. Desperately. I need to find her, find *him*. I . . . I need your help.'

Monk's face showed not the slightest flicker of response, but his eyes slid away from the stone and back to Matthew. 'That's what you said last time.'

Matthew struggled to keep his self-control. 'Can we forget the past, just for a moment? *Please*. For what it's worth, I am sure we both wish things had turned out differently. But they didn't. And it's *over*, Monk. I need your help *now*.'

Monk's reply was so quiet that he barely heard it. '*Is* it over, Matthew?'

He drifted closer again, and Matthew flinched, suddenly pain-fully aware that he was alone with a killer. 'Your past is who you are, Matthew.' Monk breathed. 'It is your purpose, your meaning.'

'Oh, spare me the claptrap, Monk. This is—'

'Why do you think I brought you here? Why are we in your wife's graveyard?'

'Don't you *dare* bring her into this,' Matthew hissed.

'But it has to do with her. It has to do with all the people here.' He nodded at the sea of stones around them. 'Dead but not forgotten – that's what they say, isn't it? And it's true. We carry our dead around with us. Our past is our soul.'

Unnerved and exasperated in equal measure, Matthew muttered, 'Fine. Whatever. Look, are you going to help me – or did you just bring me here to play some sick joke?'

Monk's face betrayed genuine surprise. 'Of course I shall help you. A life is at stake.'

Matthew couldn't contain his anger any longer. 'Oh, well, how big of you. A life's at stake. Shame you didn't think of that one before you murdered some poor sod.' He regretted his words immediately. Monk had a talent for bringing out the worst in him.

Monk chose not to reply.

When Matthew finally found his voice, there was humility in it. 'Listen. I didn't mean . . . Look, I need you. Please.' There was nothing more he could say or do: Monk would accept or he would not. His eyes remained steady and remote, fixed on something Matthew could not see.

He made one last attempt. 'I don't know what else to say, David. What do you want?'

Monk stood loosely, his eyes brown and unfathomable as a river, and fixed on something far beyond the stones and the litter.

'I told you I would help.'

Matthew said bitterly, 'Because a life's at stake.'

Monk's attention snapped back to him. He spoke softly and intensely – and behind his words Matthew sensed a force of feeling he could barely understand. 'Not just because of that, Matthew. Because of who I am.'

His eyes softened. He almost appeared to smile.

'You asked me what I want,' he said. 'The answer is, I want the same thing as you.' He stared again across the graves of the forgotten dead. 'What I want,' he said, 'is the future. Don't we all?'

Twenty

You are horrified by what you have done – and even more so by what you will do. But the horror is a small voice, and the dark tide rising inside you drowns it. In a way, *you* are not even doing these things, It is. You are driven by Rage. And, yes, you will allow that to continue.

In another way, too, you are not to blame – because you yourself have done nothing. You didn't snatch her, your associate did. You didn't film her or threaten her or call Matthew to tell him what must happen. If you had done these things, she would have recognised your face, and he your voice. It was your associate, not you, who found the woman to put the police off the scent; it was he who arranged to collect the money. All you have done is hire him, and tell him what must be achieved. And, for your pains so far, you have received fifteen thousand in cash – well, ten – and the promise of more to come.

So, if it isn't you who has done these things – what's to feel guilty about? You know what has happened is wrong, but you aren't exactly the one who did it.

Besides, these jabs of conscience are only temporary. You are dimly aware that before much longer your anxiety will be swallowed by the Thing now writhing inside you. It has changed. At first it was an itch, a spreading sore; but now It is Alive.

Fifteen thousand is not enough, not even before your vicious little associate finds a thin pretext to claw five of it back.

'Expenses,' he says. There is something evasive in his tone, and he picks at a tooth to avoid meeting your eyes.

But the lie doesn't matter to you. If he has successfully squeezed fifteen out of Matthew, then that is a start, and there is the promise of more to come. Fifteen, ten, what does it matter? A few tens of thousands cannot sustain you. This is a game with higher stakes. In every possible way, you need . . . more.

Your man sniffs, hawks and spits, then concentrates on smearing the result across the pavement with his boot. 'It's the girl that wants it. For collecting the dosh.' You don't much care – and that, of course, is why he feels safe to do this. But you are torn. Because already you can feel this slipping away from you.

And then there is the unbearable cruelty of it. (*Necessary* cruelty, whispers the Thing inside you. Necessary.) And the risk . . . Guilt is nothing – you have lived with yourself long enough to know that for every sleepless night of self-disgust there is a morning; you step into each new day with a bright new hatred in your heart. No, it's not the guilt. (Something shifts within you. *Necessary* guilt, it whispers.) It's the fear. What if you are caught, and condemned to an even worse hell? Your fearful nights are just as much a refuge from the hate-fuelled days as the other way. Every evening you return to a prison, and to a woman you have come to detest.

Set against these things there is the beast inside you, swelling, hardening. More, It roars – and It means, More pain, more money, more ruin.

But still there is the risk. The terror. You have prepared and waited – but what if you have made a mistake? What if you are making one now? Because Matthew is not behaving as you'd expected.

'The graveyard,' you snap. 'What has he said?'

Your man screws up his face in incomprehension. 'What? You mean, has he told me about it?' He spits again. 'Get fucking real.'

'Hints. Anything. Why was he there?'

He snorts. 'Listen, mate. I'm doing a fucking job here, all right? Not chatting with the fucking customers – know what I mean?'

You accept this because you have to. But you wonder. *Is* he doing the job you have paid him so handsomely to do? For the money, he should be leaping at your every word. Instead he is edgy, aggressive, even defensive. Suddenly there is something fascinating about another of his teeth, he turns half away, picking at it. Through his fingers, without looking, he says, 'Didn't talk about no fucking graveyards.' Perhaps he is telling the truth. Because Matthew Daniels is clearly planning something. Why else go to such efforts not to be followed? He is hardly likely to discuss it with his tormentor, is he?

Is it the police? You don't think so. You would have seen the signs: men at the cemetery gates trying to look casual, too many passers-by. You are sure that, in the end, he will go to them, it is in his bureaucratic nature. But not yet. But you cannot know. How are you supposed to *know*? There is nothing to guide you. The only rules are the ones that you choose, the fruits of your watching and careful planning, and the plans didn't include visits to graveyards. When Matthew finally calls the police, that is your cue to change the rules – but has he?

You stir restlessly. Your companion glances up, sniffs at you, hawks again – and smears with his boot, slip crunch, slip crunch. You sense your anger rise, and you let it. Briefly, it flashes in your eyes, then it sinks again into silence. His time will come. Soon he will be a wanted man.

Reassured, you reach a decision. Whatever Matthew is or isn't up to, it is Time. It is sooner than you expected, but what of it?

'No more contact,' you say.

That wakes him up. 'What? But the money. There's a hundred and fif— Well, a hundred,' he said, ' a hundred grand coming.'

A hundred thousand. Money is money. But pain is pain.

'Fuck the money.'

He gapes. Then his eyes flicker slyly. He is thinking, If *you* don't want it, then maybe . . .

You hold out your hand. 'The phone.'

'What do you mean. You can't—'

'The phone. Now.'

He is uncertain, you can see it in him. He is contemplating defiance. You know his type. You work with them every day, day in, day out. You know how to control them. You take a step closer, and he flinches, as though you still had your baton with you, and were wearing your uniform.

He hands over the phone – and something in you is terrified by the simple gesture. You have this power. You see it in the fool's eyes. You hear it roaring within you. And it renders you helpless. The pain, the horror, the delicious, ugly, agonising *wrongness* of it. Part of you wants to cry. You are small and scared, disgusted by your thoughts and now your deeds. Wrong. *Wrong*. But your hand takes the phone, slips out the SIM card, and grinds it under your heel. Enfeebled, terrified, you watch yourself pass the point of no return.

Your accomplice scratches heavily, wrapping an arm around himself to reach behind his shoulder. 'What about *her*, then?'

Casually, with your heart beating in your temples, you say, 'Time's up.'

His eyes narrow. 'What, you mean . . . ?'

You shrug, as if it doesn't matter to you. Your head is pounding. 'Kill her. Let her starve. Who cares? Fuck her.'

Slowly, the man's smile turns into a grin. 'You know,' he says – and his voice is thick and soft – 'I might just do that.'

Then he is gone, and you slump against the wall, horrified and elated. You can imagine her screaming, full of pain and hatred and fear. Screaming without end. The moment is all the more intimate to you because it has not yet happened, and you will not be there when it does.

Pain and death. Yes. The lessons your Rage was born to teach. It heaves inside you, once, and then is still, content to wait – for now. You have chosen. It controls you now. And you feel guilty, and thrilled. Because how can it be your fault? Because what you are doing is wrong.

Not wrong, a voice rumbles inside you. It sighs with pleasure. Not wrong, it says.

Necessary.

Wednesday

Twenty-One

The boss. If her captor was an ex-con from the Ville, then who could the boss be? It had to be someone who knew Matthew – or her . . . But she was no longer sure that it mattered. She felt cold inside, leaden. She rubbed her belly: for hours now, she had felt nothing there. Perhaps it was fear. Or perhaps she had already lost her baby. Could heparin and aspirin counter the effects of two days of terror, and then a savage blow to the belly? Who cared who the boss was. There were more important things than that. Losing your baby, for example. That was what was happening, wasn't it?

'Eyelash?' she whispered. She had no sense of the life within her responding. The warm lurch she felt every time she thought of her daughter was gone. 'Darling,' she whispered, 'don't go away.' She cupped her hands over her womb, as though the warmth from them could breathe back life. 'Stay with me, Eyelash. Please.' But something inside her was cold now, and clenched.

She couldn't cry. She rocked gently from side to side, and crooned the names she might have chosen. 'Alice, Josephine, Caitlin, Siobhan . . .' Her dry eyes were unfocused, the room a blur of meaningless shapes. 'Briony, Louie, Amanda, Jane . . .' The cold lump inside her answered to none. Perhaps there was still something there, though – because she still felt as though there was a lump, and there had been no bleeding – but it was fading, and cold, so cold. Perhaps that was a blessing. Better for Eyelash to die now than to suffer the violent assault the man had promised for the morning.

'Jemima,' she whispered. 'Maisie, Sarah, Tabitha . . .'

Tabitha. Yes, Tabitha. She liked that. She said softly, 'Goodnight, Tabitha.' For a while, she stared at the wall ahead of her. Then she added, 'I love you.'

A brief warm glow swept through her, a flutter in the pit of her, fading. Still too tired for tears, she cupped her hands a little closer. 'Sleep well,' she whispered, 'my love.'

She stared at the jumble of shapes that made up her prison: bed, toilet, the narrow girders of the roof, the door.

The blessings. She had to count the blessings. The trouble was, they were blurred by regret. There was Eyelash – but for how much longer? There was Matthew, who would be searching for her, because he loved her – but did she deserve it? She had been . . . cruel to him. She had been so absorbed in her own troubles that she had taken no interest in his pain at all. And she had never explained, never apologised. How could he forgive her, if he had never really understood? He didn't really know the woman he was searching for. He didn't know what lived inside her, alongside Eyelash: the vain, selfish, disgusting creature that she truly was. If he had seen the *real* her, he never would have married her – and she had deliberately made him suffer for his blindness.

'Matthew . . .' she whispered. But that connection, too, was fading.

The boss – the man her captor had mentioned. A man with enough power and hate inside him to do this – no, to command that this be done. Her captor was irrelevant, he was just some little runt from the Ville with a chip on his shoulder. He was dangerous, yes, but the man pulling his strings was the one to be scared of. He was the one with the desire to see this done.

How strange, she thought. Even here, locked away inside your own mind, inside a room inside a building in a place no one can find – even here, you can't bring yourself to accept that you probably – maybe – know who it is. But you can hardly think of him as the boss, can you? Not after what happened between you. He is a repulsive, self-absorbed little . . . Well, who knew what he was capable of? If it's him. But surely he wouldn't do something like this. It was too extreme. But if not him then who?

She wished now that she had told Matthew everything. Because if he knew, then finding her would be easy. He could just walk up to the right door in the Ville, and demand her back.

Of course, if he *had* known, then he would already have left her for ever.

Wearily, she closed her eyes and let her chin droop towards her chest. The wall was cold against her back, the floor as hard and unforgiving as she deserved. Behind her eyes danced pictures of the man she loved, and who loved her – but only because he didn't understand her. He strode boldly from building to building, searching – but in his eyes, doubt was growing, and despair.

'I'm sorry, Matthew,' she whispered – or meant to; perhaps she just thought it. 'I was afraid, you see. That's why I . . .' Behind her eyes, Matthew was in front of her. He reached up, touched her hair. He smiled at her, so sadly. 'I love you, Matthew,' she said. 'I do. Only, I was afraid.'

He turned away. Then darkness rose within her, took her – and a memory rose within it: a memory of betrayal, of the reason why she could never be loved.

Then, still unsure whether she was dreaming, deluded or just desperate, she staggered to her feet and studied the room. Because now she knew who the boss was – *thought* she knew – what she needed was a weapon.

It is more than a year ago. It is April. Ten months from now, she will discover that she is pregnant – and she will be overjoyed. But this is before that joy. This is five months after her miscarriage, when her life has descended from independence into misery.

She wants a baby. She never thought she would. But when she lost the baby she never knew she had, she knew – suddenly, and too late – that what she wanted was a child. A child with Matthew.

Since that day, Matthew has been withdrawn and solemn. He worries about her too much. He asks her constantly if she is all right. When she snaps at him, he protests that it is because he loves her. Perhaps he does – and perhaps not. But he won't have a baby with her, will he?

But today is the day all that changes. Because today is the day that Matthew, at last, asks her to marry him – and she discovers that she is less sure of her answer than she had thought.

It is not just the miscarriage, not just the baby. Things have been tense between them since she moved in eight months ago. Her flat is let out now. She no longer has a route of escape. She has found that what she sometimes took to be solitude when she was alone was in fact freedom. Now, as part of a couple, the more distant she becomes – preserving the part of her which has nothing to do with him, the part which is most purely her – the more persistent he becomes, and

the more distressed. He seems . . . desperate. He behaves com-
passionately, he is concerned: as though he believes that she is
suffering. And perhaps she is. In Matthew's eyes, Charlotte feels,
she is in the grip of some profound malaise of the soul: and the
painful truth is that, when he looks at her like that, when he is so
worried and unctuous and fearful for her happiness, he creates the
very problem he is so scared of. Without Matthew, Charlotte is fine;
with him, she feels hemmed in, constrained – and childless.

Em doesn't help. Em broods and watches her and signals constantly that Charlotte can never win her respect, let alone her heart.
Every meal time is a battle for authority. Every question about Em's
homework is a challenge. Bedtime is an opportunity for Em to point
out that Charlotte is not her mother and never will be.

Yet she loves Em, and she loves Matthew. When she is honest
with herself, which is all too often, she admits that there is nowhere
else she would wish to be. The problem is that, now, there is
nowhere else she *could* be. And so she has become remote, dis-
engaged. The only space she can retreat to is the one inside herself: it
is her refuge against Em's needy, over-loud rejection of her, and
Matthew's equally needy desperation that she be happy, because if
she isn't then it must be his fault. Inside, she is safe from these two
people who refuse to give her what she wants.

Em is upstairs doing her homework. Matthew is sitting next to her
on the sofa, idly stroking her leg, like it is made of glass.

It has been a bad day; not that she expects Matthew to understand.
Her period is about to start. She can feel it. She is bloated and scratchy
and tired. And if her period is starting – then that's another opportunity lost, isn't it? Another month ticking by while Matthew hums and
haws and kisses her hair too gently and tidies up around her as though
she were a precious ornament. She just wants a drink, and the soaps
on the telly. She doesn't want to talk. But Matthew does.

He opens his mouth uncertainly. Several times. Whatever it is, he
can't get it out. He's going to flap his face at her like a fish, all the
way through *Eastenders*.

She sighs, aggressively, switches off the television and stomps into
the kitchen to make herself a drink – but not him. When she comes
back, she dumps herself in an armchair and mutters, 'What, then?'

He looks flustered.

'What *is* it, Matthew?'

He gapes a moment longer, then he chuckles self-consciously. 'Well, I was just looking at you. Thinking how you're beautiful, and I love you. That kind of thing.' It is an attempt to soften her. It fails. She scowls at him to get to the point. He falters. 'Um . . . And anyway. I was thinking – you know, thinking of how I could show you – how much I . . .'

The lines were better on *Eastenders* – and it didn't matter if you didn't pay attention.

'And I . . .' he went on. He gazed at the ceiling and blew out sharply. 'Look, Charlotte, I love you. I know it's been rough since . . . Well. Anyway, I love you. And I do want to have a kid with you some day. I'm just not . . . ready. Not yet. And there's Em to worry about, and . . . Oh, God, I'm crap at this.' He holds his head in his hands for a second. 'Ahhh . . . Look, I just thought you might like to get married.'

In the future, she will understand that this is an accident of words from a man trying a little too hard. But now, here, in the moment, she turns to ice. This is not love. This is charity.

'You thought I might like it?'

He looks startled. 'I mean – I'd like it too. I love you. And—'

'Oh, you'd like it, would you?'

She is on her feet. She has no idea how she got there.

'I didn't—'

'Shut up! Just shut up!'

He withdraws. He sulks. He sits, frozen on the sofa, and looks nowhere. He says, in his lightest tone, 'OK. Fine.' He lapses into some strange place inside himself. He broods. And Charlotte soon-to-be-Daniels looks at the man opposite her, sulking because she hasn't swooned at his feet – and she loses it.

'What?' she snaps.

'Nothing. I—'

'Don't look at me like that!'

He keeps on looking at her, a wounded puppy, puzzled at the blow. And she knows she is being unfair, but she can't help herself. She's uncomfortable and confused and – yes, she's angry. She is angry at herself for being angry, because he hasn't done anything to deserve this – except mope around like she was made of crystal, and worry about her, and look at her with that gooey mix of love and dependency, as though all his feelings are her responsibility, her problem.

It is a hot evening. Perhaps that explains it. And she is tired. And Em has spent an hour shouting at her before Matthew even condescended to come home from the job he loves so much – loves more than her, she often thinks. Or perhaps she is angry because he should have asked her ages ago or said yes when she asked him on Valentine's Day just a few weeks before. But when she showed him how much she cared, he withdrew. And now she has had enough of kiss-chase. Now it is too late.

He is pouting like a child who has been punished for doing no wrong. And she's had enough of that, too, even though she knows that it's not really his fault. But knowing it's *her* fault is part of the problem.

She yells at him. 'So this is all down to me now, is it?'

'No, of course n—'

'It's that simple, isn't it? *You* decide what *you'd* like. What *I* might want doesn't come into it!'

'Darling, that's not entirely—'

'Well, you can fuck off, Matthew! How would you like that?'

'Charlotte . . .' He is pleading. She ignores him.

At the door, just before she storms out with nothing, not even her keys or her handbag and purse, she turns and shouts.

'And, just in case you were interested, I *might* have said yes.'

And she slams the door behind her, knowing that she *should* have said yes, and there is no reason that she can grasp why she didn't. Because she loves him. And needs him. And she is being suffocated. And she is a fool, she knows. Because love is love, isn't it? And she feels terribly, desperately alone.

She walks. Fast. Aimlessly. She wants to forget. She wants things the way they were before she met Matthew. She wants to be free, irresponsible in whatever way she chooses, with whoever she wants. And although she is not deliberately walking in any one direction, she finds herself on familiar streets. She passes the cemetery, then the pub that she, and everyone at the Ville, knew Matthew sneaked off to sometimes, convinced his secret was safe. That was when she still worked at the Ville, before her relationship with the newly promoted

Junior Governor Matthew Daniels made it impossible for her to continue working there.

She contemplates the building, her old workplace. Each corridor holds stories of how she used to be – friends and colleagues, casual flirtations, the laugh they all had that day when –

The Ville's blank face is a reminder of the distance she has travelled away from her friends, away from her life, away from her self. She is a stranger here now. She is a stranger everywhere. She belongs to Matthew-so-smug-Daniels, who behaves as though he is her counsellor not her lover, and who thinks it is in his gift to make her happy.

How dare he? How dare he invade her life like that? Things were fine, before, thank you very much – until he settled into her nest like some overgrown cuckoo. She realises now that he has slowly edged her out of her own life – patiently, relentlessly – and he now sits preening himself in the centre, and she perches at the margins, clutching for a grip – and soon she will fall, she will be falling –

'Good heavens! Charlotte?' A familiar voice and face. A familiar, lecherous smile – and the familiar look of the predator in his eyes. 'Charlotte, my goodness, are you OK?' He kisses her on both cheeks, his hands resting lightly on her hips. He leaves them there. 'Are you all right? If you've come for Matthew I don't think—'

She sniffs, and mutters, 'Fuck Matthew.'

And for now, she means it; to hell with him. She doesn't want to think about him. She wants her life back. She isn't here for him, she's here for her – to bump into friends, to go down to the Anchor with them after work and get stupidly drunk. To laugh.

Fuck Matthew.

There is an analytical gleam in his eye as he considers what she has just said.

'I was just leaving,' he says. He wraps an arm about her waist. 'Anchor time. Come and tell me about it.' He steers her away from the Ville, clamping her close to him. It feels good to be with a man so assured, who just *does*, without self-doubt, whose touch is intimate without needing to know her at all. She leans a little towards him and he chuckles in satisfaction. 'That's the spirit.'

She used to flirt with him before she left the Ville, before Matthew. He appeals to her. There is a danger in his eyes that others cannot seem to see. Perhaps it is a look he reserves for her.

Soon after she had got together with Matthew, he cornered her one day, and told her it was a shame because he had always wanted her himself. She had been flattered and had teased him about the fact that he was already married. He had drifted closer and murmured that married men were the ones you had to watch out for. Then he had leaned towards her and planted his lips softly on her cheek, letting them linger, brushing them over her skin, while his hands drifted round from her waist towards her buttocks, pulling her closer. She had felt the heat rise inside her. She might have fallen then – had it not been for Matthew.

But that was then. Today is different. Today she has argued with Matthew, she is unhappy and she has decided to be free.

She stops and turns him to face her – and there is something savage and excited in his face, something hungry. She bites her lip, strokes him with her eyes. There will be no deliberation, she knows, no thoughtfulness. There will just be self-abandon: no guilt, no questions.

'Where can we go?' she whispers to him. She knows this is wrong – and that is what makes it so right.

In response, Mark Thornton's eyes glow like a wolf's.

He has keys to a flat. 'A friend's,' he says. As if she cared. It doesn't matter what his story is. Nothing matters, only the now, this moment. There are no consequences – there cannot be consequences, because she is free. Fuck Matthew.

The flat is bare. There is almost no furniture, just a bed and a sofa and a television. There are no books, no clocks, no plants. The kitchen is empty, except for a microwave.

She hasn't had time even to sit down on the room's one sofa before he begins to stroke her. He is brief. He cups her cheek, lets his hand drift down over her shoulder, comes immediately round to squeeze her breast. His jaw works as though he is chewing gum. He looks thoughtful as he stares through her.

And suddenly, she finds herself uneasy. This isn't how it is supposed to be. This isn't the dizzy collision of two free spirits, this is . . .

'Mark, look, I—'

'Shhh,' he says. He puts a hand over her mouth. With the other, he is still kneading and squeezing her. There is something glazed about those animal eyes.

He doesn't care, she realises. He has no interest in how it will be for me. No empathy, no consideration.

He will hurt her as casually as she has just hurt Matthew.

She shakes her head to get his hand off, grabs his other hand and drags it away from her chest, and says it again. 'Mark, no! I'm sorry, but this is a mistake. I can't—'

He slaps her. Then he spins her round and clamps both arms around her. She is pinioned. She cannot move. And one of his hands slides down over her belly, and beneath the waistband of her skirt.

'Let's do it here,' he whispers. And he bites her neck, not gently, and shoves his hand violently downwards, clutching savagely at her through her panties.

'Mark, no! *No!*'

He spins her again, to face him, and with his free hand he grabs the top of her blouse and yanks downwards. She hears the fabric begin to rip. He prepares for another tug – and next time, it will give. His face is contorted with savage pleasure. He is somewhere else, transported. He sighs. She glimpses the white teeth in his half-open mouth.

Then she brings her knee up into his groin, as hard as she possibly can.

Home, she waits on the doorstep. She has no keys – and she has discovered that, really, she doesn't want to ring the bell. It isn't that she will wake Matthew and Em: it's that she doesn't want a scene. She doesn't want to make a grand entrance, to be questioned, or – worse – welcomed and respectfully, nervously tolerated. She just wants the way it was until last night. She wants to walk back into her cage and just live there, as though she had never left.

So she watches the dawn from the doorstep. And when lights come on inside, and she sees a shadow descending the stairs through the door's frosted glass, she knocks. Matthew opens the door. She half-smiles at him: an apology, a signal that this is the best she can manage by way of explanation. Then she bursts into tears.

'Will you stay now?' Em looks at Charlotte earnestly, fearfully.

It is three days later. They are watching television – a soap they both enjoy, a time they share every Monday, Wednesday and most Fridays.

'Daddy says he wants you to marry him. He says he loves you.'

'I love him too, Em.' Charlotte is stroking Em's hair. 'It's just . . .' She stops talking, carries on stroking. Em leans back against her, wriggles into a more comfortable position. Em smells of lemons and cinnamon and olive oil. Charlotte has come to like the smell, though she didn't at first. Patiently, she strokes Em's hair.

'What?'

'Hmmm . . . ?'

'You said it's just – what?'

Em's hair is silk. You can wriggle your fingers in it until strands are wrapped around, and then stroke downwards, and each strand unravels and her long hair is smooth again.

She does not speak.

'Do you?' Em says.

'Hmmm?'

'Love him.'

Charlotte chuckles, and muzzes her hair: it is the hair that smells of olive oil, she decides, because as she ruffles it, a rich flat scent thickens around her. She begins stroking again.

'I love you, Charlotte,' Em says simply. 'Daddy loves you too. He said.'

Silk and olives. So smooth.

'Charlotte, stay, will you?'

Olive groves. And lemons and cinnamon and soap. So familiar. So safe.

'Mmm,' Charlotte says; smelling, stroking.

And at the weekend, the two of them go out together – Charlotte Logan and Matthew Daniels – and together they choose a ring.

Twenty-Two

The London sky was a dense orange glow. The air was cool, and thick with the scent of leaves and traffic fumes.

Monk was in a taxi. The driver had tried to strike up a conversation. Monk had stared through the mirror at the man until he shut up, leaving him free to contemplate the task he had agreed to undertake: the saving of Matthew Daniels. Strictly, it was his wife that needed saving – and Monk had seen the confusion on Matthew's face when he mentioned the future and the past. Was it possible that he truly did not understand, even now? Well, perhaps it did not matter. In any case, there was time: this would take days rather than hours.

He had already made progress of a sort. He was on his way to make some more.

He had been more circumspect than Matthew about leaving the cemetery. He'd had to be. Matthew hadn't *seen* anyone following him, but that meant nothing. It would have been easy to tail him here without being seen and then wait outside the graveyard to pick him up when he left. Monk had to work on the assumption that someone was watching. Matthew had followed his instructions to the letter. He had walked back slowly through the graveyard, pausing frequently to stare into space or inspect a tombstone. When he left, he had left briskly. Monk had watched the street behind him: in case he could detect a figure scurrying after him, although it was unlikely. No one had come; but that made sense: Matthew had gone to the cemetery in a car, so if this man had followed him, he would have had to drive, too. When it had become clear that Matthew was going into a place where there was no cover, the logical thing to do would have been to retreat to his own car and wait for Matthew there, ready to follow him on his return.

He had told Matthew to drive past the cemetery gates on his way home. This was when he had expected his first glimpse of the man behind the abduction. He had crouched against a wall at the near end of the graveyard and watched through the tall railings. There was a risk that he might have been seen through the rear-view mirror – but it was tiny. After five minutes, Matthew's car had come past. Thirty seconds later, another car had followed, a cream-coloured Honda.

He had made a mental note of the registration number. Mud had been smeared over the rear plate – but a few days before, because most of it had flaked off. It was an old car – not ancient, but getting on. Its engine had growled as the car accelerated. Its windows had been inexpertly silvered with reflective film. Dark bubbles were visible on the side windows and rear windscreen.

That was interesting. If the man who had followed Matthew was a stranger, then why attract attention by so obviously hiding yourself? Was it possible that the man knew Matthew would never recognise his voice, but his face would give the game away? Unlikely. It was more likely that there were two men involved: one to follow, one to make the calls, and, presumably, guard their captive. And the instigator was the man in the car he had seen. The one who wanted to watch. The one who might be recognised.

The man was no expert. He had chosen a ludicrously impractical vehicle for surveillance. He had stuck far too close to Matthew. He hadn't realised that effective surveillance takes at least three people. This was good and bad. An amateur would make mistakes – but he might also do something unpredictable.

Satisfied that Matthew's pursuer had gone, Monk had made his own way towards Matthew's house. If the car had been there, he would have had his man.

It was not. Presumably the man had seen Matthew home and had then headed away. Did amateur hijackers take supper breaks, then? Or perhaps he had had to be elsewhere in order to keep up appearances. Or he had gone to visit Matthew's wife. Monk hoped so; because if he had been detected, or even if the man's suspicions had been aroused by Matthew's unaccustomed visit to a cemetery, then this could all be over very soon, and very unpleasantly.

Or the man might return. Monk had settled in to wait for a while, finding an empty-looking house – the owners away on holiday presumably – and settling into the dark shadow of the hedge in its front garden. He had watched the girl come home. Had watched lights go on and off in various rooms – until all that was left was the light in the living room – Matthew, he had assumed, would have struggled against sleep.

At half past one in the morning, he hailed the taxi and headed for Brixton.

He arrived in Brixton shortly before two o'clock, and climbed out opposite a night club called The Colony. In one direction, the pavement was covered by a crowd of people queuing for admission. As they trickled forward, from time to time people spilled out into the road, where they stood impassively, undisturbed by occasional buses and taxis passing so close that the wind whipped their clothes. Immediately outside the club, a red rope cordoned off a section of pavement. Here, the crowd swelled, all pretence of order forgotten. An impeccably suited man stood inside the cordon, craning to scan the crowd's further reaches. Without seeming to look at any of the people immediately in front of him, he constantly selected from them, lifted the rope and allowed a few more clubbers to ooze through. Set back from the street up a few concrete steps was the entrance: shabby purple doors, only one half open. The doorway was filled by another man, huge and packed tightly into a dark suit. He too gazed out over the heads of his clientele while he ushered them past him one by one.

Monk knew that if he stood here long enough – five minutes ought to do it – he would see tempers flare. Some would-be clubber would be refused admission. He would shout, then push, then turn on others in the crowd as they lost patience with him; and one or other of those two men would step out into the crowd, still seeming to gaze over everyone's heads, and would 'persuade' the trouble-maker to move on, more or less violently. It was normal for this part of town. It was vibrant here, and edgy; Brixton was alive, and frequently kicking.

Monk grinned inwardly. Strange to say, for a man who cared nothing for skin colour – his or anybody's – and who lived in exile wherever he was, but in some strange way he had always thought of this as home. It wasn't the houses or the people, although he had been born near here; it wasn't his memories of living and growing up here, although he had; it wasn't the fact that somewhere in this crowd there were surely people who, if he had known any family, he could greet as relatives. It was the street itself that called to him: the sense that any of these people could become . . . him. He smelled their sweat, mixed with overripe fruit from the market that had operated here earlier in the day. Hair oil, aftershave, the acid scent of the clubbers' new clothes. He knew these people's souls. He knew how they moved and thought, how they slipped through the deadly jungle they inhabited, how they survived.

The dangers here were familiar to him: the measured pace of the muggers – different depending on whether they had knives or guns – the glazed faces of the crackheads, the hawkish eyes of the dealers. And the peaceful moments, too: the tranquil squabbling over produce at the street stalls, the far-eyed look of men wearing their shabby best, sitting on the steps and watching the day.

He was one of them. He was the same as them. The truth of who he was, what made him the man he was, was irrelevant. He was faceless here – as were they all. He was home.

He slid through the traffic, and then effortlessly through the crowd outside The Colony. The man behind the cordon craned past him.

'Here for Byron,' he said. His voice was soft, yet it cut through the hubbub around him.

The man gave no sign that he had heard. He craned even higher, then lifted the barrier, without once looking at him. Monk slipped through, followed by the rising protests of those still outside. As he climbed the steps, he felt in the pit of his chest the steady bass pulse of the music inside.

The second man dwarfed him: he would have dwarfed anyone. He stood firmly in Monk's way and fixed him with a hostile stare. Monk didn't bother repeating himself; he returned the stare calmly and waited. Finally the man jerked his head, gesturing him past. He did not move to make space though: he wanted Monk to edge past him, feel his size and power, to be afraid. Monk gazed mildly at him and placed a hand gently on the man's arm. He relaxed completely, letting all his weight drain down through his feet into the ground, leaving his body as light as the wind. In his mind, he gave a tiny flick, a thought as absent as the decision to brush off a fly. His arm straightened subtly, and his palm opened and the fingers stiffened where they rested on the other man's arm – and the man slammed sideways across the doorway and into the wall on the far side. Without waiting to see the result, Monk moved on. Behind him a half-hearted cheer rose from the crowd, pleased to see one of their tormentors brought low, worried that if they showed their pleasure, their chances of getting in would be zero.

Ahead of him, the walls shivered and the air itself thickened under the savage assault of sound. There was a ticket booth with a small queue of people and a turnstile beyond, manned by another bouncer. Monk glided past the queue, and stood at the turnstile.

'Byron,' he said. The air vibrated in his chest so violently that the word was not a sound at all. The bouncer read his lips, nodded and stood aside. Perhaps he had seen what had happened to his colleague outside.

Inside, there was music instead of air, a relentless deep pounding, offset by higher notes whimsically picking out random melodies; over it all, the urgent voice of the DJ, rapping out the latest gangsta kool, a dizzy blur of words and sentiment. The space was so huge that even its twenty-foot ceiling seemed low in proportion. The dance floor was a sea of white eyes and teeth, bobbing, flashing, pulsing under harsh unnatural lights. Beyond, there were clumps of people ranged about, leaning against the velour seating that fringed the room, the men sipping at bottles of beer, the women at alco-pops, in long glasses with straws. They stood as though they were on a street corner, looking nowhere, waiting, watching the people who were watching them. Beneath the overpowering smell of disinfectant, Monk detected the sharp stench of vomit.

Next to the bar there was the outline of a small door. It was designed to be hard to spot: there was no architrave around it, there was no handle, and it was painted the same colour as the walls. The noise was far too loud for a knock to be heard. Monk ghosted through the thick crowd at the bar, mouthed 'Byron' to the bar-tender, and nodded towards the door. The woman looked at him expressionlessly, then nodded back and disappeared. Monk waited by the door. She opened it, stood aside to let him through, then closed and locked it. She didn't bother talking to him – he couldn't possibly have heard. Instead she pointed down a corridor, and then upwards. Without waiting to see if he had understood, she slipped back through a narrow corridor lined with bottles and barrels towards the bar. Monk headed down the corridor and then up the stairs at its end, the club's insistent beat battering at his back. On the second floor there was a heavy door, and more stairs beyond. When the door sighed shut behind him, the music faded to a dull thump.

At the top of the stairs there was a short corridor. The first door was open, and gave onto a spartan kitchen. There was a microwave, a sink, a tattered work surface covered with stains and half-eaten food in plastic containers – and a young man, perhaps twenty, leaning dangerously far back on a wooden chair, wolfing noodles from a plastic tub and staring at a television mounted high in a corner. A game show was on; the presenter's voice was hushed with excitement, and the audience's applause was tinny through the TV's small speakers.

Monk stood in the doorway and waited to be noticed. It took several seconds. When the man finally saw him, he jerked upright, his mouth open and full of noodles. Then he recognised Monk, and relaxed. He settled back, finishing his mouthful and shaking his head slowly.

'You shoulda knocked, bro. You freaked me.' He laughed to show that there was no disrespect. He laughed alone.

Monk knew this man's name. He was Tyrell Austin, a member of Byron Washington's inner circle, hired for his muscle and aggression, and because he was family – and certainly not for his brains. Tyrell leaned forward with his elbows on his knees and his head bowed. He cracked his knuckles loudly, and looked up and sideways at Monk; the whites of his eyes shining in the poorly lit room. He avoided looking at Monk directly. 'Boss nah wanna see you, bro. Not after las' time, y'nah?'

Monk ignored the warning. He turned and headed for the door at the end of the corridor.

Tyrell yelped. 'Shit! No, man! Wait!' Monk waited for Tyrell to catch up and stand in front of him He looked uncomfortable. 'I'm serious, bro. The boss is pissed at you, big time. An' it's me that's gotta keep him sweet, y'nah?'

'You mean, you can't let me in,' Monk murmured.

Tyrell rubbed his hands uneasily. 'Well – yeah, innit?'

'Not without a fight.'

Beads of sweat had broken out on the boy's forehead. Haltingly, he nodded. Monk drifted closer.

'So, do you want to fight me, Tyrell?'

He didn't really need to ask. Tyrell had been there the last time. Washington had tried to renegotiate the terms of a deal with Monk. Washington had reckoned that with five or six of his heavies around him, Monk would happily accept the new terms. He had reckoned wrong.

Tyrell shook his head meekly. There was a desperate look in his eyes: his mind was racing, trying to devise a way out of a situation that was a little too complex for him. Below them, the music thudded like a distant heartbeat.

Monk inclined his head very slightly – *well, Tyrell, a little lesson: every choice has consequences* – and headed along the corridor, leaving the boy standing helplessly. He opened the final door and strode in.

For a man of such importance and wealth, Byron Washington's office was unimpressive. The room was an uncomfortable shape: about fifteen feet long, perhaps ten wide, although a fireplace half-way down one wall reduced the width by two feet or so. From the doorway, he looked along the length of the room. At the far end there was a desk beneath a window with no curtains and a view of someone else's air-conditioning unit. The walls were white, and hung with several cheap prints and a single garish rug with pre-tensions of being tribal, but which smacked more of Southall than the Masai Mara. Given that no member of Washington's family had been anywhere near Africa for a couple of hundred years, perhaps the effect was doomed to be unconvincing from the start; Washington's family history was Caribbean, not Kenyan.

Washington turned slowly from the paperwork on his desk and appraised Monk, his fingers self-consciously steepled, tapping thoughtfully against pursed lips. His eyes were narrow behind austere black-rimmed glasses. His mouth was framed by a moustache and a goatee beard, trimmed to a thin line.

Monk stood at ease, a few feet inside the room. He sensed Tyrell creep in behind him.

'Couldn't stop him, Boss.'

Washington's attention drifted languidly from Monk to the boy. His eyes narrowed.

'You fucked up, Tyrell.' His voice was even softer than Monk's.

Tyrell's fear was palpable. 'Well – yeah. I know, Boss. Sorry an' all. But, shit, man. Monk – you know he—'

'What I *know*, Tyrell, is that you fucked up.'

'An' I'm sorry. For true, Boss. Only—'

'Tyrell, you're *still* fucking up. You're fucking up right now.'

'Wha . . . ? But—'

Tyrell finally got the point: he was still making no effort to remove Monk from the room. Monk could almost have laughed. He felt the boy approach from behind and reach out an uncertain hand. Tyrell gripped Monk's arm and tugged feebly.

'Boss don' want you here, man. Let's do this easy.'

Monk let his feet grow roots. Tyrell tugged harder and more insistently. Monk moved not at all. There was not even the slightest sway. He kept his eyes on Washington.

At last, Washington snarled in disgust. 'Oh, let him go, boy, before he decides to hurt you.'

Tyrell released him with great relief and stood back a few paces.

Washington sighed heavily. Then he looked up at Monk. 'I don't suppose you'd come and work for me? Teach these idiots how it's done?' Monk smiled grimly at him. Washington shrugged. 'So. You come to show off, my friend, or you got business?'

He swivelled to face an armchair by the fireplace, gesturing for Monk to sit there. Monk walked over to the fireplace, but remained standing. Washington laughed and shook his head at his own folly in imagining that Monk might have taken an offered seat.

'You's a real number, Monk. Y'nah?' In a man so measured, the Brixton patois was an affectation rather than an inheritance. Washington used it when it suited him.

Monk took him in: a discreet gold stud in the left earlobe; the skin of his face glossy and smooth except for the neat, close-cropped beard; his eyes a strangely pale brown, almost amber, reflective and intelligent. He wore a sharp, dark suit with glitter in the weave, and a white shirt, buttoned all the way up, with no tie. There were gold cufflinks, and shoes polished to a glass finish. Byron Washington was about forty-eight, very pleased with himself – and not at all afraid of Monk. Given their long history, that wasn't surprising. And, in any case, it didn't matter: he would do as Monk asked – not out of fear, but because it was far more comfortable to have Monk as his friend than to fall out with him again, and find his hired hands deserting him because they were afraid, risk patches of his turf being taken over by rival groups because he didn't have the manpower . . .

Washington was a businessman. He was in it for money not glory.

He would help Monk because it was the prudent thing to do. And because they had known each other all their lives. And because, in the sense that mattered most, they were brothers. They had sworn so, long ago.

He was staring at Monk, visibly pondering his alternatives. Finally, he sighed. 'What you want?'

Behind him, Monk heard Tyrell hiss in surprise. The boy had a lot to learn. If he was lucky, he had enough years ahead of him that he would get the chance; but he had chosen a rough profession, and the poor fool was going to have to improve his skills fast if he wanted to survive. In front of him, Washington was tapping his lips again, a little faster than before. One of his knees was jiggling lightly. Monk leaned towards him. He grinned at him: a feral smile, all danger and no warmth.

Softly – and reluctantly – he said, 'I need your help.'

He explained, and Washington listened. There were things that Monk needed done, but couldn't do himself. Chief amongst these was that he needed someone to follow Matthew – or, rather, someone to follow whoever was following Matthew. He needed to know if there had been rumours that might hint at what was happening – a 'hit' on a prison governor was far enough from normal for people to be talking about it. 'Another thing,' Monk finished calmly. 'Whoever has taken her has been using her mobile. I want to know where the calls were made from – which cell. And there's a car I want you to trace.'

Washington laughed and slapped his thigh in the slow, deliberate way an older man might. 'Heh-*heghhh*! Monk, you real funny, mon.' His impression of an elderly Jamaican man was designed to make a point. The point was that he wasn't about to help.

'I may need money, too. They want a hundred and fifty thousand.' Washington stared. Then he laughed again. Monk shrugged. 'Small price, if that's what it takes.'

Washington stopped laughing and surveyed Monk, scowling. 'Too much, Monk. By a long, long way.' His voice was hard and flat.

Monk's gaze was expressionless. 'I have no choice.'

Washington shrugged. 'I have no interest.'

This was the point. This was the territory that governed the game they were playing. Ultimately, Monk knew, any discussion with

Washington was a negotiation. He was a man who did nothing without a clear understanding of what he personally would gain. He sighed pointedly, for Washington's benefit, and finally sat in the chair that had been offered to him when he first came in.

'I think you do have an interest, *bro*.' He pointed up that single word, but kept his voice soft. It was a struggle. A lot rode on this.

Washington's usually solemn face gradually widened into a grin as he realised that Monk had something to offer in return. His eyes sparkled.

'Meaning?'

This was a dangerous moment. Washington was chimerical. Monk had been appealing to his . . . well, altruism was the wrong word, because Washington was only interested in his own advantage. What Monk was really proposing was that if Washington helped him, he would stay off his back for a while. But this, for brothers, was rocky ground. And a hundred and fifty thousand . . .

Monk gazed at him flatly. 'Meaning nothing,' he said eventually.

Washington frowned. 'You don't mean that,' he said.

Monk remained silent. If he said nothing, maybe Washington would get there on his own. He would talk himself into the deal.

'Monk, you got something, you spit it out, man.'

Monk allowed his eyes to glitter for a moment, nothing more. Washington tutted in annoyance.

At last, Monk said, 'You owe me, Byron.'

Washington's face set hard. 'Enough,' he hissed. 'Tyrell, get this—'

Monk stood, and drifted closer. Washington's eyes widened in surprise. Monk knew that it was because he had moved too fast for Washington to follow: well, if it kept him uneasy, then good.

'You *owe* me, Byron,' he breathed. His face was just a foot away. One hand was laid heavily on Washington's chest. 'Matthew Daniels is a human being,' he said softly. 'He's suffering. We both know what that's like.'

Washington scowled at him. 'True,' he muttered.

Monk regarded him until he had calmed. Then he added, 'I *need* you, Byron. I need your help.'

'Yeah, for the first and only time – right?' Washington's voice was heavy with bitterness. Monk understood: it wasn't the first time, not by a long chalk.

'Brothers, Byron,' he said simply.

Byron Washington held his gaze for an uncomfortable minute, and then sighed. 'There are limits,' he muttered.

'You didn't think that just after your father died,' Monk flashed back.

Washington shot him a glare full of cold fury – and Monk knew that he had him. In return, he gave his 'brother' one of his rare smiles – the bond between them demanded that much at least, even after all these years. 'Besides,' he said, 'you never know which time is the last – do you, bro?'

Twenty-Three

He woke from a dream that hovered at the fringes of memory. It had made him thrash in the chair. He had woken when his arm bashed against a table's corner. He stared around him, confused. There had been something about a lake. A white face beneath a sheet of water. And he should have known. If only he had seen . . .

First light. A new day. Charlotte, gone.

He reached inside himself to find her, hunting for the warm familiar certainty he always woke to – knowing that she was there, that all was well – and found a frigid void. He tried to picture her and failed. How would she be sitting? Or would she be pacing her cell, or eating, or . . . ? He had no way to know. She would know that he was doing everything he could, of course; but perhaps the link between them was as absent for her as for him. Was she in pain? Was she even alive? She had slipped away from him during the night.

Have taken away drugs. Next I hurt her. That was what the man had said. But that was before the money. So maybe . . .

Another day. She'd been thirty-six hours now, or more. And what had he achieved? He'd failed to raise a ransom. He'd spent what little he *had* been able to raise – little? Twenty-eight thousand; all the money he had – just buying time. He'd sought help from a con- victed murderer he knew he couldn't trust. And what was he supposed to do next? A hundred and fifty thousand was as unachiev- able as ever. But the only alternatives were to persuade the man to release her – or to find her. And how could he persuade the man if he wouldn't even answer the phone?

Under any other circumstances, it would have been laughable, because when it came down to it, Matthew's interests and the man's were exactly the same. Neither of them wanted this to escalate (surely, even this bastard wasn't mad enough to be happy with murder as a conclusion, was he?) – and since Matthew would gladly give everything he possibly could, the man's best course was to accept what was on offer, release Charlotte, and run. But to make the man understand that, the two of them would have to talk. And he wasn't answering Matthew's countless calls.

He hoped that Monk had made progress. *Someone* must know who this bastard was, surely. But Monk hadn't called either, at least not while Matthew was awake. And in the circumstances, he was hardly likely to sleep through a ringing phone. So what was Monk doing? Most likely, he was working out how to turn the situation to his advantage, or deliberately doing nothing for as long as possible to prolong the discomfort of his erstwhile custodian.

Perhaps, perhaps not. Monk had always been different, whether Matthew had liked him or not. He was one of very few prisoners Matthew had ever encountered who truly seemed to understand the concept of integrity. Monk had never been malicious, he was just . . . unreliable. Whatever was going on in his head, it was incomprehensible to anyone else.

But trustworthiness and reliability were luxuries he could no longer afford. Who else could he turn to? The police? No, not now. The bank? No. The loan companies that pretended to be desperate for his business? No. It was not that he trusted Monk, it was that he had been reduced to needing him, in the course of a single day.

And now what? Now, silence. Now, another day, and no idea at all how Charlotte was, or how to get her back. He didn't even know how to keep her alive.

He straightened the cushions on the chair he had not meant to sleep in. There were signs of her everywhere. The covers on the chairs had been chosen by her. Their bold pattern dominated the plain-painted room. At the time, he had thought the colour was too much; and she had told him that if she was going to stay with him, he'd better get used to a more colourful life. He loved those covers now. They brought the room alive.

Without her, they seemed gaudy and aggressive. They demanded that he be happy.

The house was silent – and all he could do was think. In half an hour or so, Em would wake up and he would have to face her. He had no idea what to say to her. He decided, guiltily, that he should keep up the lie: just because the last thirty-six hours had been an eternity for him didn't mean that they had been for her. And, by the end of today, things would have changed. They would have to change: Monk was out hunting for information, and information would make the difference. Perhaps he had already made progress – but, surely, he would have rung.

Matthew rubbed his eyes savagely, trying to drive in a little clarity. The truth was, he had no idea whether Monk would ring him or not. A normal person would – but Monk was hardly normal. It was perfectly possible that he had spent the night meditating, rather than doing anything constructive at all – or, possibly, having had a laugh at Matthew's expense, the bastard really had just vanished.

Some might say that you hung me out to dry, Matthew.

Your past is who you are, Matthew.

Matthew retrieved his mobile from the floor – it must have fallen from his hands last night – and checked if anyone had rung him. No one had: not Monk, not the man. He rang Monk's mobile. There was no reply, and no voicemail message. He rang Charlotte's mobile. It rang out.

So, he thought, to sum up. Charlotte's gone. You've spent all the cash you could lay your hands on. You've successfully made sure that the police will never believe you. And you've recruited a homicidal ex-convict who you know from past experience you stand no chance of controlling.

Nice one, Matthew. Good move.

The fact that he'd had no choice hardly seemed an adequate defence.

He went upstairs, tiptoeing past Em's bedroom. She was snoring. Nothing had changed in his and Charlotte's bedroom. The bedclothes were rumpled on his side and pristine on hers. The clothes he had worn to the Thorntons' for dinner lay in a pile by the curtains – which had now not been opened for a day and two nights. He realised that he had been wearing the clothes he now had on for almost as long. He sniffed the armpit of his shirt. It stank. He should change, have a bath. He took fresh clothes into the bathroom with him and sat on the toilet lid, watching the water run. Charlotte could be screaming somewhere, while he decided which soap to use, or whether to wash his hair.

What else could he do? Smelling of day-old sweat wouldn't help him find her. He had made his decisions: no police, use Monk; and now the only option he had was to wait – and try every new way he could think of to raise a hundred and fifty thousand pounds. It did no harm to wait without stinking. Besides, there was Em. His feeble excuses yesterday had hardly been convincing. If he looked as though he was in the middle of a crisis, she would never accept his lies. He lay in the bath, trying hard to ignore how good it felt, and the guilt-pangs that accompanied the sensation, and pondered the puzzle of his daughter.

He was half convinced that Em still blamed him for Rachel's death. She had heard them arguing so many times, had heard him crashing about the house after Rachel had gone to bed, hitting the walls out of grief and frustration, and his efficiency the day after they had found her, when she had gone. Em had lived through the police's clumsy, cruel investigations. She had answered endless questions, endured interviews with child psychologists. And when it was all over, she had never looked at him in the same way again.

Small wonder she had always been so torn about Charlotte. Whatever Em said, her behaviour made it obvious what she felt. Until a year ago, she had let Charlotte comb her hair. They had shared girlie confidences about perfume or boys or playground politics. And he, watching, had felt so glad – and relieved that another afternoon had passed without Em disappearing up into her room, lighting a candle and, he knew, whispering to her dead mother that she missed her.

In the last year, puberty had really begun to bite. These days, she kicked and screamed and stormed her way through life. Once, tantrums had been rare; now it was the moments of peace that were precious. Yet, behind the fury and postures, he still saw Emmie; fragile, devoted Emmie. He saw a girl who looked at him with reproach in her eyes, and who looked at Charlotte with confusion, but with love.

Em's alarm went off, loud even through the dividing wall. He started violently, sloshing water out onto the floor. Had half an hour really passed? How could he hope to find Charlotte if he wandered around in a daze? Fighting a rush of despair – and a towel that refused to wrap round him properly – he scooped up his clothes, dashed for the bedroom, and dressed. He had to be downstairs, ready: Em had needs, too. She deserved reassurance, comfort.

If this went on much longer, he would have to tell her, he knew; but not yet. While there was still hope of finding Charlotte alive, it was madness to risk everything by including a wild card like Em. He buried a pang at his own callousness for excluding his daughter this way, just because she was only fourteen and driven by hormones; this wasn't the time for sentiment, only for practicalities.

He put on jeans and a casual shirt – and then realised that Em would notice that he wasn't dressed for work. He changed into more formal trousers, and put on a jacket and tie. The tie felt like a noose. He could hear Em beginning to stir in her room. Heavily, he went downstairs to make them both breakfast, and to pretend.

In the kitchen, the cornflowers he had bought Charlotte were already beginning to fade. Their intense blue had dissolved to a chalky grey. The water they stood in was streaked with tendrils of green.

When he tried to make toast, he couldn't find the Marmite.

'Is she dying, then?'

His first thought was: *She knows.*

He looked blankly at her, groping for an answer. Something about how there was hope. About not giving up.

Em rolled her eyes. 'Hello? Planet Earth to Dad? Like, Charlotte's friend?'

'Oh . . . Yes. I . . . think so. I haven't spoken to Charlotte yet this morning.' Em stared at her toast. Uncomfortably, he added, 'We spoke last night. She sent her love.'

Em snorted as though she didn't believe him. Under other circumstances, this would have infuriated him – Charlotte had put in so much effort with Em – but today, it filled him with misery. What Em needed was love; and he could only give her lies.

'Her mobile's switched off,' he said. 'So she's probably still inside the hospital. She said last night that it was touch and go, so . . .' He tailed off, unsure how to continue.

'So you don't know,' Em said flatly. She pushed the remains of her toast into the middle of the table.

He scooped up her plate and made himself busy at the sink, hoping to hide his distress. Em carried on staring glumly at the table.

'I rang her last night,' she said. 'Left a message.' She wrinkled her nose. 'She didn't ring back. Of course.' Her eyes were filmy.

He took a deep breath and sat opposite her. 'She's just busy, poppet. Are you missing her?'

She gave the slightest of nods. 'Sort of.'

'Me too.'

Em sniggered. 'Only cos you can't even make breakfast without her.'

He smiled at her, wearily.

The phone rang, and his heart jolted. Somehow, he managed to keep his smile steady. He made a show of looking at the kitchen clock. 'Time to get going,' he told her, over the phone's second ring. He stood, desperate to run for the phone, but aware that he absolutely could not. 'Go and get ready. If it's Charlotte, I'll put you on before you go.'

She glared at him in disgust, and slouched out of the room. He lunged for the phone, now halfway through its fourth ring.

'Hello? Yes? Is she OK? Do you—'

Mark Thornton interrupted him. 'So, tell me, Matthew. Were you actually considering ringing back to explain yesterday, or did you decide that was too much like hard work? Do you fancy another day off?'

He could hear Em's footsteps thumping on the stairs. His heart rattled loosely in his chest. He felt hollow and dizzy.

'Mark . . .'

'Yes,' Thornton snapped. 'Mark. Who were you expecting? Social Services ringing to tell you to take it easy? Matthew, it may have escaped your notice, but there's actually quite a lot to do here. Picking up the pieces after the mess you left yesterday, for example.'

This was unfair – and absurd. What did the Ville matter? So what if a few equerries' noses were out of joint?

'I explained to you yesterday, Mark. It's personal.'

He could hear footsteps pounding about upstairs, and music: Em, preparing for the day.

'So personal that you can't even be arsed to ring in? Matthew, I think, at the very least, you owe us the courtesy of—'

Matthew interrupted. Anything to stop the idiot wittering on at him. 'It's Em. There's been . . . Well, she's got a problem.' It sounded completely unconvincing.

'Well, for goodness sake, Matthew, can't school deal with it? We need you here.'

'A *medical* problem, Mark.'

'Well, can't Charlotte—'

'Mark, Em's my daughter. Do you really think I'm going to fob her off onto Charlotte?'

There was a long pause before Thornton spoke – and when he did, his tone was humbler. 'Serious, then?'

Matthew was desperate to get him off the phone. He couldn't afford to let him ask too many questions: he knew he couldn't think of convincing answers in time. 'Of *course* it's serious, Mark. Why else would I rush off like that yesterday?'

'On that subject, Matthew, I hear you had your mobile with you. I really must—'

'Mark, Em is *ill*. I shouldn't have been in at all.'

'Well, that's for later. Now, is Em—'

'I don't want to talk about it, Mark.'

'I see. Well, of course.'

'If your daughter had just been . . .' he sighed deliberately. 'Look, forget it.'

Thornton said hastily, 'No, no. Absolutely. Take your time. We'll cover for you here. And if you need—'

'Mark, I've got to go now.'

'Of course. I understand.'

No, he didn't understand. The reason he had to go was that Em was standing in the doorway to the kitchen, gaping with horrified surprise.

'Well,' Mark Thornton said. 'Any time you—'

He rang off and faced his daughter.

'If your daughter had just been *what*?' There was acid in her voice. 'You said it was medical. What? Diagnosed with cancer? Raped? Put in a loony bin? What?'

'Em, I—'

'Who was that anyway?'

He had no idea what to tell her. He only knew that it wasn't safe to tell her the truth.

'It was work. I'm normally in by now. They wanted to know where I was.'

'So you told them it was my fault? Like, I'd got some disease? Just so you could go in late? Great, *thanks*, Dad.'

He wanted to hug her, explain that it wasn't like that, that he would never –

'You're lying about Charlotte, too, aren't you?'

'Of course not, poppet. I wouldn't . . .' But he knew his protestation sounded false.

'She's left you.'

Em was scowling. Her eyes were cast down. But, cruel though it was, there was nothing for it but to continue the lie.

'It was *work*, Em. I told you. Charlotte's in Bath. Debbie—'

'Oh, *leave* it, Dad!'

Em slammed the kitchen door, then the front door. The sound echoed in the empty house.

With Em gone, there was no need to keep up appearances. He went back upstairs and changed his jacket and tie for jeans, shirt and trainers. When had he last shaved? Who cared? Charlotte would have – but she wasn't here, was she?

He shaved.

Then he waited in the kitchen. The clock moved round. An hour. Another hour.

At half past ten, he rang Monk again. This time the call switched to voicemail. 'Monk, call me,' he said, aware of how weak his message sounded. 'I need to know what's happening.' Already, though, he half-knew the answer: Monk was sitting somewhere – or, more probably for Monk, standing – and laughing at the delightful symmetry of events: he had once trusted Matthew and in return, in his opinion, had been betrayed; and now, it was Matthew's turn, trusting him . . .

He rang off, wondering whether Monk would bother even to listen to the message. He rang again ten minutes later. There was no reply.

The only thing he could do was work on raising the money. Perhaps if he went to a loan shark . . . But he didn't know any. Monk might – but he wasn't answering his phone.

At quarter to eleven, there was a clatter at the door, and the soft flop of post onto the doormat. Some of it would be for Charlotte. What was he supposed to do with it? Because she was coming back –

wasn't she? Soon. Today, or tomorrow at the latest. He approached the letters as though they were final demands. They were all for her. There were letters with envelopes as stiff as card, and catalogues that drooped in the hand, and slithered from his grip. None of it looked important. He laid the pile on the stairs, trying to avoid the creeping sense that there was something about the act that was terribly final.

There was a catalogue near the bottom of the pile – a plastic-wrapped magazine from Monday. When he added the new post, it slipped over the letters below, and the whole pile toppled. Three days, and already the stack was too tall to stay in place.

And what had he *done*?

He left the post scattered across the hall, and hunkered down in the kitchen, dry-eyed, too exhausted for tears, wondering what was happening to him.

He rang Monk again at midday. It rang out. Just to complete the pointless ritual, he rang Charlotte's mobile. Voicemail – as if he had anything to say. But when would the bastard switch the thing on again? Was he even listening any more?

He stared blankly at the wall, numb and utterly drained. He gathered together what little energy he could and rang Monk yet again. Monk's voice said, 'Leave a message.' There was a beep.

'Monk, where the hell are you?' Matthew felt weary beyond description. When was this going to end? How? 'I asked you to help me, not to disappear.' He paused and rubbed his dry eyes. What could he say to grab Monk's attention? Either the man would help him or he wouldn't. 'I've had enough of this. I . . .' He stopped again, unsure what else he could add. He needed to *talk* with him: leaving messages only reminded him how isolated he was, and how uninvolved in this attempt to find Charlotte. 'Just *call*,' he said at last.

The silent house hung around him. Walls and dark windows. A prison just for him.

Opening Charlotte's post helped. It gave him something to do. Perhaps there were letters that needed attention. He felt comfortable making specific decisions; they allowed him to avoid the more general fear that was eating at him. He scooped up the letters and took them through to the kitchen.

He ignored the catalogues. He opened a plain white envelope that turned out to be junk mail — a letter from a local estate agent assuring Charlotte that they could rent out her house for thousands. There was a letter from the Inland Revenue: it was a statement of account, incomprehensible columns of addition and subtraction and dates: best left alone, he decided, and set it to one side. There were bills, catalogues and more catalogues. There was a bill for her mobile phone. The irony was savage: a bill for use of the phone her abductor was using to call him.

Even before he opened it, he could envisage the neat rows of calls made: the number called, and when, and the duration; each call a fragment of Charlotte's life. A call to his mobile to say she'd be late, a call for a quick chat with a friend during a lunch break. When she used her mobile, she cocked her head, and her features drew into an absent-minded scowl; and then she would notice him watching her, and her eyes would crease, her cheeks would dimple.

He opened it. The numbers she had rung were all there, her social life set out in neat rows. Most of the numbers were familiar, some were not. Their home number featured a great deal, and Em's mobile, and his. He checked the last date listed: the bill cut off at the end of the Monday a week before her abduction. In a month's time, another bill would come through; and it would show a week of Charlotte's normal life, and then nothing (he assumed) but calls to him, at home or on his mobile, each one neatly dated and time: a separate entry for each minute the man had spent torturing him, a tiny fee against each blow — eight pence for 'No police', twenty-three pence for 'Enjoying yourself, are you?', maybe seventy against each of those pictures of her in her prison. She would even be charged for the text message arranging to hand over twenty-eight thousand pounds.

She had been so small in that picture, and even in the video — a few fragile pixels, a blocky icon of fear and vulnerability. And that space around her, vast even on the phone's tiny screen: grey and oppressive and empty. And the planes roaring over as the man spoke, the noise buzzing brightly through the TV screen, and in the phone's earpiece when the man rang him.

Where was she? It must be a warehouse or something; certainly, the space was big enough. And the planes: the only explanation for them was that she was near an airport. He was puzzled for a moment why he hadn't thought of that before. But in fact, he had. He had always assumed, from the noise on the phone and in the video, and from the room revealed in the pictures, that she was being held in a warehouse or a depot near an airport – but it hadn't mattered. For all this time, he had been on the brink of getting her back. He was about to raise the money. He would be able to turn the man around next time they talked. And then he had been at work, or haggling with bank managers . . . Where she was hadn't mattered, all that had been important had been getting her back. And what little he had been able to deduce was hardly helpful. It changed nothing. How many airports were there anyway? How many warehouses?

But now it was different. The hope of a release had gone from slim to vanishing. There was no negotiating, there was no money, even Monk had disappeared. Now, at last, he was truly desperate.

To hell with Monk. To hell with waiting in a silent house. He would find Charlotte on his own. He ran to the car to fetch a map.

Twenty-Four

No knight in shining armour was going to come galloping over the hill to rescue her, that much was obvious now. She would have to escape. Her only chance to get through the door would be when the man was there. That meant that she would have to overpower him, then make a run for it.

It hadn't taken long to plan a strategy – or, more truthfully, to work out how few options she really had. A used paper plate and a plastic drinking bottle were unlikely to help her much; it was the bed or nothing.

Since the pregnancy, Charlotte had been nervous of exertion. She had felt as though she was carrying a baby spun from glass: intricate, impossible and terrifyingly fragile. Contract a muscle too hard and it might shatter – and all her dreams would shatter too. Here, though, in this stench-laced prison, with no future to cling to . . . Here and now, she knew that she was lost unless she exerted herself. She was alone. No one was coming for her – except for balaclava-face, or perhaps Thornton himself. In a way, she thought, grunting as she hauled at the bed, it was empowering to be alone: the only thing that stood between her and freedom was herself. That, and her captor, and a locked door . . . But unless she did something, she and Eyelash were dead anyway – so what was there to lose?

Grudgingly, inch by inch, the bed came clear of the wall. It scraped against the concrete floor. She waited nervously. The noise had been loud in the silence. No one came. So far so good. She wasn't strong, but she was desperate. She bent and fitted her fingers under the edge of the divan, acutely aware of the compression in her belly as she doubled over. She gritted her teeth and heaved upwards as savagely as she could. The bed came up more easily than she had expected, and ended rocking gently on one broad, flat side. The mattress sagged and curled away, flopping half onto the floor and half against the wall. Sweating more from fear than effort, Charlotte nudged the bed over on top of it. It bounced, and then was still. She surveyed its underbelly in the grey glow of the dawn.

The structure was hollow, as she had expected. It was made of sheets of wood, supported by spars and struts, some broken, some not. The main box-frame was held in place with L-shaped metal brackets. The wood around many of the screws was buckled, she assumed because of damp. Around the gaps where the drawers had originally been, were lighter spars, stapled into place. One of these was loose.

Charlotte regretfully put aside the idea of hiding underneath the bed, and hoping that the man would rush outside to find her and leave the door unlocked behind her. It smacked more of fantasy than strategy. She needed something more . . . reliable.

The first thing she tried was to pick the door lock with one of the staples that held the bed together. The first three staples she tried snapped off as she twisted them loose, but the fourth came free, and she straightened it carefully into a thin piece of wire perhaps three-quarters of an inch long. She had never picked a lock before, but she knew the principle. You had to probe for the tumblers, one by one, and tip them over.

The staple was too short. She held the very end of it, pinched tight between her fingertips and jabbed and poked inside the lock, pressing in so far that she risked dropping her improvised pick inside the lock. At the very limit of her reach, there was a hint of contact, but the tip of the pick slid off, again and again. She pulled it out before she lost it: gumming up the lock with bent metal while she was on this side of it seemed, to say the least, unwise.

It might come to that. What would she do if he really wasn't coming back? She would starve to death, separated from escape by a single door with safety glass and a few metal bars, and the kind of lock you would get on an office door: nothing special, just beyond Charlotte's feeble strength. It was ridiculous. There had to be a way. If not, she would die here.

Painfully, she extracted another staple, and bent it into a blunted

V. She fitted this into a screw on the door handle plate and tried to turn it. The staple twisted and then snapped. Calmly, she returned to the bed for another staple. It took five attempts, and by the time she had succeeded, several of her fingertips were bleeding, either pierced by the staples' sharp ends or ripped raw from tugging. The screw had not budged at all.

She wanted to cry. The unfairness of it was overwhelming. There was a child growing inside her. Didn't Thornton *realise*? This wasn't just about her any more. If he hurt her, he hurt Eyelash.

A plane ripped through the sky above her, filling her head with its demented shriek. She screamed with it, once, and kicked the bed as violently as she could. It moved a sullen inch across the floor, and hurt her toe. Still, the scream brought her back a measure of self-control, and she bent back to her task. She eyed the bed's underside. There were ten or so staples that she could see. There might be a few more hidden somewhere. Unless she was careful, she would run out.

The next one came out smoothly. She bent it to shape, and tried the screw again, more gently this time. Eventually, it budged, and with careful coaxing, loosened. The head rose slowly away from the plate. As soon as she was able to get her fingers to it, she hurriedly unscrewed it, and started on the next one.

It took her three-quarters of an hour to remove four screws. The doorplate came away easily, and she was confronted with the square metal bar that was the shaft connecting the door handles. She tugged on it: it might be useful for something, as a weapon for when he came back . . . If he ever came . . . But it would not budge. It must have been held fast by a screw on the other side of the door. Below the handle-shaft was the lock, another metal plate, this time without screws, with a central hole.

The doorplate had added at least a quarter of an inch to the depth of the keyhole; perhaps now her lock-pick had a chance of working. She began to probe. The pick met resistance. There were uneven shapes in there, close to the limit of her reach. She jabbed at them hopefully. Nothing moved. She needed to be able to turn the tumblers, not just poke them. She bent a right angle into the pick towards one end and tried again. Now it was too short.

She slumped against the door, defeated, and listened to the

melancholy howl of the planes. After a while, she struggled back to her feet. Plan B, then. The full-on attack. Damn.

She broke a couple more nails scrabbling to get her fingers under the loose end of one of the stapled spars that held the bed's two sides together. Eventually, she managed to wedge a couple of fingers in, and heaved the strut free. The staples groaned as they pulled away from the structure, then separated suddenly, sending her staggering backwards across the room, waving a two-foot piece of timber for balance.

The points of the staples protruded at both ends. She liked that; but the spar was too light: it looked as though it would break before it did any damage. She dumped it back into the bed's hollow, and set to work on one of the larger, screwed-in supports that held the thing together.

Success, inevitably, took time. It came in the form of a two-and-a-half-foot-long timber, an inch or so on a side, with a metal bracket jutting out at one end, still studded with short screws. It was as good as she was going to get. She pulled the bed back into its original position, and hid the spar behind it. Then she settled down to wait.

Hours passed. The rain stopped, and then began again. The planes began, and the sky brightened, and light seeped down from the skylights. For a while, she imagined that she was at the bottom of a pool of still grey water, the surface barely rippled by the rain. The wind rose and the rain splattered against the glass above her in soggy gusts, like catspaws across the pond. Then the wind died, and the rain faded, and a cold, bright sky bleached the grime on the windows almost white. Every ninety seconds, a plane split the silence. Hours passed. Six o'clock. Seven. Eight.

She waited, and the stupid bastard didn't come. That wrecked Plan B completely, because Plan B was to attack him.

It was nearly nine o'clock before she finally accepted that she was now alone. She was safe from him – but only because he wasn't coming: not this morning, and perhaps not ever. There would be no assault – and no food, no water, no release. He had left her, for good. She would die here, slowly, behind a single locked door in a warehouse. Because there was no Plan C at all. Perhaps it had all been for nothing.

She swallowed half an aspirin and injected a dose of heparin. Then she clasped her hands round her belly, cradling her Eyelash with all the warmth she could muster. She waited, and the hours passed. And deep inside her, beyond the reach of her cupped hands, she felt cold fingers, not her own, slowly tightening around her unborn child.

Twenty-Five

His mobile rang. He checked the screen. Matthew – again. He pressed the Cancel button – again.

Monk lay in an abandoned concrete space, his eyes unfocused, taking in the sky's blue bowl, and he pondered the strange movements of the world, and the mysteries of the human beings who crawled across its face. The sky shimmered with the calm power of all things and, pinned against the ground, he felt the energy within him rise in a column to greet it.

There was pleasure here, and purpose: for Monk, the two were one – because he was him, and the world was the world. It puzzled him that so many people struggled with such trivial questions as *Who am I?* or *What is the meaning of life?* If they lay still for long enough, if they ever just allowed themselves to be, these questions would evaporate like a cloud.

What is the meaning of pain? Now, that was a harder question. What is the value of grief? Since he was fourteen, when his journey began, he had searched for the answer to that. And, when all deeds were done, when anticipation had turned into hope and then into action . . . Peace had always eluded him. The pain remained, a rock that was covered for a few hours by the tide, and then emerged again, a little smoother for the waves that had broken over it, but still jagged, still able to cut to the bone with a single misplaced step.

He reached across his body and rubbed the shell he kept on his left wrist. Others would think it worn smooth, but he knew every flaw, each sharp grain on its surface. To him, it was scoured. Under his fingers it felt like sandpaper. Others saw a shell whose colour had long since leached away; to Monk, the patterns were deeper for their infinite faintness. He knew each line, each gradient; and the fact that they remained, after all these years, told him the depth of his pain.

His name is David Beresford Gordon, and he is fourteen. He is young and he is happy. Gloria is with him.

'Take it, David,' she says to him.

She folds into his hand a cowrie shell. It is small. Its mottled pattern is so bleached that it is almost invisible. Its surface is smooth under his fingers, but he detects a hint of ceramic roughness.

'My mother gave it to me,' Gloria says simply, 'before she died. It will keep you safe.'

David has never had a mother. He has an auntie. She comes and goes. From time to time, her name changes, and her face. For a moment, he feels jealous of Gloria – but only for a moment.

The whites of her eyes shine in her dark, perfect face. Her lips curve into a smile, and he glimpses white, white teeth and the tiny tip of her pink tongue. Her brow is slightly knotted. It does that when she is serious. Her gaze searches his, probing for the echo that she knows will be there – an echo of the joy that dances in her own.

And he is lost in her. She fills him with light.

She says, 'I think I love you, David.'

And he says, 'I love you, Gloria.' He says. 'Yes. I love you too.'

She giggles, and tickles him – and as he wriggles, he lets go of the cowrie shell, and they stop while he hunts for it among the bed-clothes – and once he has put it safely to one side, she tickles him again.

And later, spent and glowing, and slick with sweat, hiding in his room – secretly, because they are too young, and this is forbidden, and they don't care, because this thing is for them and them alone, but still they must be careful – later, she whispers it to him again: 'David, I love you. Be safe for me, always.'

And he holds her. And they sleep.

Gloria is fifteen, a year older than him, and they live in a dangerous world. Their fathers both keep the company of dangerous men. Sometimes there are guns in their houses; often there are knives and machetes. The women pull them away when these men come, scold them when they peep down from the top of the stairs.

Gloria's father is the Man. David's dad works for him. David's dad is Gloria's father's best and only friend.

Together, David and Gloria share dreams. They will escape. They will leave as soon as they are old enough, they will vanish into the night. They will marry, and they will emigrate. They will go back to Jamaica, the golden island that neither of them has ever seen. They will have a house on a pure white beach, and there will be driftwood on the shoreline, and the sea to watch, and cowrie shells to keep them safe for ever, gifts from the sea.

But, as well as dreaming, they also work towards the future that others have chosen for them. They are diligent at school, and clever. They are polite, always. They strive to be admired. They are a credit to their parents.

Outside school, David studies karate, and has already impressed his teacher. He is a brown belt. He finds karate peaceful. As his body moves and works, so his mind becomes still. There is no effort to his movements, there is only intention, and action. Gloria says he scares her – but she only says it because then he will pretend to be a monster, and he will chase her – and then . . .

Gloria Washington's brother is Byron. He knows about their love, but he will never tell. He has sworn it. He knows their dreams, too, and keeps them hidden. Mostly, Byron ignores David: he does not understand, and he does not want or need to. Byron's dream is different. When Byron grows up, he will be the Man, just like his father.

But Byron is away today, watching his father at work. David's father is with them.

There is silence between David and Gloria, a languid delight. The sun reaches through the windows to stroke their limbs.

Then there is a crash downstairs. The sound of wood, cracking and splitting. There are voices, shouting. Doors are opened and slammed. Men call to each other. There are footsteps on the stairs. Many footsteps, heavy, fast. And before David has even sat up in bed – while Gloria's eyes are still widening with fear – the door bursts open, and the men are upon them.

White men. Men who grin like wolves when they find a black girl there – beautiful, terrified, and beginning to scream. Men who laugh aloud when they see that she is naked.

After a long while, they leave her and begin on David.

'A lesson for you, darkie,' one of them snarls. 'Tell your dad, nobody fucks with Vic Bolotin. Nobody. Got that? Got that, have you, darkie?' They slice open his face, all the way from top to bottom, and down onto his chest. One man flails at him with a club – again, again, again. David loses consciousness. He thinks that this is death. But it is not.

Later, he wakes, broken, beaten, barely able to move. He is weak and dizzy, and his blood mixes on the floor with Gloria's. He tries to wake her, and she does not respond. He kisses her slack lips. Her skin is cold and swollen from the men's assault. There is dried blood on her belly and the inside of her thighs. Only later, after he has lain with her, murmuring to her, pleading with her to wake, does he press a finger to her neck, and he finds no pulse there at all.

Painfully, struggling to remain awake, David drags himself away. He goes to find Byron.

But David's house is not the only one the men raided. His father was with Byron's: now both of them are dead. Byron is only alive because he ran. One of Byron's father's few surviving lieutenants is now the Man. He is loyal to Byron, but not to David. He waits until David's injuries have healed, and then he turns him away.

David seeks out his *sensei*. *Sensei* has green tea for him, and kind words, but no answers. David needs a focus for his pain, and the skill to control it. Karate might give him that, over time, but *Sensei* detects something dangerous in David, something new and disturbing.

It is anger. David wants revenge.

'I will give you a name,' *Sensei* tells him.

It is the name of a Chinese man, a man who prefers anonymity, and who makes his money through the controlled use of terrible force. He works alone, but he agrees to meet David because of the letter from *Sensei*. And the man is drawn to him, and offers him shelter for a while – and the chance to learn. David becomes his apprentice.

He learns *Tai Chi* and *Xing-Yi* and *Choy Li Fut*. And as his body works and hardens, so does his mind. He finds a calm centre. He finds control. He finds a means to express his rage.

And when he is ready, five years after all hope of love died from his life, he searches out a man he knows only by name. A man named Vic Bolotin. A gangland leader. A dangerous man.

David kills him.

Byron is grateful. He swears to David that they will be brothers, always. But Bolotin's death, and his brotherhood with Byron – these things only deepen his pain. They are emblems of what he has lost, what he failed to do.

Years slide past, fragments borne on a slow cold river. He hides. He searches for peace – and he fails. And slowly he comes to believe that it is not anger that drives him, but regret. Perhaps he could have saved her. He could have fought them, and hit, and bitten, and kicked. He could have howled his fury to the sky. He could have refused to take the cowrie shell – and now he would be dead and she would be safe.

He should have saved her – or he should have died.

More years. Alone, he contemplates his guilt, and the grief that is still so raw inside him. He is Monk now, severed from the world by the terrible burden of what he should have been.

And as the years drift away from him, he slowly comes to understand that he must atone for the death of the only woman he ever loved.

Riverweed. What mattered was the Now. And, in the Now, he had a purpose and an identity. He had been recruited by Matthew Daniels. And that was as it should be. Naturally, he had expected it. If you stood long enough on the shore, whatever you threw out to sea came back to you. If he could help Matthew understand that simple truth, then his time would not have been wasted. Monk was Matthew's *joss*, *karma*, call it what you would. Names had no meaning. And underneath the names, really, it was not complicated at all.

It was all about pain, and patience.

He was ignoring Matthew's calls because he had nothing to say to him. Also, if he was honest with himself, which he always was, he was ignoring him because he could. It was all part of Matthew's education. And it made a change from prison, where the officers spoke to you when they wished to, regardless of what you might want or need. He had no desire to be cruel; it was just that he found unnecessary chatter distracting. Matthew wanted information: what was the point of speaking to him merely in order to tell him that there was none? When he had something to say, he would talk. Until then, he would think, and prepare.

The phone rang again – most likely another call from Matthew; but, to be sure, Monk checked the screen. It was a number only he and a handful of people knew. Byron Washington wanted to talk to him. He held the phone to his ear and waited.

The silence continued for several seconds before Washington said, 'You should work on your social skills, bro.'

Again, Monk did not bother to reply: there was nothing to say.

'Good show you put on here last night,' Washington continued, unperturbed. 'You're quite a performer, when you want to be.' When Monk did not answer, Washington chuckled. 'Hmm. Chatty this morning. Still, you put on the moves last night. Almos' convince me, y'nah?'

Washington never put on a Jamaican twinge unless he was playing a game. Monk remembered him from when he was sixteen: he had sounded like an Oxford graduate even then, even in the Brixton slums. In this case, the game was to pretend that he and Monk were collaborators, and that Washington had somehow conspired to help him barge into his office last night. The truth was more complex than that – far more complex – but then, they both knew that. Monk, therefore, said nothing.

Washington dropped the West Indian accent. 'Bro, you're not the only man who burns a little.'

In the corner of his vision, Monk could see the cowrie shell, dangling from the arm that held his phone.

He said, 'You rang me.'

This time, the silence came from the other end. Monk waited it out. Eventually, Washington laughed, brittlely. 'I did. I rang. You know, there are other people care about you 'cept just you. You know that, don't you, Bro?'

Monk found it hard to say the words. The shell twisted as he turned to find a different perspective. The light from it was flat ivory, each pore limned with a sharp glint.

'Yes,' he said. 'I am grateful.'

'I mean, someone shafts you, they shaft me. Brothers. Understand?'

This time, he did not reply. In Washington's world this meant something, but not in his. He could not change Byron any more than Byron could change him. The fact that they were . . . brothers . . . made not the slightest difference to that. Look at humanity from afar, and they might as well be ants; look close up, and you saw an individual's Way; anything between was an illusion. The connections between men – even *brothers* – meant nothing.

Washington broke the silence. 'Bro, I done my best for you, always. You know that. You went down for me. You think I'm gonna forget that?'

He knew the answer. What was the point in Monk repeating it?

'Monk, play the silent game with me some other time.' Washington, his unwanted brother and unwanted accomplice, tutted into the phone. 'I rang to tell you what your new friend is up to.'

Twenty-Six

In a way, Matthew was relieved that Monk had given up on him, because if he had chosen to stay involved but only in order to destroy, it would have been far more damaging. This way, he'd had his little laugh, he'd rubbed Matthew's nose in it by meeting in the graveyard, he'd made promises he clearly had no intention of keeping, he'd wasted some of Matthew's time – but at least he'd done no active harm. What if he'd given false information? Or, worse, he could simply have attacked him: Matthew could not possibly have defended himself against the kind of violence Monk was capable of. And if Monk had chosen to cripple him, or even kill him, what chance would Charlotte have had then?

The man's absence was a blessing. You could never really trust a criminal. And at least now, he knew what he had to do. Charlotte was being held near an airport. All that remained was to find her.

He chose Heathrow first. It was nearest and busiest – and he had to start somewhere. By the time he got there, it was two in the afternoon.

On the map, industrial estates ringed Heathrow – in Hounslow, in Twickenham, Staines, Hayes, Southall: white areas of the map, with thin, blank-ended feeder roads seeping in from all sides. Areas near canals, areas near railway lines, areas nestled in the crook of the intersections of major roads. And within a few miles of them all, the airport. When he gazed at the page, he was eerily aware that he might be looking at her, straight at her.

Or she might be miles away, near Gatwick, Stansted, Manchester.

But, wherever she was, she was under either the descent path or the take-off route. The map showed the area below the take-off flight path as a series of reservoirs: no warehouses, she must be on the descent path, between the airport and London itself. Judging by how loud the planes were, she was close to the airport itself. Beneath the descent path, the *A to Z* showed clusters of industrial estates and storage units, fringing the airport's perimeter.

Good. He drove.

The geography of this part of London was unfamiliar to him. The streets were wider and lower than the areas he was used to. Here, the city felt American: it sprawled, it was featureless, each mile was like the last. Neat suburban houses mingled with huge, impersonal industrial estates. There were low-rise warehouses, more respectable than he had anticipated: companies specialising in aeronautical engineering, general trading companies with expensive logos and manicured patches of grass and immaculate front offices, big names in the industry – BA, Boeing . . . There were guards in uniform, in mirror-glazed huts at perfectly painted barriers. And, on the other side of a wide, almost unused road: bungalows, neatly cropped hedges, rose bushes carefully marshalled and aligned. The scent of pine cleaning fluid mingled with aviation fuel.

But enough of the estates were shabby or anonymous or littered with weeds and empty oil barrels, rusting cranes and broken glass, that he suffered repeated, agonising frissons of hope. She was near – at least, she might be. Somewhere in this endless sprawl of concrete and dark glass and perfectly edged red brick – and clumps of weeds thrusting up through fractured concrete, and buildings with shattered windows – somewhere here, Charlotte could be waiting for him. Mute, terrified, undetectable.

He had hoped that he would know when he was close. Or that only one building would be a plausible candidate and he would know it when he saw it. He had rapidly found that he couldn't tell. He didn't know when he was near her, only when he hoped he was. Not the same thing at all.

He parked in one of the feeder streets. The building in front of him was derelict, or nearly so. It was two storeys high, red brick, with shattered windows. Bizarrely, a brand-new forklift stood in front of it, unattended. Along the edges where the walls met the ground, greenery grew up raggedly around freshly painted oxygen tanks. There were butterflies on tattered buddleias, broken doors with new padlocks, metal window frames with a few shards of glass standing like broken teeth – and, behind them, dark spaces, metal roofs, the tantalising suggestion of huge spaces further in.

A plane screamed overhead. The sky went dark for an electric instant. This was a place of possibilities. He climbed the moth-eaten fence.

Ten minutes later, he climbed back out. There was no sign of her.

The next place was similar. Weeds. Glass. Silence, except for the planes, each one a sudden thump of sound, a silhouette crucifix, an agonised howl – and then gone.

Broken concrete. Butterflies rising as he brushed through the shrubs. There was no smell. He found that strange. Why no smell in a place full of greenery and fractured concrete and . . .

. . . and she wasn't here either, was she?

Next.

Another drive along fat avenues, with planes shattering the sky every minute and a half. Low houses, perfect roofs, clipped roses, warehouses with walls of crimped tin and logos eighty feet across.

This was the right kind of territory. But there were another twenty or so estates to go – and that was only according to his map: what of the ones the map had ignored, or had appeared in the ten years since he had bought it? Somewhere, perhaps within a mile or two of him, in a place like the ones he had already seen, there was a shabby room within a crumbling building within an apparently derelict complex. In that room, there was space to hold a woman against her will. If the picture message was to be believed, she had no gag. Was she too far away from people for them to hear when she screamed? Or did they hear it, but dismiss it, half-dazed by the endless bruising roar of the planes? Perhaps they thought it was the scream of a drill, or a faulty compressor on a forklift – while Charlotte was yards away, battering helplessly against the walls.

He drove back along another spur road towards the main road that looped round this section of the airport. He had come so far south now that the planes were no longer overhead. He would have to try further north.

Just before he turned back onto the main road, his mobile rang. His hand shook as he clicked the receive button. Perhaps it would be *him*.

It was Monk, and his voice was hard and angry.

'What the hell do you think you're doing?'

He was wrong-footed by the unexpected assault.

'What do you mean?' After a pause to gather his thoughts, he added, viciously, 'Nice to bloody hear from you at last.'

There was a gap in the traffic. With his mobile tucked under his chin – illegally, but after everything else, who cared? – he pulled out onto the main road and headed north.

'Please turn your car round, Matthew, and head for home. Immediately.'

How could Monk possibly know where he was? Still, it was hardly a secret. He was here because Monk had failed to do anything himself. 'You'd rather I stayed at home, would you, Monk? While you disappear, avoid my calls, and do . . . What *have* you been doing, Monk? Having a good time? Sitting back and smoking weed? Staring into space like you did at the Ville? What?'

'You'd let her die, wouldn't you?' Monk hissed. 'Just because you are too stupid to think things through, and too arrogant to know it.'

The impudence of the man was astonishing.

Matthew snarled back, 'So, you reckon that *vanishing* is going to do the trick, do you? You can save her by dragging me to a grave-yard, muttering some bullshit about wanting a better future and then disappearing?'

He could feel the blood pumping in his head. His hand squeezed the wheel so tightly that the car veered across the empty road.

'What have you *done*, Monk?' he yelled. 'I asked you for information. So, tell me what you've actually done!'

When Monk answered, his voice was flat. 'You are being followed. Did you know that, Matthew?'

He looked around him wildly. He scanned the mirrors for any hint that the cars behind him were sinister. But how would he know? He hadn't been checking. The cars behind him could have been following him for hours, and he wouldn't have noticed.

Monk continued. 'Did you ever stop to think what the con-sequences might be for your wife if anyone found you snooping around Heathrow?'

Matthew was confused. Was *Monk* following him? What did that have to do with putting Charlotte in danger? And if it wasn't Monk, then . . . ?

Decision time. He was approaching the intersection with the motorway. Instead of crossing underneath it and continuing north, he joined it, and headed for home. Whoever was on his tail, if Monk knew, then others could. It was safest to stop.

'How did you know where I'm . . . ?' he tailed off weakly.

'Because, Matthew, one of the many things that I have *done* –' pointedly, he let the word hang '– is arrange protection for you. Look in your mirror.'

He had barely stopped looking in his mirror since Monk rang.

'I believe they are in a white Ford Escort,' Monk continued smoothly.

A white Ford Escort. It had been behind him as he approached the motorway junction. It was still behind him now. It held two men, both black. The passenger was talking on his mobile. He must have seen Matthew as he glanced in the mirror, because he grinned and gave a little wave. He was a big man; the gesture was incongruous and disturbing. The driver scowled.

Matthew swore softly. Suddenly, he was very scared indeed.

Monk's voice was as calm as ever. 'Matthew, please understand. This is deadly serious. Your wife is in danger, every second that you stay where you are. Please leave Heathrow now.'

'Just have,' he muttered.

Monk said nothing for a few seconds – his equivalent of approval, perhaps. Then he said, 'Can you see another car behind you, Matthew? With silvered windows. A cream-coloured Honda.'

He checked. 'No . . .' he said uneasily.

'That, Matthew, is an astonishing blessing. One that you truly do not deserve.'

'I don't understand.'

'That Honda was with you at the graveyard when we met. It followed you when you left. Last night, it cruised past your house several times.'

'But how—'

'I was outside watching, Matthew. I was away for a while to recruit . . . assistance. And then I spent the rest of the night watching your house. I saw it.'

'*Assistance?* But—'

'The same car was at the graveyard, Matthew. Same car, same plates.'

'But why didn't you . . . ?' He tailed off again. There were too many questions. He was still scanning the road behind and ahead. A hundred yards behind him, he saw a police car. He couldn't risk being pulled over for using the phone while he was driving. 'I'll call you back,' he snapped, and rang off.

He didn't call back. He drove.

He was torn between terror and fury. What right did Monk have to get people to follow him? He had asked Monk for information, nothing more. He had been very clear about that, because he had no desire to end up indebted to a murderer. But what would have happened had Monk not taken the initiative? If someone else was following him, Monk was right, that person might have thought Matthew was getting too warm; that could have spelled disaster. And at least he now knew that the man who had been watching him had a cream Honda with silvered windows.

But how much initiative had Monk taken? Who were the two men behind him? It seemed unlikely that they were members of the Salvation Army or friends of Mother Theresa's. Perhaps he was already out of his depth with Monk.

It took him half an hour to reach home. By the time he arrived, with the white Escort still in tow, he was terrified. Potentially dangerous men didn't worry him – as long as they were behind bars; but the men in that car were free to do exactly as they pleased. As he parked, the Escort pulled past him, and into a space a few houses further along. The passenger grinned at him as they drove past. Half his teeth were gold.

As he scurried from car to house, a figure emerged from the tiny front garden of a house opposite, and headed for him, unhurriedly but with alarming speed. For an instant, he thought that he was about to be attacked. Then he recognised Monk, and stood waiting.

'Who?' he said when Monk arrived.

Monk pursed his lips in a shrug. 'We are trying to find out. It may take time.'

'We? For heaven's sake, Monk, I didn't ask you to go on a recruitment drive. *Information*, I asked for information. What the hell have you got me into?'

'I took the number plate when I saw the car at the graveyard. But I couldn't follow,' Monk said. His lips twitched. 'I don't drive. It seemed sensible to arrange for someone to do some research.'

'*Someone?*' Matthew waved angrily at the Escort. It was facing away from them, but he saw the white flash of the driver's eyes in the mirror.

Monk shook his head. 'Associates.'

He asked, 'What about the number plate?'

'It's being traced. Takes time,' Monk replied calmly. He leaned closer. His eyes were hard, his face set. Matthew tried hard not to flinch. 'It's information my associates can obtain, and I cannot.'

'Who, Monk? Who are they? Because if they're friends of yours, believe me, I am *not* happy.'

Monk raised an eyebrow. 'Friends? No. But they are the people who can help. They work for a man I . . . trust. His name is Byron Washington.'

Matthew turned away in disgust and headed towards the house. Over his shoulder, he snapped, 'Get them out of here.' At the door, he turned to face Monk again. Monk contemplated him without expression. 'Didn't you hear me? I want them away!'

'That would be a mistake, Matthew.'

Matthew gaped at him incredulously. 'I didn't ask for your *opinion*! I told you to get them out of here. Why would I take advice from *you*?' His anger got the better of him and he strode back to confront him, shoving his face into Monk's. 'You proved you were unreliable in the Ville and you've proved it again here. What the hell are you playing at?'

Monk arched an eyebrow. 'Playing? This is hardly a game, Matthew.'

Enraged, Matthew roared, '*I* know that!'

Thoughtfully, lightly, Monk placed a hand on his shoulder. 'Please calm down, Matthew.'

He could feel the heat of Monk's body. His eyes gazed up at him, intense and white-rimmed. The hand weighed an astonishing amount. It was just resting there – Monk was exerting no downward pressure at all – but Matthew found his knees buckling under the sudden load. Monk murmured, 'We are on the street, in public.'

With a huge effort, Matthew pushed upwards until he was able to lock his knees. It made no difference. The pressure was unrelenting, and the strain in his lower back rapidly became intolerable. Between gritted teeth, Matthew ground out, 'Fuck – you.' Then his knees gave way.

Instantly, Monk's hand closed tight around the shoulder and held him upright. An onlooker might have noticed Matthew stagger very slightly, but that was all.

'Perhaps we should go inside,' Monk suggested.

Unsteadily, Matthew nodded.

As he turned towards the house, he heard a car's engine, accelerating hard. Monk whipped round; Matthew turned more slowly. He caught a glimpse of the car as it reached the end of the street and pulled out into the main road without checking for traffic. A cream-coloured car with silvered windows – a glimpse of *him* – gone before he could do anything at all.

Behind him another motor gunned. The white Escort executed a hasty three-point turn in the narrow street, then roared away in pursuit, perhaps thirty seconds behind its target.

Monk shook his head. 'Too late.' He turned to face Matthew and something hardened in his eyes. 'Inside,' he said again. 'They'll call if they find him.'

Reluctantly, Matthew climbed the steps.

In the hallway, Monk surveyed him unhurriedly. When he spoke, his voice was crisper than usual. 'If you had got too close, he would have killed her.'

Matthew digested this in silence. The idea rattled him. What if she *was* being held near Heathrow? If he had stumbled on the right place, what might they have done to her?

Monk continued. 'The associates you dislike so much might just have saved your wife's life.'

He couldn't meet Monk's gaze. He hated the fact that he was – possibly – right. He wanted to shout at him, but the memory of that hand on his shoulder cautioned against it.

For an instant, a smile flickered on Monk's lips. 'Matthew, this is my world, not yours. That is why you rang me.'

Matthew stared at him, confused.

'What were you hoping to accomplish, Matthew?' he continued. 'Were you going to walk in and ask for her back?'

He didn't have an answer. He hadn't thought that far ahead. He had just wanted to *do* something. He spoke cautiously. 'I was looking for her. Because you were providing no help whatsoever. You weren't even answering your—'

'And you risked her life in the process.'

'Look, I didn't *plan* to—'

Monk raised a hand to silence him. There were calluses along its edge, and lining the points of his fingers. 'What you *planned* is not the issue. The issue is consequences.'

'But those goons of yours—'

'They stay. My world, Matthew. My methods. My associates. That is, unless you think you can get her back on your own.'

'I want to meet them,' he said. 'I want to know who they are, and exactly what they are doing.' He didn't add that it was only by meeting them that he might be able to satisfy himself that shadowy underworld figures would not come back to haunt him in years to come.

'Reasonable,' Monk answered. 'But unlikely to be possible.'

'Now, you listen, Monk—'

Monk shook his head gently. 'I'll ask,' he said. 'I just can't promise.'

Matthew stared at him hotly, still unsure what game Monk was playing – or if he was playing one at all.

Monk's phone rang, and he snapped it to his ear, saying nothing. He listened for a moment then rang off. He shrugged at Matthew. 'They lost the car.'

Matthew let the news sink in. They hadn't really stood a chance.

'What now?' he said at last.

Monk gestured towards the kitchen. 'We wait.'

'But the money—'

'Ring and tell him you have raised some more. Not enough, but some.'

'But I haven't. I can't. And he—'

Monk leaned closer, radiating heat. 'The kitchen, Matthew. Then the call. Then we wait.'

Matthew froze in the kitchen doorway. On the kitchen table was a neat pile of cash, about the size of one or two hefty paperbacks. 'What . . . ? How did . . . ?'

Over his shoulder, Monk said, 'Twenty-five thousand, Matthew. As I said, my associates can be quite helpful when they choose.'

Matthew became aware that his mouth was flapping, as he tried to frame a reply. He stopped himself, breathed slowly and deliberately, tried to focus. Eventually, he said, 'You can't do this, Monk. I can't accept this.'

Because where would this end? He would become the hostage if he took the money, subject to a lifetime of blackmail by . . . who? A lifetime, though: that was more than Charlotte could expect. He shook his head firmly, but his voice wavered. 'Get it out of here.'

Monk slipped past him into the room. 'Leaving aside the minor issue of saving your wife's life, may I ask what makes you think this has anything to do with you? This money is a favour to me, not to you. For you, I doubt my . . . friend would do anything. And the plan is to get it back anyway.'

Matthew was dimly aware of looking confused again. Monk's impassive features twitched slightly. 'It goes like this,' he said. 'You offer the money. Someone has to come and collect it. When they do, we follow.' This time, the twitch was definitely a smile. 'We're good at following.'

Matthew muttered bitterly, 'And *we* means who, exactly?' But he stared at the money. It was a small neat block, and it meant so many things. It meant that Monk had broken into his house while he was out at Heathrow – and what could he do about it? Go to the police? It meant Monk's friends were rich and, presumably, powerful. It meant a choice between signing Charlotte's death warrant and ending up in debt, financially and morally, to some person he'd never met, and whose involvement had been brokered by a man he didn't trust. What kind of a choice was that?

An obvious one. Save Charlotte. Worry about the future later.

Monk's mild gaze followed him as he paced the room. 'If you fuck this up,' he ground out at last, 'I'll kill you.'

Not that he could, of course. Monk could flatten him with a finger.

Monk had the grace not to laugh. 'The call, Matthew,' he said gently. 'Ring him.'

He nodded, and headed across the room towards the phone – then froze. Em was walking down the hall towards the kitchen. She stopped in the doorway, staring open-mouthed. She took in his haggard appearance. She took in the money on the table, and her eyes widened. Then she took in the motionless figure of Monk.

'Who the fuck,' she said calmly, 'is that?'

Twenty-Seven

He started to speak. Stuttered. Found nothing to say.

He should have told her at the beginning. Except, how could he ever have been sure of the actions of a hormonal teenager? It seemed insane that he had thrown himself on the mercy of a known criminal – and yet he couldn't trust his own daughter.

Em looked from him to Monk and back again, her tear-streaked face pale in the weak afternoon light that filtered into the kitchen. 'Yeah. Whatever,' she muttered.

As she left, she slammed the kitchen door behind her. Matthew groaned and lowered his head into his hands.

Monk broke the silence, his voice flat and unemotional. 'You should not make her suffer, Matthew. She is in pain.' He fingered a bracelet as he spoke – blue string, with some kind of bead.

'Fuck off,' Matthew snapped – and was disturbed to find that he didn't entirely mean it. Monk's accusation was a fair one. Em was his daughter.

'There are things you can do,' Monk said, 'and things you cannot. You cannot find and save your wife.' He waited, as though his point was clear. When Matthew didn't respond, he went on. 'I cannot talk to your daughter for you.'

Again, true – and unbearable.

Reluctantly, he dragged himself upright and confronted Monk. 'If you're playing games here, I'll . . .' Monk stared back at him, unruffled. Matthew's glare cooled, then wavered. Then he trudged up the stairs.

For once, there was no music.

'Em?'

'Go away!'

'I need to talk to you.'

'Leave me *alone*!'

He cracked the door open, enough to signal that he wasn't going away, but not enough that he could see in. Privacy was important to her.

'Just a few minutes,' he said gently.

'Dad, go *away*!'

He waited.

'*Oh* . . .' He heard her thump across the room. She ripped the door open and confronted him, with a surly expression on her face, and a teddy bear in one hand. 'What?'

On the dressing table, a candle glowed in the blue bowl she loved so much. The bowl Rachel had given her. Looking at her defiant, unhappy face, he felt helpless. He could see her pain – they had both lived with it for years – but, even now, he had no idea how to reach her.

He said, 'Can I come in?'

She favoured him with an exaggerated groan, then turned and flung herself onto her bed. He perched on a corner and tried to smile at her.

'Bad day?'

She threw a cushion across the room. 'Patch is a bitch. I hate her.'

'Is it . . . ?' He faltered. He wasn't good at this, even after fourteen years, even after the pain they had shared. How had the gulf got so wide? 'You . . . you miss her, don't you?'

'Miss who?'

'Charlotte.'

Em pouted. 'Let me guess,' she muttered. 'The bloke's a private eye. She's left us. Like, *big* shock. Like, I hadn't even *spotted* that all that stuff about her friend is bullshit.'

'Em . . .' He reached towards her, and she pulled away. He drew his hand back, feeling hurt, and knowing he had no right to. She glowered at the bowl. It glowed under the candlelight, a bright blue smear in a room dulled by a hazy afternoon.

'It's me,' she said, 'isn't it?'

'Listen, poppet—'

'She hates me.'

Perhaps, under other circumstances, he could have laughed; but all he could see was pain. His, hers. Charlotte's. In a way, they had been here before.

'Em, she loves you,' he whispered. 'She loves us both.' He reached again across the bed towards her. She froze, and he withdrew.

'Hasn't stopped her leaving, though, has it?'

'Em, she loves you. She does.'

'Yeah, *right*. That must be why she shouts at me.'

'But—' He stopped. How had he let this happen? Had she always felt this unhappy? When had he stopped noticing? And when had he stopped trusting her?

And look who he was trusting in her place.

'Em, there's something I have to tell you. It's about Charlotte. I . . . I lied to you. Well, you'd worked that out. But she hasn't left us, I swear. It's—' He broke off, fighting a rush of unhelpful emotion. 'Ah . . . She's, ah . . .' His hands were shaking. He studied them, transfixed by the fact that he couldn't stop them.

'Dad?'

He dragged his gaze up to meet hers. Her expression was puzzled and concerned – but not fragile. She looked . . . strong. How had he never noticed that in her? Whatever the reason, he was grateful for it.

He told her.

The details took time. Em broke in with questions, and he allowed her to. It was a relief to unburden himself, even if it was to a fourteen-year-old girl who couldn't possibly help in any way.

He studied her earnestly. 'The main thing is, you have to promise not to tell a soul. Especially not the police.'

'Why can't—'

'*Promise* me, Em.'

'But if they—'

'*Em!* No police, OK? It's not up for discussion.' She looked hurt. He hadn't wanted to go here. 'Poppet, you remember when your mum died?' Her eyes flicked to the candle in the bowl. He sighed. '*Afterwards*,' he persisted. 'When the police said it was me.'

'Dad, that's got nothing to do with—'

'Em, it *has*. They were so busy trying to prove foul play that they never really *saw* the situation at all. They nearly had you put in care, poppet. Not because it was the right thing, but because it was the standard procedure. That's how they work. Paperwork first. Doing what needs to be done comes second.' He waved his hands, agitated. She had to understand this. How could he make this clear? 'Em, imagine Rachel hadn't drowned. Say *she'd* disappeared. How long would it have been before they got up off their arses and started actually looking for her?' Em opened her mouth to answer. He rode over her. '*Days,* Em. Days and days. Because that's how they do it, that's the procedure. And if you want them to do more, then you get the standard lecture: they haven't the time, there aren't the resources.'

'But—' Em's voice was a squeak.

He was on his feet. 'Come *on*, poppet. You *saw* them on Monday night.' Bitterly, he mimicked them. 'She'll be back tomorrow, Mr Daniels. Had you been arguing, Mr Daniels? Let's just leave it a few days, Mr Daniels, while we process the fucking *forms.*'

She was staring at him as though he were a stranger. He flapped his hands uselessly, then sat next to her again. It was an effort to stay calm. 'If some tart from nowhere can just step into the house, looking nothing like her, and fool them into thinking it's all over, then what's the point?'

Em stared at him, contemplating losing her temper. 'Great. It's like, we can't tell the police, so then you just tell this *guy*?'

He couldn't explain – because she was fourteen. He could tell her the truth about herself, and she would deny it, even if her life depended on it. The truth was that she lied when it suited her. If she was excited or angry – which was a lot of the time – or simply unaware. She had proved, time and again, that she was unreliable, untrustworthy and unpredictable. It wasn't her fault: it was her age and her hormones. If someone put enough pressure on her – if she was sulking for some reason, if someone teased her enough – then she would tell. If he explained this to her, she would accuse him of being unfair, but this wasn't about fairness. As Monk had made unpleasantly clear, it was about consequences.

He sighed, and was horribly aware that the gesture was patronising. 'Em, we're dealing with very dangerous people.'

Em glared at the carpet. 'Patch's dad was in the SAS. She told me. He could help.'

His response was more reflex than thought. '*No!*' The hunted look in her eyes melted him immediately. 'Poppet, we can't tell anyone.'

'But—'

'*No one*,' he insisted. 'If anyone gets wind of this,' he explained gently, 'anyone at all – then they'll kill her.'

When she answered, her voice was small and afraid. 'Patch says—'

'No one, Em. You can't talk to her. You can't talk to anyone. Come to think of it, you can't even go to school. We'll ring you in sick.'

She was pleased at that – for a moment. Then she said sharply, 'Yeah, *great*! So, like, now you don't trust me? *Thanks*, Dad.'

'Em, I do trust you. It's just . . .'

'Yeah,' she muttered. 'Whatever.'

He pressed his advantage. 'And no phone calls either.'

A shifty look crept over her. He could see her calculating her options. Exasperated, he held out his hand. She studied it, knowing what it meant: he wanted her mobile.

'Oh, *great*!' she snapped. She snatched the phone from her bedside table and slapped it into his hand. He pocketed it, and thanked her, as gently as he could.

There was silence. He stared at the candle flame, and knew that she was doing the same. The flame was a dim, swollen light. A thin line of dark smoke rose from it. Beneath, the shards of stone that were set into the bowl glittered and seemed to shift in the unsteady glow. It was a new candle. It stood high and proud, unblemished except for one trickle of wax down its flank.

'Will we get her back?' Em said at last. For that one moment, her voice was as small as a six year old's.

'I . . .' He couldn't answer.

'*Feuhl*,' she muttered. Her way of seeking contact.

He smiled at her sadly. 'Yes. I am.'

They said nothing for a long time. Eventually Em asked, 'What about the baby?' Again, he had no answer for her.

Suddenly, Em screamed, and scrambled away from him into a corner. Instinctively, he jumped to his feet, searching for the danger. In front of them stood Monk. There had been no noise; one moment, the room had held just the two of them, the next he was standing several feet inside the door.

He gazed impassively at Matthew. 'He'll see you,' he said.

'Monk, you *have* to stop—'

'My associate. The one you wanted to know about. He will see you. Now.'

Matthew contemplated pursuing his line; the fool had terrified Em half out of her wits. But it would accomplish nothing.

'Now?'

Monk didn't answer him. Instead, he transferred his attention to Em, who whimpered and shrank as far away from him as she could.

'I'm sorry,' he said, his voice oddly hoarse and faltering. 'I . . . scared you. I wouldn't . . . I'd never . . .' Hesitantly, he reached a hand out towards her. A pale shell dangled from his wrist.

She yelled, '*Get away from me!*' and clawed at Matthew's arm.

The man froze, then nodded and took a few steps backwards, fingering his bracelet uncertainly. He turned his attention to Matthew. 'The phone call. It's time. Where does he want the money?'

Em was still clinging tightly to Matthew, her wide eyes fixed on Monk. He sighed. 'Give us five minutes, Monk. Then I'll make the call, and we can go.' Monk nodded again, almost imperceptibly, and withdrew.

Em clung to Matthew and sobbed. He held her tight, and whispered to her that everything would be OK – knowing that, in all probability, he was lying.

'He's scary,' Em said, when her crying had subsided.

He kissed the top of her head. 'He scares me too.' He wrapped his arms even tighter around her. She rested her head on his chest. He stared over her hair at the candle. 'Love you, Em,' he whispered. She pressed closer, her eyes shut. He felt her jolt gently under his arm – a last, small sob.

A thin line of smoke twisted through the room, and the flame, cupped in blue, wove an unreadable pattern in the air. After a while he asked her, and himself, 'Am I doing the right thing?'

His daughter didn't reply.

Twenty-Eight

'Fulham,' Monk said, leaning into the taxi window. The driver nodded. Monk scanned the street before climbing into the back. Matthew gave Em the front seat, and sat directly behind her.

It was not surprising that she'd hated Monk on sight. An hour ago, she had thought that perhaps Matthew was lying to her about Charlotte's friend's illness. She had thought that, at worst, Charlotte had walked out on them. Now she knew that Charlotte had been abducted, and that this unsettling and dangerous man was all that stood between them and disaster. If Matthew was uncomfortable with him then, to her, his presence must seem like insanity.

'Fulham?' Matthew asked incredulously. You would be more likely to meet a banker there than a gangster.

Monk, impassive as always, stared straight ahead. 'Fulham,' he repeated. The driver chewed his gum expressionlessly, glanced at them in the mirror, wall-eyed, and set off. Behind them, a white Ford Escort pulled out and followed.

Monk had the money in a plastic bag on his lap. The man hadn't answered any of Matthew's increasingly desperate messages and texts. When the taxi driver had rung the doorbell, Matthew had buried his head in his hands. Because, if the man wouldn't even take the money then it was over, wasn't it? Monk did not think so. 'We take it with us,' he said. Then, when Matthew ignored him, he had leaned closer. 'Byron doesn't wait.'

In the taxi, no one spoke. Monk had made it clear that silence was preferable. In particular, he'd said, if the name Byron Washington was mentioned, he would stop the car, climb out, and they would never see him again. Em had looked at Matthew frantically, as though she might change something by communicating her alarm to him; but he was alarmed himself, and her distress changed nothing.

He didn't expect Em to understand. That was why she was with them: now that she knew, the only safe place for her to be was wherever he was. If he left her alone, she might take it into her head to call the police, or Patch's dad, who had surely never been anywhere near the SAS, whatever Patch claimed, or . . . She might do anything. If she had a feeling, she acted on it. It wasn't her fault. Mature consideration was not one of her strengths.

They were somewhere near Notting Hill when Monk leaned forward and dangled a twenty-pound note over the driver's shoulder. 'Here is fine.'

The driver eyed the money suspiciously. 'But you said—'

'Here,' Monk said firmly. He let the note drop onto the man's lap.

'Suit yourself,' the man said, and pulled over.

'Out,' Monk said to them. 'Now.'

The driver fished under the dashboard for his wallet. 'Hang on. It's fifteen to here. Got a fiver somewhere.'

'Keep it,' Monk said, and slammed the door. The driver didn't wait to make sure he meant it.

Monk pointed to a side road a few yards further on. 'There.' Meekly, they headed for it. Before they were halfway down the road, the white Escort roared up alongside. The passenger leaned back and threw open the rear door. 'In,' Monk said tersely.

'Dad?' Em sounded terrified.

'We'll be fine, poppet.' He wasn't sure he believed that – or that he cared.

Had Charlotte been taken this easily? Had she willingly, blindly, got into a car full of dangerous-looking strangers? He ushered Em ahead of him, and followed close behind, to act as a barrier between her and Monk.

The moment Monk was in, before he had even closed the door, the car set off, fast, throwing Matthew half on top of Em. Monk, somehow, stayed upright, swaying very slightly as the car took a corner at speed.

'Were you followed?' he asked calmly.

The passenger turned to glance at him. He had pale brown skin, bloodshot eyes and gap teeth. 'Didn't see no one, man. You cool?'

Monk didn't answer. He leaned back, apparently satisfied. Em yelped as they hit the next corner at forty or more. The tyres squealed as they scraped round it, and the car's tail smacked against a parked BMW, setting off its alarm. The passenger chuckled. The driver grinned, chewing gum. 'Yeah, mon,' he murmured, to himself, and pressed down harder on the accelerator. Em shrieked. The driver flashed yellow eyes at her in the mirror and grinned again. He was enjoying scaring her.

Monk leaned forward and said softly, 'Slow.'

The man glanced at him. 'Fuck no, man, Byron said—'

'*Slow*,' Monk repeated. His voice was quiet, but it didn't invite discussion. The driver spared him one more glance, calculating his chances, then he slowed. Monk twisted past Matthew to peer at Em. 'They get excited,' he said. 'But we did have to move fast. It looks as though no one followed us, but the only way to be sure is to be unpredictable.' He settled back. 'These days,' he said, half to himself, 'it seems that means fast.'

Matthew laughed bitterly. 'As if it matters who's following us now.'

Monk frowned at him. 'It does.'

'Oh, wake up, Monk! The man hasn't contacted me for over a day. In case I need to spell it out to you, that means—'

'What it means, Matthew, is that we don't know the situation at the moment. But we didn't know it before either, did we?'

'That's not the point.'

'I think it is.'

Em screamed, loudly, to get their attention, then reduced her voice to a simple yell. 'Grow *up*! Dad, do you *know* it's over?' He opened his mouth to reply, but she ignored him. 'Do you? No. You couldn't know, could you?' She slumped back in her seat. 'Well, then.'

Monk was staring at her. For a moment, Matthew thought he detected something troubled in his face; then a smile appeared, and turned to ice.

'There are reasons, Matthew,' he said. 'Explanations. What if he is somewhere where he can't respond? He might not have the phone with him. Perhaps he has relayed the information to someone else, and now he's waiting.' Although he was already wedged tight against Matthew, he managed somehow to lean closer. His words had an edge as hard as a blade's. 'If you fail to fight, Matthew, you fail completely. The man who risks killing her is you.'

Matthew looked away uneasily, and muttered, 'If she's not already—'

Em punched him in the ribs. After that, they travelled in silence. It began to rain and the streets blurred by.

They were heading roughly south. It was already nearing five o'clock: if they didn't arrive soon, they would be caught by the rush hour. The traffic was already thickening on Vauxhall Bridge as they crossed the river.

'Not Fulham, then,' he said to Monk. One of the men in front laughed.

'Brixton,' Monk replied tersely.

It made more sense; it was a rougher area, which made it a more natural home for the two thugs in the front – and for Byron Washington, their boss, whoever he might turn out to be. Em looked about her wildly. He gripped her hand, and shook it gently. 'Sorry,' he murmured. 'It's just . . .'

It was all the reassurance he could offer.

They had just passed the Oval Cricket Ground when Monk's mobile rang. He held it to his ear without speaking. His face was a shadow. 'Say again.' Then, after a pause, 'Thirty-two. Yes.'

He cut the line, and leaned forward to tell the driver, 'Sudcroft Road. On the corner.' The driver nodded. His companion flicked through an *A to Z*.

It took ten minutes to get there. The car pulled up just before the corner, and stayed there when they got out. Monk led them round the corner along the edge of the housing estate that took up one side of the road, a wall of dulled brick, studded with mean windows, and broken only by narrow alleys that sank away from the road. On the other side of the road was a school behind high fencing, and a row of tiny terraced cottages with boarded windows.

Halfway along the road a group of boys sat on a wall in the rain, with their hoods up and the heels of their over-large trainers bouncing off the wall. One of the boys called, 'Yo, bro,' followed by a stream of words in a deliberately exaggerated West Indian accent. It was aimed at Monk, but it was clearly about Matthew, or – he shuddered – Em. He gripped her hand tighter, and felt her lean closer to him.

Monk waved at them to stop, and approached the boys himself. He stood in front of them, perfectly relaxed and completely silent. One of them made a joke, and the others sniggered. Two of them swung off the wall, and sauntered round behind him. Monk stayed motionless. The boy immediately in front of him – the one who had called out – hopped down and faced him, cracking his knuckles and hulking his shoulders. He was at least a foot taller than Monk. He said something indecipherable – and suddenly there was a knife in his hand. He waved it in front of Monk's face. It wove from side to side, glittering in the street's damp light.

Monk reached out, and took it from him. There was no effort, no struggle; Monk's hand extended – and suddenly he had the knife. The movement seemed as natural as a handshake. The boy yelled in surprise. Monk studied the weapon idly, shaking his head as though he was astonished that anyone could consider such a poor choice.

The boy lunged for the knife. Without looking up, Monk flicked his free hand idly outwards towards the boy's chest. He jolted back and smashed hard into the wall. Monk ignored him. The others circled him, wary now, but scenting a fight.

Monk cocked his head, then grinned, and handed the knife back to the boy he had just brushed away. He snatched it, and held it nervously in front of him, unsure what to do next.

'Yeah, man,' he said, trying to sound cocky. 'You know it.' The others laughed softly, circling.

'Go away,' Monk advised softly. 'Now.'

To Matthew's complete astonishment, the boys complied. First one, then another: they stretched tall in front of him, fixed him with their eyes, then drifted away, weaving down the street on high white shoes, their shoulders jostling as the pack reformed, and vanished into the darkness of an alley.

Monk beckoned for them to join him. He muttered, 'Kids.'

Fifty yards further on, there was a narrow doorway with *BLOCK B 26–50* stamped onto a metal plate by the door, and a row of numbered buzzers. He pushed number thirty-two. The lock hummed, and they went in.

The flat was on the second floor. They climbed a concrete stairway with a black metal rail. The gritty sound of their footsteps echoed through otherwise silent halls.

'Not his actual place,' Monk said over his shoulder. 'He's borrowed it specially.'

There was a man at the door. A big man. He held them in front of him long enough for them to register his oppressive bulk, then stood aside.

A man waited in the room they were ushered into. He was tall, with an immaculate suit and a sombre face, and he gazed at Monk with an expression of mild annoyance. Another huge bodyguard stood against one wall, making the cramped room feel even smaller – but it was the man in the centre of the room that held Matthew's attention. His skin was the colour of darkened butter. His lips were pursed and pointed. Expensive cufflinks peeped out from his suit sleeves; and behind his fine-rimmed glasses, wise eyes surveyed them all with controlled curiosity.

Monk said nothing.

'Not even an introduction!' The man laughed, and his face widened into a boyish grin. His teeth were perfectly even, and brilliant white. He leaned forward and extended a hand towards Matthew, who took it, reluctantly. The man said, 'Byron Washington. Monk tells me you're not happy with what I've been doing for you.'

Washington looked, and sounded, more like a businessman than a gangster. True, his suit was a little over-sharp; but his poise and grooming suggested very expensive habits. He had sophisticated taste, and an accent to match. He watched Matthew assess him, with an expression of wry amusement.

'Never judge a book by its cover, Mr Daniels. You of all people should know that.'

'If you're suggesting—'

Washington laughed. 'You have a stereotype of what someone like me should be, Mr Daniels. Have the grace to admit that much. I don't fit that mould.' He gestured at a chair. 'Please.'

'Dad?' Em sounder nervous and uncertain. He wasn't surprised. He was scared himself. He smiled weakly at her, and sat. She perched on the arm of his chair, eyeing the massive bodyguard uncertainly.

Washington glided to a chair opposite and folded himself elegantly into it. Monk remained standing.

Washington smiled at the bodyguard. 'Thank you, Tyrell.' The man glared at Monk, then left.

'Mr Daniels, first, let me apologise for the crude accommodation. It is not how I normally entertain. Well, to be blunt, I would not normally choose to spend time with a prison governor and his daughter' – he smiled at Em; she bridled – 'at all. I thought it would be best to meet on neutral territory.'

He gestured at the room. The three armchairs didn't match. Two of them had wooden arms, and seats covered with clashing tones of orange. The third chair was covered with ripped brown corduroy, and had huge rounded wing arms that filled one corner of the room. The carpet was dark and had a florid design in swirls a foot or two across. The still air smelled of candle wax and raw meat.

'Not my taste at all, Mr Daniels, I do assure you,' Washington purred. 'In fact, its usual occupants have no idea that we're here.'

Nudged by the memory of something he had half-noticed as they came in, Matthew twisted in his seat and squinted back into the hallway. The architrave of the front door was splintered: fresh wood showed in shards through the cracked paint.

'The point is, Mr Daniels,' Washington continued cheerfully, 'that I haven't been here – and neither have you. And, most especially, we have not met. We never will.' He scowled suddenly. 'You have caused me a great deal of inconvenience, Mr Daniels. Or perhaps I should say that Monk has.'

Monk stayed immobile, but his presence suddenly seemed to fill the room. 'The point, Byron,' he said softly, 'is that they *are* here.'

Byron Washington scowled at him. 'True.' He turned his attention to Matthew again. 'Monk tells me that the issue is trust, Mr Daniels. I am sure that you find it difficult to accept that Monk here is acting in your best interests.' He smiled coldly. 'You wouldn't be the first.' He leaned back in the chair, sampled the fabric with the tips of his fingers, and pursed his lips disdainfully. 'And now,' he went on reflectively, 'you are being asked to trust a colleague of his. A partner in crime.'

He fixed Matthew with a mild gaze.

'That *is* how it appears to you, isn't it, Mr Daniels? You look at me and you see the devil in an expensive suit. But however I dress, however I behave, in your eyes I will always be just another criminal, as rough and dangerous as them all.'

'Worse,' Matthew muttered. 'At least with Monk . . .'

Washington hunched forwards suddenly, elbows on knees, his fingers steepled. '. . . you can control him? But I don't think you can. Do you? He chose to come straight to me, after all – and I am sure that was not what you had in mind at all.'

Matthew shifted in his uncomfortable chair. Washington had a point. The difference was that he had *chosen* Monk, and he was just one man. Washington was an unwelcome extra, he came with a mob of henchmen, and was, he suspected, far more dangerous than Monk. He also had money. Until a couple of hours ago, that might even have been a point in his favour.

He felt in his pocket for his mobile. It was still there – and still silent.

Washington was talking again. 'I could spin you a yarn, Mr Daniels. About how, if I didn't do what I do, someone else would – someone *bad*. I could argue that I keep the peace in places where the police fear to tread. It's me or it's anarchy. Did you know that, Mr Daniels?'

There was a tightness about his eyes. His arms were rigid beneath the costly fabric of his suit. A muscle ticked in his jaw. He sucked his teeth reflectively, took a heavy breath, and sighed it out.

'But that is irrelevant. So is the issue of whether you can control Monk or not. So is the fact that your little friend has not called you back. It would have helped us if he had, but there are other ways to find your wife.' That piqued Matthew's interest. Washington waved away his words. 'But that is not why you wanted to see me. You came here to find out whether you can control me. It's not every day that someone delivers twenty-five grand in cash to your door, is it? And I am delighted to be able to tell you, Mr Daniels, that you *cannot* control me, not in the slightest. I will do exactly as I see fit.'

'Then there's nothing left to talk about, is there?' Matthew stood abruptly, angry enough to ignore the bodyguard who took several steps towards him before Washington stopped him with a single raised finger. Em stood, too, clinging to his arm. 'You stay the hell away from us,' he snapped. 'And your goons. Call them off immediately. I want you out of this completely.' He shot at Monk, 'You too, *David*. Forget it.' Em was tugging uneasily at his arm. He patted her hand, and said, 'We'll take our chances. Come on.'

He turned to leave – but there was a bodyguard in the doorway, and he didn't stand aside. Monk remained motionless, his expression sphinx-like.

Behind him, Washington said, 'I have no interest at all in whether *you* want me out or in, Mr Daniels. I am helping Monk here, not you.' He gestured languidly at the chair. 'Please sit. I haven't finished.'

The guard at the door seemed to swell slightly, radiating threat. Hesitantly, Matthew guided Em back to the chair, suddenly very frightened indeed.

Washington smiled brightly at them both. 'Thank you. Now, let me make a few things clear.' He leaned back and rubbed his chin thoughtfully. 'First, I would ask you to remember that it was my men who warned Monk when you strayed around Heathrow. In effect, I prevented you from killing your own wife.' He laced his fingers and cracked his knuckles loudly, peering over the top of them at Matthew. 'We are doing everything that we can to return her safely to you.'

Matthew spat, 'How do you know she's even—'

Washington waved him to silence. 'She's an asset. Only a psychotic would throw away an asset.' His lips twitched at some private joke. 'Mr Daniels, I have a question for you. When did you . . . *throw away* Monk? When did he stop being an asset to you?'

Matthew gaped at him. Was he genuinely suggesting that there was some kind of similarity between Monk and Charlotte? Washington continued, leaving him still groping for words. 'Oh, I know all about it, Mr Daniels. How he helped you; then, when he got attacked for it, and had to defend himself, you punished him, revised your parole recommendation.' He scowled at Matthew over his glasses. 'I have to say, it gives me great pleasure to see you suffering now.'

Em was staring first at Matthew, then at Washington, visibly torn between distrust of this man, and horror at what he was saying.

'It wasn't like that,' Matthew snapped.

Washington laughed. 'Oh, I agree that it wasn't like that for *you*, Mr Daniels. But then, you weren't the victim, were you? You weren't the one who suffered, and had to take it, because you were powerless to change it. It was your world, not his. And Monk is, shall we say, naïve when it comes to matters of power. He has a nasty tendency to trust people. He wants the world to be a better place than you and I both know it to be.' Washington's smile was no longer there as he fixed Matthew with a stare and added, 'He trusted you. You took advantage. In all honesty, I would have, too.'

'I—'

Washington slapped his hands down hard on the arm of his chair. 'Enough!' Briefly, his face hardened into a contorted mask; then, in moments, he recovered his composure. He chuckled softly to himself, shaking his head.

'You do know Monk was innocent, don't you, Mr Daniels? He didn't commit that murder.'

'Don't be ridiculous,' Matthew spat. 'The courts—'

'He *allowed* himself to be convicted,' Washington snapped. Then he added, more softly, 'To protect a friend. A brother.'

Matthew didn't reply. Washington stood, heavily, his hands pressing down on his thighs, and paced around Monk, as though he were a statue. Monk bore the inspection impassively. Washington gave a contemplative hum, and moved towards Em and Matthew, whom he assessed with a long, cool gaze. He was a slight man, but he towered over Matthew. The chair was saggy, and he felt trapped in it. Washington carried a waft of dry aftershave with him. His clothes smelled now.

'You see, Mr Daniels, unlike you, Monk has compassion. He sees in other people the pain he himself has suffered in the past. If someone turns away from him, he learns the importance of steadfast-ness. If someone hurts him, he learns the importance of kindness.' He pursed his lips. 'Now, if you had crossed *me*, it would have been very different.' Washington registered his unease, and smiled in satisfaction. 'Except in a way, it *was* me you crossed. Monk and I are . . . close.'

Matthew felt pinned by the man's stare. The menace in his words was palpable. He was very aware that he might not get out of this room unharmed.

'Em has nothing to do with this,' he croaked. 'Please, there's been enough . . .' He couldn't find words. At last, he said weakly, 'She's suffered enough.' Washington looked down on him, his eyes creased in amusement.

Suddenly Monk was next to them. He didn't touch Washington, but he stood so close that Washington started backwards before gaining control of himself. With his gaze locked on Washington, Monk slowly extended one arm, and turned it so that Washington could see the wrist. Matthew noticed, beneath the shell on its blue thread, a hard white scar.

Washington made a show of contemplating the arm. Then he nodded subtly – and Monk moved away.

Washington turned again to Matthew. 'Perhaps your daughter *has* suffered enough, Mr Daniels. But what concerns me is: have you?' He waved a hand wearily, and returned to his seat. 'Perhaps,' he said, 'perhaps not. Time will tell.'

He studied the sleeve of his jacket, and picked at a fleck of lint.

'Monk could never have helped you on his own,' he said at last. 'I have resources. He does not.'

'Oh, who *cares*?' Em had leapt to her feet and was standing, red-faced. Matthew twisted round in surprise. Tendons stood out on her neck and arms. 'Charlotte's *dying* somewhere, she might even be dead. And you're busy giving lectures! You're – you're – *useless*!' She glowered at Washington, who regarded her mildly. Then she slumped back into the chair, arms crossed, and muttered, 'Oh, what's the point?'

Washington thought for a while. At last, he said, 'We've wasted enough time here already. I am telling you this to prevent you doing something stupid like going back to the police.' He gazed at Matthew mildly. 'If you do, you will be getting me involved with them, too. And I assure you, Mr Daniels, that would have unfortunate consequences. Do we understand each other?'

Appalled but powerless, Matthew nodded.

Washington smiled coldly. 'Very well. This is what is happening. I have had people tailing you ever since Monk spotted a silver-windowed car following you. If it turns up again, my men will . . . let's say, *discuss* the situation with its owner. In addition, we have persuaded a member of the Met to trace the car's number plate. We should hear back tomorrow. Another member of the Met has kindly agreed – at some expense to me, I might add – to trace where your wife's mobile calls are being made from. With luck, it will turn out to be a small enough cell to allow us to start a search. Again, we won't know for a day or two. Plus, as you know, we put up enough cash to keep your man interested – at least, so we thought.' He spread his arms. 'We only started our enquiries this morning, and already we're making progress. Is it more than you could have accomplished alone, Mr Daniels? I'd say so, wouldn't you?'

'Progress is getting her back,' Matthew said hotly. His anger was obvious. Washington ignored it.

'Also, my men have been asking questions. Putting out word amongst people who might know.' He shrugged. 'That, too, takes time.'

He rose, signalling that their meeting was over. 'My men will see you home, Mr Daniels. We will not be meeting again. I hope that you will have your wife back in due course. Until then, I suggest you spend your time contemplating this: responsibility is the price of another person's trust.'

Matthew had had enough. 'What the fuck's that supposed to mean?'

Washington smiled. 'For now, Mr Daniels, it means goodbye.'

When they stood, Monk drifted over to join them. Matthew bit back his instinct to turn him away. He was powerless to keep the man away. He was powerless to do anything.

Byron Washington stood, too, waiting for them to leave.

Matthew gazed at Monk's unmoving face with barely disguised fury. 'So if you didn't kill that man, who did?'

Monk did not answer, Washington did. His smile did not slip for an instant.

He said, 'It wouldn't help you to know.'

Home, he made sandwiches for himself and Em, from bread that was already stale. They ate in silence.

Monk had parted from them on the doorstep, after a wordless journey. 'I will be watching,' he had said. Somehow, Matthew had not found the idea reassuring.

When they finished, Em scooped up their plates and dumped them in the sink before sitting again, her chin in her hands, scowling. 'Fuck them,' she said at last. 'Go to the police. We have to.'

It was a seductive idea. In contrast to an underworld gang led by an uncontrollable man with some obscure grievance, the police were saving angels. But . . .

He sighed, utterly depleted. 'Em, we *can't*. Those were threats he was making, poppet. He could do terrible things to us if we crossed him – and I think he would.'

'What, worse than losing Charlotte because you trusted some geezer from the Brixton mafia?'

'Em, believe me, I'd love to. But we can't risk it. The first thing he'd do is make sure we lost Charlotte anyway. What if we got her back then one of his goons shot her a week later?'

Em slumped across the other side of the table, her face a mixture of anger, fear and disgust – and he knew that, in a way, she was right. When had the last fragments of control slipped away from him? Was it when he had asked Monk for help? Earlier, perhaps, when he had allowed that woman to put off the police. But, at the time, he had been holding in his hand the print-out from Charlotte's last scan. He had only been trying to save their child. Back then, even losing Charlotte hadn't seemed likely. And now . . . What might Byron Washington do to them all if they didn't cooperate? He might lose Em, too. For a man like that, there were no boundaries.

Looking at her, he felt the same helpless love for his daughter that he had felt in the years after Rachel died, watching her sleep, keenly aware of the world's casual brutality – when he had sworn that no harm would ever come to her, that she was safe with him, even if her mother had not been.

Em fidgeted under his gaze. '*What?*'

'Nothing. Just . . . I'm sorry, Em.'

'Dad, it's not too late. We could still go to the police. We—'

'*No*, Em!' He could see the clouds gathering, and moved to prevent the storm. 'Look, poppet, with this guy at least we have a chance. If we go to the police, then *he'll* kill her even if the police do find her. I don't like it any more than you, and I know it's my fault, but we're stuck with him.'

'But—'

'No buts. He's a dangerous man. We can't afford to cross him.'

She lapsed into silence, tracing the table's wood grain with a finger.

Satisfied that they had reached a truce for now, he fished out his mobile, and texted:

Please just talk

He tried ringing again. Nothing.

He settled to wait, suddenly haunted by an unwelcome thought. Yes, Byron Washington was dangerous. But he had also been . . . angry. Hadn't he?

Twenty-Nine

The man came towards the end of the afternoon. She heard his feet in the corridor and scrambled away from the door to what remained of the bed, frightened – and also relieved. She was still in terrible danger – she hadn't forgotten what he intended to do to her – but this way there was at least a chance.

She had her weapon. It was hidden behind the bed. She didn't have much of a plan, but it would have to do because it was all she had got. In all its glorious detail, the plan went: sit on the bed, let him get close, fish out the stick while he wasn't looking, and whack him with it. Miraculously, this would result in immediate and prolonged unconsciousness. She would grab the keys from his pocket and make good her escape. In a building she didn't know. Pursued by a man who *did* know it – and who was likely to be very, very cross.

But she had to try. For Eyelash, if not for Matthew. She had a scan this Friday that she couldn't afford to miss.

She squatted on the floor next to the bed. Her back was to the wall, and the handle end of the stick poked a few inches out from behind the bed on her right. If she tried to swing it from there, it would snag on the bed as it came out, or on the covers. In the few seconds she had, she pulled the weapon out of its hiding place, and shifted her position round ninety degrees so that she was bent double with her head on her hands, resting on the bed's end. The stick dangled from one hand, concealed from the door by the bed. She moaned – convincingly, she hoped.

It was all she could think of.

He was at the door. She ignored him, and moaned louder. She rocked back and forth for effect, and scrabbled for a better grip on the end of the spar. The key clattered in the lock, and she heard him come into the room.

'Did you miss me, then?' She could imagine his strange eyes, the sharp tendons in his neck.

She stayed as she was, moaning. Let him think she was ill, desperately ill. He wouldn't hurt her if she was ill. He would come closer to check how she was . . . and then—

He laughed. 'Trying to pull a sickie, are you? Think the boss won't let me touch you if you're sick?' He came closer, too close. He crouched behind her. She felt his hands in her hair, not stroking, tugging, wrapping it in his fingers. 'Got news for you, doll,' he whispered. 'The boss don't care no more. Told me to let you starve.' He chuckled coarsely. 'Now, I couldn't do that to you, could I? Least, not without paying a visit first. See, the way I reckon it, if the boss doesn't want you then you're mine.'

He stood, and yanked violently on her hair, tumbling her backwards into the room. She screamed, more from fear than pain – but she kept her grip on the stick. She landed on her back, looking up at him. His hands were already at his flies. His head, the only place the stick might do any harm, was out of reach. When he saw the stick, his eyes widened.

'You little—'

She jabbed it into his crotch. It wasn't much of a blow, but it made him stagger backwards slightly, and gave her a chance to stand. She raised the stick menacingly, and his eyes narrowed as he assessed its weight. Before he could think further, she kicked him violently in the balls. He let out a little grunt, and buckled at the knees, his head tilting forwards as he doubled up.

She let the end of the spar drop, twisted her body away from him as though she was practising a golf-swing, and brought it up towards his head with all her force, distantly aware that someone was screaming. It wasn't him.

It caught him slightly low, where his neck met the angle of his jaw below his left ear. His head jerked sideways ahead of the blow, and his arms flailed upwards ineffectually. Then his whole body twitched as the spar struck him, and he tottered backwards, his eyes closed. He forced them open, and began to straighten, shaking his head and rubbing his neck. His gaze was not quite as focused as normal.

She swung again. This time, she hit his temple. The point of the metal bracket connected, and the stick bucked and twisted in her hand so sharply that she nearly dropped it. The man howled in pain, and doubled over again, holding his head in both hands. She stepped round to the side and kicked him savagely in the face. Then she smashed the spar down on the back of his neck, where the skull met the neck. He flopped onto the grimy floor, curled in a ball. She circled behind him, and kicked at the back of his neck, again, again. The screaming was louder now, and the effort was jerking her body in huge spasms.

He wasn't moving. She hoped she had killed him – but she knew that she hadn't. At best, she had bought herself a tiny window of time. That time was now.

Hurriedly, she bent over him and grabbed the keys peeping out of his back pocket. Then, risking precious time to do it, she pulled off his balaclava. She needed to know. And if she succeeded in getting away, she would make sure he suffered.

She knew him, but just barely – not well enough to remember his name. He was no one special, just one of hundreds of staring prisoners from the Ville, a vulgar face leering at her as she passed, sidling up to her to stand close during Association. He could have been anybody. This was only personal in his own sick mind. And she was not going to give him the satisfaction. Besides, he was only a minion. The man she needed to get to was the boss. Thornton – could it *really* be him? It just seemed so out of proportion, even for a bastard like him with a savage, hidden temper.

For a moment, she panicked, disorientated. She was using her only chance at escape to debate who she was, ultimately, running from. What the hell did it matter who the boss was?

The man wasn't quite unconscious. His face was contorted and clotted with blood. A thin whine trickled through his lips. With one last scream, and with a strength that astonished her, she lifted one end of the bed high in the air, swung it round, and dropped its edge directly onto his head. He gave a small groan, and twitched a little. For good measure, she kicked him once more in the balls. Then she ran.

The other side of the door was an unfamiliar world. At the corridor's end, it branched left and right. Left was another run of offices, and a corner at the far end. To her right was a short stretch of corridor and then a red padlocked door. She hurried towards it, already sorting through the keys. Mercifully, there were only a few.

None of them fit. She babbled something meaningless as she tried them all again. She glanced back along the corridor. He wouldn't stay lying down. He would be here any second – and none of the keys fit. Not one of them. She screamed in frustration, and dashed along the corridor in the other direction. It continued for another four doors on each side, then there was a right-angle turn to the left. She took it at speed. Another stretch lay ahead of her, then another left turn. This was bad. She couldn't run for ever.

Fleetingly, she imagined hiding in one of these rooms, listening to him dash past her. Then she would creep out and head in the other direction. Towards what? A prison cell she had just escaped from, and a red padlocked door she couldn't open.

She whimpered again, a series of staccato sounds that marked out the rhythm of her stride. What if she'd passed the way out already? What if it was behind one of those doors?

Shut up. Keep running.

Round the next corner, there was a short stub of corridor that ended in a half-glassed door, so caked with grime that she couldn't see through it. It squealed open without a key, and she found herself in a vast metal shed. She slammed the door behind her and cast about for something to wedge it shut with: the man must surely be up and after her by now. There was nothing. A pair of rusted barrels. An unidentifiable piece of metal sheet. A tractor tyre. Pigeons clattered in the high metal roof spaces.

She looked about her, desperately. There was an opening to her left: a rusted metal frame that had perhaps once held large sliding doors. Weeds poked up through the rails in the floor. She ran through, in to another area like the one she had left. She crouched to one side of the opening, out of sight of the door from the corridors, her chest heaving.

Behind her, she heard someone running. Tap, tap, crunch, crunch: concrete floors, broken glass, office detritus.

Diagonally opposite her, there was a door-shaped outline of daylight in a corrugated metal wall. It was too dark to be sure – but what else could it be? She sprinted towards it. Behind her, the door she had originally come through screeched open.

She reached the metal door. And it was locked with a shiny new padlock on a welded metal hasp. She fumbled with the bunch of keys desperately. Tried one. Failed.

There were running footsteps behind her. Close now.

Another key. It wouldn't even go in.

Then he was with her, and she had no more time. He barged her aside, and smashed the keys out of her hand. They jangled to the floor a few yards off. She stared at him. His mud-coloured eyes were feral and bloodshot. He snarled something meaningless – and then a fist crashed into the side of her head, lifting her off the ground and flinging her sideways.

As her feet left the ground, and his rage-twisted face shrank to a dark thing at the bottom of a deep black well, she realised that she must have dropped her stick. If she'd had her stick with her, it would have all been all right. Or if she'd had the sense to lock him in the room when she left.

If only—

Thirty

They use a knife. They cut their wrists and touch the open wounds together.

'Brothers,' Byron says.

The weeds weave in a tangled wind, and high above them a plane scratches a thin bright line across the sky. There is perfect silence.

It is a time long ago, over thirty years. He stands with Byron in a field, overlooked by no one. Wind nods the weeds. The air carries the rich smell of the river.

Monk has yet to turn twenty. He is young, and still burning with memory. It roars through him.

– she said, David, I –

Regret.

Byron understands this pain. Byron knows. He stands now where his dead father stood. Byron is now the Man, as his father was before.

He says it again. 'Brothers, David. Always.'

Monk – David – does not reply. There is no need. There is nothing to say. They were brothers before. They were brothers the moment Gloria died. Both of them lost her. But Byron sees it differently. Byron sees the man that Monk has now killed – and he rejoices. Byron feels bonded to him now, because he has taken revenge, for both of them. She was just fifteen.

'Brothers, whatever comes,' Byron says. And Monk nods, just barely. Because he knows that, as the death of this one bad man recedes in their memories, they will once again remember how different brothers can be.

'I may fight you,' he says softly.

Byron laughs, also softly. Because he knows this too.

'Then we'll fight,' he says.

'There is a Way, a path,' says Monk – and he believes it to be true.

Byron chuckles. 'Then you'll walk yours and I'll walk mine.' He rests a hand on Monk's shoulder briefly. Then he pulls Monk into a sudden, close embrace. 'We are one,' he whispers. 'Your pain is mine. I will kill for you.' Monk can smell the dry, bitter scent of aftershave. He can feel the slight trace of tomorrow's stubble against Byron's polished cheek, and the crush as the arm of his expensive glasses bends.

'My brother,' Byron whispers to him. And Monk hears in his voice the grief that he carries, too: Byron has lost his sister, he has lost his father. Monk has lost the only girl he will ever love. In Byron's voice, Monk hears the sadness of a man who is truly alone.

He watches him leave, towards the dark, expensive car waiting for him at the field's distant edge. Before he reaches it, Monk calls to him.

'Byron!'

Byron turns and looks – and returns, straightening his glasses, and looking hard at the ground. When he confronts Monk again, his eyes have the texture of shining glass. Monk looks at his brother, and sees a mirror of his own still-fresh grief.

'It will pass, Byron,' he says.

Byron says nothing. His shoulders shake beneath the pads of his expensive suit, and his eyes shine brighter. Monk pities him.

'Don't you believe in redemption?' he asks gently.

Byron Washington smiles, a hard, bright, brittle smile; and turns away.

Riverweed. After thirty years, surely things should have changed. And yet . . .

They stood together in a doorway, watching Matthew Daniels' house. Next to him, a cigarette tip briefly lit the arch of the doorway that concealed them. He heard Byron's breath sucked in, smelled sweet tobacco and new fabric.

Monk settled himself more comfortably into his stance and let his eyes absorb his whole field of view. He saw everything, and gave labels to nothing. In the darkness outside Matthew's home, there were shapes, colours, textures. They were not things with names, they were patterns of energy. It was a form of meditation, and a form of preparedness. *Chi* swirled around him, and through him.

He watched, and he waited.

'So,' Byron Washington said softly, 'what will he do now?'

After a pause, Monk replied, 'Nothing.' And then, because Byron was still waiting: 'He wants to trust us. Needs to. He will wait.'

'Good.'

Some words did not need a reply. Monk let the sounds of the night-time streets answer for him: the remote roar of traffic, sporadic voices, the gentle wind as it strummed fences and shrubberies.

They waited. Watched.

But for Monk, the abstract shapes of the night had meaning, even if they did not have names. In the houses in front of him, in the energy curling around them both, in the sudden yowl of cats: in all these things, he perceived the echo of that day, very long ago, when his journey had begun.

At last, he said, very softly, 'I could have saved her.'

Regret. Riverweed.

Washington placed a warm hand on his shoulder, and said nothing. Then he threw away the stub of his cigarette, and lit another one. Monk moved not at all. The silence grew. Because they both knew it was the truth. All those years ago, he *could* have saved her. And he didn't.

Washington laughed softly. His cigarette tip gleamed in the night. 'That's the difference between you and me, Monk,' he said. 'You think. I *do*.'

Thirty-One

Is there an afterlife? If so, then perhaps you will meet her again. Will she forgive you? Will it be like it was, before? Will there be love? Maybe the love was never real, you only imagined it: what then?

And who are you, now that you have changed? Who were you before? A man in a car, munching endless packets of crisps, watching, calculating, and empty. There is no more doubt now, and no more fear. The part of you that was unsure is cut off. It is adrift and dreaming. It asks questions with no answer. Who are you? Have you ever deserved love? Will she forgive?

You have made a decision that your smaller voice had hoped would never be necessary – but you always knew that the hope was an illusion. This moment was always inevitable. So, you had prepared – and, earlier today, the moment came.

You were in your car. You had hurried to Matthew's house as soon as you could get away – to watch, to savour the pain. His car was not there, and, of course, you knew that he was not at the Ville. You had no idea where he was – and that was proof that you had made the right choice last night. Perhaps he had gone to the police at last. Well, let them come. Only the phone ever connected you to Charlotte, or Charlotte to Matthew, and you have destroyed it. And soon she would be dead, perhaps was dead already. But you never touched her, did you? *He* did. So you settled to wait, hunched in your seat, and opened a packet of crisps, safely invisible behind the car's silvered screen.

You pondered your progress. Your associate is no longer answering his phone. This is worrying. Has he been found? Has he turned? Or is he just hiding, now that he has done his . . . work? He is being silent deliberately, to protect himself, perhaps. It is what you would do; but you cannot be sure.

This doubt alone might have forced the decision on you, given time. But then Matthew returned, and you discovered that you had no time at all.

A figure crossed the road to greet him on the pavement. A short man, his skin dark. He held himself curiously upright. Something about this man tantalised you. You started up the car. By the time you passed the pair, you were travelling at twenty-five miles an hour – not a speed that would arouse suspicion, but fast enough that, to them, your face would be a blur. The man talking to Matthew turned immediately, and his eyes locked onto the car. He stared, as though his gaze could penetrate the mirrored glass – and you accelerated away with your heart clattering in your chest.

You know this man. His name is David Gordon. He is a murderer. He flattened two convicts and an officer in the Ville – in seconds, they say – and did it without blinking.

Not the police, then. Something far worse. You drove towards home as fast as you could, with your vision hazed, and fear curling in your belly. It is not that Monk is dangerous, it is that he cannot be alone. If Monk is involved, then others will be, too. Faces you don't recognise. Men with the power to hunt you down.

And Monk has seen the car.

Before you reach home, your mind is made up. The car is tainted. Monk might track it down. And if he tracks the car . . . then he has you. It was bought specially – but you bought it from a dealer, using your own name. There is no time to feel ashamed, though that will come. For now, you must act. There is a connection now between you and Matthew. It is no longer safe to be yourself. The voice inside you laughs at that, distantly. It asks a question, then drifts away. Who are you anyway? You ignore it. You must do . . . something. But you didn't plan for this. Do what?

You must ditch the car. Yes. But if the car is not safe, then your home isn't either. You leave the car at home, hurry inside, take what you need and leave. You have cash, plenty of it. It will buy you new places to hide. Already, it has bought you a new car – beaten and blue, bought for cash.

Yes, the voice says. Hide. Please. I'm scared. We can't—

But you know that hiding is not the answer, not any more. You must be bold. You must finish what you have started. Your Purpose is beating thickly in you, a second heart, the Thing that sustains you. It is your destiny, and you cannot fight it. And as you drag a half-filled case along the road, you realise that it can be done. You climb into the new-old car, and fire the engine. You know what lies ahead. You are free now. This is the start of your future.

It is time for you to disappear.

Thursday

Thirty-Two

Em woke him, with a cup of tea.

'Hey, Dad.'

He jerked upright. 'Shit! What? What is it?'

'Chill, Dad. It's morning, that's all. It's nearly eight.' She rubbed his arm gently.

He bounced off the bed. 'Eight? What's happened? We have to . . .' Em watched him, still in her pyjamas, holding two mugs of tea. He flopped back onto the bed with a groan.

She handed over a mug. It was warm against his hands, and its smell was almost reassuring. 'I've only just woken up,' she said. 'I didn't set the alarm, cos you said I shouldn't go to school.'

He nodded, still bleary. And confused. And scared. He had slept. How could he sleep while Charlotte—

'I still think you're wrong,' Em said. He glanced up at her, squinting through sleep-smeared eyes, and sipped his tea. 'About the police and stuff,' she added.

He sighed. 'Em, I've explained this.'

'But what if no one finds out?'

He almost laughed. 'Oh, they'll know.'

'Yeah. Like, the police are *really* going to come and see you in cars and uniforms?'

All the reasons that he hadn't wanted to tell her in the first place came back to him. She was headstrong, and nowhere near as worldly wise as she believed she was. She was moody. She might decide to do . . . anything. If she took it into her head to phone the police, she could destroy everything.

'Em, you haven't—'

She rolled her eyes at him. 'No. *Thanks*, Dad!'

'Look, I'm not . . . Em, you just have to promise me you won't. I know it feels like I'm being mean to you, but I need to know that you won't – absolutely won't – call the police.'

She avoided his eyes.

'*Em!*'

She muttered at the carpet. 'Yeah. All right.'

'*Promise*, Em!'

She yelled, 'I just did, didn't I?' and thumped out of the room.

When he followed her downstairs, she had made breakfast. Two plates were out on the table, with the teapot and a jug of milk.

She didn't look up at him. With her eyes locked on the table, she said, 'Stale toast and Marmite, OK?'

They ate without talking.

Thursday. Another night gone. For the last ten hours, he hadn't even noticed time passing. Now, there was a cold space inside him, and it horrified him. Even when he had lost Rachel, there had been pain. But for Charlotte and for their unborn child, all he could muster was a distant feeling of exhaustion.

And no word. No phone calls from the man who had taken her. Nothing from Monk and his gangland friends. It was over, surely. He tried Monk's phone, and was unsurprised to get no answer. He tried Charlotte's mobile. It was unobtainable. He tried Monk again.

The worst of it – of this intolerable silence from all sides – was the knowledge that he was dealing with someone he knew. There was something intimate about everything that had happened. It had been tailored to fit: his fears of losing Charlotte, the pregnancy, the money. This had always been personal, and he still had no idea who it was.

And now the sadistic bastard had cut and run. Something must have spooked him – probably Washington's goon squad, or Monk. But if the bastard was scared, then why hadn't he left Charlotte somewhere safe and sound? Because he must surely know that until he had Charlotte back, he'd keep hunting. Or until he had found the . . . Even after all this time, the real words felt grotesquely *wrong*. Body. Corpse. Remains. Unthinkable – but, most likely, true. So, if he was running, why hadn't the man at least told him where to find her? At the very least, it would have bought him time.

Em had found a magazine. She sat slumped at the kitchen table, turning the pages without reading. Monk's number rang out again.

He cradled the phone and stared out of the kitchen window at the blank wall that lay just a few feet beyond – the London equivalent of a garden.

So. Either he had already killed her or the sick game was still afoot. He was watching somewhere, enjoying all this, pulling Matthew's strings just to see him twitch . . .

But *who*?

He had been here before, early on, countless hours ago, seemed like years: trying to access his work computer and finding it blocked, combing through his memory for any of the countless prisoners who might plausibly hold a grudge against one of their jailers. What more did he know now? That the money was not important. It was personal. That the man behind this – the boss, the other one had called him – was sophisticated, calculating and powerful or well-connected or rich enough to arrange for Charlotte to disappear. How many men like *that* had passed through the Ville? None.

Frustrated and unable to sit still, he wandered towards the living room, and peered out at the street. Washington had changed the bodyguards. A different car was parked outside, and he only recognised one of the two men, the massive bodyguard who had driven them home. What had Washington called him? Tyrell.

What kind of an ego trip had that man been on? All that talk about how he was helping Monk out whether Matthew liked it or not, how he was glad Matthew was suffering, that superior air, the intimidation . . .

As soon as he realised where his thoughts were leading, he bolted for the phone, and called Monk's number again. He had no idea how to contact Washington – but Monk did. It rang out again without voicemail. Which left just one option.

He took the bodyguards a mug of tea each.

Tyrell wound down his window as he approached. 'Get away!' he hissed.

'Thought you might like a drink,' he replied cheerfully.

Baffled, the man gestured him away frantically, then wound up the window again. Matthew set the mugs on the roof and leaned down to peer in. The other man was even bigger than Tyrell. He pointed upwards, and shouted through the window at them, as though they were a couple of grannies with their hearing aids switched off. 'They're on the roof.'

Tyrell slumped in his seat and stared straight ahead. The other man pulled a phone from his pocket, with some difficulty, and dialled a number. Good.

Matthew returned to the house.

'Feeling better now?' Em looked sideways at him, unimpressed. She sat with her cheeks squashed upwards by the heels of her palms, the magazine unread in front of her.

'Just rattling the cage.'

'Whatever,' she muttered.

Three minutes later, the phone rang.

'Mr Daniels, that was not only foolish, it was dangerous.' Byron Washington's voice was calm, but the venom was unmistakable. 'You are putting my men at risk, *and* yourself and your daughter. Not to mention your wife. Just what did you hope to accomplish?'

He fought the urge to shout. He said, evenly, 'I hoped to force you to talk to me, Washington. I don't even have a number for you.'

'That is exactly as it should be.'

Matthew sighed. 'Let's cut to the chase here, shall we, Washington? I don't trust you, and you made it abundantly clear last night that I was right not to. You've got a misplaced grudge against me.'

'Oh, hardly misplaced, Mr Daniels. Your actions added at least a year to Monk's sentence.'

'We went over this last night, and it isn't what I wanted to speak to you about. I wanted to speak to you because you're hiding something. You know more than you were saying.'

There was a long silence.

'Washington, this is my *wife* we're talking about. She has done nothing – not to you, not to anyone. She's pregnant. For God's sake . . .'

Em looked up apathetically. She rolled her eyes at him, then turned her attention back to the magazine.

'Are you trying to imply, Mr Daniels, that I may have had a hand in your wife's disappearance?'

'Well, you don't seem to care what happens to her, do you? And the guy on the phone kept talking about his boss. You've got a grudge and you're enjoying watching me squirm. You only met me so you could gloat, didn't you?' He took a sharp breath. 'What do I have to do to get her back? Whatever it is, I'll do it.'

Em glanced up again, expectantly. He avoided her eyes.

There was a pause. Then Washington laughed.

'Mr Daniels, you are delightfully naïve. Do you really think that, if I *did* have your wife, I would admit it?'

'You *have* got her, you bastard! If—'

'Temper will get you nowhere, Mr Daniels. Surely you realise that.'

The fury drained out of him. He wanted her back, that was all. Em was gaping at him now. Again, he turned away. He needed to concentrate.

'Please. Just don't hurt her. I . . .' There was nothing more he could say. 'Just please . . .'

Washington's laughter was bright and long.

'Let's do a thought-experiment, Mr Daniels. Let's see what would happen if I do have her – and if I do not. If I have her, I would only admit it if I chose to, as we have already established. Until then, I would deny it. So – if I deny it, you learn nothing about whether I have her or not. You will simply face the choice of whether or not to believe me.'

'I'm tired of games, Washington. Please. I'll do anything.'

'Furthermore, if I have her, my offer to rescue her is a charade, aimed at making you suffer. Wouldn't you agree?'

It was clear that Washington was going to play this latest game out to the end. Miserably, Matthew said, 'Yes.'

Em said, 'Dad?' Understandably, she wanted to know what was happening. He shook his head at her and shrugged miserably.

Washington went on. 'That's the spirit, Mr Daniels. Now, remember, this is only a thought-experiment, a bit of harmless fun.'

His words were designed to cut – and Matthew's only choice was to sit there and take it. He waited until Washington continued.

'Now, if the rescue *is* a charade, I think we can agree that it's one which I am determined to continue with until I see fit. Do you follow? And when the charade is done, either I will produce your wife or I won't, and either she will be unharmed – or she won't be.'

Washington paused. Matthew could hear him clicking his tongue thoughtfully.

'Now, here's the tricky bit, Mr Daniels. Please pay close attention. It makes no material difference if the rescue is a charade or a genuine attempt. Either way, it will persist until it ends. Either way, I will deny involvement. And either way, there is nothing at all you can do about it.' He sucked in a breath. 'So, I would suggest that it's hardly worth us discussing any further, wouldn't you?'

He was tired: too tired to find a way out, and perhaps Washington was right, there wasn't one. Eventually, he said, as calmly as he could manage, 'If she is hurt, Washington, I will hunt you down. I'll find you.'

Again, Washington laughed. 'That might be bad for your health.'

'And for yours. I don't care about mine.'

'*Dad?*' Em looked strained.

'You'd leave your daughter to cope alone in the world? I doubt it, Mr Daniels.'

To Washington, he hissed, 'I'll wait.'

Em mouthed at him: 'What's going on?' He mouthed back: 'Nothing.'

Washington was unconcerned. 'I admire your bravery, Mr Daniels, if not your common sense. But shall we move on? You might be interested to know that we have made some progress.'

'Or invented some,' Matthew muttered.

Washington chuckled. 'Quite so. It amounts to the same thing. Either way, I am about to tell you what is happening.'

'Get on with it, then.' Matthew hesitated, then added, 'Please.'

'Certainly.' Washington paused before continuing. 'I was reluctant to tell you this, Mr Daniels. Monk felt that I should. I am afraid it is all too obvious to me how you will react.' He paused again before continuing. 'We have found the cell her mobile calls were made from.'

'Her cell!'

Em looked up again, sharply. He turned away from her. He needed to concentrate. He focused on the sideboard. An empty vase stood there, and some of the breakfast things from three days ago.

'Not *her* cell, Mr Daniels. The phone cell. It seems you were right to be searching around Heathrow.'

'Where? Have you found her? Is she—'

'Mr Daniels, if we had found her' – Em pushed herself in front of him. Her eyes were bright and anxious, searching his. He mouthed 'Wait' at her, and concentrated on Washington – 'don't you think perhaps we might have told you?'

'But *where?*' he insisted. 'This cell, is it—'

Washington's laughter was light and merry. 'You might want to *listen* for a moment . . .'

With questions still tumbling inside him, he took a deep breath and was silent.

'Thank you,' Washington said. 'We have been very lucky. The cell is only a mile and a half across, because there is plenty of phone traffic in the area. Some of the larger cells are—'

'But *where* Washington?'

'Do you mean, where is the cell, Mr Daniels? I am afraid it really wouldn't be appropriate to tell you.'

'What? But—'

'Why? Because if I tell you, you will go there. And if you go there, you will do exactly what we prevented you from doing last time you travelled there. You will blunder around; you will be highly visible. Whoever has her will panic – and that will be that.' He paused, and then said, 'If, that is, someone else has her. Either way, at present, the greatest threat to your wife, Mr Daniels, is you.'

There was a certain logic to Washington's words. He would be instantly recognisable to the man who had Charlotte; with luck, Monk would not be. But what were they planning to do? He knew from experience that the area was a wasteland of industrial parks and semi-derelict compounds. With nothing more to go on, they couldn't possibly hope to find the one small room that held her, could they? But it was something. After three days, it was a start.

Three days, and only now was there any sign of progress. A day since the man following him had been seen. A day since the last call.

Part of him was sure that it was already too late.

'I . . . won't interfere,' he said hoarsely.

'You know what will happen if you do.' Washington rang off.

Hurriedly, Matthew dialled 1471. A message told him that the caller had withheld their number. He rang Monk. There was no reply.

He dashed into the hallway and grabbed the car keys. Em scuttled after him, calling nervously, 'Dad?' By the front door, he stopped. Whether Washington was bluffing or not over who had taken her, he might be right about the risks of chasing after her. If he did have her, then who knew what he might do? And if he didn't . . . The man who did have her had already proved himself unpredictable and utterly without feeling.

Reluctantly, he set down the keys, and muttered to Em that he would explain in a moment.

He rang Charlotte's mobile hoping, even if she didn't answer, to hear her message – the echo of a happy-go-lucky woman he might never see again. For all he knew, she might already be dead. The number was unobtainable again.

Em looked at him expectantly. He shook his head and trudged past her towards the empty kitchen.

In a way, he realised, horrifying though the idea was, it might be better if Washington *did* have her. At least that way the situation was under some sort of control. Either way, though, his options were the same. He could risk everything through unconsidered action or he could wait.

Thirty-Three

A plane's engines tore the air above him, vibrating the roof. High-pitched echoes rattled between the walls. Before the sound had fully faded, the roar of the next plane was building.

Monk ignored the noise. He held himself still. His arms hung loosely, floating free from his sides. His head was light as air, his feet sank into the hard ground. His senses rippled outwards, sound, smell, memory; and his fixed gaze looked everywhere and nowhere. He was searching for signs, for some subliminal hint that he was near – that someone had been here recently, perhaps. He searched his memory, too: had he missed something in the corridor that led here? He could not possibly search even this one small complex in its entirety. It had eight separate buildings, many of them two or three storeys high.

The metal windows had teeth of broken glass. Weeds rose from the cracked cement floor in high arcs, drooping back down towards the ground, softening the hard edges of the immense space. It had been abandoned for years. It was a perfect hiding place. Unfortunately it was one of many.

This was the third compound he had visited since getting the call from Byron. This was the area that all the mobile calls had been made from. He had not searched them fully; there was only time for a quick check at each. And how many more were there in this one small cell of the phone network? Perhaps twenty. The area was littered with derelict warehouses, industrial estates, workshops. A rapid search of the first three had already taken an hour and a half; to search the whole area could take days – and, already, he could not swear that he had not missed her.

Dried rust-stains tracked across the floor from leaks in the roof.

Shards crunched softly beneath his feet, and bounced sunbeams high up into the metal rafters. The peeling walls were stippled with faint splinters of light. Pigeons clattered in the eaves, beneath roof-windows grimed with filth and moss.

He was useless here. His intuition was unreliable. What was needed was men, lots of them, all searching methodically; not two of Byron's men chauffeuring him around – a failed martial artist, a man who could only prowl and hope for some flash of insight.

Nothing here spoke to him. He picked his way back, along corridors obstructed by upturned filing cabinets and office debris, out through the door he had smashed through on the way in because it was padlocked, into the complex's central courtyard. Beyond a wall with a locked wire-mesh gate, Byron's two henchmen waited in the Escort. He ran at the wall, jumped lightly to the top, then dropped into the street without a sound.

He settled into the back seat of the car, and it pulled away.

'Where?' the driver said.

'Nowhere. Wait.'

The driver rolled his eyes, and pulled in again.

Monk flipped open his mobile and called Washington. 'I'm coming back,' he said, without introduction. 'You need four or five teams out here. You don't need me.'

The driver glanced at him in the mirror, pursed his lips, and started the engine again. He swung the car round and headed towards London.

Washington tutted as he considered Monk's request. 'Four teams?'

'Five would be better.'

'That's a big commitment.'

'Less than twenty-five grand. You agreed to help.'

There was a chuckle. 'Yes. I did, didn't I?' Monk waited him out. This was Washington's way: the long pauses were to keep you in suspense, to remind you that he was the one with the power. It didn't work on Monk: he had known Washington since they were boys, and he was comfortable with silence.

Eventually, Washington said, 'OK. You come back, then send your two boys out again. I'll get more teams on it. It'll take time.'

'We may not *have* time.'

Washington laughed merrily. 'Monk, my friend, I can't work

miracles. That's your department. You reckon you can get people there faster, you do it.'

Monk did not reply. Thoughtfully, he closed the phone, and pocketed it. Then he leaned towards the driver, and said, very quietly, 'Faster.'

Washington sat in a café two blocks away from Matthew Daniels' house, sipping a double espresso and reading the business pages of *The Times*. Monk slipped into the seat opposite him.

Washington did not look up. 'In a hurry, Monk?'

Monk ignored the implied challenge. 'The men?'

'On their way.' Washington rattled his paper into a more comfortable position, then peered over the top of it with a mischievous grin. 'Like you said, I agreed to help.'

Monk fingered the cowrie shell on his wrist, and wondered how to get through Washington's apparently impenetrable shield. 'She might die,' he said at last. 'She might already be dead.' He did not look up. On his wrist, the cowrie shell was bleached, and worn smooth with rubbing. The twined cotton thread that held it had faded from blue to grey. A charm with no colour. It had faded so many years ago, when Gloria . . .

But Washington knew all that. It was why they were brothers – of a kind. Yet not once in all these years had he seen his blood-brother mourn the loss of his sister. Why should he suddenly care now?

Washington was watching him intently. At last, he said, 'Is it the woman or is it the girl?'

Monk took a moment to absorb Washington's question. What did he mean, the girl? Gloria? But he would never call her a girl. Matthew's daughter, then. Charlotte or Emily, that was what he had asked. He didn't reply. He couldn't. He was unused to people questioning his reasons. He did what he did, without thought.

'Or,' Washington raised an elegant finger, 'is it Daniels, after all?'

That was a possibility, too. Matthew had been the first person Monk could remember who had ever approached him with respect – at first.

He wrestled with feelings he could not name. Eventually, he managed to speak. 'All.' His voice was hoarse.

All of them: Matthew, to learn, and to trust – and because what happened to Monk when he lost Gloria should never happen to anyone; Charlotte, because no one should be forced to live in fear. And the girl, Em . . .

Gloria had been that age when—

'Without us, Charlotte Daniels dies,' he added flatly.

But that wasn't quite the truth, was it? The truth was, she would die without *Washington*. It was his contacts and resources that had got them this far; alone, Monk would have accomplished nothing. Now, he personally was no more in control of this than Matthew was. He made a helpless gesture with his hands. The cowrie shell clattered on the metal table top. It showed a dull, flat white against the metal.

Washington scowled. 'Monk, you know how much trouble you have caused me?'

The answer, Monk knew, was that he had caused a great deal. He lived by his morals; Washington did not. On many occasions, Monk had seen injustices in Washington's domain that demanded correction – and Washington had refused to act. The arguments had frequently been fierce – and on more than one occasion, Monk had damaged Washington's property or his staff. On those occasions, Washington had denied that the fault was his, or that there was anything he could do. It was only shortly before his spell in prison that Monk came to believe that his almost-brother might have been telling him the truth.

A woman had come to him. A man was terrorising her and many of her neighbours. He had a gang. Several teenage boys had been beaten severely. Monk had assumed it was Washington's doing – and Washington, as usual, had denied it. Monk had decided to deal with the problem himself; it was the best way to send a clear signal to Washington that his actions were, once again, unacceptable. He would do to the gang what the gang had done to those boys. He would catch the man leading them, and explain to him the error of his ways. He was not afraid: the men would be armed, of course, but that made little difference to him.

The next morning, the man was dead. His head had been hacked off with a machete. It was Monk who found him, and the machete – and then the police found Monk, and he knew he could not tell them the truth.

'I went to prison for you,' Monk whispered.

'So?' Washington shrugged impassively. 'That was your choice.

You cause trouble, Monk. If you hadn't got involved, that man would be alive. So, he was bad – so what? You caused trouble then, you're causing it now. Nothing changes, bro.'

Monk stared at the cowrie shell, the faded reason for all that had ever passed between them.

– *David, I –*

'She'll die,' he said again.

'Maybe she deserves to,' Washington shot back.

'She doesn't, and Matthew—'

'Matthew Daniels made your life a misery when you were inside,' Washington snapped. He threw himself back in his seat. 'The bastard deserves to suffer.'

Slowly, Monk looked up from the shell, and stared. Washington glowered back, his nostrils wide, anger shining in the whites of his pale eyes. There was something here, Monk realised, that he hadn't fully taken in. He and Washington had always fought; but, now, was Washington angry with him – or *for* him? And, if he was angry with Matthew on Monk's behalf, what might he be prepared to do about it?

Monk leaned forward and hissed. 'She'll *die*, Byron.'

Washington's brows creased. 'Monk, do you really think—'

'She's done *nothing!*' He was half out of his seat. People had turned to watch. They were frowning at him. Awkwardly, he sat back down. Immediately, they looked away: this was London; it was none of their business.

The silence stretched. Washington gazed at him, unmoved, while he fought for self-control. Then he said, 'Matthew Daniels thinks I took her.'

Monk glared at him, waiting. He was beginning to think the same.

Washington shrugged indifferently, then laughed. 'I'm used to being misunderstood by you, Monk. Why change now?' Then he leaned forwards and said, intensely, 'I loved her too, Monk. Don't forget that. She was my sister.'

Monk stared back, unmoved. It was true – of course. But the fact that they had shared a loss together so many years before was scant reason to trust him now.

Washington's phone broke the deadlock. He snapped the tiny wedge of silver out of his suit pocket and held it to his ear.

'Speak.'

He listened, his face creased in concentration. Then, without farewell, he pressed a button, put the phone away.

He raised a mocking eyebrow. 'It seems we have found our man.' Monk returned the gaze coldly. Eventually Washington shrugged and continued. 'The car with silver windows. We've traced the plates.'

Monk waited. He was comfortable with pauses. Washington's eyes sparkled with amusement: he could wait, too. This was an old, old game between them.

Monk gave first. 'Who?' Energy fizzed inside him. Almost, his hand trembled. Pure pleasure spread across Washington's face as he held the pause. Then he told Monk the name.

Thirty-Four

Who cares that it is not quite how you planned it? It is still a victory. Matthew Daniels has lost the woman he loves. This is the endgame. There is only one more thing to do. Your last encounter with him at the Ville plays through your memory: blah blah disappointed, Larry, blah blah responsibility, blah blah teamwork, blah blah formal warning . . . And all the while he droned at you, you were thinking: *Just you wait, Matthew, just you wait. Tonight, you go home to an empty house.* Your heart was full of savage joy.

You feel no pity for him, although the voice inside you is horrified at what has happened to the woman. But the smug bitch had it coming. She was only one of tens of staff who mocked you; but it is good to think that she has learned her lesson.

And Matthew: he has lived through the terror of not knowing whether his beloved would live or die. But although you would love to see him continue to struggle with uncertainty, then half-certain knowledge, and then with grief, you know it is no longer practical. They saw the car. They are hunting for you.

Well, let them come. You are ready. You are poised and patient. They will come soon, or sometime, it doesn't matter. Until that moment, memory will keep you warm.

It is two years ago, a work day, and your moment with Matthew Daniels has finally arrived. This is the moment when Matthew will save Mother's life. You have it all planned. Matthew is a good man; he will understand the need, and he will give. You have requested a half-hour with him in private. Matthew takes you to the conference room. You look at each other. You don't know how to start.

He has always been kind to you – in that distant you'll-never-really-belong manner that you experience from all the senior officers. He greets you each and every morning: Hello Larry; how are you, Larry? He asks all the right questions, he asks after Mother, he makes you feel respected and at ease. He cares. And he is rich: everyone knows that he received a massive payout when his wife drowned. That money could fly Mother to America, pay for the brain surgery that only one doctor in the world can perform.

That money can remove Mother's cancer. It can make you whole again, and safe.

Selling Mother's flat has raised a hundred and fifteen thousand pounds. It is not enough. You need more. You have tried collecting door to door – but nobody admits to knowing her well. She has always made enemies more easily than friends, she has always been misunderstood, except by you. The collection only raises forty pounds. So, you run in a sponsored marathon: you do eight miles before you collapse, and get seventy-five pounds from your fellow prison officers. Afterwards, you know what they are saying behind your back. Heard about Larry Tysome? Clapped out on the starting line. Imagine him shagging; wouldn't make it past the tits.

The humiliation makes you angry.

A month after the marathon, Matthew calls you in and tells you that they've had a whip-round. Seven hundred pounds: and he gives it to you with a sad smile.

'It's not much,' he says.

True. It isn't. If your fellow workers were here now, you would spit at them – but your heart swells nonetheless. Matthew organised the whip-round; he cares enough to try. He will do what he can. He understands that you and Mother are special. You thank him, for the signal he has sent you more than for the money, and you leave. It is still not enough. Nowhere near enough.

Life is not the same now Mother is dying and you are both living at Mandy's. Mandy's cats crawl all over her; they make her sneeze. You worry about her headaches and her allergies: she has always been sensitive. Mandy should do something. She should keep the cats outside, or send them to friends – not that she has any. But she doesn't. 'They're my babies,' she whines. She doesn't see the problem – doesn't care, more like. She doesn't even want to care. Mandy wishes you and Mother were back where you came from.

She argues with Mother. There are endless screaming matches:
— *You never tidy up.*
— *Why should I? It's my fucking house.*
— *You're a slob, girl.*
— *Bossy old witch.*
— *Where did I go wrong with you?*
— *You should have put me up for adoption, Mum, at least I might have had a chance at a decent life.*

On and on and on.

You intervene. You try to make Mandy understand: the conflict is killing Mother, it's speeding up her cancer. Doctor said to keep her calm. Can't Mandy, just for once, bite the bullet and behave like a daughter should?

I hope she fucking dies, the dizzy cow. And you're no better, Larry. Mum's little fucking poodle, aren't you?

Are you a poof, Larry? Fancy boys, do you? None of them queers'd look twice at you. They look after themselves properly, but look at you. You're just the way she wants you — rushing around after her, do this, do that, yes Mother, no Mother, what's for tea Mother.

Ever kissed a girl, Larry? Ever fucked one? Of course you haven't. What if Mother didn't approve?

It all blurs together in your mind: the endless reproaches and accusations, the relentless monotone of confrontation and bitterness. Mandy has always been spiteful. She loves to make Mother angry. And she revels in your shame. She digs for it with a mindless gleam in her piggy eyes. For Mother's sake, you do not fight back. You beg her to be reasonable. But Mandy seems to think that taking you both in is already more than duty demands.

If you can just get Mother well again, you and she will escape from this hell-hole. Then Mandy will see. You'll make her realise that she should never have made you angry.

And that is why you have come back to Matthew Daniels, two weeks after the whip-round. Because he cares. Because he can save Mother's life.

'What can I do for you, Larry?' he says. He smiles warmly.

You smile back. 'It's about the fund to get Mother to America. I've got a hundred and sixteen thousand, give or take. But I need two hundred.'

You expect Matthew to get the hint. He doesn't.

'I'm sorry about that, Larry. If there's anything we can do . . .'

You don't like the sound of that 'we', but you press on regardless. 'I was hoping you might see your way to helping out.'

Matthew Daniels frowns. 'Well, I put a fair amount into the whip-round—'

'No! No. See, I'm short by eighty-odd thousand. You could help. Loan it. I'll pay it back, soon as I can.'

The frown deepens, and Matthew Daniels closes off – and this is when you realise that things are not going your way.

'I don't think that's a good idea, Larry.'

Frustration stirs in you – and resentment: who the fuck does the man think he is? He won't even help a dying woman.

'Why not? It's not like you need it.'

Daniels manages an embarrassed laugh. It gives his words the lie.

'Well, actually, Larry, I don't even *have* it . . . Goodness, eighty grand – can you imagine!'

'You *have* got it!' You realise that you are bellowing. This is desperation talking. You struggle for calm. 'You got all that money when your wife died, didn't you?'

His face turns hard.

'I . . . I meant . . .' you stammer. 'That's what people say, anyway.'

You would give anything to play this conversation through again, to find what you said wrong and unsay it. But the only choice is to move forwards.

There is controlled fury in Matthew's expression. 'For your information, Larry, when my wife died, she did leave some money. The money was given to her by her father to pay for my daughter's education – and that's exactly what it's doing.'

He slams a biro down onto his desk. It makes a feeble click. Some papers flutter in the wind from his palm. Outside, a bell rings. It seems a long way away. Then it stops.

Matthew continues. He is cold. His words are neat and precise – scalpel, forceps, swab. Suddenly, America is very far away.

'My personal life is none of your business, Larry. Please remember that in future. Even if I did have money to spare, frankly it is inappropriate for you to ask for it.'

You stare at him, weakened by his fury, and by the draining away of hope. Matthew has just ripped away everything inside you. You are empty. There is no dream left.

Mother will die.

'I'm sorry about your mother, Larry.' He is using a softer tone now, offering reconciliation. 'That's why I organised the whip-round. And I did put a fair amount in, too. It's all I could do.'

You snort.

'Is something funny, Larry?'

You snort again, contemptuously. Matthew waits.

'*All you could do?*' you say finally. 'What, a tenner in a collection box? Well, thanks a bloody million.' You tell yourself to stop, but you can't. You don't really want to. Destruction is all that's left to you. 'Thanks for nothing,' you mutter bitterly.

Matthew gazes at you for a frosty instant before replying. 'I put five hundred quid into that, Larry. I cleaned out my bank account – because I felt sorry for you. I'm beginning to wish that I hadn't.'

'*Sorry for me?*' You snort again – but you are horrified. Five hundred pounds! If only everyone . . .

But your thoughts are out of step with your mood. You look up at Matthew Daniels and see a smug, self-righteous, self-satisfied, arrogant worm.

Two months later, Mother dies in your arms. She is delusional, rambling. Her last words are for you to sort yourself out, get a proper job, a girlfriend.

You try to buy her flat back with the money you have been collecting – but the new owners want almost twice as much for it as they paid. The housing market is booming, they say. So you stay at Mandy's, and you brood, and time passes.

Work is hell. No one cares. No one understands. They whisper behind your back. The inmates needle you – got a girlfriend yet, boss, fancy a shag, boss? You ignore it. You do just enough work to get by. Reprimands come and go. Matthew Daniels is worried about you. Then he is annoyed. You are failing to perform. He sends you on courses, offers you counselling. It doesn't help. You don't want it to. You perform your duties – just. You return home, ignore the jibes and moans of your sister. You kick the cats when you get the chance.

A year drifts away.

Matthew Daniels walks the corridors with a glowing face, smug and full of happiness. My life is wonderful, he is saying. I am wonderful. And every time you see him pass, you look away and you wish him misery.

It is the anniversary of Mother's death. No one at work mentions it. Mandy doesn't mention it. You mark the day alone.

In the dark hours of the night, with Mandy asleep and the cats vanished, you think of him, all happy and shining and glistening and new.

And you come at last to understand a truth that has eluded you these last long months. Before you can find peace, you must have revenge.

Thirty-Five

Washington arrived at the house just as Matthew, Em and Monk were clambering into the car. He stood and watched them.

'Really, Mr Daniels,' he said, 'you are wasting your time. My men have a massive head start. They'll be at Tysome's house in minutes. It will take you, what, an hour from here?'

Matthew ignored him. Just before he slammed the door, Washington called out, 'You might find his exact address useful.'

Matthew drove. Em was next to him, Monk in the back. He wished he could have left Em at home, but he couldn't, because potentially, Tysome could be anywhere. The only safe place for her was with him. And he couldn't leave her with Monk, because he needed Monk with him. Besides, Charlotte belonged to her, too.

Behind them, a white Ford Escort pulled out into the traffic and followed.

It was raining. The windscreen wipers battered against the edges of the glass. The sounds of the streets outside were sighs. As they travelled, it felt to Matthew that they were wrapped in intimate silence.

He would never have thought of Larry Tysome – even now, he couldn't work out *why*. There had been friction with him over the last year and a half – but all of it, from a professional point of view, had been trivial. The man had been affected by his mother's death: all of his problems stemmed from that. It was understandable. But although Matthew had done his best to support him, there was really only so much you could do.

He had always had the creeping sense that Tysome somehow thought he owed him something. There had been that ridiculous conversation where Tysome had demanded that he personally pay for his mother's operation. He remembered now the hurt in the man's eyes when he had handed over the proceeds of that whip-round – and how that hurt had slowly turned into insolence over the months that followed. His mother's death must have affected him far more profoundly than anyone had suspected.

To some extent, then, Matthew had brought this on himself: ultimately, he was responsible for Tysome's welfare. But Tysome had made it almost impossible for anyone to help him. And who could have imagined such terrible consequences from such a minor failure of care?

Well, Tysome had imagined it, for one. Then he had gone ahead and done it.

Vast concrete blocks loomed above the streets, dull orange in the glow, and glistening with the rain. A tramp staggered along the kerb clutching a can of lager, struggling not to fall into the road. Matthew veered round him, and accelerated. In the rear-view mirror, he saw the poor man give up the unequal fight, and collapse with one leg draped into the gutter. Under other circumstances, he would have stopped to help him. As the man shrank from view, he silently wished him well.

'What will we find?' he said at last. Monk said nothing. Matthew hadn't really expected that he would. 'Aren't you scared?' he pressed.

They travelled in silence for a way. Then Monk said, 'We will find what we find. We will do what we can do.' He turned towards Matthew, with genuine warmth in his eyes. 'I will do my best, Matthew.'

It was hardly a comfort.

Suddenly, Monk snapped his phone to his ear. Matthew hadn't even heard it ring. He could hear a voice at the other end, but he couldn't discern what it said over the hiss of the car. Monk rang off without speaking at all.

'Byron's men are already there,' he said tersely. 'Tysome's gone.'

It was Matthew's turn not to answer. What was there to say? Byron's men would be looking for Tysome – but where? He continued towards Tysome's home: it was hardly as though he had anywhere else to go. They drove in silence, until Monk spoke again.

'Apparently,' he said, 'there are cats.'

On the street outside Tysome's house, there was a shabby pale-coloured Honda with adhesive silver film stuck clumsily to the windows; and, inside, as promised, there were cats. There was also an irate forty-something woman who answered the door in a dressing gown that was a repellent shade of green. Her hair was greying, thin and in disarray. Her skin was blotched, her eyes were wild.

She yelled, '*You* can fuck off an' all! The police are coming, mind! I called them, soon as those other fuckers left. He's not here, and that's that!'

Monk ignored her and slipped past her into the hallway. A cat yowled and bolted for the stairs. There were two more, hidden in the shadows further along the corridor. The stench was appalling.

Unperturbed, he turned to face the woman. 'Where is he?'

'How the fuck should I know? I'm not his bloody mother. All I know is, the middle of the night, he slams in, scares the cats half out of their wits, poor mites, then buggers off up to his room. Ten minutes later he's down again with a suitcase, and he's off. Drove off in some old wreck of a car.' She pulled her chin in against her neck, as though she was suddenly scandalised. 'Never so much as a *Thank you, Mandy*, or *So long, Mandy, see you around*. Just buggers off, the little wanker.'

She eyed them suspiciously. Matthew vaguely recalled Tysome mentioning that he and his mother were moving in with his sister; they'd needed to sell her house to finance the operation that never happened.

'You can 'ave the bastard for all I care,' the woman said. 'Little runt. I never wanted 'im 'ere in the first place – or the old witch, come to that.'

She noticed a cat skulking in a doorway, and scurried over to it, cooing. She switched on a light as she passed it, revealing an interior that Matthew would rather not have seen. On the stairs, half the stair-rods were jagged stumps. The wallpaper was covered with stains the colour of tea, and gaped away from the plaster. The carpet was so torn that it looked more like an old roll on a dump than an actual floor covering. Ripped, sodden sheets of cardboard poked out from under it. Near the door, there was a pile of what looked suspiciously like dung. He heard Em gagging behind him and trying to conceal it with a cough. Monk seemed utterly unaffected.

Mandy Tysome crouched over the cat, crooning. 'It's all right, darling. The nasty men are just going.' She glared up balefully. 'I told you. Fuck off.'

'Where is his room?' Monk asked.

'Top of the stairs.' She didn't look up from the cat. 'Come on, puss, let's 'ave yer.' She scooped the animal up. It stared at the visitors with savage yellow eyes.

Monk headed up the stairs. Uneasily, Matthew and Em followed.

Em stood in the middle of the chilly room, hugging her arms. It was in the attic, with one mean window giving onto the concrete landscape beyond the house. A single naked bulb hung from the ceiling. From the top of the wardrobe, two more shabby cats followed their movements with hatred on their mangy faces. One of them crouched and hissed.

Tysome's uniform hung in the wardrobe. Apart from that, the cupboard was empty; so were two drawers in a battered chest standing at an angle to one wall – and the four empty slots where the other drawers should have been. There was a lumpy rug covering part of the floor. When Monk kicked it back, it concealed nothing more suspicious than the tattered remains of the carpet underneath. There was a wooden chair with a cup perched on it, half full of murky water.

There was a bed. Matthew would have preferred not to look too closely at it, but that was not possible – because on it there was a note.

He picked it up gingerly, trying to avoid touching the covers. It was scrawled on a sheet torn from a spiral-bound notebook, and it read:

SHES DEAD YOULL NEVER SEE HER AGAIN

'What now?' Em said.

They stood outside, unsure what to do. All Tysome's sister had been able to tell them was that she thought the car he had driven off in was blue.

Monk punched a number into his mobile. 'He's in a blue car. No details,' he said without preamble. 'It may turn up round Heathrow. Warn them.' He listened for a while. 'Not relevant,' he said tersely. 'If you're helping, Byron, then help.' Then, after another pause. 'And see if Tysome has any other cars registered. Blue.' He pocketed the phone without waiting for a reply.

He shrugged at Matthew. 'Time.'

'But we don't *have*—'

Monk interrupted. 'Think it through. We can drive round Heathrow, looking for a blue car that may well not be there – or we can wait. Byron has men at Heathrow already. It will take us at least an hour to get there – and I don't think he'll be there anyway.'

Matthew exploded. 'To hell with Tysome! Where's *Charlotte?*' Monk gazed at him impassively, saying nothing. Matthew gaped. 'You don't even understand, do you?'

An engine gunned, and the white Escort that had been shadowing them roared away. The man in the passenger seat mouthed 'Later' as the car passed, and waved. Washington, presumably, had called them away; certainly they were no use where they were.

Em tugged at his arm. 'Call the *police*, Dad. We know who's got her now. Just—'

Monk interrupted again. 'Actually, Emily . . . we *don't* know who's got her. We only know Tysome *arranged* it. Someone else did it.' He looked along the road, his face unreadable. Em opened her mouth to argue. Matthew put his hand on her shoulder to quieten her. Monk was right.

He pulled out his own mobile, and rang Tia Hannaford at the Ville. She was the only person he could think of who might be in a position to help – except for Thornton, of course, who would flatly refuse to do anything that wasn't in the rule book, and applied for in triplicate. Tia wasn't much better, but there was always a chance. Briefly, he was horrified to realise that he had no close friends at work at all. It was his secretary or nothing.

'Tia, it's Matthew,' he said when she answered.

'Matthew! Well, at least you've rung this time. Are you—'

'Tia, I haven't got time,' he said hurriedly. 'I need you to do something for me. It's a work thing. For Thornton. You know Larry Tysome?'

There was a slight pause before she replied. 'Yes. But—'

'I need his mobile number.'

'May I ask—'

'*No*, Ti. No questions. Confidential. I need his number *now*. His mobile. It'll be in the contacts file.'

'Well, I think you should ask Mark before—'

'*Tia!* I need his number *now!* No time, no discussion. *Please.*'

There was a long silence.

'Tia?'

'I'm *looking*, Matthew.'

Relief washed over him. 'Thanks.'

'I'm not a complete dragon, you know.'

So. Another person he had completely failed to win over during their years working together.

'Tia, I never thought you were.'

'I'm going straight to Mark with this,' she warned.

'He already knows.' Lies – but who cared?

She muttered the directory names as she clicked on them. It took for ever. 'Local Network . . . Admin . . . D-Wing . . . Resources . . .'

Em was fixed on him. Monk was looking nowhere.

'OK . . . Ready?'

'Hold on . . .' He waved his free hand frantically at Em and Monk, miming something to write on. Em had a biro. He wrote the number on the message Tysome had left for him, so hard that the pen poked through the paper.

There was no time for farewells. He thanked her tersely and rang off.

He dialled Tysome's number. It rang twice, and then switched to voicemail. There was no recorded message, just a computerised voice: '*Telephone – number – oh – seven – seven – nine . . .*'

Is not available. Yeah. Matthew rang off and hit Redial.

Em grabbed his arm and dragged the phone away from his face. 'Dad, the *police*! *Now!*' He wrenched his arm away from her, and pressed the phone to his ear. There wasn't time for this. '*Dad!*' He turned away from her.

The phone rang twice. The automated voice kicked in. He rang off and tried again.

Behind him, he heard Monk's voice, talking to Em. 'The police can't help,' he said gently. 'We're doing everything . . .'

250

The answering service: '*Telephone – number – oh – seven—*' He hit the redial button.

Monk's voice continued, intense and strange: '. . . her back, OK? He . . .'

Tysome's phone, ringing again. One ring.

'. . . anything. You know that. This . . .'

Two rings.

'. . . best chance.'

'*Telephone – number – oh – seven—*'

Em's voice was miserable: 'But that message said she's dead.'

Redial.

Monk's tone softened: 'We can't be sure of that.'

Tysome's phone, ringing.

Suddenly, there was a whirl in the corner of his eye and Monk's hand slapped him on the shoulder. 'Keep ringing.' And he was gone. He turned in time to see Monk moving rapidly towards the street corner, twenty yards away. He wasn't running, but he was covering the ground extraordinarily fast. Without looking back, he called again, '*Keep ringing!*'

He vanished round the corner.

Tysome's answering machine kicked in.

Matthew was confused. To buy himself time to understand what was happening, he left a message.

'Tysome, it's Matthew Daniels. What the—' He bit off his instinctive anger. 'Listen, you're angry. Obviously you are. And I'm sorry. But, whatever it is, it's *not Charlotte's fault*. Please, just let her go. Take me. I'll come. I swear I will. She doesn't deserve this. Please.'

Em was staring at him, her eyes full of reproach. He rang off. 'I . . .' he muttered. But he couldn't think what to say. He pressed Redial. Em was still staring. 'I love her, Em.' Then he turned away.

The phone rang. Once. Twice. Voicemail: '*Telephone – number – oh—*' He rang off and redialled. Through his handset, he heard Tysome's phone ringing again.

Suddenly, Em's head jerked round, and her eyes widened. As he turned to follow her gaze, he caught a blur of motion. It was a man. His skin was blue–black, he was short, and he moved with impossible speed and grace. He had appeared round a corner and crossed the road, a half-defined streak along the pavement. He stopped next to an unremarkable blue car parked neatly in line with the others.

There was the sound of breaking glass, a car door ripped open with extraordinary force. Then, from somewhere, a howl of rage and pain. Then there was silence.

Thirty-Six

You were right to wait, because here they are. The white car that's been following them has gone, and that is good, too. Because this is private. It is between you and Matthew. And now here he is on the street, a gift just for you; and he is so scared, so desperate.

Pain. So much pain. The hope, the futility, and then the grief. You know how it feels. It is something shared. And at this moment, when you can see written in his haggard face the same pain you have endured for so long now, you finally see what your Purpose truly was.

This isn't about rage. It is about love.

You are glad now that you have chosen this path. More than anything, it always bothered you that Matthew would never know who had done this. He would never understand that this was *your* pain, a gift to him, of hatred. Now he knows.

Unseen in your car, less than fifty yards from him, you drink in his agony, and a delicious sadness slides through you. Poor Matthew. Poor you. Together, you have stripped away the layers to reveal the harsh and brutal truth of the world. It is all about misery, and grief – and the futile horror of that one small voice, still inside you, still pleading, *No, please no. NoNoNoNoNoNoNoNo.* You see now that the voice is part of a greater whole. Its fear, its uncertainty: you hold it close, with love.

Matthew is standing outside Mandy's house, with his precious daughter and David Gordon – and they are about to watch him die. Your engine is running, ready. All he has to do is step into the road and you will put your foot to the floor. Your car will roar towards him. He will turn – too late – and his jaw will drop in confusion, and then in horror. And then you will be on him, and he will scream, and the car will glide into him, slowly, so slowly, each moment of his slow death perfect . . .

Your phone is ringing. Fifty yards away from you, Matthew is standing with his mobile pressed to his ear. David Gordon has gone somewhere, the girl is kicking at a car tyre. You glance at the screen: the call is from him. You press the cancel button. Seconds later, it rings again, and you do the same. Then again, and again. And each time is a terrible delight. He knows that it's you. He feels what you feel. And there is nothing he can do about it at all.

Your phone rings. You let it ring. You press Cancel. It rings again.

The spray of glass strikes your face before you hear the noise. Your body jolts in shock. A dim flicker of memory reminds you that, just moments ago, you half-noticed a blur of movement in the rear-view mirror. Your head jerks away from the flying glass. You begin to turn it back. The noise was loud, the glass is still falling. What . . . ?

There is a man in the seat next to you. His skin is blue-black, and a scar runs down his brow and his cheek. His eyes are deep and dead.

'Hello, Larry,' David Gordon says. 'Long time no see.'

Thirty-Seven

Monk dragged Tysome over to them, hunched and whimpering, steering him with one hand laid lightly on the side of his neck.

'How . . . ?' Matthew said.

'Heard his phone,' Monk said tersely. He pointed his chin at the house. 'Inside.'

Em was too busy gaping to be useful. Matthew hurried to Mandy Tysome's door and rang the bell. She opened it almost immediately.

'I told you wankers, you can fuckin'—' She stopped when she saw her brother being steered towards her, his knees twisted, staggering to stay upright, and moaning softly. Just behind him was Monk, his face expressionless. He lifted his eyes to her.

'Out,' he said.

Her mouth flapped noiselessly for a moment before she found her voice. 'You can fuckin' shut up an' all,' she yelled shrilly. 'This is *my*—'

Monk did not seem to move at all. Tysome suddenly flew past his sister and into the hallway of the house, landing in a sprawl on the filthy floor. Monk gazed calmly at the woman. 'Out,' he said again.

Her jowls wobbled, and her bloodshot eyes narrowed as she studied him and calculated the odds. Then, clutching her dressing gown about her, she scurried down the short path that separated the house from the street. Monk strolled into the house as though nothing out of the ordinary had occurred.

Perhaps, for him, it hadn't.

It was brief. Monk only touched him once.

He manoeuvred Tysome into his sister's front room in the same mysterious fashion that he had brought him to the house: two fingers at Tysome's neck seemed enough to enforce absolute obedience. Once in the room, a small twist of his wrist sent his captive flying. He crashed to the rotting carpet in a heap.

Em and Matthew crowded into the doorway. Neither dared speak.

'Where is she?' Monk's voice was barely audible.

Tysome stopped moaning and looked up. 'Fuck off,' he said thickly. 'I know you, Gordon. You can fuck off.'

Monk took a soft step closer. 'Where?'

'I hope you fucking die. I'll kill you. I'll take out a contract. I can pay. You should respect me. I'll send them after you.'

Monk squatted next to Tysome's head. His voice was level, quiet, almost intimate. 'Where?' he said.

Tysome raised his head, and locked his eyes on Matthew's. 'Know what it feels like now, *Matthew*?' He almost spat Matthew's name. 'You've lost her. Just like you . . . you . . .'

His eyes flicked back to Monk, who leaned over him, and stretched one gentle hand towards Tysome's chest.

'Where?' he said again.

'Fuck you.'

Tysome hawked, and prepared to spit at him. Monk jabbed downwards with a single finger, striking a point somewhere just above his collarbone. Tysome howled. The finger probed deeper. Matthew saw Monk say, 'Where?' again – but he couldn't hear the word above Tysome's scream.

The finger stayed in place, and the scream continued. Em screamed, too. Matthew put an arm round her, clamped her tight to him – and watched, horrified. Monk did not move. Tysome writhed beneath a single finger. When his breath ran out, he began to cough, in small dry gasps, unable to breathe in, and clearly still in agony.

Monk leaned closer, until his mouth was next to Tysome's ear. 'Where?' he said. His voice was gentle, almost loving.

When Tysome's mouth began to work, soundlessly, Monk carefully, slowly, released the pressure. The man gasped, moaned, rolled away. When he had gained as much distance from Monk as he could in the tiny room, he said, 'Fuck the lot of you. You can all—'

Calmly, Monk took a step towards him. Tysome screamed.

'*Where*, Larry?'

He crouched next to him, and reached out his hand again.

Tysome told him where she was.

They drove towards Heathrow. Monk rang ahead to Washington, prompting Tysome for details as the need for them arose.

'He has men close by,' Monk reported.

Tysome sat next to him in the back, hunched and very still. From time to time, he moaned or babbled something incoherent. Matthew wondered whether Monk had done permanent damage with that apparently gentle touch. He didn't much care.

In the passenger seat next to him, Em huddled against the door, crying softly and without cease. He had no idea how to reach her. He wasn't even entirely clear why she was crying: relief, perhaps, or fear. Perhaps both.

They hadn't yet found her. Tysome could have been lying – although he found that hard to believe. But until they actually saw her, until they could touch her, this was just hope. In a way, Matthew felt as though he had been here before.

His hands shook on the wheel. Movements that were normally automatic took an effort of will. Worst of all, he couldn't even drive fast. At this time of the day the roads should have been clear, but they weren't. The traffic crept towards each set of lights a few feet at a time. Where he was confident of the way, he swung off onto side roads and drove as fast as he dared; but, even now, he had to be careful. What if the police pulled him over and didn't believe his story? He drove as fast as he dared. Em cried quietly beside him, and Tysome whimpered in the back next to Monk, and London's traffic crawled forwards at a glacial pace.

They were less than halfway to Heathrow when Monk's phone rang. He listened briefly, then rang off.

'They've found her,' he said.

Matthew's heart lurched. 'Is she—'

'She's alive.'

Em immediately began to wail. Matthew reached towards her, but she wrapped her arms around herself, and turned as far away as she could, sobbing into the window pane. In the mirror, he saw Tysome staring blankly at the floor.

Monk gazed out of the window. 'They're taking her to your house,' he said. 'They'll be there in ten or fifteen minutes.'

At the next junction, Matthew turned round and headed for home.

Somehow, Washington's men had let themselves in, through the locked front door. Washington himself was waiting on the steps.

'She's in the living room, Mr Daniels. My doctor's taking care of—'

Matthew barged past him, and into the front room. She was lying on the couch, her dressing gown half open. A man bent over her, wrapping a bandage around her arm.

Matthew heard Washington, behind him, say, 'Marcus.' The man looked up, then straightened slowly.

'Mr Daniels,' he said, 'she's sustained some serious injuries.' Matthew pushed past him, and knelt beside her. Somewhere far away, he heard the doctor add, 'There's a risk of internal damage, but I haven't yet . . .'

Matthew tuned him out and gazed at his wife. Her eyes were swollen shut. Her skin was blotched, purple and brown, and streaked with dried blood. Her mouth flopped open, and spittle smeared the cushion beneath her head. There was blood in her hair, a gash on her unbandaged arm that had scabbed and cracked, and now seeped yellow liquid onto the sofa. Snot bubbled in her nose as she breathed.

She had never looked more beautiful.

After

Thirty-Eight

You hate them, all of them: David Gordon, who Matthew Daniels keeps claiming is a monk; Daniels' bleating daughter; and Daniels himself, who has made such a show of letting you go. He looks at you with complete contempt. He doesn't even talk to you, he speaks to the two huge men who have asked him what to do. 'The police can have him,' Daniels says. 'But later. I don't want them anywhere near Charlotte, not yet. Just take him back to his sister's.'

Outside, the goons bundle you into their car, and drive. They stop by some waste ground, drag you out and beat you. You curl up on the ground, and they kick you, punch you, drag your head back by the hair and batter your face until you can barely see. It lasts minutes, or perhaps hours. Then one of them hauls you back to the car. They throw you in, and drive again. Your eyes are swollen. You can hardly open them. You keep them closed. Your head nods and sways with every bump. You are only half-aware.

You hear one of them say, 'White boy, you got *lucky.*'

The other one laughs, and adds, 'This time, whitey. This time.'

Your mind drifts. Your thoughts wander through dark rooms full of cats and clanging doors with violent men locked behind them. One of those doors hides a familiar voice, a man with a guttural laugh, mocking you. He has stolen something from you, but it is too late for that now. You are searching for a bed, somewhere you can rest, but the laughter follows you everywhere. There is no peace from it. And it is not a man's laughter any more, it is a woman's. It is Mother, mocking you, coughing up bile and contempt with the last of her breath.

'Hey, white boy.'

Someone slaps you. Then there is something cold against your face. It slides grittily over your skin; a knife. A hot trickle creeps down onto your neck, then cools and tightens.

'You feel that, fucker? That's a message. You fuck with that guy again, you dead. Understand?'

Your head lolls as the car takes a curve. The man holding the knife digs its point into your cheek, and you jolt upright, moaning.

'I *said*, understand?'

Vaguely, you nod. The men both laugh. They take the knife away.

They push you out of the car, onto the hard surface of a familiar road, then they roar off. Bruised, scared and humiliated, you grope in your pocket for the keys to Mandy's house. You clamber up the stairs, tripping over the torn edges of carpet, and sleeping cats.

One of them has crapped on your bed. You sit on the very edge of the mattress, and gaze around your one-room empire, king of all you survey: a ripped and piss-sodden carpet, a chair with one broken leg, an empty wardrobe, a window with a view onto a graffiti-covered street.

Who are you now? You are the same disgusting worthless *thing* you always were. The object of Matthew Daniels' contempt, and Mandy's, and Mother's. *Do this, Larry. Do that, Larry. Why couldn't I have a proper son? You're a waste of space.*

Mandy will be back soon. She will laugh at you, call you useless, just like Mother did. And your humiliation will be complete.

You sit and you dream, and time slides reluctantly by.

Then David Gordon appears. You did not see or hear him coming, but suddenly he is there.

You yelp. You cringe away. His stare digs into you.

'I want his name,' he says.

'Fuck off,' you mutter. Your voice is thick, through bruised lips.

'The man who helped you, the one who took her,' he says. His voice is so soft, but his fingers are hard as iron. You have felt them. 'The one who hurt her,' he whispers.

You try to spit at him, but your mouth isn't working properly. His hand reaches for your shoulder, softly; and his fingers probe. Agony roars through you, white flame along the nerves. Your limbs twitch and spasm. Pressure grows behind your eyes, and his voice reaches gently through –

'The name.'

– and bolts sear inwards from your skin. Roaring pain swells along your thighs and arms, through your armpits, and the whiteness builds, and –

'The name, Larry.'

– and why fight? Why protect him? Let him suffer.

You gasp his name.

'From the Ville?'

You nod mutely, and Gordon nods back. He releases you. The pain, instantly, is gone.

You collapse back onto the bed, groaning. Something soft and damp squelches across your back, seeping in through your shirt. Seconds later, the stench of cat shit rises around you. Helpless, you lie in it, whimpering – and David Gordon stands over you, unmoved. He tosses something onto the bed next to you. You squint at it through puffed eyes. It is a brown pill bottle. It rattles as you move.

'Take them,' Monk says.

Your arms are made of lead, but you reach over to pick up the bottle and hold it closer to your eyes. Your shirt is tacky against your back, the humiliation makes you want to weep – but you mustn't give him the satisfaction.

The bottle says it contains paracetamol. It is full of pills. You struggle to open the screw-cap, and eventually you succeed. You sniff them suspiciously. Bitter-powder smell. You shake one out, and touch it to your tongue. The taste is familiar: blunt and sour. You swallow two of them, and mutter reluctant thanks.

Gordon leans closer to you. He seems immune to the cat-smell rising from you. Very quietly, he says, 'All of them.'

It takes you five minutes. He watches. He waits ten more minutes, standing over you, not moving. Staring. You close your eyes. You feel strangely light-headed. When you open your eyes again, he is gone.

Briefly, you wonder who will find you, but you know it will be Mandy: who else? When she sees your body, perhaps she will understand at last; but you doubt it.

What will you look like, after? In the Ville, every few years, an inmate killed himself with the bedsheets. The trick was to twist the sheets into a rope. If it pressed on the right part of the neck, he could even kill himself lying down. Once, you helped carry the corpse. The man's body was rigid. His tongue was blue. It bulged out from his bloated face. It would be nice if you could shock her, if at the very last, you could make her scream. But that's unlikely. More probable, she'll shoo her cats from the room, snarl at your body in disgust, and then just close the door.

One of her cats jumps onto the bed beside you, and presents you with its arse. Feebly, you try to swipe it away. For your trouble, you receive a row of deep scratches on your hand. As soon as the animal is out of your reach, it stops and stares at you with evil yellow eyes. *You are nothing*, its eyes tell you. *You are a hollow space filled with empty dreams*. From a safe distance, it purrs.

You hate them all. But that doesn't matter any more. They will get all the misery you have wished upon them, and more. Because everyone does, because that's life: you try and you try, you hope for change and happiness, and your dreams just dance away and mock you. And you lie there, helpless, in the same shit as before. But it doesn't matter anyway. Nothing matters at all.

The purrs are deeper now, and further away. And that doesn't matter either. You are tired. Your body aches. So you close your swollen eyes, and you remember.

And you wait.

Thirty-Nine

Matthew drove – methodically, cautiously. Each shift of a gear was a slow, deliberate act; he began braking – very gently – a good thirty yards before the end of each street. He said nothing, which was just as well. Neither did Em, who was sitting in the back, apparently sulking.

It all felt unreal. Perhaps she was still trapped in that room, and this was the continuation of a dream – perhaps her last dream, because that beating had been . . . she couldn't really remember how it had been. After a while, it had stopped hurting. She had watched him beat her from a strange distance, somewhere up in the tin vault of the roof. He screamed at her, kicked, pounded her immobile body with both his fists as though he was thumping a table. His bared teeth were blunt and spaced, and yellow against his brown skin – he hadn't bothered putting the balaclava back on. Blood ran down his temple in a thin red trickle, and drops flicked off his chin and spattered onto her face and clothes. From the roof, idly, she had wondered if he was going to rape her, but he hadn't. Eventually, he had given her one last half-hearted kick and muttered something about leaving her to rot. Then he was gone.

But he had been wrong about her rotting there. Already, she was out in the sky beyond the tin roof, with the planes flocking around her like fallen leaves, because it must be autumn by now, and it was time to go.

Then Matthew woke her, with careful words and a kiss so soft that she barely felt it. And she was in her own bed, which was impossible.

He whispered to her. 'It's all right, darling. You're safe. It's over.'

The curtains were closed, though it was light outside, and there was birdsong, and the endless roar of traffic was like the roar of her pulse.

Then it was dark again outside, and she imagined she could feel Matthew lying next to her – although that was impossible, wasn't it? Because there was something about a big room with a tin roof, and a man standing over the beaten form of a woman.

Light again, and the curtains were open, and someone brought her food. In her mind, it was Matthew, and he said something to her about a scan, and they should try to do it because if there was still the slightest chance that Eyelash –

But that was impossible too, because Eyelash had only ever been a dream. A dream, yes. None of it real.

She slept.

'Can you move, darling? Come on, try to move.' His tone was bright, but he spoke so quietly that she could barely hear him above the din of the birds and the cars and the breeze at the window.

She tried to move, and it hurt.

'Well done. Good. Try to stand,' he urged softly. 'Let's try to get you to the car.'

She didn't move. After a while, he said, 'I'll ring them. Tell them we'll rearrange.' He sounded uncertain. Nervous.

Wordlessly, and unsure why she was making the effort, she forced herself upright. But then, if it wasn't real, why not? And if it was, then Matthew had found her after all.

And now she was in a car, dreaming. And Matthew was driving as though the car – or someone inside it – was made of glass.

The nurse helped her to her feet, and she shuffled through a door, dazed, into a dark room full of white machines. The nurse closed the door. Through the narrowing strip of light, she saw Em. She was scowling at the floor, her face drawn and distressed.

Poor Em. She understood too much of what had happened. And perhaps Matthew did too – a little, in his own way.

Poor Matthew.

He held her hand, squeezed. She did not squeeze back. She was too tired. She hovered near the ceiling, and watched. The machine beeped every time the woman pressed a button. Black and white speckles drifted on a tiny screen. Then the woman smiled tightly, said that was all, and suggested that they wait outside.

There were tears in Em's smile when she came back out into the light. Matthew's expression showed only raw exhaustion. He moved over so that she could sit between them, then stood to help her sit.

The radiographer stared at him sourly, then turned away. Her shoes squeaked on the rubber floor. She vanished into a room.

Matthew opened his mouth, then closed it again, and placed a hand on her arm instead. She was glad to feel it there, but had no idea how to respond.

Not real. Not real at all.

'Mrs Daniels?'

Heavily, Charlotte stood. Matthew stood, too, steadying her arm.

The nurse frowned. 'If you don't mind, Mr Daniels, the doctor would like a moment with Mrs Daniels alone. I'll call you in as soon as they're ready for you.

Matthew opened his mouth to object, hesitated, then sank wearily back into his seat.

The nurse smiled at her briefly, and turned to lead the way.

Charlotte went in, without looking back, and heard the door close softly behind her. A man sat at a desk in a small room. Next to the desk was a spare chair. The man was studying some papers, and scribbling notes with a fat fountain pen. He looked at her over the top of his glasses, and gave her a short, unfriendly smile.

'Sit down, Mrs Daniels.'

I've been here before, she thought distantly. She couldn't quite remember when, because she didn't want to. And anyway, she wasn't really here. Being numb was nice. It was safe.

'I'm Dr Raschid,' he murmured. He gave her a smile, too brief to be warm, and concentrated on writing again. Each word glistened briefly under the desk light before the ink dried. She could smell the ink. She said nothing.

Finally, he reached a full stop. The nib tapped tartly against the page. He slipped the pen into a jacket pocket, and swivelled to face her.

'Mrs Daniels,' he said, 'the radiographer was very concerned to see your bruising.' He took off his glasses, and studied her skin. Then he looked at her expectantly.

She waited for him. She was too tired to talk. Anyway, what was the point?

The doctor cleared his throat uneasily. 'Mrs Daniels, I do assure you that we take this kind of thing very seriously indeed.' He pursed his lips, and perched his glasses on the end of his nose again. 'Abusive relationships are not as rare as you might think. There are organisations that can help.' He scooped up a handful of leaflets he just happened to have lying on his desk and offered them to her. 'I realise you might not want your husband to see these, but you are very welcome to read them here, maybe take down a few numbers—'

She laughed, bitterly. Because, really, it should have been funny. He actually thought that Matthew had done this to her – her gentle, over-considerate husband. And the irony was that this man's concern was so genuine, so earnest. He meant so well. Just like Matthew.

'I was mugged,' she said abruptly.

He raised his eyebrows, startled. 'Well . . . Have you reported it?'

She actually chuckled at that one.

'I'm serious, Mrs Daniels. The police—'

'I don't want to report it.'

He studied her mildly. 'Mrs Daniels, assault of any kind is a serious—'

Painfully, she stood to leave. 'Thank you, Doctor.'

He stood too, and gestured her down again with the palms of his hands. 'Please, Mrs Daniels. It's entirely up to you. Just – well, please be aware that you do have choices. I know that it's easy to feel you have nowhere to go, no one to turn to . . .'

She made no move to sit. She stared at him, over bruised and swollen cheeks.

He fidgeted uncomfortably, and took out his pen. Turned it in his fingers, end for end for end.

'Well,' he said at last, 'of course, it's completely up to you. Please.' He gestured again at the chair. This time, reluctantly, she sat.

'Thank you.' He gazed briefly at the papers on his desk. 'As you know, Mrs Daniels, we were scanning you today because of your previous miscarriage.'

He looked up at her over the top of his glasses. His eyes were warm and intelligent.

'Mrs Daniels,' he said, 'I have some good news for you.'

Forty

The house was empty when he arrived. Two hours later, there was still no sign of Matthew, or any of them. He wouldn't wait for ever.

He stood in Matthew's living room, his knees unlocked and relaxed, and let his arms float up in front of him, carried on the currents of energy that rippled through the room. The cowrie shell dangled from his wrist by its thin blue thread. His eyes traced its contours. Each curve was a familiar memory, each faded colour a separate glimmer of history, a moment from a story he had never told, or lived. Hopes and dreams. Ancient things. The seeds that never grew.

Sometime during this last week, he had turned a corner. A moment had come, an opportunity – and he had taken it. Now, there were farewells to say, and one small item of unfinished business – the man who had so nearly killed Charlotte Daniels. But these were small things. The future lay ahead, a river stretching on towards an unseen distant ocean, broad and bright and unfamiliar.

Tysome was dead: he had stayed with him long enough to be sure that there was no way back. He had watched him fade, muttering and complaining, and stinking of shit, all pretence of dignity finally abandoned. He . . . evaporated. And now he was gone. Dead. Killed.

Monk did not believe in regret – but he was puzzled. Dead *why*, exactly? Killed why? Why had he done it?

Of course, the answer was that it was the wrong question. He had done it because he had done it. Killing Tysome had seemed necessary – and symmetrical. People who cared so little about pain should be removed. Efficiently. Painlessly.

He lowered his arms, distracted. Energy exercises required

concentration, not thought. The cowrie swayed, wobbled, then settled coldly against his wrist, a tiny, comfortable burden. For a moment, he saw Gloria, laughing. Then screaming. Then gone.

Yesterday, he had stood in the doorway of this same room, and watched as Matthew wept over his wife – alive, just; damaged, and mute. He had watched the girl, too – Em – as relief turned to uncertainty, and then to silence. A numbness had crept across her face. He remembered the feeling behind it: the exhausted aftermath of horror, a gradual realisation of the casual brutality of the world.

And, with her expression still burning in his thoughts, he had slipped away. Hailed a taxi. Visited Larry Tysome, and done what needed to be done. As he intended to do with the man Tysome had hired. As he had all those years ago with the man who killed Gloria.

He ran the cowrie's blue thread back and forth through his fingers, feeling each subtle twist of the fibres. There was no room for regret. There were things still to do.

Why was he waiting here? Could Matthew Daniels' gratitude change the past? Unlike Byron, Monk bore Matthew no resentment for his time in the Ville; he understood that Matthew had been trapped by his job, he had only done what the rules required.

Besides, what did it matter that he had been convicted for a killing he had not committed? He was a murderer nonetheless. He had killed; and he knew that he would kill again. For Monk, there was no redemption. There was only regret and revenge. Perhaps the likes of he and Matthew would always carry their chains. He shut the door carefully behind him when he left.

Byron was waiting for him, hidden from the street by the hedge that fronted the house. When Monk appeared, he tossed his cigarette onto the gravel and ground it out. He said, 'What now?'

Monk shrugged. What was there to say? There were things to do. Reckonings still to be made.

Byron frowned at him. 'Leave it, bro. The woman's safe. What more do you want?'

Monk shook his head, and moved a step closer. Byron edged backwards warily. Monk reached out a hand, and laid it softly on Byron's shoulder. 'Goodbye, bro.'

He glided past him onto the street.

Byron called after him. 'What do you want, man? Dead is dead. She's *dead*, bro.'

No. She wasn't, though Byron would never understand. Gloria wasn't dead in any way that mattered.

But Monk paused, wondering. Byron's question was still a good one. What now? For him, the answer was clear enough – and what was next for Matthew, Charlotte, Em? It occurred to him, quite suddenly, that there was one thing still to do. He turned and walked back past Byron towards the house.

'Wait here. Five minutes.' Byron looked at his watch, rolled his eyes and sighed.

Monk picked the lock and entered. Then he drifted up the stairs as softly as rising smoke, and into the girl's bedroom. There was a dresser, and on its top there was a bowl, a bright blue bowl with shards of stone set into it that glittered in the afternoon sun. In the bowl's centre was the stub of a candle, a fragile sliver of ivory against the blue. Beside it, fresh candles lay in a row, and a box of matches perched on top of them – and he knew that he had been right to come here.

Words came to him from long ago – the thoughts of a man who had been wise beyond years, and who was so skilled in violence that he could kill with a touch.

– *Sifu, how can you be sure what you do?*

– *You will find your path inside you. It is who you are.*

– *But how do you explain misery, Sifu? How do you avoid mistakes? What about pain?*

– *Every day in training, you hurt yourself. You harden your fingers, your bones, your muscles. You choose pain every day, David. Now tell me – where is the mistake?*

Monk reached down to his wrist, and slipped a finger under the blue thread that circled it. He snapped it, and gathered into his palm a bleached cowrie shell, loose and warm. He ran the blue thread through his fingers, sensing each strand and wisp. He hefted the tiny shell. It was smooth, and as translucent as the candle's stem. He set it gently in the bowl, and laced the thread around the candle's base.

Perhaps, one day, it would keep her safe.

As he glided down the stairs, a breeze slid through the silent house. On it, he heard the faraway sound of Gloria, sighing, as she woke for one brief moment from her sleep and found him, as always, by her side.

Forty-One

Monday. Three days, and still Charlotte would barely talk, nearly four. But at least there had been the scan. For now, the baby was safe.

He would have to ring Monk and thank him – although how he was supposed to thank a man who never answered his phone was a puzzle. But it could wait. First, there was Charlotte to nurse back to health. There was Em, too: he could see that she was struggling with everything that had happened. She was in pain. He hoped she didn't see his inattentiveness as some kind of betrayal. But how could he find time for her? Charlotte had to come first, at least for now.

As they had helped Charlotte up the steps into the house, still stubbornly mute, he had whispered over her head to his daughter, 'Thanks, poppet. I'll see you a bit later, OK?'

Em had shrugged, and headed for her room. Alone, he half-carried Charlotte up to their bedroom, changed her, and then drew the covers up around her. Through bruised lips, she groaned. Then she muttered, 'Sorry. It's . . . I . . .'

He kissed her hot forehead, and whispered, 'Shh. You're safe. We're here.' She mumbled something that he couldn't catch. Then her eyes, already blank, fluttered closed.

He watched her from a chair in the corner. Washington's doctor had pronounced her stable before he left the night before: there was no serious internal damage, and no injuries that would not heal without intervention. A miracle, of sorts.

Eventually, he spoke. 'I was afraid, Charlotte. So afraid.' But her breathing had deepened into sleep.

Em let him into her room without meeting his eye. A thin line of smoke drifted upwards from the candle in the bowl on her dresser, as though it had just been extinguished. The smoke steadied for a moment, then it faded and was gone.

Em flopped onto her bed, and kicked her heels, staring grumpily at nothing in particular. Cautiously, he settled next to her.

'It'll be a while,' he said to her. 'But she's OK. That's the main thing.'

Em scowled. 'No she isn't.'

'It'll be fine,' he insisted. 'She's just . . . hurt, that's all.'

'Yeah. Whatever.'

He ignored the jibe, and let the silence grow. 'Not easy,' he said at last.

She sniffed loudly, and hauled herself upright. She crossed to the chest of drawers opposite her bed, struck a match, and held it to the nub of candle. Then she slumped back onto the bed, avoiding his eyes. They watched the flame together as it flickered, steadied, then wove a slow pattern in the air. Sadness lurched inside him. There was so little he could do. Always, there had been so little.

'Still missing her?' he asked, as lightly as he could.

Em pouted at him. Then, irritably, she muttered, 'It's for Eyelash.'

He nodded, unsure what to think, and unable to say anything. Good. Perhaps, at last, she was taking her first steps away from the past. He knew that he should, too.

Sorry, Rachel. I have to go now.

Perhaps, now, he could think that, and mean it. Things changed. So did people.

Together, they watched the flame.

'I couldn't have told them,' he said at last. 'The police. You understand that, don't you? If they'd blown it . . .'

Em did not answer. Out of the corner of his eye, he could see her clenched fist, the knuckles bleached white with lack of blood. A braided blue thread trailed between her fingers. It looked familiar. He didn't ask.

'What about now?' she said. 'You could tell them now.' She glared at the carpet.

He blew out heavily. 'Now . . . I think Charlotte has to decide.'

He was surprised to realise that he didn't much care what happened to Tysome, or even his sidekick, whoever he was. There would be time for that later; and, truth be told, the idea of wading through report forms with the police, with Charlotte still so fragile, filled him with dread. He was happy enough to wait, even if it meant a cold trail for the police to follow. For now, he just wanted back the Charlotte he had first fallen in love with, two years ago.

He reached out a hand towards his daughter, and wriggled his fingers expectantly. She hesitated, then put hers in it. They lay side by side, sharing a moment's peace.

'I'm proud of you, Em,' he said at last. 'I don't tell you that enough.' He added, after a pause, 'Give it time.' She didn't reply; but she squeezed his hand, hard, and he thought he heard her sniff.

The rich smell of candle smoke curled through the room.

What comes after a fear is conquered? Relief, fatigue, satisfaction. More fear. He had Charlotte back – but that didn't guarantee that he would not lose her in the future. She had barely spoken yet – understandable, given what she had been through. It was almost as though she was still only half-conscious. She was functioning but she wasn't really there. The numbness would fade with time. He hoped.

But he sensed a change in her, too. A new determination. The willpower that had dragged her out of bed that morning to go for the scan. She had refused all but the smallest support from him, trudging to the car one painful step ahead. It was as though she wanted to be alone. Was she *angry* with him for getting her back? Or perhaps, she was angry about what had happened to her, and this was the only way she could express it. So, maybe she had changed – or maybe she was slowly changing back.

Either way, he could only do what he could do: be there, and be strong. Support her as she healed. Listen when she chose to talk. Wait for her.

What comes after fear? Patience.

He lay beside her, torn between exhaustion and absolute alertness, propped against the headboard in the darkened room, watching Charlotte sleep, horrified at the terrible injuries he could see and the ones he knew that he couldn't. She stirred from time to time, or moaned. When she did, he brushed the hair back from her forehead and whispered to her. Whenever she woke enough, he gave her sips from a water bottle.

Early in the afternoon, her breathing became lighter, and she slowly opened her eyes. He gave her a moment, and then moved gently to her side.

'Hello, darling.' He stroked her hair. She twitched as he touched her. He pulled his hand back, uncertain what to do, then he stroked her again. This time, she didn't resist. She closed her eyes and let out a weary sigh.

Through damaged lips, she mumbled, 'Thornton.'

'Hmm?'

'Thornton. Did you . . .' She trailed off. Seconds later, she added thickly, '. . . catch him?'

He kept his voice as gentle as he could. 'Thornton? Mark Thornton? *Catch* him? Why would I . . . ? Oh. No, darling, you mean *Tysome*. Yes, we—'

Charlotte's whole body was twitching. Her mouth opened, and wet sips of air slipped out of her.

'*Shit!* Charlotte? Charlotte! Are you—'

Seconds passed before he realised she was laughing. 'Not – Thornton, then.' She squeezed the words out between gasps. 'That's – blown it.'

He watched her convulsions. 'No,' he said at last. 'Not Thornton. Larry Tysome.'

Eventually her gasps subsided. He watched her, his mouth half-open, framing a question he had never wanted to ask. After a long while, her breathing deepened and she began to snore.

Perhaps that was best. What use was there in questions about the past? And what difference did it make? He had always known anyway, or suspected. So, now she had mentioned his name: what had changed?

Strange that she should think he had something to do with her abduction, though. He knew that it was just the confusion of a terrified and wandering mind, but it was disturbing nonetheless. But he could live with the uncertainty. He was good at that, these days.

Anyway, she had been dreaming. That was all. Just a nightmare. It was gone now.

The snoring stopped after a while. And then some time later, a tear rolled down from the corner of her eye to the pillow. She trembled.

Gently, trying not to disturb her bruised body, he settled lower, and lay with his head propped on a hand so he could see her face. He stroked her hair, and murmured to her.

'Hey, darling. It's all right. You're safe now.'

She rolled her head away to gaze at the window. It was grey outside now, and darkening. The constant moan of the traffic had faded, and the breeze had dwindled to nothing. The trees hung limp and still.

'It's all right, darling,' he whispered. 'I'm here.'

She sniffed, clumsily because of her bruising. 'I'm . . . Oh, Matthew, I'm sorry.'

'Shhh,' he murmured. 'It'll be fine. Everything's fine.'

That morning in the shower, he had washed the blood clots from her hair. It was smooth, now, and shining. He brushed it from her scratched and swollen forehead.

'I love you, Matthew,' she said at last. Her voice was cracked and faint.

He answered, 'Shh.'

He stroked her hair, patiently, until she slept again. Then he lay next to her, and stared past her, out through the window, at the failing light of the day.